Ghost of Briar Rose

ANNA ROMER

THE GHOST OF BRIAR ROSE
Copyright © 2024 by Anna Romer
All rights reserved. No part of this book may be reproduced in any form or by any electronic or mechanical means, including information storage and retrieval systems, without written permission from the author, except for the use of brief quotations in a book review.

This is a work of fiction. All characters, names, places, and events are either the product of the author's imagination or used fictitiously. Any resemblance to real persons, living or deceased, is entirely coincidental.

ISBN: 978-1-923019-09-6 (paperback)
ISBN: 978-1-923019-08-9 (ebook)

First Edition: Published in Australia, July 2024
Visit the author's website: annaromer.com

*For Hailey
Who believes in
fairies, magic, ghosts,
the power of dreams
... and me.
Love you, Bean*

1
ROSALBA

NOW

He said he loved me.

He said he'd come back for me after the war and marry me, that nothing could keep him away. Not even death.

But he lied.

I fisted my skirt in my hands, glaring across the garden.

Dew sparkled in the moonlight, glistening on the petals of fragrant peonies and lilac, while beyond the flowerbeds and imported trees, rugged bushland stretched away into the night.

I had tried to move on.

To forget the way his eyes lit up when he smiled at me, the warmth of his hand clasping mine. His promise of a beautiful future together. But every night, as I stalked the gravel pathways and trails that meandered between the tree shadows, his face tormented me.

"Leave me alone!" I yelled into the dark. "Haven't you haunted me long enough?"

The breeze lifted my hair away from my face, but I didn't bother raking it back. There was no one to see me. No one to run screaming in fright. Just the owls and insects, the frogs in their muddy hollows, and the stars gazing down from the inky bed they shared with the moon.

I envied the stars, twinkling and dancing in the endless expanse above. They were free while I was trapped in this leafy prison forever. A monster, my father had called me. An evil spirit, the locals said, warning each other not to come here.

They were right to be afraid.

Right to stay away.

No one was welcome here. No one. All my secrets were buried here. All my lies, and the bad things I'd done that made me tell them. Buried in the earth that sank under my feet as I ran past the prickly roses and blackberry vines, the shadowy tree trunks, under the tangled branches, always restless. Always searching for that one truthful thing I had misplaced, yet dreaded to find.

I slowed to a walk, my toes sinking into the damp grass.

Mosquitoes buzzed and nagged around me, even though their quest for a feed was pointless. I could feel their confusion as they circled me, the scent of my blood stirring them into a frenzy, but of course it was unobtainable to them and anyway probably deadly.

I snatched a little bloodsucker from the air and caged it in my fingers, puffing my icy breath on it. When I opened my hand, its tiny, lifeless husk floated silently to the ground.

William once told me that true love's kiss could break any spell—or curse or affliction, even one as terrible as mine. He hadn't called it terrible, of course. *Your father has a lot to answer for, Rosalba. Putting those ideas in your head, filling your heart with fear and self-loathing. To me, you're perfect ... if only you could see yourself the same way.*

Typical William, always the shining knight. Back then, as a naïve girl, I had believed him. At least for a while. And when he said he loved me, I had believed that too. *I'd cross endless deserts to be with you again, Rosie girl. Scale deadly peaks, and swim raging rivers. Nothing will keep us apart, not even death ...*

"Then where are you?" I shouted, my voice echoing in the treetops like an owl's cry. "If you loved me, why did you stay away?"

I listened hard, but there was no reply.

There had been no reply for a hundred years, yet the silence still dragged on my heart. *If only I knew why you broke your promise, William. Were you rotting in a foreign field? Or was our love a lie, as Father said? I've been waiting for more than a century, and my heart still hasn't healed.*

"So many years alone ... yet I keep hoping you'll return for me." Return and break the curse that trapped me here in an endless, timeless loop.

Time was a funny thing, wasn't it? The way it slipped through your fingers like flakes of rust, or dead leaves. Or broken heartbeats. It was a trickster, a magician. Making a hundred years pass in an eye-blink, while stretching out the moments till you wanted to scream—

A noise rumbled through the night.

The growl of a car motor echoing up the mountainside.

I stopped walking, holding my breath.

Was that shouting?

Yells and catcalls, drunken laughter.

My heart began to punch against my ribs, my breath quickening as I turned back along the track and hurried uphill. When I climbed the ridge that overlooked the dirt road beyond the front gateway, I saw headlights carving through the dark.

Tyres screeched as a beat-up ute came over the rise, three youths bellowing and hooting as they leaned out the windows. The vehicle skidded onto the gravel driveway at the front of my garden and the boys tumbled out.

One of them clutched a shotgun.

I darted into the shadows and ran downhill, dodging between the tree trunks as I raced towards the gates, my palms damp, my blood turning to ice. The chirp of insects and night-time rustling in the surrounding garden fell silent. There was just the drunken calling and laughing, the harsh voices invading the night and making me giddy with fear.

Why did they do this?

Why couldn't they leave me alone?

And why now, during the waning moon, when I was most vulnerable? I never left my garden. I craved solitude and tranquility, tending to my memories and weeding out the things I needed to forget. Why did the outside world insist on tormenting me?

One boy elbowed his mate, his gaze flicking towards me as he searched the darkness. Could he actually see me, or was his sixth sense suddenly aware of my presence? The three of them started jeering and yelling obscenities. The one with the rifle fired a shot in my direction. Then another. Bullets whooshed past me, and one even zinged right through my body.

I glared at the intruders.

Hateful creatures.

"You'll be sorry for this," I hissed under my breath.

I moved closer, my torn dress billowing around me in the night air, tentacles of dark hair lifting around my head as though electrified.

One youth whipped his head around in my direction, still searching. "Oh-ooh, spooky Briar witch! You don't scare us!"

They couldn't see me, but they could sense me. Sense my agitation, my anger crackling in the air, turning it electric.

Another bullet zipped past my ear, striking the trunk of a beautiful old elm—one that William had planted a century ago—and a spray of bark splintered off its side. The tree moaned softly. Or maybe it was me.

I swallowed my fear and rushed towards the youths, my arms spread wide, my dark energy gathering between my shoulder blades and then exploding from me as I screamed like an avenging angel. For a heartbeat, the night stilled. There was just the roar of my fury, deafening and monstrous. Then the wind rose and screamed too, gathering leaves and twigs and grit into gusts and hurling them in a gale force at the intruders.

One boy clutched his eye and cried out, blood trickling through his fingers.

The other boys exchanged glances. Their smiles fell away as they backed towards their vehicle.

I inhaled the night and screamed again.

Suddenly, the intruders were piling into the car, all panicked limbs and harsh voices. The motor choked to life and the car lurched away, pebbles and dust flying in its wake.

I could see how terrified they were as they spun out of control on the gravel road and careened down the mountainside. I was glad. They wouldn't return. News would spread, and others would come, but I'd send them away as well.

No one was welcome here. No one.

I stood panting and trembling, watching until the car had

disappeared around the curve of the mountain road. Then I dropped to my knees in the dirt.

My garden was safe—at least for now. My secrets still buried, my past unexposed.

Yet my father's warning echoed in my mind. *The world does not tolerate monsters like you, Rosalba. People will hunt and kill you. Is that what you want?*

"No, of course not." My father was long gone, yet his words continued to taunt me even more than a hundred years later. I lifted my gaze to the sky. "All I ever wanted were the things you couldn't give."

Acceptance. Respect. A family who cared enough to love and protect me. But those were for others, not me. Who was I to wish for them?

"You were right about me, Father. I really am a monster." My breath caught in my throat, the weight of the surrounding darkness crushing me. "I never wanted to be this way. Never meant it to happen. I've just forgotten how to be anything else."

2
CLEARY

A BEAD of sweat trickled down the side of my face and into my scruff. I scratched it away, shifting my boots on the creaking staircase, locking eyes with the spectral figure of a boy on the top step above me.

My prey.

The entity I had bought this old house especially to banish. To send into the next world, even if it meant forcing him over against his will.

The boy glared back at me through the dimness, his dark aura radiating outwards. Despite having all the lights blazing, the clammy shadows that darkened the stairwell had seeped through the rest of the place like a black fog—a cold black fog that pulsed with desperation and clung to everything it touched.

Especially me.

I clenched my teeth, fighting to stay focused, but I could feel the aura overwhelming me, a cobwebby rankness that stuck to my hair and skin and made the air go stale in my lungs. If there was one thing I loathed more than a ghost, it was the fog of toxic energy they always emitted.

"We can do this the easy way," I told the boy. "Or the hard way. It's your choice."

He scowled, shoving a lock of greasy black hair off his face. He was fourteen, only a handful of years older than my daughter, and his clothes hung off his bony frame like rags. The collar of his shirt gaped from a missing button, revealing a neck blackened by bruising.

"What do you want with me, mister?"

I stepped back down onto the next riser. "I can help you find peace."

His frown deepened. "I don't want peace. I just want you to leave my house."

"It's my house now, Lewis."

It had taken me six months to strip away everything in the derelict old Victorian. Rotten floorboards, defaced plaster walls, sagging ceiling. I gutted it and rebuilt from scratch, investing all my money from my last house sale. It was a steal. Way below market price on account if it languishing unsold for so long. Neglected. Derelict. Haunted, people said.

Someone died on those stairs, you know. A woman, years back. One rainy night, her son pushed her and then strung himself up.

Slowly, I took a small tin from my pocket and eased off the lid, sprinkling a line of black salt crystals across the step.

As a dank odour filled the air, the boy recoiled.

"What's that smell?"

"It's a blend of salt and bone ash, mixed with earth from your grave." My voice came out harsher than I intended, no trace of the gentle calmness Elsie would have used. "It'll weaken your attachment to the house and help you cross over to the other side."

"Cross over? If anyone's crossing anywhere, it's you."

A pulse throbbed in his bruised neck as he descended towards me, angry shadows swarming in his eyes. But as he neared the salt line, he looked down suddenly and then scrambled backwards, slapping at his limbs, shrieking and howling.

"It burns! You tricked me, mister! You're as bad as my mum. But I got rid of her. And I'll get you, too!"

He charged towards me in a sudden blur of dark energy, yelling as he crossed the salt line I'd made. I gripped the bannister, dragging myself out of his path, but his fingers still managed to claw down my arm.

The shock of contact was instant. I buckled forward, my skin turning ice cold as everything grew dark. I was no longer myself, but seeing, feeling, breathing inside the mind of Lewis's mother—

Stout and unsteady on my thick legs, the taste of tobacco and cheap liquor souring my tongue. My face twists in disgust as I stand on the stairs, shouting at the boy. "You no good loser. Why don't you get a job? Lord knows we need the money, but you're just like your useless old man!" When he shoves me, my scream is so loud and drawn out it tears the lining of my throat. I'm flailing as I fall, my fingers clutching at nothingness, my body crashing onto the floor below, bones snapping—

I gasped the air back into my lungs, clutching the bannister like a lifeline. Fighting the nausea my visions always brought on.

"Jeez, kid."

Lewis had reached the bottom of the stairs. He frowned as he approached the open back door, peering outside into the courtyard. Another trail of black salt glinted in the porch light, but he seemed unaware. Something beyond it had spellbound him.

He stepped across the salted threshold with barely a shiver, heading into the yard. Strange. He'd been so resistant to leaving the house before, now he seemed almost eager.

The salt turned blacker as it soaked up the fog while the boy's aura grew fractionally lighter. When the bright, waning moonlight struck him, he gasped softly and began to shimmer.

As I stepped into the doorway after him, my breath caught. A small, slender figure stood in the courtyard. Her dark hair jutted up from her head, gilded by the porch light, her baggy shorts making her legs look like matchsticks.

I froze in place. My daughter was only nine, already a talented hunter, but she was also still a kid and way too vulnerable to be doing this.

"Elsie, get back!"

She ignored me and walked towards the boy.

"Hey, Lewis! I found something of yours." She put out her hand, revealing a glinting metal button. She had found it while we were gutting the place, and later noticed loose threads on the boy's shirt.

Lewis's hand drifted to his collar.

"My mum grabbed me. On the stairs." His voice was barely a whisper. "I was angry. She drank too much and smelled funny, and sometimes she thrashed me with a belt. I wanted her to stop shouting at me, so I pushed her, but I never meant for her to die."

"It's okay, Lewis," Elsie said encouragingly. "She'll forgive you. Once you cross over, you'll feel better." She kept her eyes on him, her pixie face serious.

She had known the button would lure him out under the waning crescent moon, when the lunar energies were weakening and entities at their most vulnerable. It hadn't been part of our plan, but she knew what she was doing.

She was like my father that way. Observant. Focused. A

regular little Sherlock Holmes. Once she set her sights on something, not even a nuclear blast could sway her. For her, this was personal, and she took immense pride in her work. Unlike me. Hunting supernatural beings was purely a job, and the less emotionally invested I was, the better.

"Elsie, get back." I lifted my arm in warning. "You can't trust him."

She gestured to the boy to put out his hand, then dropped the button on his palm. It slithered through his fingers and clinked on the path, but he didn't notice. His gaze stayed fixed on her.

I started patting my pockets for the matches.

"Elsie? Move away!"

Her shoulders twitched, as though my voice was an irritating fly she could shrug off.

"Look around, Lewis," she told the boy gently. Then she smiled, her blue eye gleaming like a raindrop, the other darker iris lost in shadow. "Can you see a shaft of light somewhere? Like a moonbeam? It's your doorway to the other side."

Ignoring her instructions, Lewis clenched his hand as if gripping the button. He leaned closer to Elsie, his eyes dark and intense.

"You're the only light I'm seeing," he murmured. "I want to stay here with you."

Elsie shivered, as if a cold gust had shot up her spine. Lewis forgot the button and inched his hand towards her face—

"Dammit, Elsie!" I struck a match and dropped it on the salt line.

The crystals crackled and spat. The boy's head turned at the sound, and then he was running back along the path, his hair electrified around his head, the bruise on his neck glowing angrily. He started towards me, his eyes alight with the same shock and fear all entities got when they began to untether.

"Dad, no!"

I stepped back too late. Lewis reached out to me, his arms passing straight through my body.

The shock of cold numbed me. Dead cold, like I was drowning in a sunless ocean. I buckled over, gripping the door frame. Fighting the nausea, and the flashes in my mind of his mother writhing broken on the floor as she died—

The boy's eyes widened, and he stumbled back outside. The sky and fence, the dark yard with its manicured trees, became visible through his body. His cry of rage was barely audible as he evaporated like morning mist.

Elsie stalked along the path towards me, swiping her foot through the crackling salt and killing the embers.

"Why'd you burn the salt, Dad? He was going peacefully. Now he's probably tetchy again. He might come back."

"He won't come back. He crossed the salt three times. Did you see him?"

She scattered the remaining salt with her foot.

"Lewis wouldn't have hurt me."

"He reached for you, Else." I shivered, my stomach clenching. "It's too dangerous. I don't want you ending up like your granddad."

She swiped under her eye. "I'm okay with it, Dad. I don't get sick from their touch like you do. You're the one who shrivels up and dies if one of them even breathes on you."

She was right, but that didn't make me any less afraid for her. My daughter loved befriending trapped spirits. If she could, she'd send them over the rainbow with a hug and a packed lunch.

I was more like my mother. I had seen what they could do.

What they could steal from us. Fear was healthy. It kept you on your toes. Kept you alive.

Elsie huffed, her thin little eyebrows inching closer. "You need more faith in me, Dad. In them. They're not all bad. Even the bad ones don't always mean to be. They're just lost."

"You're too trusting, kiddo. That's what scares me."

"And you're not trusting enough, Dad. They're people, not monsters. People who need our help. You can't just trick them into doing what you want. It's mean."

"It keeps us alive, kiddo."

She grumbled something under her breath and stomped off.

I left her to it and headed back inside for the dustpan and broom. Shaking my head at her words. Trust one of them? That'd be the day. I'd sooner trust a busload of maniacal axe-wielding killers than someone who'd made such a royal mess of their life that not even death could fix it.

3
CLEARY

My mother offloaded two huge jars of black salt onto the kitchen counter, and then followed me out to the lounge room. Her long hair was pink today, and the charm bracelets around her wrists jangled as she patted my arm.

"Nice job, Cleary. The place looks wonderful."

She approached the stairs and looked up at the bright light coming from above. "It's so welcoming now. No more gloom and doom. I'm impressed."

"Let's hope the new buyers agree."

She shook her jangly bracelets, smiling. "You should take a moment, Cleary. Be proud of what you've achieved here. You've transformed a sad old rundown house and given it a new lease on life. Why not stay and establish yourself?"

I shrugged, already restless, feeling the tug of impatience to get started on my next project.

"That's not how I roll, Ma."

"What about Elsie? Constantly moving around is not ideal for raising a child. She's only nine. She needs a permanent home. She's attended so many schools, yet never made any lasting friends. Why don't you settle for a year, let the grass grow under your feet?"

"Elsie's fine, Mum. No friendships are lasting at her age. We're good."

Mum pinched her lips together, and lifted her hands as if in defeat, but I knew her better than that. Once she got an idea in her head, she couldn't let it go.

She sighed. "Elsie said the boy you untethered was close to crossing peacefully. She said he only panicked at the last moment because you ignited the salt. She thinks you don't trust her."

"It's not her I don't trust. It's them."

"You mean Lewis?"

I nodded. "Elsie let him get too close for comfort."

Mum jangled her bracelets, adjusting the charms. "She told me all about it. And Cleary, I know you were trying to protect her. But isn't it better to teach her the ropes while she's young so she can protect herself, rather than wrap her up in cotton wool and hope for the best?"

"She gets too attached to them. Wants to be friends with them."

"That's why she's so good at untethering, Cleary. She's a natural. Which is why you need to teach her how it all works. In our game, knowledge and experience mean safety."

"It didn't help Dad."

"After forty successful years in a dangerous job, your father made one mistake—and it cost him everything. It cost us, too. Elsie can learn from it and use her grandfather's experience to protect herself. But only if you let her."

"I let her do plenty. Within reason."

Her gaze softened. "After what happened to your father, I

understand you're wary. But it's not just the others, is it? Maybe if you'd trusted Jolene more, she'd have stayed?"

"Jolene didn't leave because I lacked trust, Ma. She left because she found someone else who could give her the things I couldn't. Flashy things. Diamonds. Gucci handbags." I shrugged. "I'm just glad she agreed to sole custody."

"Me too. I mean, I cared for Jolene. But she was a handful. And Elsie's just so …" She hugged her hands to her heart and gave a besotted smile.

I laughed. "Glad we agree on something."

"So, silly question. Have you found the next place?"

"Yeah. Snapped it up a few days ago."

"Of course you did."

I pulled a rumpled contract of sale from my back pocket and passed it across.

"The place is stunning, Mum. Or it will be once I work my magic on it. An hour north of Melbourne in Woodhill. An enormous house on the mountainside with views to die for and an old historic garden. It's been on the market forever. I got it for a song."

"And the entity?"

"The locals reckon there's a young woman haunting the place. They call her Briar Rose. Past tenants claim they heard her screaming, and someone reported seeing a ragged figure stalking the grounds at night. I reckon she'll be a breeze to untether."

"Why, because she's a young female?"

"Because I know what I'm doing."

Mum looked dubious. "That's what you said about Lewis. You'll be careful, won't you? Not let your guard down."

"Always, Mum."

She handed back the contract and wandered to the window,

peering outside into the yard. Elsie was poking paper flowers she'd made into the grass, dotting the expanse of perfectly trimmed lawn with rainbow shades. Making everything pretty for the new owners.

"Look at her, Cleary. I know you hate me saying this, but that girl needs a mum in her life. And I'm not talking about Jolene. She needs someone who gets her, who appreciates her uniqueness. Someone who'll stand by her no matter what."

"And I don't do all that?"

"Yeah, sweetheart. Of course you do. But Elsie needs to settle and form connections. You both need that. Far more than you think." She looked at me. "Love has the power to transform someone for the better, Cleary. Take me and your father. Apart, we were a couple of shambling messes. Together, we were strong. That deep connection still sustains me. Even with him gone all these years."

I huffed. It broke my heart a little each time she mentioned my father. Regardless of what she said about their bond sustaining her, I knew she still missed him every day. I knew the pain that still dogged her. Maybe if she'd loved him less, she would have moved on already.

I didn't plan on making the same mistake.

"There's only one connection I need, Mum. That's the one leading me to the next property. The next challenge. The next ghost I can flush out and send to the afterlife." I folded the contract and pushed it back in my pocket. "And I think I've found her."

4
CLEARY

Golden sunlight streamed into the kitchen, casting a warm glow over the sleek granite countertops and pristine tap fixtures. Today was the big move, with all our belongings boxed and stacked by the door.

Only two large glass jars remained on the kitchen countertop, full to the brim with black salt. In the bright morning light, they seemed to glow, their crystals shimmering like specks of charcoal ice.

I wrapped the first jar in paper and stowed it in a cardboard box. The other jar I unscrewed and tilted back and forth, making the grains glitter as they scented the air with ash and bone.

My mother's secret recipe for black salt was never much of a secret in our family.

Growing up with the odour of burning bones—the organic beef bones Mum bought in bulk from the butcher—we all knew she used only three ingredients. Salt, of course. A string of incantations. And greasy bone ash scraped from the base of the big iron skillet she positioned low over the flames on the brick barbecue in the yard.

She could have achieved the same result by using powdered charcoal or black chalk dust to colour the salt. But Mum wasn't taking any chances. When it came to her family—first Dad, then my sisters, and now me—she refused to cut corners, determined to do everything in her power to protect us.

"Dad?" Elsie's voice chirped from outside. "You ready to go?"

"Sure, kiddo."

I pinched out some salt and tossed it over my shoulder. For luck. Or a final, parting insurance policy. The faint gummy smell of bone ash wafted in the surrounding air.

Mum's words drifted back. *After what happened to your father, I understand why you're wary. But it's not just the others, is it? Maybe if you'd trusted Jolene, she'd have stayed?*

My father had trusted the others—the poltergeists and wisps and funnel ghosts he routinely untethered from the properties they haunted. He called them lost souls who only needed a nudge towards the light. Towards peace.

Until one of them latched onto him and refused to leave. A young female, a girl my father felt sorry for. He used to joke that she was the baby of the family, coddling her and playing to her whims in a way he never did with my sisters.

Mum took it in her stride. She called my father the most careful man on the planet and said she wasn't worried. But she started putting extra bone-ash in his salt, and fortifying her incantations. Even tying the jars with bright crimson blessing threads she knotted herself.

I gripped the counter and gazed into the yard, inhaling the familiar scent drifting from the open jar.

I could still see Pa crumpled on the ground that day, outside the old house we had restored together. He wore the navy three-piece suit he was so proud of, the suit he got married in and claimed was his lucky charm. He lay flat on his back, a broken jar of Mum's black salt scattered beneath him in the dirt. The air reeked of bone ash and death, and the clammy fog of a malevolent aura.

Pa stared up at the grey sky, his lips moving, his face chalk-pale and his eyes ... heaven help me, his eyes.

Andrew Branchwood had seen so much death in his 48 years, you'd have thought his own would come as no real surprise to him, especially in his line of work. But what I glimpsed in his eyes just before his spirit slipped from his body left me cold to the core. The weight of the world in their depths, the silent terror. The realisation that someone he'd been trying to help had brutally slain him.

And me crouched helplessly at his side, pounding his chest as the tears slid down my face. An entity had felled the man I hero-worshipped, cut him down like an oak tree, and there was nothing my mother or I could do to bring him back.

Pa always used to joke that if anything happened to him, he'd come back as a ghost and haunt us himself. I could still hear the pride in his voice as he delivered the motto he lived by. *True love is putting someone else's happiness before your own needs, Cleary. And if that means giving up a prize perch in Heaven to hang around with my family a bit longer, then I'd do it in a heartbeat.*

But the salt he'd fallen on, the same powerful black salt my mother had concocted to keep him safe while he untethered the spirit he was hunting, had instead untethered my father. Leaving my mother broken, my sisters consumed by grief, and me with a burning appetite to make everything right again.

Restore the balance. Make someone pay for taking him from us too soon.

At eleven, with no genuine talent for the business at all, I had stepped into my father's oversized shoes and set out on a journey to finish what he had begun. I'd been hopeless at it too, learning everything the hard way, making more mistakes than progress, even with my mother's wise counsel. But when Elsie was born nine years ago, all that changed.

She was like my father, with her sharp features and wispy dark hair—and an alarming connection to all things otherworldly. A connection that even outshone my father's. It felt wrong to bring a small kid into frightening places. But since she could walk, Elsie insisted on coming with me. Her only tantrums were when I tried to leave her behind. She was never afraid. Never. And I had never seen anyone, not even my father, clear an aura fog as quickly as Elsie could with a smile and a gust of her bright, babyish laughter.

With her around, my job got easier. The money flowed in as we cleared one house after another. We became a team and stayed that way ever since—

"Dad!"

I lurched around, gripping my chest.

Elsie stood in the doorway. "You're taking forever!"

I slumped. "Thanks for the heart attack, kiddo. Why aren't you waiting in the car like I asked?"

"Got bored. You said five minutes."

I rapped my knuckles on the jar lid. "Just packing these."

She sighed, and I'd have sworn my father was peering back at me from her bright nine-year-old eyes.

"Come on, Dad. Woodhill's over an hour away."

I tucked the jar into the box and collected it under my arm, then grabbed my keys. Before we left, I quickly scanned the room.

Lewis and his mother wouldn't recognise the place now. Pristine white walls offset the gleaming floorboards, and floating concrete and steel had replaced the old wood staircase. I was especially proud of the cottage garden brimming over with roses.

The old Victorian terrace had sold for a breathtaking sum. Even I was surprised. A retired Sydney couple looking for a quieter life in Melbourne had quickly snapped it up. Their deposit alone had allowed me to purchase our next project, sight unseen, online.

According to the website, Loch Ard had been on the market for years. It was a secluded property with fifteen acres of sprawling gardens and breathtaking views of the town. The real estate agent had confirmed my suspicions.

No one stays very long, and the property's fallen to neglect, which is why they're selling so cheap. Apparently a young woman died tragically there a hundred years ago, and the locals swear it's haunted. But most historic places have a story, don't they? I hope the hearsay won't put you off—

Elsie had already buckled herself into the passenger seat, kicking her heels on the footwell mat. While we reversed out, she glanced over.

"Who do you think lives there, Dad?"

She'd been asking this for weeks, and my answer was always the same.

"They reckon a young woman."

"I hope she's nice."

"When are they ever nice?"

She tucked in her chin and glanced over. "Lewis was nice."

"He pushed his mum down the stairs."

"Nobody's perfect, Dad."

I grumbled under my breath. Hunting entities wasn't just a job, but a burning passion that consumed me. Sometimes there were hiccups, but when it ran smoothly, the feeling was addictive. Banishing one dark fog after another, making the world a safer place. Especially for kids like Elsie—kids who were sensitive to the darkness and psychic pollution that all ghosts dragged around with them.

I glanced over at her.

"Whoever's inhabiting the next place, Else, I'm pretty sure 'nice' doesn't come anywhere close. I want you to stay away from them this time, okay?"

She nodded, pretending interest in the passing scenery. But the brightness in her eyes told me she had no intention of doing anything of the sort.

5
ROSALBA

THE GARDEN GLOWED in the bright midday sun as I raced barefoot along the track.

Up the hill and through the shady pines, along the wild perimeter where the gum trees grew. Passing the wrought iron shade house and running down the wide gravel track until I reached the lightning tree.

I stopped in front of it, gazing up into its twisted branches, black against the sky. I saw it every day, but it still filled me with wonder. After more than a hundred years, it was tall as the sky, its knotted old arms sprouting grey-green leaves that tickled the clouds, its tiny, spiky flowers filling the air with their peppery scent.

The night I was born, a massive thunderstorm tore across the mountain. Lightning struck the tree and set it alight. It had blazed for days, even in the deluge, the core of its great trunk continuing to burn. Eventually, the rain had put it out, leaving a blackened cavity at its base. Yet somehow the tree continued to grow. Like me, it survived that night against the odds.

I leaned against the vast trunk, gazing down across the valley.

Far below, the little town of Woodhill snuggled in the river's curve, the surrounding woodlands growing thick and green along its banks. Trees had grown up over the years, hiding William's stone farmhouse. Perhaps they'd torn it down, built another in its place. What it once symbolised for me—having my own family, and a place to call home—had faded but not vanished entirely. Just knowing it had once stood there made me feel William's presence close by. It hurt, but it was sweet too, as I remembered that long-ago day he held me in his arms and kissed me, whispering goodbye—

A car door slammed.

I went still, my eyes suddenly wide as I stopped breathing to listen.

A voice called shrilly from across the garden. I couldn't make out the words, they came from too far away. But one thing was certain.

It was a child's voice.

Time froze. Or maybe it was my heart. From my depths, a memory emerged. A tiny starfish hand clutching mine, and large blue eyes framed by thick lashes peering up at me from the time before. Before I got trapped here in this bright, sun-drenched garden. Before I destroyed everything that mattered most to me and became the monster my father always feared I would be...

I turned and ran back uphill along the track. Past the shade house with its ferns and choking vines. Past the old piper's cottage, and the thickets of blackberry and wild rose, past shady beds of violet and thistle. Past the loch, the horrible loch, with its mossy boulders and deep, unforgiving water. Up higher until

I emerged onto the bright, bushy ridge overlooking the dirt road that ran past Loch Ard's front gates.

I could see them through the trees.

A young girl and a man.

She was about nine years old. Scruffy and boyish, with cropped hair and oversized shorts, sandals on her small feet. Skipping from foot to foot, chirping like a magpie. Beside her, the man stretched his back and yawned at the sky.

Lord.

Like a protective giant, he loomed over the child, scanning the road for hidden dangers. Then he shrugged, as if satisfied the coast was clear. After all, what dangers could lurk along such a pretty, deserted country road?

What indeed.

He walked along the verge to a thicket of ironbarks below me. His shaggy hair was black as ink, and a thin shirt hugged his muscular torso. Shadows hastened to touch him, enfolding him in their dark embrace. Through the foliage, small inquisitive fingers of sunlight jealously caressed the beautiful scruff of his jaw.

I leaned further forward, squinting through the leaves. He seemed familiar. Had he been here before? Surely I'd have remembered a man like that?

Hands in pockets, he continued along the dirt road for a way and then pivoted his head in my direction. Shading his eyes, he looked up the hill—straight at me.

My hand shot up, pulling my hair over the ruined side of my face. Impossible, he couldn't see me. Could he? I stood rock still, hidden behind a thicket. But still I lowered my head, the old shame burning through me. I hadn't worn my veil in years. What was the point? No one could see me except the birds and possums. But I wanted it now, that veil. I needed somewhere to hide.

And yet.

This man...

He stepped onto the sunlit verge directly below me, still searching, as though sensing me here. As he looked up, the sun hit him. The shadows retreated from his face. A frown line cut between his brows. His scruff softened his jaw, but there was no hiding the challenge in his eyes. Then his frown fell away and he scratched his chin, the gesture achingly familiar.

I gasped. "William?"

He scowled, stepping closer, his lips parting as if to speak—

Then the child called to him, and he tore himself away, heading back along the road to join her.

I dragged my fingers through my hair. *Of course it's not William. You're seeing things, you dill. William's been gone for a hundred years, his bones rotting in the mud of a forgotten French battlefield.*

I clung to a branch, staring at them.

The man and the skinny girl. *You can't be here! I don't want you! The garden is mine. I won't have you coming here and trampling my memories. Unearthing my secrets. Ruining the fortress of solitude I've worked so hard to build. Just climb back into your car and return to wherever you came from and leave me and my garden alone.*

They continued up the hill, oblivious to me. The girl skipping along and chattering like a grass wren, the man clomping through the weedy grass, checking over his shoulder. Searching the ridge.

He felt me, then. Was sensitive to my presence. Good.

Sensitive people were easier to scare away.

6
CLEARY

The back of my neck prickled, and the hairs along my arms stood to attention. I twisted around, searching the slope again. Further up on that ridge, sunlight streamed through the branches of a tall gum tree. I'd have sworn something moved. Just a bird, probably. A shadow.

Or maybe the entity I had come here to drive out.

I pushed through the heavy white gates and ducked under a weather-beaten sign—LOCH ARD—then headed up the grassy driveway with Elsie hot on my heels.

"Dad?"

"Yeah, possum?"

"I like this place. It's perfect for us."

"It's a neglected mess, is what it is. A money pit. It's gonna blow out my budget and drive me into the poorhouse."

She beamed. "Is it our forever place?"

Whenever we bought a property, she asked the same thing. She already knew the answer, so I didn't bother replying. Instead, I climbed to the top of the rise and gazed down the mountainside. Between the trees, I could see farms and bushland stretching to the horizon, the river winding through it like a blue snake. In the distance, a mountain range glowed faintly purple in the clear midday light.

"Oh Daddy, it's lovely."

"Hmm."

She slid her fingers into mine and peered up at my face. Her cheeks were pink, her freckles dancing on skin far too fair and sensitive for the Australian sun.

"Dad, do you like it?"

"Where's your hat?"

"In the car."

"Go get it."

She kicked the toe of her sandal in the dirt. "I wish we could stay here forever."

"We haven't even seen the house yet."

"It feels like *the one*."

I made a dismissive sound. "Don't get your hopes up, kiddo. We're only flipping this place. Not living here permanently."

"Oh, but could we keep it, please?"

"Next one, possum. I promise."

She slumped, letting go of my hand.

"That's what you always say. But then we move again and it's like we're stuck in a loop. Always moving. Never really living."

I sighed and crouched in front of her.

"We talked about this, remember? What do we always say?"

She heaved a sigh. "A rolling stone gathers no moss."

"Right."

"But what if I like moss?"

"No one likes moss. Moss is the worst. It bogs you down

and gets you stuck in a place. Next thing you know, you're stagnating. Right?"

She nodded. "I guess."

"So, we're good?"

"Sure."

"Now run and get your hat before you turn into a beetroot."

I continued up the driveway, recalling what the agent had said. *A wealthy Scotsman built Loch Ard in 1890 to replicate his childhood home. It has a small manmade loch, imported iron shade house and a piper's cottage. Sadly, the cottage is derelict, you'll probably need to pull it down ...*

I climbed higher, then let out a whistle as the valley opened up before me. "What a view."

Far below, a green patchwork of farms and bush corridors stretched for miles. The purple haze of hills smudged the horizon, and in the middle distance a lazy blue river meandered along a leafy course. Right below us, the sleepy village of Woodhill nestled at the base of the mountain, surrounded by farmland and sparse pockets of bush. The highway bypassed the town like a silver ribbon, tiny cars rushing north to the border or south back to Melbourne.

A view to die for. Except for one towering, blackened eyesore.

The huge old gum tree had been struck by lightning at some point, but had continued to grow. Partially blackened by fire, some of its branches were bare and broken. A real blight on that breathtaking view. Nothing a chainsaw wouldn't fix. I could hire a bobcat and clear the entire garden back to its former glory in a few weeks.

Rattling out the keys, I went along the wide gravel driveway. Elsie skipped up along behind me, the brim of her sunhat flapping around her face, chattering to herself and swishing about in the grass.

"Don't wander off," I called.

She answered with a baby bird chirp that made me smile. But then, a twinge of guilt as I remembered her words. *It's like we're stuck in a loop, Dad. Always moving and never really living.*

It won't be forever, I silently promised. We were just a couple of house flips away from buying our forever home. Maybe we could finally retire and settle down, something my father dreamed of but never achieved—

I inhaled a lungful of sweet air, but as the house came into view, I puffed it out again.

Holy heck.

The website photos hadn't done it justice. It sat amid the overgrown garden like a stately colonial queen, head held high and majestic. Its creamy sandstone walls nestled behind wooden fretwork eaves and sweeping verandahs. White timber shutters framed the vast picture windows, and the height of the steep iron roof made me dizzy. A tall paperbark cherry tree nestled against one flank, littering the ground with a froth of white blossoms. On the other side grew a rambling cypress, scenting the warm air with pine.

Climbing the front steps, I went inside.

The air was a little musty. And cold, as if the air-con had been running overtime. I sent out my feelers, but despite the icy chill in the air, there was no sense of anyone inhabiting the place. Strange. Maybe local hearsay had got it wrong.

Rubbing my arms, I ventured deeper. Shadows sprang around me as I crossed the glossy old floorboards towards a wide, welcoming staircase.

The walls needed a coat of paint, but the bones were good.

More than good. Wonderful. Enormous rooms. An open fireplace. Wide windows overlooking views that made me catch my breath. The garden was lush and inviting. I was already itching to get lost in it.

Little sandals slapped across the floorboards. Elsie slipped her hand in mine.

I gave her hand a gentle squeeze.

"You sense anyone?"

She glanced around, then frowned out at the garden.

"Not in the house."

"We've been wrong before."

"I don't care if there's no one here. I already love it, Dad."

The yearning in her voice touched a nerve in me. After so long in the city, hemmed in by crowded buildings and noisy city streets, this leafy paradise seemed overwhelmingly beautiful. Almost too good to be true. Like stepping into a different world.

When it came time to sell, we'd make a bucketload. Maybe more than ever before. Dollar signs flashed before my eyes. Elsie could go to an elite progressive school. I could get that flashy ute I'd been eyeing off. Heck, I could buy a fleet of them. I pictured Jolene begging to come back, and me taking great pleasure in turning her down. I smiled.

Selling this property was going to make all our dreams come true. We could have anything we'd ever wanted. All I had to do was flush out the ghost of Briar Rose—if she existed—and banish her from this place forever.

7
ROSALBA

I'D BEEN WATCHING them for days, the man hauling boxes from his vehicle, dragging furniture around the big empty house, filling the old barn with tools and whatnot. The girl prancing and chattering in the garden or rocketing her bike along the pathways, her face glowing pink.

Didn't she own a sunhat?

She seemed like an annoying child. The way she larked about, ignoring her father's calls. Venturing up the hill or poking around in the shade house, despite his warnings not to wander off. Her feet were wearing new trails in my grass, and her chirpy chatter setting my teeth on edge. Her presence in the garden was a thorn in my heart, pricking open old wounds. Old memories that made the dark places in me ache.

A child ... I can stand anything but a child.

As dusk fell, I walked up the hill to the lightning tree and gazed back down towards the house. They'd been here a week. Already their television invaded the soft damp blackness of the night, the blaze of electric light swamping the stars.

I sank into a big fallen log, taking comfort from its solid reassurance. High above me, the leaves whispered. *He won't be satisfied to dwell here peacefully. You know that, don't you? He'll want to leave his mark, change the house and garden to suit him. Erase your presence here and replace it with his own ...*

Everything I cherished was in danger.

My solitude. My memories. My secrets.

The intruders had to go. It should be easy enough. Scaring people away was my superpower. I could strike now, tonight, while the garden was at its darkest.

I sighed up at the pale crescent moon. It was a silver fingernail tonight, dangling up there in the cold blackness of space. Not even a solitary star for company. It looked lonely. Lost. Almost afraid.

I stopped by the lily pond on the hill overlooking the house and found my reflection in the moonlit water. Matted hair. Wild eyes. Ragged dress and bare, grubby feet. What a shame they couldn't see me. My appearance alone could send them screaming ... but I had to make sure they wouldn't return.

I pushed back my tangled hair to reveal my face, far more disturbing than the other attributes combined. I clenched my fists, my heart rate quickening as adrenaline coursed through my veins. Bright, dark anger bubbled up inside me, giving me a boost of strength.

Think of the loch. The horrible loch. Remember how cold the water is, how the slimy mud sticks to your skin. How the weight of terror drags your limbs under till there's nothing left to cling to but your screams ...

As the little moon climbed higher, my body began to tremble, and then shake uncontrollably. All around me in the glow of my rage, the garden had grown treacherously dark, the shadows even darker. But I needed more. More power. If I was going to drive away the intruders so they never returned, I needed more might, more potency.

Think of him ... think of Father. What he did in the stables, how he hurt you. Made you kneel on thorns. How he said wicked things, and forced you to say them as well. Making you hate him. Making you hate yourself even more—

8

ROSALBA

1909

"What are you, Rosalba?" My father's voice echoed in the rafters of the old stables behind the house, his leather shoes creaking as he shifted his weight. "Let me hear you say it."

I rocked forward on my knees, wincing as the thorns dug deeper into my skin. I lived to please him, but sometimes—like now—he demanded too much.

"Please, Father. I don't want to."

The cane switch struck my bare shoulders. I flinched, but didn't cry out.

Today was my birthday, always a dark day for my father. He had been cursing this day for the past fourteen years, fifteen if you counted the day I burst from my mother's broken body and ruined his life.

I knew he would be irritable today. Usually I stayed hidden in my room, reading or sewing, treading softly so he did not have to bear the memories of what my birth had stolen from him. So why had I thoughtlessly barged in on his visitors today? A group of ladies from the church, come to thank Father for his latest donation.

I hadn't meant to scare them.

Their laughter and merry chatter drifted through the house, and I'd not been able to resist. My veil forgotten, I crept into the doorway to look at the lovely creatures chatting with my father. Being church ladies, they dressed modestly, but in my eyes they were goddesses. Their pale smooth faces, their liquid eyes and shiny hair. Their prim, perfect smiles.

How I yearned to capture one of those smiles for myself. To let it warm me, as only a kind smile could. So I crept into the sitting room, my slippers rasping softly on the floorboards, my eyes wide in wonder.

One lady glanced over, and for a fleeting, glorious instant her smile alighted on me.

Then she screamed.

Another of the ladies had fainted—

"Say it, Rosalba."

The stables were stuffy and hot. Shards of afternoon sunlight burned through holes in the iron roof, but despite the heat, I shivered.

"No, Father. Please don't make me."

He whisked his cane through the air again, making it sing.

"Tell me what you are."

"Please, no—"

The cane struck my bare back. The shock of pain roared

through me, catching my nerves alight. My legs trembled, and from the corner of my eye I saw a fleck of crimson land on the whiteness of my good petticoat. It bloomed like a tiny sad flower. I tried to recall what Nanny said about getting blood out of things. Soak it in hot water or cold? Rub salt into it, or was that sugar—?

"Say it, Rosalba."

"No."

The cane whistled softly and struck a diagonal across my shoulder blades. A scream tried to shove its way out of my throat, but I clenched my teeth against it. Tears burned in my eyes like kerosene.

My father's shoes creaked.

"Say it, child. And the punishment will end."

My silence prompted another strike. I whimpered and crumpled forward, forcing the rose thorns more savagely into my knees. My hair swung forward, stringy with sweat. The cane whistled as my father swished it through the air, impatient.

"I grow tired of your disobedience, Rosalba. Straying from your room this morning when I had company. What were you thinking?"

"I don't know, Father."

"After everything I've told you about the outside world. Do you know how people treat creatures like you? They hunt them down and kill them. Is that what you want, child? To be hunted and killed?"

I bent my head. "No."

"Then say it."

My eyes watered hotly and tears were slithering off the end of my nose, but I could not lift my trembling arms to wipe them away. Rules were rules, and I had already broken too many today to risk breaking another.

I swallowed the tightness in my throat.

"I'm a monster."

"And how do monsters survive?"

"They hide."

"Where no one can see them. In their room, or in the garden's darkest shadows where they belong. They don't climb fences and run wild in the paddocks, do they?"

"No, Father."

"They don't barge in while the church ladies are visiting. They don't forget to wear their veils. And they don't cause havoc with their monstrous antics."

"I'm sorry, Father."

He sighed wearily. "The rules might seem harsh, Rosalba. But they're for your own good. Once I'm dead and gone, what will become of you? You'll stay here, of course, at Loch Ard. Out of sight. You'll tend the garden, as I've shown you. Live off the geese and hens, the fish in the loch. But how long until the world discovers you? What will become of you, then?"

Icy fingers crept along my spine. "I don't know."

"If only you hadn't been born. Your dear mother would still be here with me, while you—" His voice cracked, and he released a long shuddering sigh. "Your mother was the most beautiful woman I've ever seen. Her beauty was renowned. Even back in Scotland she'd been famous for it. People visited just to admire her. Did you know that, Rosalba?"

"Yes, Father."

"Perhaps it was best that she died before seeing your face. A woman like her giving birth to a creature like you is one of God's harshest mysteries."

I drew inwards. Hearing him speak of my mother that way made my crippled heart try to grow wings and fly away. I hated him talking about her beauty. Her saintliness. Her unfortunate death in the birthing of me. I had seen pictures of her, and she was every bit as lovely as Father described. Smiling from the photograph, her brows arched imperiously, as if knowing the effect she had on lesser mortals.

I had an effect on people, too.

The church ladies could testify to that.

I had read about other mothers in my storybooks. Sometimes they were kind as well as beautiful. Leaving magic combs or wishbones to help the daughter they left behind when they died.

Would it have horrified my own mother to have a daughter like me, as Father said? Or would she have seen past my ruined face and loved me, anyway? Loved the girl I was beneath?

It's for your own good, Rosalba.

Sometimes, when the night-time shadows gathered too close and the coldness of my upstairs bedroom grew unbearable, I imagined warm arms around me. Gentle fingers stroking my hair, and a voice whispering to me. *One day, you'll have a daughter of your own, and her appearance won't matter to you. You'll love her for who she is on the inside—*

My father's shoe leather creaked again, his soles crunching grit beneath them. I stole a glance, but his attention had drifted away from me. The cane hung limp in his hand. The anger had drained from his whiskery face, leaving him grey and withered.

He caught me looking and tossed the cane in the dirt. Then he stalked away.

I wiped my tears and glared after him.

The old blunderbuss. One day, I'd pack my things and sneak over the fence, down to the gate and beyond. I'd keep going along the road until I reached the town. I might bypass the town and head straight to the city. I would explore the world on my own terms, and if anyone tried to hurt me, I would lash back and hurt them instead.

I rolled my shoulders, wincing.

One by one, I picked the thorns from my throbbing knees. A thread of blood worked its way down my backbone, and I wiped it with the back of my hand.

The Devil take Father and his rules.

I would play his cruel games and bow my head, be the obedient girl he had shaped me into. But I would bide my time. One day, when I was older and stronger, I'd show them all just how monstrous I could truly be.

9
CLEARY

NOW

Stalking through the house, I turned on all the lights, driving the shadows back into their dark corners where they belonged.

Night fell quickly up here on the mountain.

The garden outside was sunk in blackness, the waning moon too frail to hold the dark at bay. It was October, and the spring weather was warming up all over the country ... meanwhile here at Loch Ard, the air was still crisp and cool.

I raised my arms and yawned, feeling the pull of tension along my spine.

After shifting furniture and lugging boxes and scrubbing

walls and floors and bathrooms for the past week, every muscle in my body ached. I needed a bath.

While the tub filled, I got dinner started. Peeling potatoes, marinating salmon steaks in garlic oil. Opening a bottle of red. When the bath was ready, I headed down to the bathroom.

The antique cast iron tub was so big that even I could comfortably stretch out in it. Lavender scented steam wafted from the diffuser and out through the open window into the dark. Having four sisters meant knowing how to bathe in style.

Stretching back into the tub, I breathed in the tranquillity. The city seemed a million miles away, the rest of the world even further. All I could hear was the chirp of crickets outside and my daughter's voice drifting from her room as she chatted on the phone to her grandmother. *You should see it, Gran! It's big and lovely and there's a ginormous garden. I went looking for fairy rings like you told me and I found one ...*

Crazy kid. Crazy-cute.

Mum's words came back to me. *The poor little mite needs a mum, Cleary. When will you meet someone and settle down?*

"Never."

I'd been there, done that, and discovered it wasn't for me.

I'd fallen hard for Elsie's mum. Jolene had caught my attention right away, her striking face framed by pin-straight hair and lit by a warm smile. She was cultured and witty, with intelligent brown eyes and tanned legs that went on forever.

Being with me was her idea of roughing it, and from the beginning, I sensed she wasn't committed for the long term. Being a flight attendant with Qantas, she always put her job first. Which I'd been super proud of—until Elsie came along. Jolene complained through the entire pregnancy. *How can I regain my figure after carrying around a giant melon for nine months? Really, Cleary. I blame you for this. You should have been more careful.*

Out in the kitchen, the oven timer chimed. I stayed submerged. One glass of vino and my bones were jelly. Nudging the hot tap with my toe, I ran more water, then shut my eyes and melted back into the heat.

Jolene was right. I should have been more careful. But after Elsie was born, my regret vanished. She was a big baby with rosy cheeks and the most amazing eyes—one grey-green, one clear liquid blue—and a chirpy little laugh that lit up her entire face and touched everyone around her. I lost my heart the minute I saw her. Jolene... not so much. She had lasted exactly three months as a mum. *Honestly, Cleary... I've got bags under my eyes and rolls around my middle that won't leave. I'm over cleaning up poop and wee and sick! I feel like a fat, leaky zombie and I've had enough.*

When I refused to dump Elsie on my mother to raise, Jolene had packed her things. *You'll soon see what it's like, Cleary. I grew up with a single parent, and it's no picnic. You won't cope on your own. You can barely commit to shaving every day or getting a haircut, let alone raising a child. So you'd better find someone else to do it. One of your bimbos, if any of them can be bothered. I'm done!*

For a while she had drifted in and out of our lives, visiting when she found time. I had hoped as Elsie grew, Jolene's mothering instincts would kick in, but that never happened. After a couple of years, her visits stopped. It was her loss.

"Here's to you Jolene." I raised my wineglass and drained the dregs. "I was okay with cleaning up. The pigtails, the skinned knees. The wee and the sick. Me and Elsie are perfectly happy without your drama, thanks very much—"

A bird shrieked outside.

Wine sloshed over my hand.

I set aside my glass and sat up. An eerie sound, whatever it was. An owl. Or maybe a fox. Shrill and angsty, it caught me off guard. Perhaps it wasn't a bird.

Had someone screamed?

"Elsie?"

Out of the bath, I dragged a towel around my waist and ran down the hall. Shoving open Elsie's bedroom door, I barged in. She lay on the bed with her phone. When she saw me, she slapped a hand over her eyes.

"Gross, Dad!"

"Did you just scream?"

Her eyes went wide. "We thought it was you."

"Me?"

"Gran said you must've seen a spider." She returned to the phone. "I dunno, Gran. No, it wasn't him. Maybe the TV. He's naked."

"I'm in a towel!"

Back in the bathroom, I pulled on jeans and a clean T-shirt, shaky with adrenaline. Dragging on my boots, I thrust open the window and stood rubbing my hair with the towel. Looking outside and searching the darkness.

Bloody Jolene. Thinking about her always made me jumpy. I put on a tough façade, but deep down, I knew she was right. I wasn't cut out for this parenting gig. Desperate to prove her wrong, I had poured all of my savings into bigger, fancier houses—an old mansion in St Kilda, even a former orphanage —trying to create a feeling of stability and normalcy for my daughter. But no matter how much money or time I poured into these illusions, they never felt like home. And the nagging fear that I was failing as a father ate away at me every day. *It's like we're stuck in a loop, Dad. Always moving. Never really living.*

"It'll be different this time, kiddo. This property will get us back on track—"

Another scream cut through the night.

Muffled now, as though the bird had flown deeper into the garden. Up the hill, towards the damp thicket of trees and brambles that surrounded the loch. There'd been no mention of adjoining properties, but that didn't mean we were totally alone on the mountainside.

When it came again, I flinched.

Bird, my arse.

It sounded nothing like a boo-book owl and everything like some poor woman lost out there in the dark. Calling someone's name. Or maybe crying for help. My feelers prickled, forcing the hairs on the back of my neck to attention. I hadn't felt them since the day we arrived, when I sensed someone watching us.

I clawed my fingers over my scalp.

It was her. Briar Rose. It had to be.

Stalking back to Elsie's room, I went in. "Did you hear it that time?"

She shrugged, but seemed a little wide-eyed. I gestured for her to pass me the phone so I could speak to my mother.

"Hey, Mum?" I sent Elsie a warning look. "Stay on the line with her till I get back, okay?"

"Cleary, what on earth—?"

"I heard a noise outside. I'm sure it's nothing, but I need to check."

"You sound jumpy. Have you been drinking?"

I sighed. "Just stay on the phone, please?"

"All right. Put her back on."

Elsie took the phone, but I caught her eye.

"Don't leave the house, hear me? I'll be two minutes."

She suppressed an eye roll and went back to her grandmother. "I know, right?" she whispered as I slipped out. "I think he's overtired."

Delicious smells wafted from the kitchen, and my stomach growled. Too bad, dinner would have to wait. As I hurried through the house, the scream came again. A long drawn-out wail that sounded anguished and definitely human.

"Bloody hell," I muttered, rummaging under the sink for a torch. "I've barely been here five minutes and already the place is a madhouse. It sounds like someone's being murdered…"

10
ROSALBA

He was easy enough to follow. A big beardy bear of a man crashing noisily uphill along the track, following the jerky cone of torchlight he was shining around in the dark, his boots crunching on the gravel as he headed towards the trees.

Quiet as a shadow, I crept along behind him.

"Hello," he called. "Anyone here?"

He didn't expect an answer, did he? Out here in the pitch-black garden, surrounded by bushland. High on the mountainside, miles from anywhere. The darkness leaping around him, his breath rasping in the stillness.

I moved closer.

My own feet were bare, my tread silent. I was close enough to reach out and run my fingertips across those broad shoulders. Give him the tingles, a rush of icy cold. I'd have loved to shove him or trip him, but alas, that sort of contact was beyond me.

Besides, it would spoil the surprise.

A single scream, delivered right next to his ear, should just about stop his heart. Years ago, one poor fellow had been on this same track seeking me out. Hoping to frighten me off with a bundle of smoking sage and a mantra. I had rushed up and screamed into his face. Not just a short sharp screech, either. A good long bellow, full of angst and fury. He turned ashen, stumbling backwards, the sage sailing off into the dark, the mantra swallowed by a scream of his own. He rolled down the hill and fled Loch Ard that very night.

This man tonight was calm. Like someone who did not startle easily. Well, we'd soon see about that. I went closer, right up close, drawing the night air deep into my lungs...

And screamed right next to his head.

The man lurched sideways, but then planted his feet square on the ground and whipped around. He didn't flinch, or even seem all that surprised to find me standing there.

Rather, it was me who reared back, clutching my throat.

"William—?"

The garden stilled. The night air grew thin, impossible to breathe. William was dead. He'd been gone for over a century. This man was flesh and blood, heat radiating off his skin. His black hair curled down to his shoulders, and a dark scruff covered his jaw. Drawings twined over his thick arms, and his jeans and T-shirt were just a murmur too tight ... but his face. A familiar face, and dear to me.

He frowned. "Who's William?"

My lips parted. My mouth dropped open. Not even a breath escaped. His eyes, the same eyes that once undid me, now met mine, ocean-blue and unforgettable. Then his pupils bloomed, black engulfing the blue, and his gaze turned sharp as he stepped closer.

"More importantly, who the heck are you?"

11
CLEARY

"You can see me?"

The woman emerged from the shadows, her eyes wide and luminous as planets. If not for the tangled hair, she could have been breathtakingly beautiful.

I dipped my torchlight. "Of course I can see you."

"Oh, dear."

I stepped closer, but she skittered back into the shadows. Her long knotty hair and old-fashioned clothes made her look vaguely hippyish. The once elegant dress was now torn and mud-stained, its ankle-length hem frayed, and the embroidered flowers on the sleeves coming unstitched, the threads poking up like tiny antennas.

I flicked the light back to her face. *Jeez, what was that? Difficult to see in the gloom. Was it a bruise ... or blood?*

She shielded her eyes. "Quit that, will you?"

"Sorry. But you seem ... hurt."

"You'll get hurt if you stay here."

"Is that why you were screaming?" I shone the torch into

the bushes behind her. Shadows scurried from the light, but there was no sign of anyone else. "Did someone attack you?"

"I'm not hurt!"

"Your face..." I'd meant to say it gently, but it sounded like an accusation. "It's just that—"

"You need to leave." She raked the dark curtain of tangled hair forward to cover the massive bruise or whatever it was swallowing the entire left side of her face. "That's why I was screaming. Because this is my garden, and you're an intruder."

I scoffed. "Your garden?"

"Yes, mine. The flowers and trees. The birds and insects. It's all mine."

"I suppose all those blackberry vines taking over the place are yours, too?"

"Of course."

I inched closer. She seemed human enough. Despite a vague chill in the air, there was no malevolent fog around her. Yet my feelers sharpened, the hairs on my arms prickling. She had a faintly dreamlike shimmer, as if she'd invaded Elsie's glitter stash. I stepped closer and frowned.

"Have we met before?"

She bristled up, glaring at me. "You look like William, but you're not him. You're different. The way you speak. You're loud and sure of yourself. Your hair is so ... long. And those drawings on your arms..."

"Tatts?"

"William never had those."

"Who's William?"

"Never mind. What matters is that you're not him. And you and your child are trampling all over my garden. Leaving trails and breaking my links to ... well, to the time before. Scaring the shadows. It must stop."

The back of my neck tingled. It was her, Briar Rose. It had to be. Her talk of us breaking links to the time before, and wanting us gone so badly. Yet she seemed so real. Not spectral at all. Even the shimmer had faded. My hunter radar had barely stirred.

"You live here, at Loch Ard?"

She adjusted her hair, peering at me from behind the tangled curtain. She seemed perplexed, as if my face puzzled her. Her lips tightened and her single eye flashed in the gloom. She lifted a slender arm and pointed down the hill.

"I live down there."

"The house?"

She lets out a pained sigh. "Not the house. Lord, the house, I'd rather die than set foot in that horrible place again. See that black cypress hedge below the shade house?"

"Yeah."

"There's a cottage tucked behind it."

"The cottage is derelict. The estate agent recommended I pull it down."

She made a scoffing sound, then turned abruptly and stalked off down the hill. For someone so irate, her tread was oddly silent, while my boots thumped along the track after her, crunching on dry leaves and twigs.

"Hey, wait. What's your name?"

She glared over her shoulder. "Rosalba."

Pretty name. Unusual. She had to be Briar Rose, although part of me hoped I was wrong. Maybe the cottage really did have a tenant no one knew about? She was intense, wary, a bit of a kook. Lovely, though. Radiant as a moonbeam. If only she'd pull back her hair and let me see her better.

I caught up with her. "I'm Cleary."

She slipped past and darted off down the slope. When she

reached the hedge, she ducked behind it and ran ahead towards the dark shape of the cottage.

"See?" Her voice was bright in the darkness, triumphant. "I told you! It's lovely, isn't it? It has such a pretty view of the valley, especially when it snows. Besides, it's where William and I—"

She cut off, glancing over at me, her eye gleaming warily in the dimness.

I shone the beam over the cottage.

According to the website, the original owner had built the old piper's cottage in the late 1800s to accommodate the bagpipe player he'd brought with him from Scotland.

It would have been charming back then. Now, it was a mess. Weeds choked the path leading to the buckled door. The roof was missing tiles and the gutter hung down like a torn hem. Most of the windows gaped empty, shards of fallen glass glinting from among the overgrown grass and weeds. The tiny dwelling looked leaky and desolate, in need of attention.

"No one lives here, Rosalba." My voice was no longer gentle.

Seeing the derelict cottage made me sway more towards the likelihood that she was our entity. A shame. She was intriguing. In another life I might have enjoyed getting to know her better. I thought of the jars of black salt in my pantry. "Why don't you come back to the house with me so we can get you sorted?"

"I don't need sorting. I need you to leave Loch Ard and never return."

I blinked, and suddenly she stood inches from me. The earthy scent of violets wafted around me as she leaned in closer, her pink lips parting into a smile. My pulse faltered as I tried to decipher the look in her eyes—was it playfulness or something more dangerous? And why did she seem ever so vaguely familiar?

I'm sure I know you from somewhere. Rosalba, Rosalba ... your name doesn't ring any bells. Of course, I'm hopeless with names, yet I know you.

No warning sirens were going off, my feelers barely prickling. As a hunter, I should sense a restless entity the minute I met one—but I was strangely undecided about the person in front of me. If only I could see past her hair, maybe then I'd remember if we had met before. Reaching out, meaning only to shift her hair gently aside so I could see her better, my fingers grazed her face ...

And passed right through her.

She gasped and lurched away, running towards the cottage. I buckled, fighting the roll of queasiness that always accompanied contact with one of the others. A jumble of images flashed behind my eyes, too fleeting to make any sense. I quickly shook them off and managed to stagger after her, shining the torch between the trees and along the track. I thumped up the steps and pounded on the door, shining my light through a broken window.

"Rosalba?"

For a while I stalked around the little dwelling, hoping she'd return. My ears still rang from the echo of her screams. Maybe if I waited long enough, she'd start up again so I could follow her. But nothing stirred. Briar Rose had disappeared into the deathly stillness of the night as if she'd never been.

12

ROSALBA

As the moon sank lower and the sky lightened by degrees, I darted through the garden, trying to lose myself in the shadows. Cold, wet leaves clung to my legs and branches snagged the thin fabric of my dress, but nothing erased the memory of his warm fingers brushing my skin.

Had he really touched me?

I shivered. My plan to scare him away had backfired. He hadn't been scared at all. Not even rattled. Rather, I was the one to take fright and run. And I was still running now in the fragile morning light, my feet barely touching the ground as I bounded along the misty trails.

"He touched me."

Or at least, he had tried. His fingers passed through me like a puff of breeze. Yet the simple gesture made my heart pound so cruelly I could barely breathe.

So I kept running.

Veering through a patch of flowers, inhaling their syrupy perfumes. Trailing my fingers over the soft petals, the furry leaves and smooth leaves, over rough bark and prickly blackberry stems.

Midday came and went and now somehow it was afternoon. The sun trailed her tendrils of light across the sky as she sailed westward towards the horizon. The heat of the man's hand still clung to my skin like an imprint, and the flicker of recognition in his eyes haunted me. Did he sense the bright pulse of connection between us, just as I did?

"He's not William."

Saying it aloud didn't help. Not when my voice wavered with uncertainty. William had died on the battlefield long ago. But perhaps in another lifetime this man had once *been* William. Perhaps fate had somehow brought us together again?

"He's not William!"

Rather, he was a threat. Hadn't he said so himself? *The cottage is derelict. The agent recommended I pull it down.* What else was he planning to destroy, the garden? And me along with it?

The sun blazed overhead, and the back of my neck began to burn. I paused to mop it with a hanky. *The next time I see him, I'll be stronger. Better prepared. I won't let him sway me with his deep blue eyes and gentle words. He's a threat, and threats must be driven away.*

I wandered uphill to the shade house. It was cooler here. Tree ferns sprouted thickly through the wrought iron bars, their hairy trunks clogged with moss. With each step, the crumbly soil squished beneath my toes, releasing a rich, earthy aroma. I closed my eyes and took a deep breath, letting the scent soothe me—

A peal of gleeful giggling shattered the stillness.

I straightened up, my breath catching. Someone was at the loch. It could only be the girl, but what was she doing? The loch was a horrible place. Damp and gloomy, its dark waters churning with danger.

I ran up the hill, following the shrill sounds. Chatter now, and more giggles, merry as birdsong. By the time I reached the deep little lake, I was faint with dread and fear. I looked around.

The trees grew thickly here. Sunlight fanned through their upper branches, but closer to the ground the shadows were dark and dank and over there, on the muddy banks, in between the mossy boulders, little pockets of water gleamed like spilled ink. The scent of mud filled my nostrils, the gagging smell of rot and decay and raw panic—

'Hello!' chirped a voice.

I whipped around, my hand on my throat.

A mighty tree trunk had fallen across the deepest part of the water, forming a natural bridge from one side of the loch to the other. The girl was stepping along it, her arms out for balance, her reflection dancing over the black water. In one hand, she held a small bouquet of wild roses. *My* roses. She was smiling ear to ear.

"Get off that," I barked. "You'll fall!"

She gave me a wave, then skipped along the trunk and bounded over. Her freckled face was pink from the sun, her dark hair jutting up uncombed at the back of her head. Her sneakers were muddy, and one glittery shoelace had come undone.

She looked up at me with big, trusting eyes. "I'm Elsie."

My heart squeezed. Oddly, she resembled her father, but there was no trace of William in her small face. Had I only imagined a likeness, wishful thinking, after a century of loneliness?

"Stay off that log, you hear?"

"Okay."

"Why play in such a terrible place?"

"I was looking for tadpoles. But there aren't any, so I climbed up on the bridge—" She pointed her wilting flowers at the fallen tree. "I thought it might lead to a magical realm."

"The only place it leads to is trouble. That water's deep. A young girl like you could easily drown. Anyway, why are you in my garden?"

"I just moved here with my dad."

"What about your mother?"

She tilted her head as if pondering one of life's thornier questions, then shrugged.

"She ran off and left us."

"Why?"

"Dad says she had stars in her eyes."

I peered from behind my hair. I should stop. She was safely away from the hungry water. Not my responsibility. Talking would only encourage her, but I had to ask.

"Stars?"

Elsie nodded. "She works for a big airline. Travels a lot. She thought a family was cramping her style. At least, that's what Dad says. I don't remember her much." She looked back at me, her eyes narrowed in interest. Curious eyes. One dark green, the other seawater blue.

"Does—" I stopped. My head was spinning. A conversation. With a child, of all things. The sudden rank, mossy smell of the waterhole filled my lungs and a feeling of foreboding swept through me. "Does he know you're wandering around up here on your own?"

"He thinks I'm in my room reading."

"Why aren't you?"

She shrugged. "Got bored."

"Hasn't anyone told you not to talk to strangers?"

"Dad tells me all the time."

"Then why are you talking to me?"

Her freckles rearranged themselves as she grinned. "You're not really a stranger though, are you?"

"I am most definitely a stranger."

"What's your name?"

"None of your business."

"Aww, go on. Tell us. Please?"

I huffed. Could this child be any more annoying? I could actually hear time ticking away. Or maybe it was my heart, reminding me I had one job to do, and I was right now doing exactly the opposite.

"Is it Rumpelstiltskin?" The girl tapped her sandalled foot against a rock. "Your name, I mean?"

"Are you always this nosy?"

She grimaced, nodding. "My dad says I'm incorroborable."

"Indeed."

"Go on, tell us your name. Ple-ease."

I scowled at her. "Rosalba."

Her face lit up. "What a lovely name! Oh, I'm so jealous. I wish my name was lovely like yours."

"What's wrong with Elsie? It's nice enough."

She flapped her ragged bouquet against her leg. "You think so?"

"Of course."

"Have you seen the ghost yet, Rosalba?"

I pulled back. "Ghost?"

"She was crying last night like a boo-book owl. We heard her." Elsie gestured past me down the hill towards the house. "Maybe the other tenants used to hear her too. They never hung around long. I guess she scared them off."

"Why aren't you scared?"

Her little eyebrows shot up. "Oh, I love ghosts! Things that go bump in the night. Glimmers. Ghouls. Spirits. Glimpses from the corner of your eye, you name it. They're my thing. Besides, my dad already met her! He reckons she's not scary at all. That she's kind of nice. At least, when she's not scaring the stuffing out of a person. You know what else he said?"

I blinked. Nice?

The girl leaned in. "He said she was super pretty."

I went still.

She nodded. "Or at least, she would be if she brushed her hair."

I huffed. Annoying little trickster.

"Go home, Elsie. And stay away from the water. It's deeper than it looks."

She squinted up at me, shading her eyes against the sun. The rays through her fingers caught the blue iris and turned it luminous.

"Okay, Rosalba. See you round like a rissole!" She gave another wave and scooted off down the track towards the house.

I bellowed after her. "And don't come back!"

Rissoles. Boo-book owls. Ghosts. Lord, what an exasperating child.

But as dusk settled over the garden, the house drew me, and I stood watching from the darkness. One by one, the windows lit up, glowing like big, friendly eyes. Behind the curtains, a large bear-like shadow moved deliberately, while a small one flitted like a butterfly. After a while, the lights blinked off. All but one. The man paced silently behind the window, back and forth, his shoulders hunched against whatever thoughts were keeping him awake.

My dad reckons she's super pretty.

I lifted my hand to my face, tracing the ruined left side with my fingertips. It felt smooth in the dark, as though it perfectly matched the good side. But by daylight ...

I drew back into the shadows.

Why weren't they scared of me?

The girl. The man. Cleary. What sort of name was that, anyway? It made me think of cloudless skies and sunlight, and piles of freshly raked grass.

"You should be scared of me. I'm a monster who's done monstrous things. And you should be scared for your daughter. Especially for her."

My fingers lingered on my cheek where he had touched me. Gently, carefully, as if all he wanted was to brush aside my hair. Had he seen? Had he glimpsed the part of me I tried hardest to keep hidden?

The house was fully in darkness now.

The man and child slept, their dreams shimmering in the night like bright cobwebs, altering the energetic landscape of the garden as they faded. Covering my own memories like a layer of ash, so that they faded, too.

13
ROSALBA

A WEEK HAD PASSED since I saw the girl by the loch. She and her father had been quiet, and I started to hope they had taken my hint to leave. But as I did my early rounds of the garden's perimeter, there he was, the man, stalking uphill along the western boundary fence, a big glass jar gripped in his hands.

As the first rays of sunlight crested the horizon, he unscrewed the jar and poured a blackish substance onto his palm. Then he began casting it along the fence line.

I followed him uphill, keeping my distance. As he passed the lightning tree, he looked out across the valley below. Darkness still lay over the town, and fog swirled on the river. He stood steadfast as a sea captain at the helm of his ship, gazing out across the ocean of space.

If I squinted, he could pass for someone else. A man returned from war, perhaps. His broad shoulders slumped a little after battle, his perfect features bronzed by the rising light.

Please don't move and break the spell ... you are so like William and I don't know if it hurts me or helps to see you standing there so proud and unattainable, and I can't explain why but I really don't want you to move...

He looked back over his shoulder. Did he sense me watching? If so, he made no sign of it, just continued up the hill along the fence, casting his black substance around as he walked, as though feeding grain to invisible hens. I waited until he was out of sight, then went across to investigate.

It was not grain, but small blackish crystals. Like salt dusted with black powder. Some crystals were fine, others the size of little stones. As I crouched beside them, my head began to spin. I was suddenly woozy, lightheaded, as though the day had grown uncomfortably warm. Sunlight flared off the crystals, making them wink and glitter like black glass.

I bent nearer. My nostrils flared. A scent lifted from them. A whiff of decaying bones and scraped campfire ash. I reached out to touch them...

Then pulled back, gasping.

My hand burned, my throat alight too, the air scorching my lungs. My eyes streamed, and a terrible trembling gripped my limbs so intensely that my teeth chattered.

As I lurched away from the crystals, the burning eased.

Others had tried to get rid of me—and failed. The fellow with the sage. Another lot who lit candles at midnight and sat around a board, pushing a glass back and forth and calling out to me in strained voices. Fools. Children playing with fire, who startled easily and ran when I bashed on the window pane or screamed blue murder in the garden.

But this one. Cleary. He was no child. He was a genuine threat to me and the garden I was protecting.

As I glared up the hill, my rage quickened. "If you want me to leave, you'll have to try harder than this!"

14
CLEARY

A FLURRY of dry leaves and dust lifted off the ground and swirled around my ankles. Strange. I looked across the valley. No clouds, just a peaceful blue dawn sky.

I emptied another handful of salt from the big jar, scattering it across a trail worn into the grass. Careful to sprinkle it lightly, so the crystals blended into the pebbles and dirt. Rosalba had ventured this way often in the past few days to gaze down at the view. The salt wasn't enough to expel her completely, but if she crossed it even once or twice, her tether would weaken. It would give me a head-start until I could find her gravesite.

When I reached a rocky ledge, I paused under a thorny rose vine to admire the view.

The first rays of sunlight painted the landscape with gold, glinting off the river, which hugged the sleepy little town in its gentle curve. Farmland extended in all directions, rolling pastures bordered by bushland. Majestic hills rose to the northwest, their dense forests full of shadows. As I inhaled the crisp morning air, a sense of peace settled over me. *Imagine waking up to this every day. A man could get used to it—*

"Steady on, you sound like Elsie. A rolling stone, remember? You've got a job to do, and once it's done, you're outa here."

I turned away from the view and returned to my task, scattering salt along the narrow track. When a gust of wind came out of nowhere and snatched the grains from my fingers, I braced myself against the force of it. Another more powerful blast came straight after, knocking me off balance. I stumbled back and collided with the rose vine's trunk, the thorns clawing my skin through my T-shirt, their poison tips setting my flesh alight.

"What the hell?"

The wind punched into me again, shoving me so hard against the vine that the jar slid from my grasp. It shattered on the rocky ledge, spilling salt on the ground beneath me.

"Damn it!"

I rubbed my throbbing shoulder. A moment ago the day was still and serene, barely a puff of breeze. Now it was rising into a gale, causing trees to sway and leaves to swirl and dance in the air like confetti. I squinted against the updraft, searching the garden. Further up the slope, half-hidden among the trees, stood a figure.

"Rosalba?"

As I moved towards her, she raised her arms. The wind grew stronger, pushing against me like a solid wall. Grit and leaf litter stung my face. Rosalba flicked her hands and more leaves ripped from the trees and swarmed towards me. The air came alive, whipping sticks and debris into what felt like a cyclone.

I shielded my face with my arms. Had she been watching me and guessed what I was doing with the salt? Was this a warning?

"Quit it, ghost girl," I called out to her. "You can't scare me off this easily."

Rosalba stood tall, her dress whipping wildly in the violent wind. Her arms lifted higher and her hair lashed around her head like angry horsetails. With a sweep of her arm, more debris surged down the hill towards me.

Grit flew into my eyes, stinging and burning. I struggled to breathe. I raised my hands to shield my face, yelling at her to stop, but the attack intensified. Cursing under my breath, I ran for cover.

Debris surged after me as I raced through the garden, veering off the track into the undergrowth. By the time I ducked through the cypress hedge and across the weedy garden that surrounded the piper's cottage, dust and grit covered my hair and clothes. Dragging open the cottage door, I stepped inside, recoiling a little from the musty smell. Glass crunched under my feet. The wind howled through the broken window panes, and a branch crashed onto the roof, sending down a rain of dust.

I slumped against the wall.

Rosalba had created this.

The violent wind. The churning debris and fallen branches. She was somehow controlling the weather, using it as a weapon. My chest tightened. I had underestimated her. She wasn't the lost young girl I had taken her for, but a dangerous force driven by elemental energy. A poltergeist, far stronger—and angrier—than I'd imagined. Powerful. Maybe even vengeful.

"She has to go, before—" I thought of Elsie's tendency to slip out of the house and go wandering in the garden, and my fingers curled into fists. "Before she hurts someone."

The howling wind died down. I stumbled outside, blinking in the bright sunlight. Leaf litter and twigs carpeted the ground, but Rosalba had vanished. Probably back into the shadows, no doubt still watching me.

I rubbed the dust from my face, then brushed leaves and debris from my clothes and hair. *Think, man. You need to get rid of her fast. It's no longer just about the property. She's dangerous, and there's too much at risk. How can you use her anger against her?*

I headed back to the wild rose ledge and collected the pieces of my broken jar.

I left the salt.

The wind and rain would scatter it, but its potency would linger. Maybe Rosalba would trip headlong over it and untether herself, saving me the trouble.

"Yeah, not likely. But a guy can dream."

15
CLEARY

By the time I had washed off the dust and started on breakfast, Elsie emerged from her room. She wore her uniform, ready for her first day at the new school, her damp hair poking up as if electrified. She flopped on her perch at the table, her gaze fixed on the window, as if hoping to see someone out there.

I set a plate of fluffy pancakes in front of her.

"You planning on brushing that bird's nest on your head?"

She scooped a pancake onto her plate and topped it with bacon and fried tomato, then smothered the lot in maple syrup.

"I'll do it in the car."

"Got your brush?"

"In my bag." She dug into the pancake with her fork, devouring it hungrily. Wiping a smear off her chin, she beamed over at me. "Any sign of Rosalba this morning, Dad?"

"Just a glimpse. She was hiding in some trees."

"Hiding? Did you frighten her?"

I rolled a pancake into a tube and bit into it. Rosalba had

kicked my arse with that windstorm, but I wasn't about to admit it to my daughter.

"She got feisty, but I showed her who was boss."

Elsie's face fell. "Oh, why? I like her!"

"You know how I feel about you getting involved with the others. It's not safe."

"But she's lovely."

I poured myself a coffee and sat opposite her. "You've known her for five minutes."

"I can just tell."

I scooped some bacon and tomato onto another pancake. My mother was right. It was tough for parents to risk their child's safety repeatedly, but leaving them unprepared for dealing with the others was even worse. Elsie had proved she was more than capable. What worried me was her big, kind heart.

"Why do you insist on making friends with them, kiddo? Once they cross over, you're always sad."

She studied her pancakes. Her shoulders twitched, and when she finally looked up, there was a fire in her eyes that reminded me of my father.

"I need to make friends with them, Daddy. Because you can't."

I shoved my plate away, my appetite gone. "Hunters don't make friends with their prey, Else. It gets too messy."

She glared up at me. "They're not prey, they're people! They have feelings, just like us."

"I just don't want you getting hurt, possum."

"The others can't hurt you." She mopped her pancake through a pool of maple syrup. "It's just your fear of them that's dangerous. And I'm not scared, so I'm safe."

I gulped my coffee. She was wrong. People got hurt all the

time. My father, for one. I considered reminding her how her grandfather died, and how I vowed the same fate wouldn't befall us. But she was already nervous about her first day at school, and I figured that talk could wait. Besides, the sun was fully risen now, and if we didn't leave soon, she'd be late.

We hopped in the car, and Elsie was quiet for the whole twenty minutes it took to drive down the mountainside and into town.

She hated school. She got teased about her mismatched eyes, and for what she called her weirdness. I had mentioned it all to her new teacher last week, who reassured me the school didn't tolerate bullying. When I told Elsie this, she hadn't seemed convinced. Right now, she was glaring through the window as if expecting the worst, and I had a niggling sense she wasn't just cross about school.

"You okay, sausage?"

"Yeah, Dad."

"Nervous?"

"Maybe a little."

I frowned over at her. "Want me to come in with you?"

"Nope."

"You sure?"

"I'll be fine, Dad."

As I pulled up at the gate, she gave me a quick peck on the cheek and bounded out of the car, adjusting her backpack.

"Later, alligator."

Before I could reply with my usual—in a while, crocodile—she ran off along the concrete path that bypassed the playground, probably to locate the library. I watched until she disappeared inside and then drove across town towards the outskirts.

Elsie hadn't stopped talking about Rosalba since she met

her the other day. I'd been hoping her interest would be short-lived. Now, though, after seeing the glow on her face at breakfast, I worried it was already too late. I had to get rid of Rosalba before Elsie had her heart broken. Again.

Getting a spirit to cross a charged salt line wasn't the only way to break their tether. If I found Rosalba's grave, I could scrape up some loose soil and mix it with the salt and set it alight. This could be traumatic for the entity, which was why we usually avoided it. A traumatised entity was unpredictable and dangerous. Besides, it relied on locating the gravesite, which was often impossible.

The upside? It was fast.

And, if done correctly, permanent.

16

CLEARY

On the outskirts of town I found Woodhill's tiny cemetery nestled behind an iron gate. Morning sunlight warmed my back as I followed a gravel trail to the old section, stopping at each headstone to trace my fingertips along the rough edges, reading names and dates as I went. My heart sank with each name that wasn't hers. The sun burned hotter, making sweat drip down the back of my neck as I glared around.

Insects hummed and birds sang, bringing the day to life. But as the heat grew more intense, so did my frustration.

Rosalba's threat haunted me.

You need to leave Loch Ard ... don't make me force you.

Her words hadn't rattled me until the windstorm. That was proof enough she was dangerous, and that she'd stop at nothing to see us gone. She seemed so harmless that first night. Gentle, almost timid. But then she'd drawn on some hefty poltergeist rage to summon that wind. I had felt it in every gust.

Retracing my steps through the headstones, I circled back towards the gate.

"Where the heck are you buried, ghost girl?"

Not at Loch Ard. I'd scoured the property soon after we arrived and hadn't seen a grave. Which meant she had to be somewhere here at Woodhill. Maybe she'd taken her own life? In earlier times, suicides were buried outside the consecrated grounds of a cemetery, often without any marker.

I stepped through the gates and onto the surrounding land, walking the perimeter.

Many entities became tethered to our world after committing heinous acts in life, or having them committed against them. Murder. Suicide. Some got stuck here because of unfinished business, like a family betrayal or deception. But all tethers had one thing in common: negative emotions so strong that they stopped a person's spirit leaving after they died.

When I first met Rosalba, I thought she was sweet and sensitive, a probable victim. Clearly I misjudged her. What terrible deed bound her to this place, stopping her from finding peace?

The surrounding land yielded nothing even remotely grave-like, so I returned to the car.

"Looks like I'll have to find another way to get rid of you."

With the new moon approaching, this may be my last chance to untether her. Once the moon began to ripen back towards fullness, its potent energy would strengthen her connection to our world even more. I'd have to wait a whole month to try again. That would give my daughter time to form an attachment.

The longer I waited, the more brutal Rosalba's departure would be.

17
CLEARY

The next morning I dropped Elsie at school and then returned to Loch Ard, determined to find Rosalba's grave before the new moon.

I wasted a couple of hours searching the outer reaches of the garden, but found only brambles and weedy, forgotten flowerbeds. Even if Rosalba's family had buried her here, I might have to tear the whole fifteen acres apart to find the site. Weeks of work. Time I didn't have.

I gave up looking and headed back towards the house along a kangaroo track, mulling over my options. What else did I know about Rosalba? She had mentioned someone called William. She avoided the main house and lived in the cottage, but it was the outdoors she seemed to love most. *This is my garden ... the flowers and trees, the birds and insects ... it's all mine—*

A shadow fell over me and I flinched, but it was only the big old gum tree with the blackened trunk. The one I'd been meaning to cut down to open the view. I stopped and gazed up past the damaged bark into its gnarled branches.

Leaves danced delicately in the breeze, and one or two tiny blossoms still clung to their bracts, a solitary butterfly pausing to taste them.

As I breathed the warm air, a feeling of calm settled over me.

I could see why Rosalba loved the garden, but did she really believe it would stay untouched forever? Eventually someone, most likely me, would come along and clean it up. Replace the tired old flowerbeds, drag out the weeds. Chop down this ugly, burned out old tree. Still, I couldn't imagine her letting that happen without a fight—

I huffed, smiling up at the contorted branches.

"Maybe a fight is exactly what I need."

I practically ran back to the house, collecting my remaining jar of black salt. And my chainsaw.

A few minutes later, I was back at the towering red gum, scattering salt in a wide trail around its drip line. If Rosalba wanted to stop me chopping down her precious tree, she'd have to get right up close and personal. And to do that, she'd have to cross my salt line.

I eyed up the cuts I would make on the lower branches.

The old girl must have witnessed a lot. Thunder storms, hail and floods. Bushfires. The black scar that gutted half the trunk was probably lightning, forming a narrow cave almost large enough for me to stand inside. Incredible, the way it had regrown around the damage and kept going, bright green leaves still sprouting from its twisted limbs.

I cracked my knuckles and picked up the chainsaw. Holding it steady, I pulled back the safety bar and gave it a few revs. Fine black oil spattered the ground, and then I set it roaring like a savage beast. Angling the chain up under a low-hanging branch, I eased it against the rough bark—

A shriek tore the stillness.

Right behind me. Long and shrill enough to crack glass. My heart stopped. Something inside my head seemed to shatter, probably my eardrums. Stopping the chainsaw, I staggered around.

"What the heck—!"

Rosalba stood beyond the salt line, her green eyes flashing. She had replaced her torn green dress with a clean apricot one. Her hair still hung loosely over one side of her face, but she had brushed it free of tangles, and it gleamed darkly in the morning light.

"Hello, Cleary."

I blew out a breath. "Trying to give me a coronary, are you?"

"I won't let you cut it down." She glanced behind me at the tree, frowning. "Why would you want to do that, anyway?"

"To open the view."

"Or to lure me here." She glanced pointedly at the salt trail. "I know what you're up to. You think you can trick me into walking across those crystals, but it won't work. I know they'll burn me up. They'll send me into the void, won't they?"

I felt a pinch of admiration. Smart cookie. But she didn't have to cross the salt completely. If I could lure her close enough, the charge could still damage her tether.

"You seem kind of lost over there, ghost girl. Why don't you come closer?"

The glimmer of a smile. "How's your heart?"

Racing like mad, but not because you just nearly blew out my eardrums.

"My heart's fine. What the hell's your problem, anyway?

Sneaking up on a bloke like that, especially while he's holding a chainsaw. Someone might have got hurt."

Her lips curved into an annoyingly smug smile.

"That big old chainsaw can't hurt me, Cleary. You could slice it through me a thousand times, and it wouldn't make a scratch. However, you ... well, it takes a lot of focus, doesn't it, to wield a machine like that? Imagine if I screamed while you were mid-cut." She drifted closer, her gaze dipping over me. "Such lovely strong hands you have. Beautiful hands. What a shame to lose one."

I swallowed. "What do you want?"

"I want you to leave Loch Ard."

I laid the chainsaw on the ground, sighing. "The minute I leave Loch Ard, someone else will arrive. But the next people could bring bulldozers and demolish the house, clear the garden entirely and build a block of units. Is that what you want?"

She deflated. "Units?"

"Yeah, or worse. A concrete high-rise. How would you like that?"

"Would they really come here?"

"I did."

"But you ..." She drifted off, sinking small white teeth into her lower lip.

"Look here, Rosalba. I get it. We have a problem. You want me to go, but I'm refusing to. And if I stay, you're worried I'll change your garden. But here's the deal. If I revamp this place, it'll allow me to sell it for a king's fortune."

"This is about money?"

I tipped my head towards the valley. "Isn't this view amazing? If we opened it up, made it visible from the house, can you imagine how much more incredible it would be? It would make this property way too valuable to bulldoze. A nice rich city couple will buy it as a weekend escape." Even I could hear the falseness in my voice, but Rosalba's cogs were ticking over, I could see it in her eyes. "Chances are they'll leave you in peace most of the time. That's what you want, isn't it? Peace?"

She frowned.

Heck, she was pretty. Even scowling, even with her dark hair shadowing half her face, there was something about her that intrigued me. I took a step closer. I had meant to lure her, but here I was inching closer, drawn like an iron filing to a magnet. My heart punched hard as I crossed the salt, the grains crunching under my feet, glittering darkly in the afternoon sunlight.

"What's keeping you here, Rosalba? Why can't you just move on?"

Shadows engulfed her eyes. "Move on?"

I waved my hand at the salt line. "Cross over. Follow the light. Don't you want to find peace?"

She pulled back, glowering at me. "You think it's easy? You think I can just hop over the fence anytime I wish and simply vanish?"

"Have you ever tried? Maybe stepping outside the garden will break your bond to it?"

She huffed. "I've no intention of leaving the garden. It's my home."

"You must be lonely, living here by yourself. Don't you have loved ones you want to see again?"

Rosalba blinked rapidly. She adjusted her hair and then peered at me. A deer in headlights. Or maybe that was me. I stepped closer, the salt behind me now.

"What about William? Maybe he's waiting for you on the other side."

Her chest rose and fell, her small hands fisting by her sides.

"William's not waiting for me! He promised to return after the war and marry me, but he never did!"

A flock of cockatoos erupted into the sky and flew away. Rosalba took a step closer. And another. Then without warning, she launched at me, as if intending to fling herself into my arms.

My body tensed, my pulse starting to fly as I wondered how her willowy curves might feel pressed hard against my body—

But she passed straight through me like an arctic gust.

My skin turned icy.

I moaned, buckling over, shivers ripping through me.

The garden faded into a murky haze as my sight blurred. Jumbled images from another time flashed behind my eyes. The smell of gunpowder filled my lungs, and distant screams rang in the air. Suddenly, I was running across a blood-soaked battlefield, terror gripping my heart as another man's thoughts invaded my mind.

18

WILLIAM

1918

William ran across the field, the rifle in his hands slick with blood. A hot, wet river coursed from the wound over his hip, but there was no pain. Just the explosive kick of his heart as the roar of artillery fire battered him from all sides. *Keep running, man. Lower your head and keep running. You made a promise, remember? And now you'll do whatever you can to keep it.*

He trudged through mud, leaping and stumbling over fallen bodies, his boots plunging and sucking in the soil.

Run, man. Run for your bloody life ...

His lungs were on fire. A bullet grazed past his ear and he

lurched sideways, but it was the man beside him who went down. A good man. They'd been sharing smokes and stories of home for weeks, but right now William would be damned if he could recall the bloke's name. His mind was too consumed with the sole purpose of staying upright and surviving.

After all, he had a promise to keep.

I've no intention of dying, Rosebud—the minute I'm home, I'll put that emerald on your finger and we'll never have to say goodbye again.

He was almost at the trees where the rest of his platoon waited, when someone behind him started yelling. Blue murder, poor bastard. Must have been hit. William stopped and turned around. One of his mates was curled on his side, poor old Batesy, with a wife and two little ones waiting for him at home. He was clutching his chest, blood slicking his hands.

William ran back to Batesy and grabbed him under the armpits. Batesy was a big man, but somehow William found the strength to hoist him to his feet. He slung Batesy's arm over his shoulder and they set off limping back towards safety.

"Hang on, mate." William tightened his grip on his friend's arm. "You'll be back home with Mary before you know it."

Another shell exploded behind them.

The blast threw Batesy forward, and William buckled beside him. Clods of soil and metal shards rained down, driving him against the ground. When it stopped, he pushed himself up and tried to stand, but his arms and legs shook too violently. Other wounded men surrounded him, some lying prone and others hunched deathly still over their weapons. The battlefield swam like a mirage.

He tried to stand. Something was wrong. His head. What was wrong with his head? He blinked up at the sky.

It was awash with red.

Another blast hurled him forward onto his face in the mud, his rifle trapped under him. Blood poured into his eyes. He was panting for air, his lungs limp and useless. He tried to roll on his side, but nothing worked, his limbs soft as boiled rubber, confusion rolling through him.

The yelling and shouting around him grew distant. Artillery fire and the whomp of mortars became muffled. The smell of smoke and blood faded. He clung to a single thought, his only lifeline.

"Rose."

It was just a whisper, a barely-there breath, but it anchored him. He slipped deeper into his mind, blocking out the din of gunfire and shell blasts, the screams and moans of the dying.

"Rose, are you here?"

She appeared before him, her hair bundled to the side, a loop covering half her beautiful features.

William smiled. A rare bird, his Rosebud. Her face upturned like a flower to the sun, bright tears gleaming in her eyes. Of everyone he knew, she was the most deserving of happiness. Brave, loyal Rosalba with her enormous heart and luminous spirit. He remembered what he told her that last evening as they stood under the lightning tree saying goodbye.

Nothing will keep us apart, Rosie girl. Not even death. I'll find my way back to you, love. No matter how long it takes...

His promise echoed in his mind and he clung to it, even as the sky darkened and the broken world around him slithered into a black void.

19
ROSALBA

NOW

I stood up the hill by the fence, watching Cleary, my fingers clenching the fabric of my skirt, as if that could somehow ground me. He had fallen to his knees in the lightning tree's dappled shade, his hands protecting his head as if from attack.

Was this another of his tricks?

I rubbed my arms. Flying into him had shaken me. As if I'd plunged into a hot swamp, and now my heart had thrown itself around in my chest, bruised and pulpy as an overripe peach.

He was so much like William.

Not just his looks, but other things, too. His scent. The warmth of his body, almost too warm, as if his heart was pumping extra hard. The energy that radiated out of him. That similarity was starting to obsess me. Which was bad. Very bad. A hundred years ago, William had broken me.

And now Cleary intended doing the same.

"Not if I can help it."

I glared down the slope, watching as he climbed to his feet and staggered back to the house, his shoulders rigid.

My fingertips tingled, and my skin felt chafed and alight as a dark energy radiated out of me. Did he honestly believe I could hop over to the other side whenever I wished? Why would I even want to? Loch Ard was my home and yes it was lonely, and sometimes just looking up at the stars filled me with a longing so deep and wretched it stole away my breath ... but leave?

"Never."

He would be the one to leave, not me. He may have weathered my windstorm, but I would get rid of him. I would find a way.

Running back along the fence, I trailed my fingers along the weathered posts. William had built this fence. It skirted the entire garden, although these days it wasn't much of a barrier. A century of rain and snow and scorching sunlight had eroded the posts, and the wire now hung in tangled, rusty loops. No longer doing its job, allowing kangaroos to enter, and feral goats and sometimes runaway stock from farms on the other side of the mountain. The entire world could come and go. Except me.

Can't you just follow the light?

Beyond the fence, a sloping paddock stretched out before me, dotted with wildflowers. Butterflies were everywhere, the warm sun gilding their wings as they swooped and fluttered over the weedy grass.

Just cross over.

Further up the slope, under the wild roses, the dark grains

of Cleary's crystals winked and glinted like tiny reptilian eyes. I could not feel their burn from here, but the faint whiff of greasy bones and ash turned my stomach.

He made crossing over sound so easy. As if all I had to do was leave the garden. Was he right?

Secretly, I craved to be somewhere else, anywhere else in the world. But it was a craving I buried deep inside me. What was the point of wanting, when you knew having it was impossible?

Don't you have loved ones you want to see again?

"Only William."

I hoisted myself up onto a fencepost and balanced there, my arms outstretched, my toes gripping the weatherworn wood. I only had to fall forward, into the outside world ...

My heart punched my ribs. My throat went dry. I had never left the garden. Never gone to town or ridden in my father's car, or dared to climb over into the paddock. Even in the time before, this fence confined me. And before the fence, my father's words.

You will not survive out there, Rosalba. It's a cruel world. They will hunt you down and kill you like the monster you are...

I stumbled back down from the fencepost, my pulse pounding wildly. Crossing over would not help me. No light or safety awaited me on the other side, only darkness and fear. And being hunted endlessly by those who refused to accept me as I was.

I left the fence and climbed the steep hill, hurrying along the maze of tracks and gravel pathways, bypassing the tall cypress hedge, and continuing on towards the piper's cottage.

Up behind the little dwelling, in a secluded spot shaded by trees, there stood a magnificent blue atlas cedar—my safe haven. Its twisted branches drooped down to the ground like a curtain, creating a hidden nook underneath it. A vibrant fairy ring of native violets surrounded it, their delicate purple petals and sweet fragrance usually bringing me joy.

But not today. My fists clenched at my sides and a dark feeling festered inside of me as I glowered at them.

"You'll be the one to leave this place, Cleary. Not me."

I had shown him what I was capable of. How dangerous I could be. And that was just the beginning. My fingers tingled, and a rush of power burned through my veins.

"I warned you!"

I crouched over the violets. Their nodding purple heads bowed over slender stalks, like dainty maidens admiring their frilly green skirts. With gentle fingers, I caressed a deep blue bud, then watched it wither and turn black.

I flicked it off its stalk.

The light did not shine for someone like me.

I would never cross over. Not willingly. I would rather be trapped here for eternity than face the unknown.

Than face the dark shadows of my past.

Sunlight speared through the weeping cedar canopy above me, but down at the base of the trunk it was deliciously dark. The violets nodded prettily, their soft little faces modestly downcast, lavender-blue and freckled with white. And me so poisonous right now, I could wither them with a glance.

As more petals wilted and fell to the ground, something gleamed from underneath them. I knelt for a closer look. It was a piece of glittery pink shoelace, curled up like a sleeping caterpillar. As I poked it with my fingertips, realisation flooding through me.

"Elsie."

She was Cleary's weakness. If something happened to her, it would crush him. His grief would drive him out of the garden and back into the outside world where he belonged.

Images started bombarding my brain.

Perhaps the girl would have an accident? The loch was a dangerous part of the garden, and luring her there would be easy. She might venture too close to the water and fall in. Drown. The loch had claimed other young lives, hadn't it? She wouldn't be its first.

Her spirit might even linger in the garden with me. It was lonely here. Perhaps I'd judged her too hastily before. She was funny and quick-witted and really quite entertaining. She might be good company once the shock of her passing wore off. She might learn to appreciate my company, too. Hadn't she raved about how much she loved ghosts? Perhaps she'd enjoy being one.

My father's words folded around me like a breath of wind.

No monster gets a happy ending.

"Well, I'll have mine!" I shivered and hugged myself.

Elsie could be my little shadow, running around the garden, chattering like a wren, trailing me through the long nights. Perhaps, in time, I'd learn to love her like a daughter. A little ally to keep me company in the bleak eternity that lay ahead.

20

CLEARY

Scalding water ran over my aching body as I stood in the shower, soaping off the sweat that had drenched me during my vision under the lightning tree. Contact with the others always caused me to see things, only nowhere near as vividly as this.

Why had this time been different?

I felt like I'd been struck by lightning myself, my blood buzzing in my veins, my thoughts on fire. *William running across the battlefield, the roar of artillery deafening as his pulse boomed in his ears.* I could still smell it. The blood. The smoke and mud. Could still hear the shouting and moans of the dying, the crack of rifle shots.

I towelled dry and pulled on my jeans, then went out to the kitchen where I wandered around in a daze. Looking for my mug, finding it in the place I always kept it. My thoughts as sludgy as treacle. I brewed strong coffee, then drank it at the window, squinting out at the brightness.

Every part of me ached. My legs were rubbery. My fingers and toes throbbed with cold despite the shower, and a fluey hangover gripped me. Worse than that, I felt like a stranger in my skin. William's emotions still raged through me, the weight of his promise to Rosalba crushing the breath out of me.

Nothing will keep us apart, Rosie girl. Not even death.

Being inside William's head was intense. His racing thoughts as the battle thundered around him. His fear for his dying friend, and his final thoughts about the woman he had loved. The grenades exploding nearby, and the soft thump of shrapnel embedding in flesh ...

"Ugh."

I felt totally out of my depth. I had dealt with poltergeists before, and other entities with various powers—only none that had gotten under my skin this way before. *Did you really think she was going to fly into your arms, idiot? Give you a sexy spirit-girl hug?* What was wrong with me? Rosalba was a powerful entity, maybe even powerful enough to really hurt me. Or worse, hurt my daughter.

I needed more than just a line of blessed salt.

I needed my mum.

Grabbing my phone, I dialled her number and stalked through the house, describing the morning's events. Mum listened attentively to my dilemma, but not in the way I wanted.

"You're saying she hugged you? Oh Cleary, you big loveable idiot. Are you all right?"

"No."

"What happened?"

The amusement in her voice set my teeth on edge.

"I'm not sure, Mum. Entities have swooped me before, and usually it's cold and cobwebby and I end up reeking like a grave. But this was different."

"How so?"

"My vision was extreme. I lost all track of myself. I was

really there, in someone else's body, thinking their thoughts. Living their life."

"What made her run at you?"

I slumped. "I threatened to chop down a tree."

She sighed. "A tree she values?"

"It's called progress, Ma. Clearing a burned out old red gum to open the view." I carried the phone to the window. "It's an eyesore. If it was gone, you'd be able to see the entire valley."

"Did you ask her permission?"

"It's my tree!"

"She might think otherwise, Cleary. If she's still hanging around, she probably thinks the garden is still hers."

"How do I get rid of her?"

"Have you salted her hangouts?"

"Yeah, a waste of time. She figured out the salt and now she's avoiding it."

"What about a grave? Your father liked to mix salt with a soil sample and burn it."

"I've searched the property and checked the local cemetery. Nothing."

Mum was quiet for a few seconds, then sighed. "Well, the new moon's tomorrow night. If you were hoping to channel lunar energies, you've pretty much missed your window."

"Not to mention I'm shaking like a leaf right now. I couldn't untether an ant. We'll have to wait another month."

"Are you absolutely sure you want to get rid of her?"

"Damn right I am."

"Then listen carefully ..." A bell tinkled somewhere on her end, and some papers rustled. "First, you need to win her trust. Get her to open up, talk about her life. You'll be digging down deep, looking for something in particular. A triggering event.

Something she's buried in her mind that keeps her tethered here."

"Sounds like fun."

"Most entities won't tolerate that sort of intrusion into their inner world. But if you tread gently and persevere, she might come around."

"How will I know this event?"

"It'll be something traumatic. Unfinished business. A crime committed—either by her, or against her. Maybe a distressing or unjust cause of death. A secret that needs revealing. A guilty conscience."

"She's very prickly."

"Facing past trauma isn't easy, Cleary. But if you help her discover the root cause, she'll have a better chance of confronting it. And once she confronts it, her tether will break. She'll be out of your hair and winging her way to the afterlife."

"You make it sound easy."

"Trust me, it won't be. Whatever raw emotion is tethering her, I can guarantee it's a powerful one. Rage. Vengeance. Hatred. You might have a struggle ahead of you. When she's forced to face her darkest emotions, she'll be at her most volatile."

"Can't wait."

Mum let out a small, exasperated sigh. "Your father had a knack for gaining an entity's trust and uncovering their secrets. But remember the last one you two were trying to untether? He let his emotions cloud his good sense, and it ended badly. For all of us." She swallowed hard, her throat clicking. "You're dedicated and driven, Cleary. But you don't have your father's skills or intuition. What you do have, fortunately, is a strong heart. And I believe that's enough to pull this off."

"That makes one of us."

"Oh, Cleary. You need more faith in yourself."

Through the window, I could see the gnarled old eucalypt where my chainsaw sat abandoned. A wide, beautiful valley extended beyond the tree, marred only by its blackened trunk. *Imagine if I screamed while you were cutting it down, you could lose a hand.*

"Can't you come over and have a go yourself, Ma?"

She laughed softly. "Nice try, love. I'm a salt maker and spell binder, not a hunter. If you want her to leave, you'll find a way. It's your garden, your territory now. No one can do it for you. Just a word of warning, though."

Another one? Great. "What's that, Mum?"

"Make sure you truly want her gone. Once her tether is broken and she leaves, she can never come back."

21

ROSALBA

For three days, an eerie silence hung over the house, broken only by the rumbling of Cleary's truck as he took his daughter to school and brought her back in the afternoon.

As I crouched beneath the shadowy cedar tree, up behind the cottage, I watched them come and go, certain I had triumphed. Soon, the removal van would come and they would return to the city, leaving me in blissful solitude once again. The lightning tree intact, my garden safe from demolishment.

Settling back against the rough cedar trunk, I sighed contentedly. The curtain of branches around me swayed gently, dancing its shadows over the flowers and ferns. I closed my eyes, drifting on the quiet breeze of birdsong and rustling leaves—

A sharp, metallic roar tore across the valley. It revved up and down, each burst louder than the last.

I shot upright. "The chainsaw!"

Scrambling out of my bower, I ran downhill, my bare feet pounding the track as my shadow raced ahead of me. My palms were suddenly damp, my heart fluttering sickly. My tree, my beautiful tree. Where I had waited for William, where we had kissed for the first time. And the last. Could I really bear to see it felled?

But when I reached the edge of the garden, I stopped in my tracks. The tree was unharmed. Cleary stood beneath it, revving his chainsaw a good distance from the trunk. The black crystals he had scattered around its base a few days ago glittered evilly in the sun.

When he saw me, the noise cut off.

I stood tall and glared into his eyes, catching my breath.

"What are you doing? You can't come here and destroy what's precious to me without consequences. I won't allow it."

He placed the chainsaw on the ground by his feet and walked towards me, crossing over the crystals. Then he frowned.

Why is he staring at me like that?

I gasped, clawing my hair forward to cover my bad side. Too late. He had seen. Seen it all. He had seen the real me and now he would fear me. Shun me. Good. Maybe now he'd take the hint and leave, before anything too tragic happened.

But wait. That wasn't fear in his eyes. It was pity.

His lips parted. "Your face."

"What of it!"

"It's a birthmark, isn't it?"

I lifted my chin, shrivelling inside. "Does it offend you?"

"Of course not! I might be an arsehole, but I'm not heartless."

He approached me, but I stood my ground. My lips pinched tight, and my fists clenched by my sides as I fought to endure his steady gaze.

"You don't need to hide behind your hair, Rosalba." His

voice turned gentle. "It's just a birthmark. Nothing to be ashamed of."

Just a birthmark? You have no idea, you idiot. This mark doesn't merely cling to my skin! Its roots have buried themselves deep down into my soul and infected that with its poison, too.

A scalding tear streaked down my face, then another. Fury and shame were burning up my insides, leaking out of my eyes. I wanted him to start the chainsaw again, so I could lash out. Hurt him, make him bleed. Make him feel the horror and despair that had gripped me since my first frightful glimpse in a mirror.

I jutted my chin. "I'm not ashamed."

He shuffled a step closer. "It's a mark, that's all. Skin deep. Heck, you wanna see a mark? Check this out."

Rolling up his shirt, he twisted to the side and patted his flat, hairy belly. Muscles rippled beneath an angry pink scar that coiled from his ribs and disappeared around his waist.

"Fell off a rooftop as a kid." He sounded almost proud. "Caught myself on a broken gutter pipe. Fifteen stitches. Guess I won't be winning any beauty pageants anytime soon."

Was he mocking me? Showing off his muscles, displaying a mark he could easily conceal beneath clothing? A mark that only seemed to enhance his rugged masculine beauty.

I squared myself and stepped closer.

"Why are you still here?"

He lowered his shirt, tucking it into his jeans.

"I want to make a deal."

He was smiling again. His eyes held no trace of pity, if it had ever existed. William always said I looked for the worst in people's reactions. Dear, kind-hearted William. How could he understand? While he saw the best in everyone, I had learned to anticipate the worst.

"I don't make deals."

Cleary gestured at the lightning tree. "It's burned out. An eyesore. It might be dying. Why does it mean so much to you?"

I inched closer. He had flecks in his eyes, grey amid all that blue. Light freckles on his cheeks, and threads of ginger in his scruff.

"Why do you care? You want it gone."

"I'm willing to trade for it."

"Trade?"

"Rosalba, you can keep the tree. I won't harm it, I promise. But in return, I want something from you."

I peered at him through my hair. "What?"

"A story. About your life before."

Cold panic shot through me. "I can force you to leave without telling you anything!"

He shrugged, breaking his gaze off my face, kicking the toe of his boot into a grassy tussock.

"My daughter and I are hunters. Both of us. We hunt entities trapped midway between this life and the next, and then help them to cross over."

"Is that why I can't scare you away?"

He nodded, giving his arms a rub. "We hunters are a stubborn lot. But here's the thing, when someone like you touches me, it sets off a kind of mental explosion in my brain. I start seeing things, visions. Snippets of other people's lives and thoughts."

"So?"

"The other day, when you ran through me ... I saw William. He died on the battlefield, didn't he?"

I froze. I never learned how William really died, so how could this stranger know? I leaned forward, frowning.

"What did you see?"

"He was trying to save his friend, but an artillery shell exploded nearby. As he lay dying, he was thinking of you. About how desperate he was to keep his promise and return to you."

I wanted to believe, because William had once made that very promise, but how could a vision show you inside someone's head?

"How do I know you're not lying?"

Cleary shrugged. "Does the name Rosebud mean anything to you?"

I gasped and inched closer, my heart quivering. Rosebud? Only I knew about William's pet name for me. No one else. It was our secret. Could Cleary's visions be real, after all? Did William really think of me as he died? Did he whisper my name with his last breath? Did he love me after all?

Suddenly I was all ears. "Please tell me more."

"And in return, you'll talk about your life?"

I nodded, standing frozen while he recounted William's last moments. The smoke and cries of the other wounded men, the deafening blasts. And William's blood seeping into the soil of that faraway place, his precious life ebbing away. The promise on his lips as he lay down in the mud and shut his eyes. When Cleary got to William's final words, my throat closed up and tears trickled down my cheeks.

Nothing can keep us apart, Rosie girl.

Reaching for my hanky, I dabbed it over my face.

Even if Cleary had made the whole thing up, I wouldn't have cared. It moved me to hear him speak of William this way —the raw emotion in his voice, the tiny pulse galloping in his throat, his gaze fixed just beyond me to a time long lost. It touched me in a way I couldn't explain, as if his words were slowly mending the broken pieces within me. And for more of that, I would pay any price he asked.

I looked at him. "What do you want to know about my life?"

Cleary walked a little way along the track and settled on a fallen log. His long legs stretched in front of him, his eyes crinkling as he smiled. He beckoned me over and patted the log beside him.

"Start with something easy."

"None of it is easy."

"How did you and William meet?"

A magpie warbled unseen in a high branch. The shadows where I stood were frigid on my skin, damp and oppressive. Meanwhile, the sunny log where Cleary sat—with his bulky tattooed arms and gentle eyes—seemed a far, far safer place to be.

I went over and sat next to him.

Stiff at first. My ankles pressed together. My wall of hair forming a barrier between us, my gaze darting anywhere but him. Yet as I spoke, haltingly at first, my stiffness melted away. Time yawned wide and somehow I slipped into it like a warm bath, letting that long ago life wash back over me.

22
ROSALBA

1914

DRY LEAVES CRUNCHED under my feet as I crept through the shadows beneath the willow tree. My veil fluttered with each quickened breath, and shivers ran over me. Though the morning sun tried to break through the branches, its rays didn't reach my hiding spot.

Digging my fingers into the warm bark, I pressed myself against the trunk and peered around it.

Out on the grass, a sunlit figure was raking leaves into a pile. A man. He was tall, whistling off-key as he worked, his muscular arms rippling under his shirt, his face hidden by the brim of his hat.

I bit down on my lip. *He mustn't see me. Mustn't know I'm here. Those are the rules, and breaking them always brings pain.*

Growing up, my father made me cover my face with a thin muslin veil, even when I was alone. Our home was devoid of mirrors and other polished surfaces. We had only china tea sets and wooden trays, nothing silver. No shiny surfaces to reflect my image and remind us all of what I was.

A freak, the maids whispered behind their hands.

A monster, my father boomed aloud.

Whatever I was, the veil became my haven. My shelter through the stormy seasons of my life. People didn't mean to be cruel, but my appearance touched something primal in them that brought out their worst. I learned to stay away, tucked inside the stone walls of our rambling house. The veil pulled over my face. Hiding myself like a shameful secret.

Only Hattie, our new maid, showed me any kindness, whispering news of the war through my bedroom keyhole, or bringing treats from the kitchen. But even her visits were brief and secretive.

I lived for those days when Father was away and I could sneak into the garden. Relishing the warm sun on my face and the breeze in my hair. Breathing the flowers, inhaling the birdsong, feeling my spirit come alive.

Like now.

I shifted behind the willow trunk, my gaze fixed on the man raking leaves. The new gardener.

Last night at supper, Father said he'd employed someone for the yard work. Help was scarce up here on the mountain. Since the war began a few months ago in July, thousands of young men had signed up to fight overseas. The papers predicted that many thousands more would follow.

Why had the new gardener not enlisted? Was there something wrong with him? If only I could see him better. See his face. But the leaves hung like a curtain in front of me, obstructing my view.

Gripping the smooth willow trunk, I leaned further forward and peered through the foliage, twigs cracking softly under me. The gardener paused, looking up. I froze in place and held my breath, and after a heartbeat he went back to raking.

Perhaps he had a horrible defect that prevented him from joining the army? Or wore thick glasses, or had a frightful squint? My father despised imperfection, but what if the lack of strong young men had forced his hand? What if this gardener was deformed somehow?

Like me, shunned and forced to hide himself away?

I leaned out as far as I could, but still the foliage blocked my view. Standing on tiptoes, I stretched out my arm to push aside a cluster of leaves, but lost my balance and fell sideways, yelping in shock. As I struggled to regain my footing, a branch caught my veil and ripped it from my face. In a hurried frenzy, I grappled it free, shredding the delicate fabric in the process, and stumbling out into the open.

The gardener stopped raking. *Please don't see me.* My throat jammed shut, my lips—my horrible swollen lips—caught around a gasp. *Please don't look, don't see. Please...*

But he did look, and he did see, his face brightening as he gave a friendly wave.

"Hello, there!" Lowering his rake, he strode towards me with a wide grin spreading across his face.

His beautiful, perfect face.

There was no defect that I could see—no thick glasses, no squint. Just terrifying symmetry, and a smile that grew wider as he approached.

Sunlight danced across his tanned skin, illuminating every

perfect curve and angle. His eyes dragged me into their blueness, like I was sinking into the crystal clear depths of a river. His green shirt and loose dark work pants hugged a body that was strong and fit from outdoor labour. Every movement he made seemed fluid and effortless, and I couldn't tear my eyes off of him, surely a god among men.

While I ...

Frozen. Bare-faced.

A monster. A freak.

A cry tore from my throat, the bark of a wounded gull. I slapped my hands over my face and fled back into the shadows, down along the cypress hedge, fleeing back towards the safety of the house.

His voice rang after me. "Wait! Stay and chat, won't you?"

Rushing upstairs, I locked myself in my room and leaned heavily against the door. With each explosive thump of my heart, I died a little more.

He had seen me! A man had seen me. Without my veil. A man had seen me without my veil and Father would not be pleased. He would shear off my hair. Burn my books. Scatter thorny rose boughs for me to kneel on. Then he would lock me in my bedroom and take away the key until I learned not to defy him. Which would never happen, as we both knew I couldn't obey.

Whistling. Was someone whistling? I crept to the window, dashing away the wetness on my cheeks. He stood over by the stables now, his green shirt flecked with dry grass, his hat skewed back revealing longish strands of thick dark hair.

The new gardener. My gardener.

I frowned, pressing my palm against the glass.

He had not screamed. Or fainted. He had not run to Father and complained. At least not yet. He had looked right at my face—my wretched, ruined face—and smiled. Not with revulsion. Not with horror. Not even with pity. His smile was all friendly curiosity. *Stay and chat, won't you?*

My palms turned damp. I slid my hand down the windowpane, leaving a smear. When you've starved for love all your life, even a crumb can trigger a feeding frenzy.

My life's perpetual sameness was all I knew. Me and Father rattling around this big old house, keeping to ourselves. Him with his brandy and prayers, me with my books and sewing and stolen moments in the garden.

Once, I might have been content. But not now.

When the gardener smiled at me, I finally understood the nameless longing that had plagued me all my life. To love and be loved. Could there be anything more important? No one had ever looked at me that way, with such a light in their eyes. With such a smile, like it was meant for me alone and no one else. It made my pulse fly, made my heart swell with longing. It was what I wanted, what I now craved. For a man like him to love me. To cherish and protect me. To adore me. Perhaps even one day to marry me.

The patch of sunny lawn was empty now.

The leaves raked up, and the new gardener gone home. Yet I could not forget him. The friendly, handsome face. The generous smile. And the blue, blue eyes that had—I felt certain—seen past the ruined monster to the good, kind girl who was hiding beneath.

What should I do? Even as mortification flushed my skin to an even deeper, uglier red, another part of me wondered. Should I stay in the lonely shadows forever, as Father insisted I must?

Or should I dig deep and find the courage to take a chance on love?

23
CLEARY

NOW

ALL NIGHT I tossed and turned, my bedcovers tangling around my overheated limbs, the clock ticking away the hours.

What an idiot.

Displaying my childhood scars to Rosalba, who had endured so much more. The mark on her face was extreme. It covered her whole left side, a deep angry red, dark as a blood-blister. Not something you could whip a T-shirt over and put out of your mind.

I kept seeing her beside me on the fallen log yesterday, her head lowered to hide the marked side of her face.

The look in her eyes, though.

She hadn't been able to hide that.

The hungry look as she talked about William, the longing in her voice when she spoke his name. A hundred years hadn't dimmed what she felt about him, the passage of time only seeming to strengthen her feelings.

She adored him. Loved him deeply. Still yearned for him. And something in her faithfulness made me yearn a little, too.

"William's the key, isn't he?"

The key to solving her mystery and understanding how to break her tether. She seemed eager to talk about him, the way her face had glowed yesterday, her words spilling freely. Yet the cruel things she'd said about herself—*a monster, a freak*—made me wonder. Was there more to her story than a young woman who'd lost her sweetheart in the war?

I felt a curious pull towards knowing the rest, not just to unravel her secrets, but because her words had seeped into my soul. *Should I find the courage to take a chance on love?*

I gave up trying to sleep and dressed hurriedly, grabbing my flashlight. It was 2 a.m. I checked on Elsie—sound asleep beneath her polka-dot quilt—and then headed outside. The moon shone brightly, lighting my way. I climbed the hill in the dark, heading towards the old piper's cottage, the night air damp on my skin.

I knocked softly on her door.

"Rosalba?"

The place was silent. I tried the handle. It was open. The door screeched, and I went inside.

"It's me. Cleary. Are you here?"

The cottage was gloomy and cold inside, somehow desolate. Dust particles floated in my torch beam like tiny ghosts. An open fireplace faced the door, its bricks blackened and derelict. In front of it sat a dusty armchair, and pushed under the window was an old wrought iron daybed. I crossed the room and went along a narrow hallway. The deep blackness swallowed the torchlight, and shadows leaped around me as if trying to bar my way.

"Rosalba—?"

At the rear of the cottage, I found a small room. A narrow bed stood in the shadows, and beside it, a baby's cot. Other items were crammed together in the opposite corner—a church pew bench and a broken dressing table stacked with old books. Tattered curtains hung from the window, and the roof bowed inwards, festooned with cobwebs. I walked over to the bed and brushed my fingers across the dusty coverlet, feeling its icy chill. A noticeable dip in the middle, perhaps where someone had slept every night—

A shiver swept over me and I whirled around.

Rosalba's eyes were wild. "What are you doing here?"

"Looking for you."

"What do you want?" Her voice trembled, and in the flashlight's harsh beam she seemed smaller, her shoulders hunched and her breathing shallow.

I stepped back and lowered the light, cursing myself.

"I'm sorry for intruding on your private space. I didn't mean to frighten you. If you want me to leave, I will."

"You can stay."

She drew nearer until her face was barely an inch away from mine. Even in the downcast torchlight I could see the faint purple shadows under her eyes, the tiny freckles like cocoa particles dotting her nose, and her lips the colour of ripe strawberries.

I swayed forward until we were almost touching.

"Can I ask you something, Rosalba?"

She frowned from under the curtain of her hair. "In exchange for another vision of William?"

"If you like."

Her eyes dropped to my mouth, and she nipped her bottom lip between small white teeth.

"What do you want to know?"

"Did William love you?"

Her expression softened. "Yes, he did. At least, that's what he told me. To be honest, after all this time, I often doubt it."

"Maybe I can help you figure it out?"

She stilled. Reaching over, she skimmed her icy fingers along my cheekbone. I shut my eyes, waiting for the flashback to hit, but there was nothing. No dizzy whirlwind dragging me back through time. No sensation of falling. Just the cramp seizing my chest that made it suddenly impossible to breathe.

"All right," she whispered. "Where will I start this time?"

I settled on the church bench, and then patted the seat beside me. Rosalba frowned, but then her lips twitched up. She perched on the edge and eyed me through her hair.

A rush of cold swept through me at her closeness.

"Tell me more about William." My heart beat slowly, thudding painfully against my ribs. "Why do you still care for him after all this time?"

24
ROSALBA

1915

I crept past my father's room, my good black winter coat swamping my nightgown. The clock chimed midnight and I paused, a vein pulsing in my throat. On the other side of the door, my father slept, dreaming his twisted dreams.

Knowing Father, there was just one thing he dreamed about.

If only your mother had lived and you had died, Rosalba. How different my life would have been. She was a beauty, have I told you that? With skin flawless as alabaster, soft as a peach. She was never cross, her voice always lowered with respect and rever-

ence. She was a pious woman. A good wife. Why do you think God took her instead of you, Rosalba?*

"I don't know, Father," I whispered under my breath. "Maybe she wanted rescuing from you."

Unlike my mother, I was not pious.

I didn't need God.

I had someone far better.

Hurrying along the hall, I crept down the stairs and through the house, out into the dark garden. Once free of my prison, I ran. The night air was cold, the garden deep in shadow, the trees rustling and sighing as my feet pounded the track. Uphill I ran, William's note in my skirt pocket, crumpled and rubbed thin by my fingertips.

Meet me under the lightning tree at midnight, my love. There's something we must do. I have only one request—that you wear black.

My heart sang as I ran along the moonlit trail.

Something we must do? My insides quivered. Perhaps he would hold my hand again? He would tangle his big fingers with mine and lean his shoulder briefly against my arm. In return, I'd tilt my face up like a sunflower and boldly gaze into his eyes.

So many boundaries I had already crossed.

What would he ask of me tonight?

As a child, driven half-mad with loneliness, I had once vowed to be the monster my father believed me to be. But getting to know William had changed all that. He had changed me. Given me reason to be my good self and bury the bad.

I ran up to him in the darkness and caught him by surprise. A small kerosene lantern burned nearby on the ground, lighting my bare feet and the hem of my nightgown, making William's big boots gleam like molasses. Something lay by his feet.

I gasped in surprise. "Is that a shovel?"

"Indeed, it is." William took my hand and kissed my fingers. "You wore black, little Rosebud. How fitting."

I laughed, suddenly nervous. "Look at us, we're dressed for a funeral!"

His smile was full of mystery. "That's exactly where we're going."

I went still. A funeral? Here, in the blackness of night, at the edge of our sprawling garden? A sick feeling came over me.

"Who died?"

William caught my hand and drew me closer. With gentle fingers, he unpinned my veil from my hair. No one had ever touched me so gently, with tenderness and purpose—and it enthralled me. Before I understood what was happening, my veil was gone, my face bared to the world. Bare to William. As bare as it was the day I stumbled out from under the willow tree.

I tried to shrink away and hide myself, but he held me firm. I tried to grab back my veil, but he whirled away and before I could stop him, he tore it to shreds. While I wept for it, he dug a hole and buried it, even saying a prayer.

"Ashes to ashes, dust to dust, good riddance to this sorry little veil that keeps my sweetheart's face hidden from me."

Sweetheart? That dried up my tears. The flush that crept up my neck and into my cheeks was an ugly one. I could feel it flooding my face with a hot rainbow of guilt and shame. But, sweetheart? Did he really mean that?

William filled in the burial hole and stomped down the soil, placing a stone to mark the spot.

"Swear to me, Rosalba. Never cover your face again."

"But William—"

"You must be who you are. Without apology. Without shame."

"Father will be angry."

"Your father is a goat's arse who should be jailed for how he's treated his daughter. Swear to me, love. Don't wear it again."

"I can't."

He tugged me close until our bodies met, and then he gently cupped my face with the palm of his hand.

"Your beautiful soul shines through your face, Rosalba. Please don't hide yourself from me."

My soul? Did he really think it was beautiful? Me, the monster who everyone despised and feared. The freak who made the church ladies scream, who tarnished mirrors with her reflection. William thought my soul was beautiful?

I bit my trembling lip. And then, just to please him, to make him smile so I could see his dimples again, I nodded.

"All right. I swear."

Not really meaning it, not really believing. But as the words tripped over my lips, something shifted inside me. I stood taller, my shoulders unhunching themselves. The breath moved more freely in my lungs.

William lowered his face, his breath hot on my lips. The fluttery yearning in my belly returned, only this time it was a molten heat that turned my legs to jelly. It gripped me until I could stand it no longer. I lifted my face to William and when his mouth crushed mine, I fell against him, winding my arms around his neck and pressing my length to his. William moaned softly against my lips and squeezed me closer against him, as though sensing my need. We stayed that way for the longest time, William clinging as tightly to me as I clung to him.

I never wore another veil.

My father could not forgive my defiance, but when he tried to punish me, I defied him in other ways. Refusing to kneel on the rose thorns, shrieking long and hard right into his ear when he tried to force me. Running away when he brought out the shears to cut my hair. When he ordered the maids to hold me down, I bit a fleshy arm till it bled and Father had to pay for the doctor to come and stitch it.

Oh, the shame.

But this time it was his shame, not mine. And I was secretly glad. After all, shame was my personal territory, and I had learned how to navigate it. However, Father—a proud man even in his lowest moments—did not.

This will end badly, you hear? Pride cometh before a fall, daughter. And a monster will suffer the greatest fall of all...

Yet with William, I felt less like a monster and more like ... just a girl. My sweet William was the most important person in my world. He had seen my face and declared me beautiful—at least in his eyes. And that was enough for me. I would not wear that cursed veil again, and I would fight anyone who tried to make me.

I fashioned my hair so that it fell across my mark and made it less obscene. Hattie brought me a tin of face powder that lightened the dark port-wine stain by a few degrees.

Without my veil, I emerged as someone different. As William's Rosebud. The person I was inside blossomed, while the old Rosalba—the fearful one with shame dogging her every step—began to wither and die.

Father took to avoiding me. On those rare occasions when our paths crossed, he averted his eyes as though the sight of me pained him. Rather than addressing me directly, he spoke to the rafters, to the spiders in their webs, or to the mice that scuttled after crumbs on the floor. He spoke to the windows and walls, and oftentimes to his own thin bony hands.

But never to me.

I did not mind. He wouldn't have to suffer this new me much longer. William and I had a plan, and soon, perhaps in a matter of weeks, we would put it into action.

25
ROSALBA

NOW

Talking about William had made me jumpy. As though an army of ants was marching through my veins instead of blood. I sprang to my feet and looked at Cleary.

"Your turn."

He stood too, but more slowly. As if the weight of my story anchored him back in that forgotten time. I knew how he felt.

Thoughts of that long ago night floated in my head, and I wanted to remain there forever. Basking in the kindness glowing from William's eyes as he removed my veil. Loving the way his hands were always warm and how his hair smelled like sunlight and freshly cut grass ...

I had revisited that memory so many times it was threadbare. I eagerly awaited Cleary's new vision. I didn't care if it was true or not. If his visions extended the sweetness, bringing William back to me, if only briefly, then I would gladly play along with them. A hundred years was a long time to replay the same memories. I ached for a fresh glimpse of William so desperately I could barely breathe.

I stepped closer to Cleary, drawn by his warmth. A stream of soft, silvery moonlight streaked through the window, bathing his face in its gentle light.

"Are you ready?"

He nodded. "Hit me with it, ghost girl."

The corners of my lips twitched. How like William he was. Breaking the tension with a joke. Bestowing nicknames. The dimples when he smiled, the crinkles around his eyes. The intense way he squinted as he searched my face. His voice, even his laugh were all echoes of my lost love. And being alone with him in the stillness of my room made it all the more real.

I swiped the wetness off my face and moved closer to him. When we were almost touching each other, a violent shiver ran over him.

I bit my lip. "Sorry about that. Should I just fly through you again?"

He laughed softly. "Lord, no. Here, take my hand if you like. It should be enough."

His body heat radiated against me, and it was strangely soothing. As I leaned in and gently linked my fingers into his, I felt him shudder. His breath was hot against my neck as he moaned. Then he shut his eyes.

26

WILLIAM

1916

The night was icy, the winter rain streaking the windows of the piper's cottage and drumming its tin roof. Inside, the crackling flames in the fireplace made the small lounge room seem all the friendlier.

William pulled Rosalba down beside him on the rug in front of the blaze. She soon warmed under his hands. As his mouth trailed those tender places behind her ear, under her chin, and at the corners of her eyes, he felt the bowstring tension in her muscles relaxing.

"Will it hurt?" she murmured.

He gathered her closer. "At first, it might sting a little. But I'll be gentle, you'll see. And if you don't like it, we can—"

"Oh, shush." She laughed huskily, and her breath warmed his cheek. "I'm determined to like it very much, so consider yourself warned."

He smiled against her mouth, unbuttoning her blouse and slipping her out of it. As he did battle with her undergarments, her small quick hands went to work disrobing him. When he was naked, she traced her fingertips over his skin, setting him alight.

He had planned to steal her away from Loch Ard and marry her, and at first she agreed. They had plotted every detail, right down to the dress she would wear and the books she would bring. But each time it came time for them to act, she found an excuse to stall. *Please let's wait, William. Another week, that's all. Give me time to get used to the idea of braving the outside world.*

He kept pressing her, but she only lowered her face and went silent. Slowly, he began to understand. Leaving Loch Ard terrified her. In all her twenty years of life, she'd never left the property. It felt safe and familiar to her.

Maybe she was right to stay.

All his friends were signing up. The war was still raging overseas, and soon he'd have to finish filling out the enlistment papers he'd been carrying around for weeks. It distressed him to think of leaving her. They'd talked about it, of course. Joining the lads on the front, doing his duty. He only feared that it was approaching faster than Rose knew.

"William, you're miles away."

He pulled her close and kissed her, his fingers tangling in her chemise.

"I'm right here, love."

She took pity on his fumbling and expertly unfastened her own hooks and eyes, slithering out of her underthings so quickly that his head spun, all thoughts of the war forgotten. When her lips found his again, he shut his eyes. If only this moment could last forever. A stolen moment, with the rain outside creating a barrier between them and the outside world. If only the war was over, and they never had to be apart—

"William, do you really love me?"

"You bet I do, Rosie girl."

"How do you know it's real?"

He pulled back and cupped her face in his hands, stroking her marked cheek gently with his thumb as he searched her eyes.

"Love sneaks up on you, doesn't it? One moment you're carefree, racing through life without a second thought. And then suddenly you're tumbling head over heels, everything falling into sweet chaos. But that's how you know it's real. Because without that special someone, life no longer makes any sense."

"You won't leave me?"

He tensed at the flicker of sadness and doubt in her eyes, remembering how her father had treated her, and how she had been so alone before they met. He reached out and took her hand, kissing her fingers, vowing to put an end to her loneliness.

"You're part of me now, Rosebud. Nothing can separate us, not even this blasted war. And if somehow it does, I'll cross endless deserts, scale deadly peaks, and swim raging rivers to be with you again."

"You would?"

"I'll find my way back to you, love. No matter how long it takes."

"I don't like to think of us being apart, William."

"When I go, it won't be for long. I'll do my bit and then rush home so we can be married."

"But what if something happens to you?"

"Nothing will happen."

"What if it does?"

"Then I'll whisper your name with my dying breath and haunt your dreams forever. Nothing will keep us apart, not even death." He had said it with a smile and meant it lightly, but when her eyes filled with tears, he saw his mistake. He pulled her near and held her tightly, whispering against her hair.

"Don't fear me dying, Rosie girl. True love lasts forever, remember? It just keeps cycling back life after life in an endless loop, always searching for its other half. Whatever happens, we'll be together again one day."

She pulled back and stared at him wide-eyed. "Do you promise?"

He smiled, but suddenly his chest was so constricted he could barely breathe. He strengthened his hold on her, feeling her tremble under his hands.

"I promise." Drawing her to him, he kissed her gently, then more deeply. His lips moved over her jaw and neck, trailing lower, until she was giggling and gasping in the same breath. "No more talk of leaving," he murmured against her skin. "We're here now, and this moment belongs to us. For all time."

Rolling onto his back, he pulled her on top of him. Her long limbs tangled with his, her curtain of hair falling over both their faces. She crouched over him for a moment, then relaxed her weight onto him, and he guided her gently until she began to move herself, slowly at first, and then with more confidence, and then with a wild joy that set them both ablaze.

27
CLEARY

NOW

Bent double, I gripped my knees and waited for my vision-induced nausea to subside. Rosalba shuffled beside me, her cold, impatient aura washing over me as I straightened up and scrubbed my hands over my face.

I could still see them in my mind's eye, entwined together in front of the blazing fire, their bare skin illuminated by the flames, while rain drummed against the windows.

My heart pounded, whether from the intense vision or from witnessing such an intimate moment, I couldn't tell. *Not witnessing it, man. You were right there in William's body, feeling every touch, every one of her kisses. Sliding your hands over her velvety curves, your lips devouring hers as you lost yourself in her embrace.*

"Well, Cleary?" She huffed impatiently. "Are you going to make me beg?"

My gaze darted everywhere but her. Maybe I should make something up?

Her brow creased. "What did you see?"

"William was here in the cottage."

She waited. Finally, she huffed again. "What was he doing?"

I moved to face her. Those wide eyes, the way they peered through her hair as if expecting bad news. She was within reach, but touching her was impossible, no matter how much I wanted to.

As I eased out a breath, the torch slipped from my fingers. It clattered onto the floor and winked out, leaving us in darkness. Good. Hopefully she'd miss my flushed cheeks and the raging lust in my eyes that made my pulse race.

She leaned closer, and moonlight touched the side of her face not obscured by her hair. Seeing the naked yearning in her eyes sent me flashing back to the fireside. Her skin felt warm under my hands, and her smile was luminous. So carefree and radiating love. She had giggled and beamed into my eyes, and it seemed I would love her forever—

Not me. William.

"Cleary, what did you see?" She wasn't smiling now. Her old suspicious frown was back, and it brought me to my senses.

"He was here with you, Rosalba."

"Oh?"

"On a blanket by the fire. You were—"

"Oh!" She glanced away quickly, her hand going to her hair, adjusting it further over her face. "Well, it's nearly daylight. You should get back to Elsie."

"Yeah, I should."

She stepped aside, and I marched past her to the door, hurrying through the cottage, my boots echoing on the dusty floorboards. This time, the shadows sprang out of my way, as if sensing my mood. A hunter's mood, not to be messed with by shadows. My mind raced so hard I could barely breathe, my blood flowing so hotly it burned my veins, setting my skin on fire.

In the cramped lounge room, I hesitated—taking in the derelict fireplace and tattered rug in front of it with cinder burns, where just a moment ago, it seemed, I had lain there with Rosalba writhing in my arms—

Jeez, man. Get it straight in your head. It was William, not you. Reaching the door, I stood a moment, letting the night air cool my limbs.

"Cleary?"

Her voice was barely a whisper behind me. I turned and found her peering from the dark hallway.

"Yeah?"

"This cottage has happy memories for me, but mostly I avoid thinking about them. They're usually too painful, you know?" She gestured at the fireplace. "But that night was special. I'm glad you reminded me."

I nodded. "Goodnight, Rosalba."

Damn my voice for sounding so ragged. So husky with emotion. Emotion belonging to someone born over a century ago. Someone now dead.

I stole a glance at the fireplace, seeing them again in its cosy glow. Seeing her. A million questions rushed through my mind. There was still so much I wanted to know. To ask. But when I looked back at the doorway, Rosalba had vanished.

28

CLEARY

It was nearly dawn when I got back to the house. I made strong coffee and sipped it at the table, watching through the window. On the far side of the garden, the burnt-out tree loomed black in the early light, its craggy limbs clawing the moonless sky.

As I stared across the garden, I thought about William and Rosalba in front of the fire. She'd been so carefree in his arms, so happy. Trusting him with her vulnerable self, which must have taken a lot of courage. But I couldn't shake the way she'd described herself earlier, her cruel words still making me shiver.

Me, the monster ... the freak.

How she must have hated wearing that veil. Hated her father. I was starting to hate him, too. What kind of lunatic would make his daughter cover her face because of a birthmark? If Elsie's face was marked, I'd thrash anyone who dared to judge her. Anyone who said she was anything less than perfect.

Jolene had called her a fruitcake. She just couldn't comprehend why Elsie dressed like a boy and cut her hair and refused to play with dolls, preferring to ride her bike and climb trees. My ex was intolerant of things she didn't understand, and she didn't mind voicing her opinion. Yet for all her faults, she was a decent person at heart. Decent enough, at least, not to berate Elsie openly for her quirks.

But punish her? Shear off her hair and make her wear a veil? Force her to kneel on rose thorns. How could a parent be that cruel? Especially towards a child whose facial mark made her so incredibly vulnerable.

I searched online for images and interviews, trying to understand. Even now, people with differences often faced bullying, but some were finding acceptance and support and sharing their experiences. I found a woman in her twenties who resembled Rosalba—dark-haired with milky skin and a challenge in her light green eyes—who had inspired others by standing up to media bullying. But as I put my phone away, my head pulsed with unanswered questions.

I understood why Rosalba fell in love with William. He loved her for who she was, respecting her need to stay safe at Loch Ard while he was away. My vision of him dying on the battlefield would explain why he hadn't returned for her like he promised. So why did I still have the niggling sense that it wasn't the full story?

My visions were difficult to prove. Though they were historically accurate, they were often fleeting and hard to verify as actual events. They could just be psychic impressions from the entity, like shadows over a lake. Rosalba's own beliefs might have influenced my vision of William's death.

The rising sun caught me by surprise, so I brewed more coffee and sat gazing out at the garden until it was time to start breakfast. I broke eggs into a bowl and whipped the batter, mixing in handfuls of the big plump blackberries we'd found growing down behind the house.

While I worked, my mind kept flying back to the cottage. To Rosalba in her cramped bedroom.

Her eyes had been pools of ink, her face kissed by moonlight. She stood close, and the air around us felt heavy with electricity, my heart thrashing against my ribs as if trying to bash its way out and reach her. Our faces were just inches apart, and a desperate urge seized me to brush the strands of hair away from her eyes, trace my fingers along her jawline, and lean in and press my mouth against hers—

Elsie burst into the kitchen and rushed over. When she saw me, she frowned.

"You're quiet."

"Just thinking."

"About Rosalba?"

I looked at her. "Nah, kiddo. I'm thinking about how great these pancakes are gonna taste. Want some?"

She peered at the batter I was knocking around in the bowl with my wooden spoon. The berries had turned the mix bright purple.

"Wow, Dad! Blackberry pancakes? What's the occasion?"

"It's Saturday."

"You know they're my favourite, right?"

"Better than anyone, kiddo. Hey, grab the frypan, would you?"

She placed the cast iron pan on the burner and lit it the way I'd shown her.

"Dad?"

"Yeah, possum."

"When you saw Rosalba yesterday, did she ask about me?"

"Sure did. She raved about your good behaviour and asked when you'll visit again."

Elsie tipped her head to the side, narrowing her eyes.

"She didn't mention me, did she?"

I gave her a sheepish shrug. "I guess we had other things to discuss."

"Like what?"

Pancake batter sizzled as I dropped it in the hot pan.

"She's going to tell me about her life."

"Cool!" Elsie waved the spatula in the air like a magic wand. "What did she say?"

"She said her father was a muttonhead and that you're the luckiest kid in the world for having me."

She rolled her eyes. The pancakes bubbled, and she flipped them expertly.

"Did you ask about her face?"

I held out the plate, and Elsie transferred the first batch onto it. The next lot of batter hissed as it hit the hot oil.

"I think it's a birthmark."

"What's a birthmark?"

I held off saying any more until the pancakes formed a tall pile on the plate. Elsie took it to the table, and I grabbed forks and maple syrup. While the pancakes cooled, I scrolled through the pictures I discovered last night on my phone.

"A birthmark is pigmentation of the skin. Some are small, like freckles. Others are large."

Elsie shouldered against me, peering at the images on the screen. I scrolled to the young woman with dark hair. She was gazing defiantly into the camera, the blue of her eyes popping against the dark port-wine mark on her cheek.

Elsie gasped. "She looks like Rosalba!"

"Hmmm."

"Gosh, birthmarks are kinda cool. How do you get one?"

"You're born with it."

"Oh."

"Don't sound so disappointed. It's gotta be difficult for people with them. Imagine if everyone judged you by the way you looked."

"You mean like Mum?"

I eased out a careful breath. "Your mum took care of herself. That's a good thing, right? But it's not the only thing. You gotta take care of your brain, too. And your heart. Especially your heart."

Elsie's eyes widened when I came to one of a baby with her tiny hand resting on her mother's chest, a birthmark on her cheek that was almost as large as the one Rosalba had. As I watched Elsie's face, my heart sank like a stone. Her forehead furrowed and her little lips trembled. She felt it too. The raw injustice of what Rosalba had endured.

I swiped to another image. A boy of about twelve was riding his bike along a country lane, a large heart-shaped port-wine patch under his eye.

"Look at this little guy. He doesn't look all that happy, does he? Maybe he gets picked on at school for how he looks?"

Elsie's brows swooped together, angry little wings over serious eyes.

"That's mean!"

"People can be cruel."

"I'd be his friend, Dad."

I bumped my shoulder gently into hers.

"Kindness matters, kiddo."

She nodded, her lips pinching into a frown.

"Rosalba doesn't like her birthmark. Maybe people were mean to her, too."

"I'm guessing they were."

"Is that why she's trapped in the garden and can't leave?"

"It's connected, I think. But whatever the reason, it's a powerful one. At least for her."

"You want to help her, Dad. Don't you? Not just untether her, but really help her."

I shrugged, trying to look unaffected. "Maybe."

Elsie gave a little sigh, as if I was her hero.

"Kindness matters."

I grimaced, guilt pinching at me. My efforts to help Rosalba cross over were driven less by kindness, and more by the dollar signs flashing in my eyes. A haunted garden would never attract the sort of big-paying investors I needed to make a decent sale.

You idiot, stop denying it. The woman's gotten under your skin and you're half-mad with fear. You're scared of getting close to one of the others. Scared that what happened to your father will happen to you, too.

I started piling pancakes onto our plates. Rosalba wasn't getting to me. Her fragility brought out my protective side, that was all. Nothing to freak out over. Her feistiness excited me, but so what? There was no problem here. No need getting all hot and bothered.

At least, not much.

Learning about her past wasn't helping. As she related her story about the veil last night, I'd been clenching my fists in outrage one moment, the next I was aching to hold her close, soothe away her pain like William had done.

I couldn't explain these feelings. Just that they were impossible, and I had to stop feeling them. I had to clear Rosalba from my mind. Get her out of my life. Out of Elsie's life.

My mission had always been to rid the world of supernatural beings. Wreak my personal vengeance on the others and purge the lot of them. But I couldn't ignore the immense sadness of Rosalba's story.

Maybe if I could help her in some small way, it would cure this ache inside me ... at least until I discovered how to remove her from our lives forever. If only my mother's warning didn't ring so loudly in my ears.

Once her tether's broken and she leaves, there's no way she'll ever be able to come back.

29
ROSALBA

Golden morning light seeped through the trees, shimmering on the dewy grass. Bees buzzed around the delphiniums, and magpies warbled in the branches as the sun rose higher in the sky, its heat radiating off the gravel tracks.

Normally, I loved this time of day, but as I peered from my hiding place behind the cypress hedge near the piper's cottage, all I felt was confusion.

A week had passed since Cleary's pre-dawn visit to my cottage. Now here he was again, his ute parked right beside it, whistling as he dragged a bunch of broken things outside and tossed them in the tray.

Had his visit there last week inspired this?

Broken glass shattered as he pulled it from the window frames, his gloved hands working quickly. He wrapped the glass and placed it on the growing pile of broken tiles and rotten posts, old linoleum and busted furniture.

Elsie was crouched on the path, digging weeds from between the bricks and sweeping away the debris. She kept glancing over her shoulder, frowning at the hedge. Clever thing. She sensed me spying on them. Once or twice she got to her feet and shaded her eyes, searching the sunlit garden.

But I stayed hidden.

In the shadows, watching.

That first night I met Cleary, I had lied about the cottage being lovely. I knew it was a broken, rundown mess. He'd called it derelict. Said they should pull it down. Was that what they were doing now, pulling down my home?

Was it how he hoped to get rid of me?

I should fly at him again.

Shriek and wail and cause a riot. Raise another windstorm, or whip up some hail. Give them a show they'd never forget.

Yet something stopped me. If they were pulling it down, why was Elsie weeding the path? And why were there piles of new timber sitting on the grass beside buckets of paint?

I nibbled my lip.

Once, the cottage had been charming. Mounds of lavender and purple sage flanked the steps leading up to a tiny front door that William had to duck through. The rooms inside were small, but a cosy fire had roared in the hearth and a big rack hung above it to dry wet clothes in winter. Floorboards gleamed underfoot, and the windows all had scenic outlooks—white hydrangeas, or the cypress hedge, or up along the grassy trail that led to the shade house.

We still called it the piper's cottage, even after the old piper died. I used to steal the keys from Father's study and bring William here. Tucked behind the cypresses, it became our secret trysting place. Our own private realm, away from prying eyes.

It held my happiest memories.

Somewhere along the way, it had become my home. As the years passed, it had crumbled around me. I could not sweep the floor or dust the furniture. Or clean the windows or do repairs. All I could do was watch decay take hold and try to ignore it. Sometimes people rented the cottage and did repairs, but they never stayed long.

I made sure of that.

"Rosalba!" Elsie ran up to me, beaming. "I knew it was you!"

Adjusting my hair across my face, I tried to frown.

"Why are you pulling down my cottage?"

She reached for my hand, but then withdrew. "We're not pulling it down, silly. We're fixing it up for you. Making it pretty. Come and see."

I followed her over. Cleary caught sight of me and dropped the armload of rotting timber into the back of the ute. He walked over, pulling off his gloves.

"You look worried."

I gestured at the cottage. "You're wrecking my home."

"I promise, when we're done with it, you'll be much more comfortable there." He winked at Elsie. "Right, sport?"

Elsie danced excitedly, gazing up at her father's face and then at me.

"No need to worry, Rosalba. Just wait till you see what we're planning. Dad's brilliant at this. He's fixed up a ton of places much worse than this one. He's even good at picking curtains!"

"Curtains? But it—" A flush crept up my neck as Cleary caught my gaze and smiled. He stood tall in his dusty jeans and singlet, his muscular arms damp from exertion. The tattoos twining over his tanned skin—a skull on one large bicep threaded with thorns and roses, and on the other arm an owl in mid-flight—made him seem dangerous and beautiful all at once. The longish hair pulled back off his face in a band, the scruff of gingery beard. And his eyes, blue like William's, so clear and steadfast as they studied me right back—

I pushed my hair forward, thankful for the thick weight of it to hide behind. "It already has curtains."

Cleary tipped his head towards the vehicle.

"Not anymore." On the back tray, under a pile of broken plaster chunks, lay the dusty old drapes. "Once I fix the wood rot and replace the old plaster, we can freshen it with a coat of paint. We should have it finished by the end of the week."

"I thought you wanted me gone?"

He twisted the gloves in his powerful hands. "We had a deal, right? We swap a few stories, maybe try to figure out some things. It could take a while, so I want you to be comfortable."

"Rosalba?" Elsie was fidgeting, shading her eyes from the sun as she peered up at me through her fingers. "Can I hear your story too?"

Since telling Cleary about William burying my veil that night, my mind had felt lighter. My heart, too. It was like therapy. Healing old wounds, cutting old ties. Relieving my soul of old burdens. Besides, Cleary had offered to help me figure out if William had really loved me, and why he never returned. Even if his visions weren't accurate, they acted like a healing balm on my heart. Wasn't that worth another trip into the past?

"All right."

Elsie clapped her hands. Cleary huffed out a breath, as if he'd been holding it in. He took a picnic basket from the ute and we walked up the hill.

We sat on a picnic rug in the shade of the atlas cedar behind my cottage. Low-hanging branches concealed the trunk, creating a shadowy bower where I sometimes liked to hide, and being near it now seemed special somehow, like sharing a secret.

Cleary unpacked a picnic basket, laying out slices of cake, a thermos of tea and three enamel mugs. He poured some tea and placed the mug in front of me. I leaned in to inhale the fragrant steam, and Cleary smiled over. My face grew warm again. Even in the sunlight he resembled William—but that flirty, knowing smile was all him.

The scent of freshly baked carrot cake tickled my nose as it wafted up from the plate. Elsie chattered while she ate, her shrill voice mingling with the birdsong. I watched them both, their heads bent over their steaming mugs, Elsie's hair falling into her eyes as she blew on her tea, and Cleary's blue gaze drifting back to me.

Guilt tightened my stomach. Had I really entertained the idea of luring his daughter to the loch, driving him away from here so cruelly? Look at them, they were really no trouble to have around. This sweet picnic. He'd even packed three mugs. And fixing my cottage to make it more comfortable?

I watched him through my lashes.

He'd been kind the other night in the cottage. I had caught a flash of William in his eyes, and it melted the ice in my heart a little. How could I cause him grief now, without hurting myself too? Instead, I wanted to repay him somehow, so when he hinted it was time for a story, I decided to trust them with a slightly more bittersweet glimpse into my past.

This time, there was no hesitation. My words flowed like a river, quickly transporting me back to the time before.

30
ROSALBA

1916

One Sunday, William arrived while the rest of the household was at church. It was his custom to ride his bike so that he could arrive unnoticed, but that day he came on horseback, yelling as he rode up the gravel drive.

"Rosalba!" He dismounted and tied his mare to the post, then rushed over to me, gripping my arms. "We have to talk."

I shook him off, glancing over my shoulder at the house, more out of habit than fear, and ushered him deeper into the garden.

William stumbled along the path, weaving sideways and

then righting himself, the reek of alcohol heavy on his breath. I found his hand and gripped it, and he clutched my fingers damply. I'd never seen him like this before. His agitation frightened me. I leaned against him as we walked, hating the distance that seemed to have sprung up between us.

"William, what's going on?"

He wiped a sweaty forearm over his eyes and grabbed my hands. Despite the day's heat and his state of exertion, his fingers were ice cold. "There's something I must tell you, Rosalba. And I'm afraid you won't like it."

"Oh?"

"I'm going away."

I pulled my hands from his grip and straightened my shoulders. Going away? Of course he was. Father had warned me, hadn't he? I'd been a fool to believe William's love would last. And now here it was. The lie, the falsehood that would be my undoing. It came as no surprise. After all, I had been dreading it, expecting it all along—

"They've sent my marching orders. We're sailing off next week."

My blood thinned, cold as winter rain. "Sailing off?"

William took my hands again. "I'm sorry, love. We'll only have a few days left together before I leave. They're saying we'll be deployed by Friday next."

"You mean ... going to the front?"

"Or wherever they decide to send me. But I won't be gone long, Rosie girl. A few months tops."

I tore away from him. We had spoken about this possibility since his enlistment three months ago. He attended training at Broadmeadows, which he convinced me was jolly good fun. And Hattie had said only this morning that there was talk about the war ending by Christmas. Only now ... William was leaving. My heart struggled to beat as I stared at his beautiful, treacherous face.

"Father said this would happen! He warned me, but I didn't listen. And now ... now—"

I turned and ran into the garden. Off the track, deeper into the briars and close-growing trees. Up along the fence line, vines tearing at my skirt, clawing my legs. A low-hanging branch whipped my face. When I reached the shade house, I ducked inside and threw myself down on the ground among the tree ferns.

My safe place as a child.

I had taken shelter here from the various storms I had created around me growing up. Picking thorns from my knees, or with blood oozing from my shorn scalp, I had found refuge within the deep green shadows, my veil tucked over my face, soaked with tears, wishing for the ground to open up and swallow me.

"Rosalba?"

"Go away!"

William sank to the ground beside me. "Hey, I'm sorry. Come here, little Rosebud."

When he pulled me near, I fought him, smacking at his hands and face. But then I fell against him sobbing, burying myself in the damp folds of his shirt.

"Did you ever love me? Or was it a trick?"

He was silent, probably wondering how to break it gently. To confirm what my father had said all along. *Who but the devil could love a monster like you?*

Bracing myself, I looked up at him, wanting to see his face when he spun the lie that would take him from me forever. To my surprise, his eyes were pink, the skin below them damp with tears of his own.

"Ah, Rosie girl. I'll always love you. I'll never stop, not even if I die on a muddy battleground—"

"Oh, don't say that!"

"It's true, though." He brushed back a wisp of my hair and kissed my brow. "I've loved you since that day you fell out from behind the willow tree. With each day that passed, I loved you more. Crazy, isn't it? That you can love someone even before you even speak to them. Before you understand how wonderful they truly are. But that was me, poor sap that I was. Head over heels before we uttered a word. And I'll be head over heels with you forever, my Rosebud. Not even death can take that away."

I wanted to doubt him.

All this talk of death panicked me, but still I wanted to doubt. Even as I gazed up into his dear, tear-streaked face, my father's poison was drip-drip-dripping into my mind. *This will end badly, you hear? Pride cometh before a fall, Rosalba, and yours will be the longest, hardest fall of all—*

"William, please don't die over there. I couldn't bear it."

He mopped the back of his hand across his eyes.

"Aww, Rosie girl. I've no intention of dying. I'll do my bit in the war and then rush home quick and lively. Don't worry about me, love. Just keep yourself busy packing your bags. The minute I'm home, I'll put a ring on your finger and whisk you away with me."

Reaching up, I placed my palm on his face. "Promise?"

He winked. "Cross my heart and hope to—"

I gasped and leaned in to kiss him. There'd been enough talk of dying. It was making me nervous. William moaned softly and drew me against him, pulling me close along his length, warm and safe in the tree fern shadows.

We stayed entwined for a long while, the warm earth under our bodies, and the sky watching over us through the shade house bars. A delicate breeze whispering through the fern fronds as we created a moment to treasure once fate tore us apart. Sweet, and yet somehow bitter, because no matter how I tried to block my father's voice, his words were always with me.

Who but the devil himself could love a monster like you?

31
CLEARY

NOW

A MONSTER? Did she really believe that?

Sitting on the picnic rug in the shade of the old cedar tree, my fingers clenched as I fought the urge to reach over and brush back her thick hair, exposing the mark she thought made her so unlovable. But that other time I reached for her, she'd fled into the night, and I sensed she would flee again now. I could see it in her face. Her beautiful, sweet face. A face I was becoming a little obsessed with.

Beside me, Elsie sighed. "Did William come back for you?"

Rosalba looked over at me, her cheeks flushing pink.

"No, he didn't."

"Why not?"

"I don't really know. His name never appeared on the casualty list in the newspapers. Hattie heard nothing in town about his death. So I invented a tale of him being shot down in France. It was easier for me to believe that."

My daughter inched forward, peering up into Rosalba's face.

"That's so sad! Gosh, you must have cried bucket loads."

Rosalba sighed shakily. "It was a long time ago, Elsie. Wounds heal, if you give them long enough."

My heart ached for her, remembering my vision. "Maybe it's true that he died in the war, after all. Maybe there's no mystery, no betrayal. Why do you keep doubting him?"

"I thought I saw him once." She examined the carrot cake on her plate, then her gaze skated away over the grass to the weeping cypress further up the hill. "He was an old man, bent and white-haired. I never got close enough to know for certain. But he walked like William, and his bearing ... his voice..."

"He spoke?"

She studied her hands. "He called my name. At least, that's what I thought. Maybe I just imagined it."

Shadows darted over her face, pooling in the hollows around her eyes. The past was swallowing her alive, I could sense it just under her surface, vast and heavy as a body of deep water. Yet she skimmed over it like a dragonfly, never letting herself land, yet never quite able to fly away.

I had thought helping her might somehow cure the ache of longing that being near her inspired in me, but I saw now I was wrong. While she flitted over the water's surface, I felt myself sinking slowly under. Drowning.

She caught me looking and tipped her head forward, letting her hair fall over her face. If only she didn't feel the need to hide around me. She had opened up about William today and given us a glimpse into her private world. Into her pain. It took guts to do that, and it made me wonder about something else.

I emptied the tea dregs and packed up the picnic basket.

"Elsie, would you give us a moment?"

Elsie glared at me, thrusting her head forward as if she couldn't believe what she was hearing. Her eyes were huge saucers, one blue, one pale green, and still gleaming with sorrow for her new friend. I held her gaze, though, and she slumped. With a longing look at Rosalba, she stomped off in search of a tree to climb.

"Can I ask you something, Rosalba?"

She was still staring after Elsie, her brow wrinkled. Her gaze flew to me, then away.

"You can call me Rose, if you like."

"Rose ..." I inched closer, settling my fingertips near her hand on the picnic rug. "Was your father mean to you because of your birthmark?"

She raked her hair further forward. A loose strand tangled in her fingers and she tucked it back with the others.

"I suppose."

"You're still trying to hide it."

She said nothing. Her shoulders were stiff, her limbs tense as though ready to spring up and flee.

Slowly, I took out my phone. The screen glinted in the sunlight and caught her attention. She said nothing, but her lips parted, her eyes grew wide. The tension melted from her as she craned forward.

I smiled. That was easy. "I want to show you some pictures. Have you seen a phone before?"

"Phone? You mean a telephone to call someone?" Her pale brow puckered. "Yes, my father had one installed soon after the war started. But it was nothing like yours. It can show pictures?"

"It does everything these days. But yeah, pictures. Here, scoot over and have a look."

She was by my side in a flash, her cold aura pleasant in the morning heat.

I rested the phone on my knee and shaded the screen with one hand. Tapping through the folders, I located the screenshots I'd saved the other night.

"Can you see?"

She bent closer, nodding, her hair swinging forward and brushing lightly on my forearm. I enlarged one photo. It showed a tall woman in a red halter dress.

Rose gasped. "Her face."

"She's a highly paid fashion model. The biggest designers in the world fight over getting her to model their clothes."

"But those patterns on her face. Her shoulders. She's a dark girl with patches of white on her skin. How is that possible?"

"She has a condition called vitiligo, where the skin loses pigment and becomes lighter in some areas."

"Her marks ... they look like leopard spots."

"I think she's beautiful. And this woman—" I scrolled to the next photo. "Isn't she stunning?"

Rose's fingers hovered near the screen. "Her mark is just like mine." She leaned further in, forgetting to keep her distance as she shifted her cool limbs closer to me. "Yet she looks almost ... proud."

"Why wouldn't she be?"

"But her ..." She wiggled her fingers at the screen. "Her face."

"Women have so much pressure to look a certain way. To conform."

"It was the same in my time."

"But who wants to look like everyone else—that's boring, right?"

"I suppose."

She didn't seem convinced, so I pressed on.

"Women are fighting back against being judged by their appearance. Take Elsie. She gets teased sometimes for cutting her hair and dressing like a boy. Even about her different eyes."

"But she's adorable! And her quirks make her interesting."

Her indignation made me smile. "She's a character, all right. And she's got her head screwed on properly, regardless of what people think. Trying new things is important, especially when you're young."

"I wish I had Elsie's courage."

"You have courage like I've never seen, Rose." Damn my voice for coming out so huskily.

Her eyes widened, and she glanced at me. A little half-smile twitched at the corner of her mouth.

"You sound like William."

She leaned in, her attention returning to the screen. My whole side went cold. My breath caught. Could she hear my heart thumping? Feel the heat of my skin where it almost touched hers?

Without moving my head, I studied her. Her hair mostly concealed her birthmark, but the edges I could see along the side of her nose and scooping under her eye intrigued me. Spilled wine on porcelain, fading to splashes of deep blush-pink, like perfect little freckles over one side of her mouth.

I drew a careful breath.

Had her father really locked her away? Had the people of her time truly shunned her, made her feel second rate? Her words still tore at me. A ruined monster. How could people be so cruel? And yet her big heart shone out of her, made her glow. No wonder Elsie was obsessed with her. I was becoming a little obsessed, too. Rose had scared everyone away from the garden with her screams and elemental rage, yet here she was sitting beside me in the fragile sunlight, admiring images of other women who looked just like her.

"Cleary?"

I gulped a breath. "Yeah?"

She looked at me. "A simple act of kindness can make a lasting impact. Thank you."

"Huh." Lost for words. Her eyes were so clear. Grey-green like a eucalypt leaf, and large enough to fall into and drown. It was unlike me to feel this way, especially so quickly. Like I'd known her forever. That our paths were meant to cross in this lifetime, because they had crossed before.

I rubbed the back of my neck.

"Listen ... Elsie's been bugging me to invite you to the house. Why don't you pop over tonight? Say around dusk?"

"The house?" A shadow fluttered over her and she sprang to her feet. "I haven't been there in years."

I could have kicked myself. The house—the childhood home where she lived with her brute of a father, the place she'd been a prisoner, constantly shamed and diminished.

"Hey." I stood up quickly, reaching for her arm, fearing she'd vanish again. My fingers grazed her icy aura. She flinched but did not move away, just stood gazing up at me, her eyes large and liquid as rain. I moved as close as I dared. "Let's hang out on the verandah. That way, you don't have to go inside."

She glanced at my mouth and lifted her hand towards my face. My body pulsed as I leaned in towards her.

But she didn't touch me.

Instead, her fingers rose to her hair, lifting it back from the marked side of her face.

I stopped breathing.

The late sunlight glowed unearthly. The garden faded around us. There was just this woman revealing herself to me, and the trust in her eyes as she exposed her vulnerable self. She caught her lip between her teeth and then murmured something, a name.

William.

Then her small, cold fingers circled my wrist.

I inhaled. The rush of cold from her touch was icy. Shocking. Electric. The garden distorted around me. The sun burned too brightly, the air blazed. I was no longer breathing. I shut my eyes —

32
WILLIAM

1916

William couldn't take his eyes off her. She looked so relaxed and happy in the hazy afternoon twilight, the shadows of the lightning tree—their tree—dancing softly over her features. She had tied her hair back off her face, and the deep blush-red of her mark made her green eyes glow even brighter.

Reaching up, she touched his face, her palm warming his skin.

"I won't say goodbye, William. Because I will see you again. You'll come back to me, won't you?"

"As fast as I can, Rose. And then we'll be married."

"Promise?"

He huffed softly and kissed her. Then he reached into his pocket and took out a small emerald ring. Sunlight winked off its deep green facets, making it shimmer like water and illuminating the notch of deeper green at its core, an imperfection that made him think of a tiny heart.

"It was my grandmother's. She was a bold and assertive woman, never hesitating to voice her opinions and defend her beliefs. I wish you could have met her. She would've thought the world of you, Rose. She gave me this ring before she passed away, and I treasure it more than anything else I own. Will you wear it for me?"

Her lips parted, and she looked up at him. Nodded.

Gently, he collected her left hand and slipped the ring onto her third finger.

"Whenever you doubt our love, just look at this ring. Remember us standing here, under our tree. And remember how much I love you. Because I do love you, my sweet Rosebud. More than life itself."

She admired the ring, tilting it to catch the sunlight. Tears welled in her eyes as she smiled at him.

"I'll wear it always."

William led her over to the fence. He pointed down at the rolling landscape of farms and pockets of bushland that stretched across the valley below. Woodhill nestled in the river's bend, sleepy and far away.

"You see that patch of trees where the river curves northwards out of town?"

"I see it."

"That's our place, Rose. It belonged to my grandfather, and now it belongs to me. The minute I get back, I'll take you there. It's our new home, love. Yours and mine."

"It's beautiful." Her lips quivered. "I can hardly wait to live there with you. Hurry back to me, won't you? So we can start our new life together."

His throat tightened. Rosalba said her father had retreated lately, mostly ignoring her. But how long would that last? William should have insisted they marry sooner. He should have tried harder to ease her fears, convince her that his family would have rallied around her, protected her. But he had seen the terror in her eyes and given in.

"I'll hurry back, Rosebud. I promise."

She reached up, trailing her fingers over his newly shorn hair as she smiled up at him.

"Make sure you do, or I'll be cross!"

William laughed softly.

Lord, how happy she looked, despite the gleam of tears. How glowing.

Yet even as he admired her, a shadow passed over him, making him shiver. Probably just a crow flying across the sun. Nothing to get in a knot about. But it stirred his darkest fear. What if he never saw her again? A coldness swallowed his heart, and for an instant it seemed to stop beating. *Hold her again, man. Make it count, because you might never get another chance.*

He shook off the chill, sweeping her into his arms. Holding her so tightly that she went very still against him, her own arms locked around his neck, her tears hot against his cheek.

He sighed into her hair, then inhaled her.

His coarse uniform made his skin itch, and the brown leather army boots had already worn blisters on his heels. But as he drew Rosalba even closer against him in the dying light and kissed her, he knew this would be one of those bittersweet moments he escaped to again and again, during whatever dark times lay ahead.

33
CLEARY

NOW

Rose watched me wide-eyed as I stood trembling in the garden's shifting twilight, hugging my ribs against the cold nausea, and doing my best to describe what I'd seen through William's eyes.

My words came haltingly, a jumble that failed to capture the sweetness of their encounter. She didn't seem to mind that I faltered. Her hungry gaze never left my face, holding her breath as my stream of words tumbled out.

"He was worried about leaving you with your father. He wanted to return to you as quickly as possible. And he gave you a ring that once belonged to his grandmother, saying he wanted you to wear it while he was away so you'd remember how much he cared—" I stopped.

William's thoughts felt familiar, like a distant memory resurfacing. His feelings for Rose—his love for her, and his fear for her—still blazed so brightly inside me I could barely think straight. "He said, 'I'll hurry back, Rosebud. I promise.' And then he kissed you one last time and said goodbye."

Rose let out a shaky breath. "That's exactly how it happened."

"You remember?"

"Like it was yesterday."

"Then my vision ... was real."

She nodded slowly. "You know what this means, don't you? If your visions are true, then William died in the war. That's why he never came back."

"I can't imagine anything but death keeping him away from you. Maybe not even that."

The tree shadows danced over her as she tugged at her hair.

"I want to believe you, Cleary."

"But you still have doubts?"

She shrugged, nodding. "Because of the old man I saw. I convinced myself he was just another sightseer after the ghost. But that's what I always do. Make excuses to avoid facing reality."

"It's what we all do, Rose. It's part of coping with life. You can only do your best, even if that sometimes means running scared."

"I've been running scared my whole life."

"Join the club."

Her brows shot up. "What are you running from?"

"Same as you, I guess. Confronting my pain."

She huffed and shook her head. "You seem so capable, though. So robust. Like nothing could rattle you."

I shook out my hands, trying to ease the tightness in my shoulders. "I might look like a tough guy, but I'm not. Underneath, I'm just a scared kid who's trying to battle the glimmers and make sense of why they took my dad away." As soon as the words left my mouth, I regretted them. Rose was nodding, her eyes so dark they were like mirrors, reflecting her own pain back at me. I took a step towards her. "I'm sorry, that was harsh. I never meant—"

"It's okay." She shrugged, hugging her ribs. "I know I'm one of your glimmers, but I'm not offended. The past has a powerful hold on us, doesn't it? I'm sorry about your father. He must have meant the world to you."

I swallowed the sudden tightness in my throat. "Yeah. He did."

"Elsie told me you move around a lot, and now I understand why."

"Oh?"

"Moving from place to place is a distraction. If glimmers took your dad away, then you probably have feelings of guilt over not being able to save him. Deep down, you believe you don't deserve a stable, settled life. And maybe you don't need one. But Cleary, your daughter does."

"You sound like my mum. She's the wisest person I know."

Rose adjusted her hair over her face, her fingers lingering near her mark.

"That's a kind thing to say, but I'm not wise at all. I'm fighting my own battle inside my head. Every time I convince myself that William really loved me, my father's voice storms into my thoughts and denies it."

"Your father was wrong to make you doubt that William loved you."

She pressed her fingers over her cheeks, as if to cool them.

"I remember that last day with William vividly. The ring he gave me was beautiful, even more precious because it was my only link to him after he left. I always wore it on a chain around my neck."

"What happened to it?"

"It's gone. I don't remember where."

I eased out a breath. "My vision was so clear, almost like a memory. The emerald ring sparkling green in the sun as William slid it on your finger. The pleasure in your eyes." I inhaled, hoping to clear my head, but the sweet scent of violets filled my senses. "The way you reached up and ran your fingers over my hair—"

Rose frowned, stepping into the gap that lay between us, locking her gaze on mine.

"You mean William's hair."

"That's what I said."

She was standing too close. I couldn't breathe, yet I couldn't for the life of me tear my gaze off her. William may have died a century before, but part of him still burned inside me like a bonfire.

Leaving her that day was the hardest thing he'd ever done. He had read the stories in the newspaper, the reports and casualty lists. The tales of death and destruction on the battlefield. But his fear wasn't for himself ... it was for her. For Rose. As they said goodbye, standing under the burned out old tree, a terrible foreboding came over him. A shadow across the sun. A cold, hard certainty that even if he did survive the war, he'd never see his Rosebud's sweet face again—

"Cleary?"

Rose leaned in until we were almost touching, her gaze sharp on my face, her breath puffing clouds of ice against my skin.

"You don't just see through William's eyes, do you? You feel his emotions. You feel everything he feels. And you're feeling it right now."

I shook my head. "No, it's just..."

She blurred before me.

I blinked, and something hot slid down my cheek. I swiped it away with my wrist, and when I looked back again, she was gone.

34
ROSALBA

I hurtled through the garden, my strides long and fast, the sweet scent of jasmine tickling my nose.

The sun had set six times since Cleary's vision, and with each day that passed, I fought the urge to seek him out and beg him to summon another one. But I stayed away, sheltering unseen beneath my cedar tree, or racing through the shadows.

I couldn't return to my cottage, because he was always there. Hammering and sawing, painting the walls. Replacing the sagging roof beams. I was grateful for his kindness, but I needed time to process what he had said. To make sense of it all. Yet as the hours ticked by, my thoughts became more tangled and confused, like a knotted piece of rope.

Seeing Cleary that way, as he stood under the shadows of the cedar tree the other day—his breath ragged, his eyes glazed with emotion—it was William standing in front of me, saying goodbye all over again.

A shiver ran through me.

It seemed I'd known Cleary all of five minutes, yet here we

were already on the brink of something huge and terrifying ... and possibly wonderful. But was it *real*?

Late afternoon sunlight streamed between the trees like liquid gold, warming my face and arms. Magpies sang harmonies in the treetops, their voices tangling with my frantic thoughts.

Were his visions true? It was the only way he could know about the emerald ring, and our kiss goodbye under the lightning tree. Which meant his other visions were true, as well. William had died on the battlefield. He had whispered my name with his last breath, truly loving me to the end.

And now he had found me again. Just as he promised.

Cleary sensed it, too.

The way his words had faltered as he described our goodbye. His hoarse voice, the wild flush in his cheeks, as if he hadn't just seen William in a vision, but had actually *been* him.

Was he my second chance? Because why else was he so like William? Not only in looks, but in other ways. Being outraged by my father. Pretending to be gruff, and then doing something thoughtful and sweet, like showing me pictures of beautiful women he said I resembled. The way he watched me, his gaze travelling over my skin as I sat beside him. Lingering on my lips, trailing the edge of my mark.

He thought I hadn't noticed, but how could I not? His attention made my skin tingle and my heart do cartwheels against my ribs. And when he shared William's final words, he'd been teary over memories that weren't even his.

Oh, Cleary. You big lovable bear. Do you really think I'm beautiful?

Of course not. He was compassionate, not blind. Besides, he hadn't yet seen the real me. The me my father had hated with such intensity. That person—the me behind my sunny smile, the monstrous me—was very good at staying hidden.

Mud squelched underfoot, oozing up through my toes.

I blinked out of my thoughts and stopped walking.

I was at the loch.

Why had my feet brought me here? It was a shadowy place, full of dankness and rot. Moss clung to the twisted tree roots bulging from the ground. Particles of dust floated in the straggly sunbeams pushing through the canopy overhead, and the air was colder than an underground tomb.

Damp air curled around me, lifting strands of my hair and making me shiver.

I ventured closer to the water, sticky mud swallowing my feet. The mossy smell of the water reached my nostrils, and the greasy dankness clogged my lungs, filling my heart with panic.

The water called to me.

I crept nearer. The loch's dark surface mirrored the trees and sky, the dying sunlight. Right at the edge in the rippling shallows, it also reflected me.

I had to see what Cleary saw.

Did I really resemble those proud women with fire in their eyes and seductive smiles, whose marks were an asset instead of a curse? Defiant women who refused to be locked away, instead parading themselves with pride.

I ran along the fallen tree trunk to where the water was deepest and most mirror-like. Crouching there, I gazed down at my reflection. It rippled in the dark surface, a distorted blur. Leaning further forward, I dragged aside my hair. There. My face. It didn't look so bad in the dappled light. Perhaps if I squinted, I would see myself the way Cleary saw me. Someone brave and free, who deserved respect. Who deserved to be loved.

Maybe even by him—

I lost my balance and twisted in midair, grappling to right myself, but it was too late. I plunged headfirst into the water, shrieking just before the loch swallowed me. My lungs quickly filled with water. I had never learned to swim, despite having played here often as a child. I tried kicking my legs and flailing, but the water only dragged me deeper.

Memories flooded up from the muddy depths. I fought against them as bubbles exploded from my mouth. Fingers of loch-water clawed my limbs, closing around my wrists, my ankles, pulling me deeper. Deeper. Down into a hellish shadow world where the true monsters lived.

The black water tugged at my clothes, pulling my hair and limbs, as though determined to drag me back into the past.

35
ROSALBA

1916

William had only been gone for three or four months when my father found the letters. William wrote at least a few times a week, sometimes daily. Chaste topics mostly, or at least to the degree they would pass the army censor. I hid them in a bundle beneath the chemises in my bedroom drawer, where I thought they'd be safe.

What Father hoped to find under my chemises, I would never know. He claimed my maid found them, which was a barefaced lie, since Hattie was the one who secretly visited the post office for me. We had become friends, and she had no cause to betray me. Father was the culprit ... but in truth, how could I blame him?

He had seen me rush from the breakfast table, pale as a sheet. Had probably heard me retching in the washroom. Perhaps he'd also noticed my waist thickening? Now he stood in the kitchen, his face beet red as he raised the letters in his fist and shook them at me.

"You're a fool if you think he'll return for you."

I hung my head, fiddling my hair further down over my mark.

If only I had the courage to defy him. But after William's deployment, my spirit wilted back into its old ways. I still refused the veil, instead hiding my mark with my hair. Kneeling on thorns seemed a small price to pay for peace. As long as I kept receiving William's letters, everything was bearable—even Father's constant rants. What did it matter? Once the war ended, I would marry William and live in the farmhouse by the river.

"Do you have nothing to say for yourself, girl?"

"He will return, Father. We'll be happy together."

"You've brought shame on this house, Rosalba. There'll be no happy ending for you."

I stood up straight. "William is a good man. He promised to return, so he will."

Father brushed past me and stalked along the hallway to the sitting room. He crossed to the fireplace, where flames crackled in the grate.

Winter had set in and the days were bitter. The slate-grey skies meant snow might fall and turn the garden white. Snow was always magical, the way it glittered in the garden, freezing the water in the birdbath and crusting along the pathways. Yet it kept my father home more often, too.

I hovered in the doorway. He seemed awfully close to the fire, my precious letters clutched in his fist.

"Give them back. Please, Father. They comfort me while he's away."

"Comfort?" Father's jaw worked as he stared into the hearth. When he finally looked at me, his face was grey as the sky outside. "I suppose he promised marriage."

"Yes."

"Then you're more of a fool than I thought. He is stringing you along, Rosalba. Stoking the flames of his own selfish ego, knowing he has a creature like you in his thrall."

"Please give me the letters."

My fingers went to my neckline, to the ring I wore in secret on a chain. Sometimes in the dark, while the rest of the household slept, I threaded the ring on my finger the way William had done that afternoon. *Marry me, Rosebud. Let's make a life together, what do you say?*

My father's thin lips parted. "He's toying with you, girl. How can you not see it?"

"No, Father. You're mistaken. You can steal my letters and shear off my hair and make me kneel on thorns till I'm crying with shame. But there's one thing you can't steal from me, and that's William's love. It'll be with me always, no matter what you do. Always."

My fingers went protectively to my belly.

Father's keen gaze followed. His brow pinched, and something softened in his eyes.

My breath caught, hope sparking inside me. Could the bitter old man have a change of heart? He had loved my mother, and though he blamed me for her death in childbirth, part of her still lived on in me. Maybe he saw her reflected now, as life quickened inside me, flushing my cheeks and brightening my eyes.

"I'm your daughter," I said softly. "And yes, I'm carrying your grandchild. If you can't soften your heart towards me, then I beg you, at least try to love my child."

My father's face hollowed, the colour draining from his cheeks.

"Your child is a curse, Rosalba. A curse that will destroy everything that is good in your life, everything you cherish."

"I know you're capable of love, because you loved my mother. Please, Father. Don't turn your back on me when I need you most."

He shuffled nearer to the flames, his grip on the letters loosening.

"It's true, you are like your mother in many ways. Your voice when you speak. The way you light up when the kookaburras chortle outside in the trees. The way you fuss over a bunch of flowers you've picked, arranging them in a vase just so. And now ..." He slumped, as though defeated. "Especially now."

A tiny gasp left me. I took a step towards him.

"Father?"

"I've only been strict with you because you are so much like her. She was spirited too, did you know?"

I shook my head, my lips parting. I'd never heard him speak this way before, with such emotion in his voice. Such gentleness.

"You never told me."

"But while she bent gladly to my will, you defy me every step of the way." His voice turned hard again. "You left me no choice but to break your willful spirit. You were a nightmare of a child, Rosalba. The one blemish on your mother's memory. I fear for what the future holds for someone like you."

I slumped. "I can tell you what it holds. I'll marry William and be happy."

"Happy?" He laughed grimly. "Monsters don't get to be happy. William has abandoned you, girl. That is the truth. You need to get it through your skull and forget him."

"You're wrong, Father. He loves me."

"Even if he survives the carnage of war, he won't be back. Why do you think he enlisted in the first place?"

"To serve his country."

Father studied the letters, thumbing the ribbon that bound them together. The blue satin ribbon William had given me to tie back my hair.

"Foolish girl. He would rather throw himself into the firing line than marry you. The war was a convenient escape for him, don't you see?"

"That's a lie!"

"He used sweet talk and empty promises to get what he wanted from you, but would rather risk a bullet than stay around and commit. Do you know why?" Father's gaze flicked to my belly, his eyes narrowing. "Soon there will be another little monster to darken my household. And God help us all if the cursed creature is anything like you."

Turning abruptly, he threw the bundle of letters into the blazing fire and held me back while they burned.

36
CLEARY

NOW

Rose's short, piercing scream still rang in my ears, even though it had startled me a good fifteen minutes ago.

One moment I was sliding home-made pizza into the oven, setting the timer while Elsie did her homework at the table ... the next I was running uphill through the garden, calling Rose's name.

Was she in trouble?

Or just playing one of her old pranks?

It had been a week since we saw her at the cottage. A week since my vision of her bittersweet farewell with William. But her words continued to linger, haunting me day and night. *You don't just see through William's eyes, do you? You feel everything he feels, and you're feeling it right now.*

Naturally, I denied it. How could I feel anything beyond pity or suspicion for an entity? But she was right. The connection I had with William was tangible and intense, binding me to him in ways I never could have predicted. And now, thanks to him, I was emotionally connected to Rose as well.

It was a suffocating feeling, like being bound by invisible chains to these two strangers who had somehow become ingrained in my being. As much a part of my life now as Elsie or my mum.

"Rose, where are you?"

As I climbed the shady incline, I tuned my hunter senses to her. Becoming aware of small animals rustling in the bushes and worms shifting under my boots, owls watching from above. Until I felt the faint, distinctive cold ache of a supernatural presence radiating from the direction of the loch.

I started running, my pulse pounding in my throat.

"Rose, are you okay—?"

The sun was sinking behind the hills, casting eerie shadows through the maze of trees I passed through. When I reached the loch, I skidded to a stop, my boots sinking into the muddy ground. The water's surface was dark, an undulating mirror reflecting the sunset's distorted glow.

I went closer, my gaze drawn to the water, and there was Rose, floating beneath the surface like a submerged angel. Her hair swirled around her head, tangled with the water weeds, blurring the line between where she ended and the loch began. Her slender arms were loose and stretched over her head as though in surrender, her skin deathly pale, and her lips tinged blue.

"Rose!" My cry rang loudly in the stillness, but she didn't move, her eyes closed, her face serene as if she was only sleeping.

I plunged into the frigid water, splashing towards her, gripped by panic. In the short time I'd known her, she had become a puzzle I was determined to solve, an anchor I didn't know I needed. The idea of losing her now, like this, turned my blood colder than the black water she was drowning in.

I dived under, kicking off from the bank and swimming towards her, my arms outstretched. The water was icy where she floated.

As I got closer, her body jerked and her eyes flew open. Bubbles streamed from her mouth when she saw me. I could feel her terror in the way the water churned around us, the darkness below roiling like a living, malevolent presence.

Flinging out her arm, she grasped my outstretched hand.

Her icy fingers closed around mine, and I somehow dragged us both backwards towards the embankment, and then up out of the water. Mud squelched around us as we collapsed together on the bank, Rose gasping for air and shivering uncontrollably. I rolled closer to her, hoping to warm her, but already the darkness was settling over me.

"Cleary?"

"Rose ... are you okay?"

She nodded, her teeth clacking together.

That was all I needed to know. Before she could say anything else, my eyes blurred, everything around me turning dark.

I gritted my teeth and tried to fight the oncoming vision, climbing to my feet, only to sink back to my knees in the mud. It was no good. I was sliding into something I wanted no part of, unable to stop myself as blackness crashed over me like a tidal wave.

"Cleary, are you—?"

Her cold body crept closer, but her voice drifted away, growing distant. I gave in and closed my eyes, the eerie stillness of the night only broken by my quickening breath as darkness consumed me.

37
WILLIAM

1918

William tore the bandages away from his eyes, his heart hammering. The air in the hospital ward was freezing, and somewhere he could hear the patter of rain on a tin roof.

He bolted upright, his eyes throbbing in the sudden brightness. As sleep lifted, he heard the other wounded soldiers around him, their murmurs and groans flooding his memory banks with the chaos of battle. Suddenly he was no longer in the hospital, but back there on the front line—shells exploding, dirt and debris flying, and men screaming in agony.

A wave of helplessness washed over him, unlike anything he had ever experienced before, followed by a surge of panic as he shook off the memory. Had it been months since he last saw combat, or mere seconds? The fog in his mind from so long at sea was still distorting his memory.

How long had he been home?

Too long. It was coming back to him now.

The endless waiting. The bandages being applied or removed, lukewarm baths and cold hands. And then his nightmare last night. In it, Rose was crying, her face twisted in fear as she ran through the dark of night. She was holding a bundle, maybe an infant, its weak cries echoing like the call of a dying bird. The air was freezing and dirty snow melted on the ground, reeking of despair.

Before the war, as the two of them stood under the lightning tree saying goodbye, he had felt a shadow cross his soul. He'd forgotten about it until now, but it rushed back into his mind with all the ice and chill of an arctic squall.

What if I never see her again?

He swung his legs over the side of the bed and searched for his shoes. His feet were wooden, his legs wobbling under him as he stood. Grabbing his coat from the locker beside the bed, he shrugged into it and headed for the door. They couldn't force him to stay here. Not now.

A nurse bustled over. "Where do you think you're going?"

He gripped her hand. "I need to go. Something's happened to my girl. She needs me."

The nurse pulled away, looking over her shoulder for a doctor. "You're unwell, William. I know you're frustrated, but you've only been home a few weeks. You must be patient. Please go back to bed and I'll call for fresh bandages."

He turned from her and hurried through the ward, ignoring the sudden hubbub of raised voices behind him. He veered into the corridor and bypassed the nurse's station and somehow found the exit.

As he rushed along the wet Melbourne street, his thin coat flapping about his legs, already drenched by the rain, his mind was a blur. All he could think about was his dream—Rose's tear-streaked face twisted in distress, her cries echoing through the garden. Had something happened to her? Was that why his letters went unanswered? Why she hadn't come to visit him in the hospital, despite the countless notes he'd sent to Loch Ard, announcing his return?

He would go up the mountain today. See her at last. Sort everything out between them, and finally put that emerald on her finger.

"Stay strong, Rosie girl," he murmured, ducking onto the road to hail a cab. "I'm on my way."

38
ROSALBA

NOW

CLEARY KNEELED in the mud beside me, hugging his ribs and blankly gazing at the water. His body trembled and his face was pale as he struggled to catch his breath.

I crawled closer to the warmth he radiated. "Cleary—?"

He blinked, moaning as he fell back beside me. We stayed that way for an age, me still catching my breath and Cleary staring up through the branches into the dark sky, his chest rising and falling, his eyes a little wild.

Finally, he looked at me. "Are you all right?"

I nodded. "Where did you go just now? When you were staring at the water. You had one of your visions, didn't you?"

He shook his head, his face serious. "It was nothing. Look at you, you're shivering. At least let me warm you."

He sat in the mud and shifted closer. So close that if I inhaled and expanded myself, our bodies would touch. He was right. I felt better instantly. His breath warmed my skin, his body heat radiating out of him like a furnace. My shivers became less violent and my breathing slowed.

"How did you know I was here?"

"I heard you scream."

I leaned nearer, absorbing his warmth. In the dimness, he was less like William and more like himself. His tattooed arms were muddy and even his hair had sludge through it. Mud in his beard, on his face. If I wasn't so shaken, if the loch water chilling my skin did not smell so bad, if my lost memories did not haunt me so cruelly—then I might have managed a smile.

Did he care, after all?

Forgetting myself, I reached over and trailed my fingertips along the tattooed thorns on his wrist.

"You saved me."

He flinched, then tried to cover it with a smile, springing to his feet.

"Come on, ghost girl. You're like ice. Let's go back to the house and get you warmed up."

He gestured for me to follow, then headed down the hill, away from the loch and along the path towards the glowing lights of the house. I hurried after him, waiting for him to say something, anything. But he stayed silent, his eyes downcast, as though deep in thought.

39
ROSALBA

He stayed quiet until the house came into view, then he seemed to relax. Night had fallen and a quarter moon risen in the sky, small friendly stars twinkling overhead.

He shot me a glance. "I'm confused. Water and mud can touch you, but I can't?"

I smiled, shrugging. "They're elemental. Like air and heat and rain. I suppose I'm elemental too."

"Although..." His brows knotted. "Back there in the water, I'd have sworn your fingers closed around mine. Like real flesh and blood. Is that even possible?"

Ah, so he felt it too. Of course he did. I had gripped his hand so tightly my knuckles popped. But why did he get to ask so many questions when I only wanted one answer?

"My touch triggered another vision, didn't it?"

He looked away, his fingers flexing. "I was worried about you, that's all."

"Was it William?" My voice sounded shrill in the dark, but I couldn't rein it back in. "Please Cleary, if you saw him again, I want to know."

He met my eyes, shadows swarming over him. "What were you doing in the water?"

"I fell in." When he continued to stare at me, I rolled my shoulders. "I was trying to see my reflection. I don't know how to swim, and I just seemed to … sink."

"Reflection?" He searched my face for a moment, then slumped. "Damn. I should never have shown you those pictures."

My tension wilted. Why was I carrying on, pushing him about the vision? He'd just saved me from the loch, this was no way to repay him.

"I'm sorry, Cleary. You were only trying to help. I enjoyed seeing those women. You were right, they made me feel somehow less alone."

"You're not upset?"

"You'd know if I was."

We stopped walking, and he swayed towards me, his eyes crinkling at the edges. His face was close enough to feel the addictive warmth of his breath, see the glimmer of reflected moonlight in his eyes. Then he blinked and pulled back.

"Come on. Elsie's probably wondering where I am."

As we approached the house, my muscles went rigid. Despite the glowing windows, the place itself seemed dark. Shadows dripped from the boughs of the tall pine that towered over it, and the verandah light swarmed with moths.

Cleary gestured for me to go ahead.

On the threshold, my breath caught. Delicious food smells drifted out, and the crackling smokiness of a fire. Cosy smells, the promise of welcome.

Yet I froze in the doorway, my pulse thumping sickly.

The last time I was here, my father had stood by the fireplace, a frown creasing his thin face. *You were restless last night, Rosalba. What were you up to?* I had left in a hurry, my bag thumping on my hip, the weight in my heart as heavy as the sleeping child swaddled in my arms—

As I stepped over the threshold and went inside, Elsie rushed up with her arms out, as if to hug me.

"Rose!"

Cleary caught her in time. "Rose is our guest. Mind your manners, okay?"

She shrugged him off and beamed up at me. "You like pizza?"

"I've never had it before."

"Oh, you'll love it. Dad's an awesome cook."

I followed them deeper into the house. It was not as I remembered. The dark galley kitchen at the back of the place had gone. The sitting and dining rooms were now one large, open space. Bright paintings hung on the walls and a long, sleek table created a striking focal point. Mismatched wooden chairs in bright shades surrounded it like eccentric guests at a tea party.

I whirled around, my eyes wide.

"Everything's changed! It's not the same house."

Cleary checked inside the shiny oven, making blue flames dance behind its glass door.

"Is it overwhelming?"

"Perhaps a little. In a good way, though."

His gaze trailed over me. "Your clothes are dry. Who'd even guess that twenty minutes ago you were in the loch?" He grinned as he looked down at himself, brushing at his sodden T-shirt and jeans. "Me, on the other hand—I look like a mud wrestler. Nothing a quick shower won't fix. I'll be five minutes, max."

Once he'd gone, Elsie asked about the loch.

"I was a dill," I told her. "I leaned too close to the water and fell in."

"Did Dad save you?"

"Yes, he did."

Elsie tucked in her chin and beamed. "Typical Dad. He comes across all gruff and cranky, pretending he doesn't give a hoot. But underneath he's ..." She glanced over her shoulder at the hallway, and then plonked her elbow on the table and leaned closer. "He's just a big old softie."

I leaned in too. "I think you're right."

Cleary bustled back into the space with damp hair and clean, mud-free clothes. "I'm gone for two minutes and you pair have already got your heads together, whispering. I hope my ears won't start burning."

Elsie rolled her eyes and laughed. "We've better things to discuss than you, Dad! Like, when will that pizza be ready?"

Cleary went over to the oven and opened it. The scent of baked bread and tomatoes wafted out. He removed a large tray with what looked like a flat open pie bubbling with cheese and vegetables. Placing it on the bench, he cut it into wedges and served them onto plates. Elsie carried the plates over to the table and laid them out.

I settled at the table with them.

Tiny shivers kept rushing along my spine. *How is it possible I'm back here? In my father's old house, where I vowed never to set foot again?* Opposite where we sat, the stairwell was as I remembered, disappearing behind thick railings. The dark wood was now painted a soft sage green, pretty against the cheery white walls. Despite it all, my scalp tightened. In my mind, I could still hear my father's boots thumping down the stairs, still see his face distorted with anger—

"Rose?"

Elsie pushed a plate over. A generous slice of pizza pie sat beside the most delicious looking salad I'd ever seen. I breathed it all in, savouring the aromas, but then sat back.

"This is lovely ... but I can't—"

Cleary placed a knife and fork on either side of my plate. "It's okay. We just want you to feel included."

Elsie devoured some salad, then got to work on her pizza, eyeing me the whole time.

"Do you get hungry, Rose?"

"Sometimes."

"What do you eat?"

I bit my lip, glancing down at my hands. *I hunger for touch. For companionship. Love. Somewhere out there, William's soul is drifting through the universe. Does he feel alone, too? Does he yearn for me, like I yearn for him with every beat of my heart?*

I smiled over at Elsie.

"It's more a memory of hunger, I suppose. When it strikes, I recall a delicious meal I had in the time before. And somehow that seems to fill me up."

Elsie's eyes widened. "You mean before you became a ghost?"

Cleary glared at her. "Elsie!"

"It's all right. I'm happy to answer questions, if I can." I looked across at Elsie. "And yes, I still remember the meals I ate when I lived in this house with my father. Simple fare, mostly soup and bread. Nothing as grand as this."

Elsie looked alarmed. "No pizza?"

I shook my head. "Alas, the closest we came was roast mutton and vegetables baked in suet."

She looked hopeful. "Suet?"

"A kind of pastry made with hard white fat."

Her little nose wrinkled. "Yuk!"

Cleary opened his mouth as if to scold again, but then floundered.

"It does sound horrible."

"In fact, it was rather tasty."

Elsie wiped a smear of tomato off her chin. "Were you terribly poor?"

"Not at all. My father …" I swallowed. "Well, he was a very wealthy man. We had maids and a cook. Several young stable hands. A piper to play the bagpipes. A full-time gardener…"

Elsie's mouth dropped open. "You had horses?"

"Only four." I counted them off on my fingers. "Branny, Angus, Dougal, and Mrs Mac the Feisty. She was my favourite, a huge grey mare with a horrible temper and a passion for carrots. Once, I took her a treat from the garden, but the cheeky thing nipped me because I was too slow handing it over." Lifting my hand, I displayed the white notch on my wrist. "I still have the scar!"

Elsie had stopped eating. Cleary, too, his pizza slice halfway to his lips.

I looked from one to the other. "What?"

Elsie was staring at my face. My face! I gasped. How had I forgotten? Fumbling hastily, I readjusted my hair further forward over my ruined side. But Elsie wasn't looking at my mark. She was beaming right into my eyes, her short hair tufting out all over the place, and her gaze bright with interest.

"Will you tell us more, Rose?"

"More?"

Cleary smiled over, his own eyes brimming with curiosity. "I think she'd like to hear a story. About your life. Before."

"Oh."

"If that's okay," Elsie added shyly.

I settled back in the chair. Clasping my hands on the edge of the table, I took a breath.

"What would you like to know?"

Elsie glanced over at her father, who nodded. She squinted at the ceiling, then looked at me.

"When William never came back, you said it was easier to think he died. How could that be easier?"

I adjusted my hair, glancing at Cleary through the strands.

"William was the gardener here at Loch Ard. He had the biggest heart of anyone I knew. He was brave and smart and funny, and after he left for the war, I missed him dreadfully. Yet it was worse when he never returned. Believing he had died was easier than thinking he'd forgotten about me."

Elsie's gaze sharpened. "Why would you think that?"

I swallowed the moth-like flutter in my throat.

"We planned to marry, but I hesitated too long. Leaving Loch Ard scared me. I had never gone outside the gates. Then the army shipped William away for training and soon after he was deployed. It happened so fast my head spun. Father warned me not to get my hopes up about William returning for me. He said—" *William would rather risk a bullet than stay and marry you. You're a monster, Rosalba. No monster gets a happy ending.* I gulped back another flutter. "He said …"

When my silence stretched too long, Cleary propped his elbow on the table and leaned in.

"What did your father say?"

My fingers trailed the side of my mouth. Even with my hair drawn forward, it could not fully hide the mark. I straightened my shoulders. The women Cleary showed me on his phone had not cowered in shame. They had stood proudly, heads held high.

"My father said William never really loved me. Otherwise, he'd have stayed and married me, instead of rushing off to war. He said my face scared William away."

Elsie gasped. "That's mean!"

Cleary flattened his palms on the table, his eyes intense.

"Your father should have gone to jail for how he treated you, Rose. You're a sweet person, intelligent and kind. There's a ton of reasons William never returned. But I'm certain of one thing. He loved you ... very much."

The way his voice broke on those last words brought back the moth-flutter. It sounded like an admission. He spoke of William, but had he felt it too? I swallowed, blinking back the prickle of tears.

Elsie frowned, her little head tilting to the side.

"Oh, Rose," she whispered. "We love you, too."

Silence crashed around me, my limbs locking in place. I stared at the child, and something about her—the trusting eyes, the adoration in her gaze, the hint of a smile on her lips, the small freckled face tilted towards me like a flower greeting the sun—turned my heart to ice.

The smell of the loch drifted back, and I shivered.

There's something in the water, a crocheted bunny rug, the sort you'd wrap a baby in. A helpless baby with big blue eyes and porcelain skin ... but what's that unsightly stain on her face, Rosalba? Please, no. Father will not be happy. He won't let you keep her. He'll send her away and the outside world will shun her, just as it shuns you ...

I gasped. "Elsie ... you can't. It's not —"

Not safe. It's not safe for you to love me. Hasn't anyone told you not to talk to monsters?

Getting to my feet, I fled across the room and down along the shadowed hallway. Behind me, chairs scraped back, their legs squealing on the floorboards. One crashed over. Cleary called my name, his footsteps thudding behind me, but I was faster. When I reached the solid oak door—the door my father imported from Scotland a century ago—I stepped right through as if sliding through a mist.

"Rose, wait!"

I ran into the dark garden, my heart punching my ribs.

They had drawn me to their world like a moth to candlelight. It felt welcoming and safe, but I could never belong, no matter how I yearned. I was an outsider. An intruder. One of the others.

The prey their instincts told them to hunt.

Even worse, I was a threat to them. And the closer they came to me, the more deadly that threat became.

40
CLEARY

The damp night air wrapped around me as I quickened my pace, my boots crunching on the gravel path as I veered uphill through the trees. The plump quarter moon glittered in its bed of stars above, shining down on a light fog that drifted over the ground and grew thicker as I climbed deeper into the garden.

"Rose?"

Elsie was worried. *Go after her, Dad. Make sure she's okay. She's upset, and it's my fault.* If anyone was to blame, it was me. I should have told her about my vision at the loch. The vision she sparked when our hands met. But how could I tell her when it would break her heart?

"I know you can hear me." The cold caress of a breeze brushed the back of my arms and I glanced around. "We overwhelmed you tonight, and I'm sorry. But you don't have to hide from us. Just tell me you're okay."

I heard a sigh and suddenly she was standing in front of me. The fog swirled more thickly, curling around her feet like a cloud of ghostly cats.

I inhaled the scent of violets. "Why did you rush out? You seemed happy. And then…"

She glared out from behind her curtain of dark hair. "The house has bad memories for me."

"I think you got scared." I shifted closer. "Because of what Elsie said."

Her chin jutted defiantly, but tears gleamed in her eyes. "If anyone should be scared, it's you. We spend all of five minutes together and you think you know me. But you don't. I'm like the loch. Sunny on the surface but deadly beneath. Someone like me can cause a lot of damage. Getting too close is a mistake."

"What are you talking about?"

She twitched again, her shoulders creeping up protectively.

"Elsie shouldn't say those things. About love and such. I'm a stranger. She barely knows me."

"She has solid instincts. And she knows how she feels about you."

Rose's gaze turned dark, the fog surrounding her growing more restless.

"What about you, Cleary? How do you feel?"

"Rose, it's not—" I stalled. Not about how I feel, I meant to say, but the words jammed in my throat. In the beginning, I only cared about getting rid of her. She was an entity I needed to banish and then forget about. But since hearing her story and getting to know her, everything had changed.

I huffed, clawing my fingers over the stubble on my jaw.

Every new vision reinforced just how intensely William adored her. How proud he felt to stand beside her on the edge of the garden and plan their future together. How desperately he wanted to protect her, to make her happy. And now, somehow, those feelings were passing into me.

I thought about her all the time. While making breakfast. Driving Elsie to school. Sanding floorboards or hoeing weeds in the garden. Even in the shower. She crept into my alone time like a tune I couldn't stop humming. I daydreamed about kissing her, about pulling her into the bed with me and crushing her willowy body beneath mine. About loving her through the night and making her murmur my name. Which was wrong on every level. She was the enemy, a threat to everything I valued. Everything I had worked so hard to build. It was wrong to care about her this way.

"Well, Cleary?"

I scratched my beard again, resetting my shoulders. "I don't feel anything."

Rose stepped closer, her lips pulling into a line. "No?"

I stepped back, creating distance between us, but Rose closed the gap I had made, taking another step, her gaze luminous in the dark.

"When you pulled me from the loch this afternoon, it sparked one of your visions."

"Yes."

"Tell me what you saw, Cleary. I need to know."

I braced myself, inhaling the night air into my lungs.

"You won't like it."

"Tell me."

"William survived the war. He came home."

Rose's eyes popped wide. "What, no. You saw him die on the battlefield. A shell exploded and killed him…"

"In my vision at the loch, I saw him waking in an Australian hospital."

"He lived." Fog coiled around her, tendrils advancing higher as if offering comfort, but then retreating to the ground. "So why didn't he—?"

"Come and see you? He wanted to. To make good on his promise to marry you. He hadn't recovered properly, but he tore off his bandages and checked himself out."

Her lips parted. "Then what happened to him?"

"I don't know."

"Why didn't you tell me this at the loch?"

I shrugged. "You seemed .... vulnerable. Besides, it was so brief. Barely a glimpse. I can hardly even remember."

Sudden fury lit her eyes, the coiling fog rising again, clinging to her like a shroud. "We had a deal, Cleary."

"Yeah, I just—"

"Just nothing." She swept closer, her silky hair fluttering against my chest. I felt her icy breath on my face, and something in her gaze chilled my blood. She trailed her touch lightly down my arm, then gripped my hand in her icy fingers.

"Remember it this time. And tell me what you see—"

41
WILLIAM

1918

After leaving the hospital, William caught the train back to Woodhill and walked across town to his farmhouse on the outskirts.

He shaved and bathed away the antiseptic smells, then hurried out to the old barn where his father's Model T Ford was housed. He drove up the mountain to Loch Ard, rattling over the gravel and choking on dust, his nightmare about Rose replaying in his mind. Curse the war, and curse his injuries. He should have ignored the doctors and escaped the hospital sooner.

"I'm here now, Rose. I won't leave you again. Not ever."

He drove through Loch Ard's big wooden gates and parked outside the house. Rosalba's father was waiting. He stepped aside, watching William stalk through the door, his gaze sharp and snakelike. Jedrick McGregor had become even more skeletal with the passing of years. He had aged badly, his craggy face deeply lined and his eyes swollen with bitterness. A missing tooth gaped from his insincere smile.

"I'm surprised to see you, William."

"Why's that?"

"Rosalba thought you were dead."

William met the older man's gaze. Once, he had worked side by side with Jedrick in the garden, helping him to recreate the McGregor's ancestral home in Scotland. Together they had planted thickets of maples and firs, ancient oaks. They had planted ferns around the wrought iron shade house, and filled the loch with trout fingerlings imported from Aberdeenshire.

William left part of himself in every corner of the garden, as did Jedrick. The older man wasn't afraid of hard work, yet no genuine friendship had ever sparked between them.

William took off his hat.

"I'n still alive, as you can see. I got hurt, but I recovered and now I'm here. To make good on my promise."

The old man offered him a brandy, which William declined. He was growing impatient. He wasn't here to make conversation with Jedrick. It was Rose he wanted to see.

"Where is she?"

"If you think she'll be leaving with you, you're mistaken."

"That's her decision, not yours." He went to the stairs and called up into the darkness. "Rosalba? Please come down so we can talk."

Jedrick ambled over to the sideboard. Opening a drawer—with infuriating slowness, William noted—he took out a box of cigars and offered him one. William declined this as well, and Jedrick lit his own with a match. He drew deeply on the cigar, his face disappearing behind a puff of smoke.

"She had a child, you know."

William took a step back, suddenly unsteady.

"A child?"

"A baby daughter."

His pulse picked up. A child. Rosalba had hinted in her letters two years ago, but when he tried to press her, she skirted the issue. Then in 1916 her letters stopped abruptly. He hadn't heard from her since, unsure if his own letters were reaching her. Wartime mail was notoriously unreliable. Rose may have felt a distance develop between them, but once he saw her again, that would change.

"I want to see them."

Jedrick pressed his thin lips together, jerking his head towards the window.

"She's up in the berry patch. With the child."

The injured side of William's head throbbed as he processed this. His bad eye streamed, but he elbowed away the tears.

"It's freezing out there. They'll catch their deaths."

"Maybe that's her intention."

William scowled. Crazy old coot, wasting his precious time with vitriol. He retrieved his hat from the stand, eager to be gone. As he stalked to the door, Jedrick caught his sleeve.

"You don't know my daughter as well as you think you do, Will. Rosalba is unfit as a mother. She destroyed our family. And she'll destroy you too."

William clenched his teeth, his fingers curling into fists. He had never wanted to punch someone as badly as he did now. But this was Rosalba's father. When did the man ever have a decent word to say about anyone? Wicked and poisonous as Old Nick himself, he wasn't worth William grazing his knuckles on.

42
CLEARY

NOW

My stomach twisted into knots as the vision faded. A searing pain erupted in my head, spreading over my body as if a sledgehammer had struck me. The world spun and I stumbled, grabbing onto a tree trunk for support.

Rose drifted nearer. "Cleary, are you all right?"

"Yeah." I wasn't. Every time I surfaced out of a vision, my stomach roiled with dread that I'd lost another piece of myself and gained a part of someone else. The aftereffects were becoming more intense—a noxious mix of vertigo and existential despair that left me gasping for breath—but worse was the sense of forgetting myself.

Once it calmed, I explained my vision as best I could, and for a moment Rose was silent. Clutching the front of her dress with white-knuckled fingers, her gaze fixed on my face.

"William came back to Loch Ard?"

I probed my memory of the vision, my breath catching as a fist of something joyless and cold closed around my heart.

"He had a nightmare. He was worried about you."

"Then why didn't I see him?"

"He seemed determined to find you."

She pinched her chin, her fingers leaving red marks.

"Why would I visit the berry patch in the snow ... with my child? Up the hill, so far from the house. It doesn't make sense ... unless—"

Her lips clamped shut, and she made a choking sound. Turning, she retreated into the darkness.

I stepped in front of her. "You never said you had a child. Why don't you ever talk about her?"

"What's the point?" She sidestepped me, shaking her head as she stumbled deeper into the shadows.

I caught up with her. "Hey, please. You can tell me."

Her hand swept out, as if to ward me away.

"I don't know what happened to her! I try to remember her growing up, but all I see is a chubby-cheeked baby in my arms."

"You've forgotten?"

"No, it's not that. Mostly, I can't bear to think about her, so I push the thoughts away. Then sometimes, in the night, or when my guard drops, there she is. So tiny. Peering up at me from the time before. I always wonder if she grew up to be happy. If her children and grandchildren are still out there somewhere, living wonderful lives because of the love Odette showered on them. The love I tried to shower on her."

The night converged around her, and she trembled, her skin

as pale as moonlight. She seemed to blend into the surrounding darkness, fragile and delicate.

I inched closer. "Maybe if you talk about her, it'll spark a memory?"

"What if it's a memory I can't face?"

"Think of something happy, then. Her first tooth, learning to read. Growing up and going off to school. What was something she loved?"

Rose shut her eyes, drawing a shaky breath, trying to smile.

"She loved the snow. One afternoon, I took her outside to see it falling. She was so funny, giggling up at the snowflakes, trying to snatch them in her tiny hands. Wriggling and shrieking as they melted on her skin…"

43
ROSALBA

1917

Snow lay thick on the ground at Loch Ard that winter, blanketing everything in white. It floated from the sky like tiny glittering petals, transforming the garden into a fairytale place.

I crunched along the path, cradling Odette in my arms as I bypassed the flowerbeds, heading uphill.

With the war still going, most of our staff had left. Which increased my workload around the house, but it also gave me the freedom to venture into the garden as I pleased. So I walked every day, showing Odette the insects and birds, the thistles and thorns, and the damp green shadows where the tree ferns grew. And of course, the snow.

Odette's chubby arms flapped excitedly at the icicles twinkling in the leaves, and at the glittering frost and swirling snowflakes. I hugged her against me, enjoying her enjoyment of the magical landscape, wishing we could stay here forever. But soon it grew too cold, and I retraced my steps reluctantly back down the hill.

In the sitting room, my father was stoking the fire.

When I bustled in with the baby, he stalked over to the window and stood with his back to us, silhouetted by the afternoon glare. Had he been lingering there already, watching us? He glanced over, his gaze colder than the snow on the ground outside.

"Did you enjoy your walk, Rosalba?"

"It was lovely, thank you."

I rocked Odette in my arms. She was such a pretty baby, with her large liquid blue eyes, and sweet face framed by feathery dark hair. Her birthmark was a fraction paler than mine, but the sight of it still broke me. My own mark had always caused me insecurity and shame, and I feared hers would do the same. Every day, I prayed it would fade as she grew.

She gazed up, cooing happily, as if to say, Silly Mama, my mark won't stop me from having the most wonderful life imaginable. I kissed her head and squeezed her close, my breath tickling her ear, making her giggle.

My father made a disapproving noise in his throat.

"It's a bitter day outside."

"Yes, Father."

His attention shifted back through the glass to the garden. He rarely looked at me when he spoke, preferring to address an object or a view. Which suited me fine. These days, I barely noticed the revulsion in his eyes when he glanced at me—but when he looked at my daughter that way, it brought a pain to my heart that was increasingly difficult to bear.

He pressed the back of his hand against the windowpane. "Babies are fragile. They can die in the snow, you know."

"I'm always careful, Father."

Odette shoved her fingers in her mouth, making a loud sucking noise. She was heavy, and it was nearing her feeding time. As she fussed in my arms, I made a beeline for the door, eager to escape Father's stern gaze and depressing conversation.

"Wait, Rosalba." His gaze dropped to my child. "Don't you worry about her future?"

"She'll have a happy life, Father. I'll make sure of it."

"Happy?" His mouth turned down. "But surely you can see how frightful she is?"

I clutched my baby protectively, my anger blazing up at his words. You are the frightful one, I wanted to scream. You are the monster! But I bit my tongue and kept my eyes downcast. I didn't need him to drag me to the stables and belt me for being impertinent. Instead, I murmured my excuses and fled into the freezing hallway. As I hurried towards the stairs, footsteps hastened behind me.

My father's wiry fingers closed around my arm.

I froze. "Father?"

"When you were born," he said in a quiet voice, "the doctor gave me a choice. Save the mother or the babe. I chose the mother, but she slipped away despite his best efforts. While you ... somehow, you survived."

I tried to pull away. "Father, you're hurting me."

His fingers dug deeper into my flesh. "What sort of life will Odette have? Locked away, unseen. Treated like an outcast? Shunned?"

"I won't shun her! She'll know only kindness from me."

"But the world will shun her."

"Then the world can go to hell!"

My father recoiled at my words, but his grip on me only tightened.

"You wicked girl! If you truly care for her, then take her out into the snow. Leave her there. Let nature run its course. She won't suffer for long, the cold will take her quickly. Be brave and think of the miserable life you're saving her from."

I wrenched free and backed away, gripping Odette against me. I was glad he saw me as a monster, for that's how I felt right now—wild and untamable, raring to lash out.

"God help me," I whispered harshly. "How can you even think such a thing? She's my child, I'd never harm her!"

"Then you are a fool."

Unable to hear anymore of his poisonous words, I fled upstairs to my room and shut the door.

My bedroom was my sanctuary, even though Father always locked it from the outside. Cheery curtains hung at the window and Father had allowed me to use the wooden cot that had once been mine. Every spare space was decorated with treasures collected on our daily walks—lorikeet feathers and pinecones and such—bringing my beloved garden inside. But there were moments, like now, when my room felt more like a prison.

I heard footsteps. The key rattled, and the lock clicked, and then my father's tread retreated, fading to silence.

I stood at my window, watching the snow fall.

What sort of life will Odette have?

"Is there so little hope, Father?" I hugged Odette tighter and bent to kiss her feathery head. "Oh, my little one. How I love you. But what will become of us now?"

I did not want a miserable life for her.

I did not want it for myself.

But what could I do?

Outside, pure white flakes clung to the branches of the tall paperbark cherry that shaded our house. As the snow softened and ran down its trunk, the pinkish bark turned blood-red. And all the while I heard my father's words whispering, whispering like the wind.

Take her into the snow, Rosalba. Be brave and think of the life you'll be saving her from.

44
ROSALBA

NOW

A SOB CAUGHT in my throat as I broke away from Cleary. Gathering my skirt, I fled through the misty darkness, all the way back to my cottage.

In the room out the back, I tried to steady myself, but the tears only streamed all the faster down my cheeks. Stumbling over to the wooden cot in the corner—the same cot my daughter slept in all those years ago—I gripped its wooden rail as a tidal wave of memories flooded back.

The soft coos of my baby girl, her tiny hands reaching out for me as she opened her eyes. Her warm weight as I cradled her against me.

"Odette." A hot tear splashed onto the thin mattress. "How can I speak of her, Cleary? It was so long ago. I don't even remember how it felt to be a mother—" That was a lie. My sweetest memories were of being a mother to my little girl. She had given my existence meaning that nothing else had. She'd been my world, and even now, a century later, I still missed the weight of her in my arms.

But did I dare remember her?

My baby watches the snowflakes drift down, mesmerised by their dance. She snuggles closer, cosy inside the soft white blanket I crocheted for her. Her blue eyes meet mine, and I hold on to her tighter, not wanting to let go of this perfect moment together in the midst of our snowy fairytale.

I hunched into myself, the roar of my conscience drowning out all other sounds. My grip on the cot rail was fierce, as if releasing it would shatter me into a million pieces. As if the tide of remembering might wash me away into an abyss of shame and guilt I could never return from.

Rose, please ... What happened to her?

"I don't know what happened to her, Cleary. That's what scares me." My voice trembled, catching in my throat like thorns. "I tell myself she grew up to be happy. That she had everything I wished for her. Love. Adventure. Peace. Her own child to love and be loved by. But what if that's a lie? What if I did something monstrous to her?"

Crumpling to my knees on the floor, I rested my forehead against the side of the cot and closed my eyes. That was a mistake. Another memory assaulted me, this one brighter and larger and a thousand times more vivid than the one before.

My father's features twist in horror as he stares down at my baby. "Look at the child, Rosalba. Her birthmark is even worse than yours! She'll be cursed unless you do as I told you." I gather

Odette from her cot and run out into the garden. Snow is dancing all around us, and the wind shepherds us up the frostbitten hillside. My fingertips grow numb, and Odette wails, her mark flaming crimson in the cold. Her little eyes turn up at me, searching. I try not to look at her. Black shadows carve the snow-crusted pathway, and far above us the oyster-shell sun drowns in a soup of grey clouds. My breath grows ragged, and one by one, the tears turn to ice on my face—

"No, no ..." My eyes sprang open, spilling more tears. "I would never hurt my child!"

But what if I had?

Not knowing would haunt me forever, wouldn't it? And now that the floodgates had opened, no part of the garden was safe. The roses, the willow, the cypress tree—each corner held memories I had carefully buried.

Unearthing the past to share with Cleary had stirred something inside me, and now secrets were rushing out uncontrollably. The harder I struggled to contain them, the harder they fought back. Soon they would erupt, destroying me and everyone else in their path.

45
CLEARY

By the end of the following week, Rose still hadn't made an appearance. Elsie had spent another afternoon searching the garden, despite my warnings, and was now pacing the lounge room, tears streaking her flushed face.

"It's all my fault!"

"She'll show up when she's ready."

"But, Dad! You always tell me not to ask so many questions, and I never listen. I just keep asking and asking. And now Rose is upset, and it's all my fault."

"She was overwhelmed, that's all." I dug my hands deep into the pockets of my jeans. If anyone was to blame, it was me. Pushing Rose too far, prompting her to remember things she clearly wasn't ready to face. I looked over at my daughter and forced a bright smile. "She's still getting used to us, Elsie. You'll see her again soon."

"Promise?"

"Yeah. Hey—" I picked up the remote and switched on the telly. "Why don't we watch Digger's Delight? See which garden they're making over this week? There's ice-cream in the freezer..."

Her gaze flickered past me to the kitchen, but her lips were trembling.

"What if she never comes back, Dad?"

"She'll be back. She's too curious about us to stay away for long."

"Tomorrow's the new moon. Her hold on our world is weakest now. What if something happened to her? She might have gone back to the loch, fallen in the water again." She smudged away fresh tears. "What if she's already crossed over?"

I stood in the doorway, biting my lips shut.

Rose had been distraught when I saw her last. Talking about her child had rattled her in a way I hadn't seen before. But while my heart went out to her, I couldn't help wondering if it wasn't such a bad thing.

I wanted no more visions. No more time in William's head. His feelings for Rose were too intense. They made me uncomfortable. Or maybe William's feelings were becoming my feelings, too. Was I falling for Rose? There were moments when being near her felt sweet and tangible. Addictive. But it wasn't real. I was a hunter with one job only. To untether Rose, sell the property, and then move on to the next entity who needed untethering. All this extra contact—seeing her from William's point of view, getting to know her—was making my job impossible.

You need to harden up, man. Get your priorities straight.

I was used to the transient nature of my relationships. The fleeting moments of connection that eventually gave way to the cold, existential reality that we were all alone. Rose had changed my outlook. Her laughter, her bright eyes as she talked about the garden or shared bits of her past, or even just interacting with Elsie—it all opened up the potential between us. But where could it go?

We could never touch. Never hold each other. Not even kiss. All that was frustrating, yet not essential. What about Elsie? She needed a mum who could hug her, be present in ways that Rose couldn't. What if something happened and Rose couldn't protect Elsie?

I had always been a lone wolf, keeping my distance from others. Avoiding closeness, wary of getting hurt or hurting someone else. But with Rose, that all changed. She was like a big warm bath that I had fallen into willingly and eagerly. I sensed she was developing feelings for me, too. And not just because she saw something of William in me. It was because of us, the way we connected. The gleam in her eyes sometimes, the comfortable way she sat beside me. The way she tilted her head back when she laughed, forgetting to adjust her hair.

Lone wolf, yeah right. You're more like a lovesick puppy.

I scooped ice cream into a bowl and then rummaged in the drawer for Elsie's favourite spoon. She was slumped in front of the TV, her gaze glued to the screen as Digger's Delight came on. Upbeat music blared into the room, and a montage of garden makeovers flashed past.

I handed her the bowl of chocolate chip.

"Why don't we work on the cottage tomorrow? It could entice her out."

She took the bowl without looking at me.

"It's okay, Dad. I know how to get her attention."

46

ROSALBA

Golden sunlight filtered through the canopy of trees, casting long shadows on the pebbly trail as I did my morning rounds, walking uphill towards the shade house.

The scent of ripening November apples drifted down from the orchard, and I inhaled it deep into the bottom of my lungs.

I was determined not to let my memories of Odette consume me. Weaken me. I had to stay strong to fight the doubt and uncertainty. But the thought of leaving her in the cold to die, as my father insisted, still haunted me.

I stopped walking and gripped my ribs.

Was I capable of doing such harm? Of course not. I had loved my baby more than life itself. But what if Father had gotten under my skin somehow? Influenced me to do his bidding? It had happened before. What if my need to please him had driven me to do the inconceivable—?

A watery, splashing, plopping sound broke through my misery.

I frowned. It seemed to drift from the loch. And was that a child singing ... or crying?

Gathering my skirts in one hand, I ran downhill towards the waterhole, pushing the undergrowth out of my way. Thorns caught on my hem, and my breath escaped in little hisses as I forced my way through the thickets of vegetation. I burst through a wall of brambles and finally halted in front of the loch.

Moss-covered boulders littered the shore, and in among them was a small figure. She stood ankle deep in the shallows, tossing stones across to the deeper side and making an occasional splash herself, the water gulping hungrily at her legs.

"Elsie!" I shrieked. "Get out of the water!"

She whipped around, her eyes popping wide. Then she grinned and sloshed along the bank towards me.

"I thought you left!"

As she reached dry land, I clutched my chest. "Oh, my heart!"

She laughed, her eyes lighting up. "We missed you!"

"You wanted to lure me here, didn't you?"

She tucked in her neck, shrugging guiltily. "Where did you go?"

"I had things to do." Important things, like wallowing in my unhappiness, if you must know—but of course I didn't say it aloud.

"What things?"

I rolled my gaze at the sky. Lord, what a child. First giving me a coronary, and now an inquisition. Did her questions never cease? I beckoned her to follow me, and we walked uphill along the track until we reached the orchard. I looked at her, puffing along beside me, her freckled face pink from the sun.

"I've been busy counting fireflies," I told her. "That's why I haven't seen you."

She frowned. "What's a firefly?"

"They're bugs. At night, they glow like fairy lights."

"Will you show me?"

The sun burned overhead. I stopped walking and stretched, the bones in my spine popping. I hated to admit it, but I'd missed her bright, funny company.

"Maybe."

Settling beneath a gnarly old apple tree, its branches weighed low with fruit, I ran my fingers across the soft grass, rippling the blades.

Elsie flapped her hands excitedly. "When?"

"Tonight around sundown? Meet me at the shade house and I'll take you."

"Yay!" She flopped beside me. "Rose, are you cross?"

I looked at her. She was slight for a nine-year-old. A smear of dried jam clung to her chin. Her dark hair was dragged carelessly into an elastic band that made it spike from the back of her head like a stumpy horsetail. With her muddy legs, she looked like a scruffy doll that someone had played with too many times and cast aside.

"Why would I be cross?"

"The other night at dinner. I said the wrong thing, and you left."

"I wasn't cross, Elsie. I just had to ... go."

"Dad thinks the house might've spooked you. He said you were unhappy growing up there. Is that true?"

"Well, I was content in my way. I had a roof over my head. Enough to eat. An entire library of books to keep me busy." I gestured at the garden. "And all this to escape into. This was my happy place."

Elsie settled back on her elbows. "What about your mum and dad?"

"My mother died when I was born. And my father ... I suppose he meant well, but he was strict." Elsie fixed her full attention on my face, the side I hid behind my hair. Before she could ask, I hurried on. "What about your mum, Elsie? Do you miss her?"

She shrugged. "Not really. She visits every few years. She's okay. She thinks I'm a fruitcake."

"Oh?"

"Nutty as a fruitcake, she calls me. I heard Dad telling Gran on the phone one time."

"That must have hurt."

She shrugged, her thin shoulders making her seem vulnerable. "Maybe she's right. I'm not like other kids. I see things no one else can. The others. People mostly." She gave me a little wave. "And sometimes animals."

How could she be both hilarious and so heart-wrenching all at once?

"That doesn't make you a fruitcake, Elsie. It makes you unique. Which is a good thing, right?"

"Hmm." She gazed at the grass, plucking, plucking, as if the soft green blades were the most fascinating thing in the universe.

I leaned closer. "Once you find your purpose in life, you'll be so absorbed by it, you won't care what people think."

She sat up and pondered her bony knees. "How do I find my purpose?"

"You could start by learning more about the garden," I told her gently. "Reading books and exploring with me. I learned about plants and insects from a wonderful teacher."

"You mean William?"

"Yes."

"How will that help?"

"The more you explore the world, the more you begin to understand yourself. What fascinates you or bores you. What delights you. It's a good place to start."

"I love frogs. And climbing trees. Finding nests and hollows."

"That means you're connected to the natural world. One day, you might study those things and discover new ways to conserve them."

She sat up straight. "Like a scientist?"

"Why not?"

She blinked, her gaze roaming the garden as if it was all suddenly new to her.

"I almost can't wait."

Warmth washed over me. Odette had been different, too. Her face was marked like mine, and my father said people would shun her for it. But I pictured her having a friend like Elsie. The two of them growing up together, being strong for one another. Never caring what people thought. I smiled to myself. *Sweet girl, it's all ahead of you. I hope you find your purpose and that it brings you a life of meaning and happiness—*

"Rose?"

I swiped at my eyes. "Hmm?"

"How old are you?"

"Over a hundred."

"Gosh, you don't look it."

"I'm really twenty-one."

"I can't wait to be twenty-one. What's it like? No one bossing you around. I bet that's the best part."

"Your dad's bossy?"

She bugged her eyes and nodded. "He says it's for my own good. He reckons being a parent is tougher than it looks."

"It can't be easy on his own. A young girl like you needs a mother to ... well, mother her."

Shock registered in her eyes, but she blinked it away in a flash. Her chin tucked into her neck and she gave me a grin that transformed her mousey face into something glorious. I remembered her words from that night, and the lump in my throat returned. *We love you, Rose.* I bent over my legs, pretending interest in a dry leaf that clung to the hem of my skirt.

Elsie wriggled over for a closer look.

"Oh, I love leaves! Sometimes I press them in my books like little bookmarks. Do you like books, Rose? I do, I read tons of them. Dad says one day I'll wear out my eyes from too much reading."

Her cheerful little face made me smile. Reaching down, I cupped my fingers under the leaf and scooped it into my palm. Elsie's eyes grew wide.

"Take it," I told her. "Something to remember me by."

Her mouth popped open as she stared at the leaf. "How are you doing that?"

"Sometimes I can."

"Does Dad know?"

I thought of the windstorm I'd created. "I'm sure he has an inkling."

Elsie plucked the leaf from my palm, her warm fingers brushing my cold ones. She gazed at me for the longest time, then tucked the leaf into her pocket and sprang up.

"See you tonight?"

"Right on dusk."

She waved and scampered away down the hill towards the house.

I stood in the sunlit orchard watching her. Seeing her so full of life and brightness, the garden didn't seem as lonely anymore. The shadows retreated, and my spirit grew lighter. I could hardly wait for the sun to sink.

So much for keeping my distance from them. Staying aloof. Driving them away. Now those thoughts couldn't be further from my mind. What had I gotten myself into? I exhaled slowly, hugging my arms around me.

Oh, Rose ... we love you—

But Elsie was a flesh and blood girl who could never truly be mine. Just as her flesh and blood father could never be mine. Fate had brought us together, but at some point, it would tear us apart again. Elemental rules allowed spirits and humans to coexist in the world for a time ... but it was fated to end unhappily. The thought made my heart want to shatter into a million tiny pieces, and it took every ounce of my strength to hold it together.

47
ROSALBA

As the sun began to set, I walked down to the shade house, pacing back and forth among the tree ferns, eager to see Elsie again but nervous about facing Cleary.

His curiosity about Odette last week had reopened old wounds that I was still struggling to cope with. I knew he could help me uncover the truth about what had happened to her, yet fear paralysed me from facing it head on.

You have courage like I've never seen, Rosalba.

If only that were true. The bravest thing I ever did was to peel off my veil and let William see my face. A devastating moment for me, but in the larger scheme of things?

Compared to those who'd taken up arms and gone to war, seen the horrors that William had skirted around in his letters? The hidden things between the lines that would have ravaged his soul just as deeply as the physical injuries that I once feared had ended his life?

"You're wrong, Cleary,' I whispered, hugging myself. "I'm terrified every moment of every day. At least I was."

Before you and Elsie arrived.

The sound of voices drifted along the gravel trail, and soon Elsie came bounding towards me, carrying a large tartan rug. Cleary followed closely behind, his muscular arm straining under the weight of their picnic basket.

He saw me and stopped walking, his eyes intense, a little wary, as if expecting me to bolt again and dissolve into the ether. Yet when he smiled—oh damn!—his whiskery dimples sent my pulse racing, as his blue gaze travelled over every inch of me in one appreciative sweep.

"Looking good, ghost girl. New dress?"

I smoothed my fingers over my hips, laughing at the ridiculous nickname, hoping he wouldn't notice the pleasure I could feel radiating from my eyes.

"Ha, this old thing?"

It had been William's favourite, snug and silky against my skin, hugging my curves and swishing pleasantly when I walked. Wearing it always gave me confidence, and I liked the way Cleary's gaze fell over me in it, the hungry look that came into his eyes.

Elsie hopped impatiently from foot to foot. "Are the fireflies out yet?"

"They will be soon," I said, glad for the distraction. "Follow me."

As the sun sank lower, I led the way uphill, the three of us walking past a rocky outcrop and winding around the steep hillside. We emerged onto a flat grassy area surrounded by a grove of tall, shady gum trees overlooking the valley.

At the centre of the grass was a bare patch where past tenants had built a fire pit. On the other side, down the steep incline at the mountain's base, was the start of Lion's Head Road that led into town.

Elsie dropped the blanket and ran across the grass, searching the sky for fireflies.

Cleary sat the picnic basket on the ground and came over, hands in his pockets. He seemed thoughtful, and when he licked his lips, I knew what was coming next—more questions about Odette and what had become of her.

I sighed inwardly. *Can't we just have one night where it's not about the past, and be solely focused on each other in the present moment?*

But then he surprised me with a soft chuckle as he shook his head.

"I need more nights like this."

I looked at him. "What do you mean?"

"Doing something for fun. Hunting fireflies, instead of ... well, you know."

"Hunting me?"

He glanced across at Elsie, who was skipping around the fire pit, still watching the sky. Then he turned to me, his eyes burning darkly.

"I have to admit something, Rose," he said, his voice low. "When I told you that I don't feel anything, it was a lie. I can feel William's emotions, even when I'm not in the middle of a vision. And right now, I'm feeling them so strongly it scares the hell out of me."

A shiver ran across my shoulders, and I leaned in. "If it makes you feel any better, I'm scared, too."

He ran his hand through his thick, unruly hair, sending strands in every direction.

"When I first arrived at Loch Ard, all I cared about was sending you over to the other side. But as I got to know you, things changed. You know that, right?"

I nodded. "And now?"

He gazed up through the branches at the sky, dark now and dotted with pinprick stars.

"It's the last night of the waning crescent moon and the start of a new one. The lunar energies are draining away as the sun's shadow grows weaker. When that happens, an entity's hold on this world grows weaker, too."

I swayed back. "The perfect time to force me over?"

He blew out a breath, nodding. "But I need you to understand that it's not about that anymore. At least for me. I'm here for you, Rose. I want to help you figure out the things that are troubling you. Not as a hunter trying to untether you, but as a friend who genuinely cares—"

Elsie stampeded over and elbowed her way between us, beaming up into my face.

"How much longer?"

I squinted up into the darkness, my nostrils flaring as I drank in the warm air. Hoping neither of them noticed the way my lips were suddenly trembling.

"They're on their way."

"How can you tell?"

"I can hear their tiny heartbeats."

Cleary chuckled softly and got to work unfolding the rug and spreading it on the grass, unpacking the basket. Then he wandered over to the pit and started building a fire.

Elsie flopped onto the tartan blanket and tucked her legs beneath her. She studied me, her head tilting like a curious bird.

"I like your face, Rose."

As I settled beside her, my fingers went to my hair, raking it over my mark. "Oh."

She tucked in her chin, beaming. "Dad's right, you're super pretty."

"What? Oh, no—"

She nodded. "Yeah, you are."

I inhaled the night, Cleary's words from before still lingering like a dash of honey on my soul. *As a friend who genuinely cares...*

"That's sweet of you, but I'm not really. I'd have to change a few things."

"Your birthmark?"

"Yes." My voice was a whisper. "I would change ... that."

"Oh, why?" Her words sank in disappointment as she peered up into my face. "I think it's lovely. I wish I had something special about me like that. My freckles, I suppose. But everyone has those. Even Dad, and he's boring. Your mark is like one gigantic, awesome freckle that beats everyone else's by miles. Without it, you wouldn't be you."

Her little voice chirped brightly in the warm darkness, the forbidden words—your mark—sounding less like a death-sentence and more like birdsong.

As she babbled on, a shudder tore through me. It wasn't my usual shame, but something releasing. The thorn festering in my heart dislodged, and I no longer felt like myself. As though another person had slipped inside my skin, making me dizzy and lightheaded. Free.

Elsie smiled at me, the firelight catching her eyes.

I ached to reach out to her, wrap her up in my arms. Press my lips against her spiky hair, repay the comfort she'd given me. She was a tiny replica of her father—skinnier, frecklier—but there was a gentle kindness in her. Not pity-kindness, but a simple uncomplicated acceptance.

She made my disfigurement sound so normal, so ... mundane. Not monstrous. Not even a shortcoming. *It's like one gigantic, awesome freckle.*

I couldn't help smiling. "In my time, people considered it a curse."

"That's a cruel time."

"It was, I suppose. People don't mean to be cruel, but sometimes they are unintentionally."

"Then it's good you found us."

A glow burned suddenly inside me. Us. Like I was one of them, instead of one of the others. Laughing softly, I reached out and ran my fingertips over the shaggy tips of her hair. They wafted faintly under my touch as though in a breeze.

She grinned. "I felt that!"

I bit my lip, grinning, trying not to let it matter too much. "You did?"

She nodded, her eyes going wide. "Do you have kids, Rose?"

My smile fell away. I gazed down at this curious little human. How had she suddenly become so precious to me?

William's words from long ago drifted back. *Love sneaks up on you, doesn't it? One moment you're carefree, then the next everything's tumbling into sweet chaos, because without them life no longer makes any sense.*

I shook my head. "I had a little girl, but she died."

"Oh no! You must miss her."

"Every moment of every day."

Elsie's little hand slid over and settled on the rug next to mine. "I bet she misses you, too. You'd be a great mum, Rose."

I swallowed the lump in my throat, bracing for more dark things to bubble up from my subconscious. But there was only warmth, and the unexpected glow of courage this sweet girl inspired in me.

Suddenly, the prospect of facing my past was no longer so

daunting. *I want to help you figure out the things that are troubling you, Rose. Not as a hunter, but as a friend...*

"Oh, look!"

Elsie squealed and jumped to her feet as a lone firefly flickered into view, wobbling through the darkness towards us. Before long, others joined it, and the swarm flitted around, illuminating the clearing. Elsie twirled and skipped among them, her laughter ringing out as they twinkled around her like tiny, living stars.

48
ROSALBA

My warm glow stayed, even as the fireflies drifted down the slope, dispersing into the darkness. Elsie followed a little way until Cleary called her back. He threw some pinecones and branches onto the fire and then settled on the rug beside me.

The flames lapped the night's chill, sending tendrils of heat towards us. Elsie eventually lay down on the rug between me and Cleary and shut her eyes.

Soon she was asleep, one small hand tucked under her face, the other resting on the rug near me. Cleary gathered a blanket over her and tucked it round her chin, then rested back on his elbows, watching the night.

I rested back, too.

If only this moment would never end.

I could stay bundled inside it forever, a warm cloak against the cold eternity I'd already spent alone. As my eyes drifted shut, I felt hunks of ice break off my soul and fall away, melting through the spaces in my bones. I felt my blood clog and crystalise, my withered heart swell, my body fill with shifting shadows like continents adrift. I wanted to float away into the night, leave my body here in the grass, and return to my essence. Dissolve into air, into water, into the breeze, into nothing, into everything. I wanted to leave with the wind, as tears and gusts, in snow and rainfall. I wanted to become all that remained of myself, return to my past, my future, my being, my heart, my senses, to the place left in the wake of my body—

"Alright there, ghost girl?"

I opened my eyes, shaking off my thought stream. My smile came easily, and then somehow I was a prisoner of Cleary's slightly amused, watchful gaze.

I hesitated, nibbling my lip, but then took a breath and let the words tumble out in a rush.

"In your vision before, you said William went looking for me in the berry patch. He must have found me there, but I can't remember. Why do you think that is? Did I do something bad? Is that why he never married me? I think—" I gulped the air into my lungs, reaching for Cleary's arm. "I think I'm ready to find out."

Cleary shifted out of reach.

"I've got another idea," he said softly. "You said you're elemental, and can connect with the trees and the earth. Stones too?"

When I nodded, he took a heart-shaped pebble from his pocket and placed it on the rug between us. It was pearly pink with a glossy patina that shimmered in the firelight.

"It's rose quartz," he explained. "It opens the heart and helps you face buried memories. Would you like to try?"

Still feeling brave, I nodded eagerly and ran my fingers over the smooth stone. An electric current seemed to pass through me, tingling and fizzing as my senses burst to life.

My mouth was closed, my tongue still, my breath held as I

tasted my long-ago memories of chocolate and spice and wine. Then I could taste the grass and the earth and the blood pumping through my veins, and the ache of something delicious and vaguely painful pulsing through me.

"Focus on the crystal," Cleary instructed, his voice low and hypnotic in the stillness. "Let your mind wander ... till you find yourself somewhere peaceful."

Closing my eyes, I concentrated on the crystal and let its energy sweep over me. I imagined walking through a lush green garden surrounded by tall trees that reached up towards the sky like pillars of light. Every step brought more peace and clarity than the one before it until my fear shrank away and only serenity remained.

I was floating.

I looked down and saw a tiny house nestled in among the trees. So pretty, and strangely inviting. As I drifted closer, I gasped.

"It's Loch Ard!"

Cleary's voice came from far away. "Breath, Rose. Surround yourself with the quartz's energy. Don't be afraid, I'm right here. When you're ready, go closer ..."

I let myself sink downwards towards the house. My heart kicked against my ribs, but I brought the pink quartz glow around me like a cloak and it calmed me.

It was dawn. Chickens clucked softly from their roosts. Somewhere down in the valley, a rooster crowed—once, twice, three times. I passed the old stables, freshly painted with the dark ochre red my father preferred. The household still slept. Smoke drifted from the chimney stack. Someone was up early. As I drifted closer, I saw a muddy trail leading down from the loch to the front door. Strange. The servants always used the other entrance—

I tried to pull back, but a dark force had me in its grip, tugging me towards the house. My body tensed, but I couldn't fight it, even with the pink glow. I tried to find Cleary, to tell him I needed to stop and return to the picnic rug, but something was wrong.

The force of energy sucked me right through the panes of my old bedroom window, and in a violent rush of darkness, it thrust me into my sleeping body on the bed and stole away the light.

49
ROSALBA

1917

I AWOKE in the predawn darkness. A faint orange glow seeped through the window, but my room was still dark. Something had woken me. Not a noise. Rather, a silence. As if the house had gasped and was now holding its breath.

I sat up and clutched my head.

"What—?"

My brain throbbed and my tongue felt dry, and a filmy haze obscured my vision. I blinked to clear it. Why was everything so still? No ticking clocks, no creaking rafters. No servants stirring downstairs.

I forced myself out of bed, my limbs like deadweights.

"Odette?"

Normally by now she'd have woken me with her hungry cries. It was not like her to sleep through her early feed. In the dim light coming through the window, her cot looked empty, so I stumbled over.

She was not there. Her bunny rug was gone too, leaving just the bare sheet. I about-faced, frantically searching the room, as if she might have escaped her cot somehow and crawled across the floor into the shadows.

Impossible, of course. At six months, she was too small to climb from the cot. Maybe I had risen in a daze and bundled her into the bed with me? I threw back my covers, but still no Odette.

As I whirled around, a watery trail on the floor caught my attention. Was it mud? Thick, sludgy footprints went from my bed to the door. I saw that mud splashed my feet too, and the hem of my nightgown. A dank smell lifted from it, and my lips parted in shock.

Had I gone up to the loch in the middle of the night?

My pulse drummed in my ears, but my father's voice was louder. *The cold will take her quickly, Rosalba. Be brave and think of the miserable life you're saving her from.*

The walls closed around me, my breath coming in sharp, shallow puffs.

"Odette!"

I bolted across the room, flinging open my bedroom door with a crash. My bare feet pounded the hardwood floor as I sprinted down the stairs and through the house. Bursting outside into the thick, suffocating fog of the morning air, I stumbled up the steep hillside, my nightgown billowing around me like a parachute as I pushed myself higher and higher towards the looming darkness of the loch.

50
CLEARY

NOW

Rose whimpered, her eyes darting beneath her closed lids as a cool blanket of mountain mist settled on us. Tiny glittering droplets caught in her eyelashes and the strands of her hair.

I leaned closer. "Rose?"

Her hair had fallen aside, revealing more of her mark than I had seen before. It sat like a deep red handprint across the left side of her face, fringed with tinier marks like splashes of red wine. I imagined her velvety skin as I traced my mouth over those splashes, kissing the soft darkness of her mark—

I tore away my gaze, staring at the dying firelight, but it made no difference. Her face was scored in my mind. Other faces, the faces of women I'd cared for in the past, even Jolene, whose beauty had turned heads in the street—faded in my mind. I could barely remember them. But Rose was imprinted there. Not just her sweet face, but her energy and spirit.

She could summon a windstorm with her fury yet banter and giggle with my daughter for hours. Her sheer audacity had touched my hunter's soul, while her vulnerabilities stirred my protector. She was like a wild, broken bird whose wings were crushed beyond repair, and suddenly all I cared about was helping her mend them.

She cried out softly as she emerged from the trancelike memory, her eyes wide, tears streaking her face.

"Cleary—?"

"I'm here."

A tear leaked along the side of her nose, and she brushed it away. "It's raining."

A moment ago it hadn't been, but now large droplets fell around us, ice cold on my arms and face. I started gathering our things, then gently shook Elsie awake. As we hurried down the slope, Rose remained silent, her face turned away from me, her cheeks glistening with rain and tears. Whatever memory she had confronted back there had clearly shaken her.

"Did the crystal unearth anything, Rose?"

"Oh—" She dragged her hair back over the exposed mark, glancing at me from the corner of her eye. "Not really. I think I fell asleep."

The rain started falling harder, and soon the three of us were drenched. We broke into a run, detouring through the cypress hedge to the piper's cottage and stumbled inside, rain dripping from our hair and clothes.

I collected an armful of kindling from the porch and knelt in front of the cold hearth. With a few strikes from the matches

I'd left after our renovation, wisps of smoke were soon curling up the chimney. Elsie was shivering under her damp clothes, so I settled her on the daybed across from the window and draped a crocheted blanket over her, rubbing her hands to warm them. The fire roared in the grate, and eventually she fell asleep.

Rose perched on the daybed arm beside me.

I watched helplessly as tears started rolling down her cheeks again. If only I could wrap my arms around her willowy frame and tell her that everything would be okay, but the distance between us in that moment felt like an insurmountable barrier.

"You saw something before, didn't you?" I took out the heart-shaped crystal and placed it beside her. "Why don't you try again?"

She sprang to her feet and backed away, hugging herself.

"I did see something." She eyed the crystal warily. "But can't go back there, Cleary. I thought I could confront it, but I was wrong. Memories can be cruel. I don't want to be reminded of what I've lost."

"You mean your child?"

She nodded. Then a quivering sigh escaped her.

"I always hoped she had grown up. I imagined her losing her baby plumpness, running through the garden. Becoming a teenager, then a young woman. A wonderful person whose courage and kindness made the world a happier place. It would have been sad for her growing up without a mother. Especially living under my father's shadow, but she was such a sunny little thing. I'm sure she'd have won him over eventually—" She shuddered. "But what if something happened to her, and it was my fault? I can't face that."

"You won't have to face it alone, Rose."

She looked surprised, but then nodded and swiped at her tears.

"I can't decide which is worse. The constant torment of not knowing, or the heartbreak that comes when you finally discover the terrible truth."

I smoothed my hand along the daybed arm where she'd been a moment before. I understood how it felt to be haunted by the past. To have memories that cut deep and refused to heal. But so much of Rose's story remained untold. She needed to confront it directly in order to find peace. But not like this. Not with tears. And not while her heart was breaking.

I had to find another way.

51
CLEARY

The rattle of passing cars on Woodhill's main street was a jarring contrast to the peaceful silence of Loch Ard. Shoppers scurried past carrying bulging bags, while others lingered under shady trees, engrossed in conversation.

Gravel popped under my soles as I crossed the road to a sandstone building, home to a quaint second-hand bookshop. I pushed through the heavy wooden door and stepped inside.

The air was thick with the smell of old paper and dust. Dodging a neglected fern, I made my way to the counter, eyeing the chaos. Stacks of books teetered on every surface, spines facing out in a wild disarray. Bookshelves threatened to collapse under the weight of worn and aged tomes.

"Help you, mate?"

The man behind the counter was scratching his unkempt beard, eyeing me with a frown. His corduroy jacket strained against his belly, and bits of cat hair clung to his sleeves.

I explained what I was looking for—a history of Loch Ard and its original owners—and his frown turned to a scowl.

"I rented it a few years ago. You know it's haunted, right?"

I shrugged. "I've heard the rumours."

The man scratched his whiskery chin. "About the ghost, you mean? I never saw her myself, but by God, I heard her. Night after night, wailing like a banshee. I even took a burning sage stick into the garden to chase her away, but …" He cleared his throat. "Bloody irritating place. No one ever stays long. You're after some info, you said?"

"Anything at all."

His gaze travelled over me, his frown disappearing into his bushy whiskers.

"The original owner was a wealthy Scotsman, renowned for his generous donations to the local Presbyterian church. A group of women, including the pastor's wife, would make the trek up the mountain just to visit him. Oh, to be a fly on the wall, eh?"

"How do you know all of this?"

He disappeared into a doorway, returning a few minutes later with a water-damaged notebook, which he thrust at me.

"It's a dry old memoir," he explained. "Written by a lady who ran the historic society. There's a chapter on gardens in the area, and some notes on Loch Ard. Not even sure why I kept it. A bit of a hoarder, I guess. Here, take it. Saves me the trouble of binning it."

I flipped through the buckled pages, finding some interesting insights about the property—the origin of a trout hatchery, a French shade house from 1890, and the loch, which was completed in 1901. The garden was built as a labour of love by the owner Jedrick McGregor, as a tribute to his late wife.

There was no mention of Rose or William.

Until the last page.

A black-and-white photo showed an elderly man seated on a

bench in the sun, his face partially obscured by a large straw sunhat. I felt a strange sense of recognition as I stared into his piercing, disapproving eyes. Like looking into a mirror at a future version of myself.

Below it was an acknowledgement.

The author would like to thank William Nolan, gardener at Loch Ard from 1914 to 1916, for his huge contribution to this book. He tirelessly spoke about his time there, providing the author with invaluable accounts of the garden's construction and design. They remained friends until William's death in 1978 at age 87.

52
ROSALBA

Silent as a breeze, I crept up behind him. Wanting to observe him a moment before I made myself known. He sat on a fallen log by the lightning tree, wearing torn jeans and a frown. The frown eased when he spotted me ... but not by much.

"Hey, Rose. Elsie can't stop talking about the fireflies. She's been chattering my ear off for days, and I blame you."

I smiled, a flush burning up my neck. "She's a wonderful girl, Cleary. You're lucky to have her."

He patted the log beside him, and when I sat, he took out a notebook and smoothed his hand over its buckled front cover.

"It seems I was right about William surviving the war."

"Oh?"

He opened the book and flipped through. Lines of tiny handwriting and diagrams filled pages, some photographs glued in. When he reached the back page, he flattened the book open on his knee and tapped a photograph.

"Recognise him?"

I leaned in, studying the man for a moment. Then I gasped. His face, the battered old sunhat that shaded it. The fuzzy brows clenched in a frown, and the creases bracketing his mouth. Lord, where had all those wrinkles come from? He was ancient, cross and unhappy-looking—but there was no mistaking him.

My eyes stung. "William."

"Are you sure?"

I swallowed the lump in my throat, nodding. "But I don't understand. Why did he grow old and I didn't? We know he returned after the war and found me in the berry patch. But why didn't we get married?"

"I don't know."

I gripped my elbows, blinking back the needle-prick of tears. At that moment, I hated William. Hated him with an ache that stole my breath away. Here was proof that he'd survived the war and returned home ... only not to me.

"Can't you have a vision and find out?"

"I can't control them, Rose. They're random."

"Then we'll keep trying until they make sense!"

Cleary looked at his hands, his jaw working.

I'd gone too far. The visions hurt him, made him ill and depressed afterwards. And the aftereffects were getting worse. Why should he go through all that for me?

"I'm willing to try again," he said soberly. "But I'm not sure that's the answer."

I slumped over my knees. "Then what is?"

"Facing your memories, Rose. It's the only way."

"They're random, too, it seems."

"Maybe you need to remember the day you died. It could be the key to understanding how the other pieces of the puzzle fit together."

I gulped. The smell of dank water drifted in the air, filling my lungs. The shadows tugged at me, memory trying to drag me under, but how could I let it? I clawed my fingers into the splintery wood of the dead log and shut my eyes.

"I can't, Cleary. I'm afraid."

He scooted closer. His body heat usually calmed me, but now it just made things worse. Warmth radiated off him like small, insistent rays of sunlight, taunting me with the physical love and comfort I could never have.

"You're not alone anymore, Rose. I can help you."

But that was just it. I *was* alone, and I'd never felt it more keenly than now.

"I probably died of a broken heart!" My back straightened and I glared at Cleary, sudden rage tingling through me. "William promised to marry me, but he lied. It was all a lie, wasn't it? A trick. All our plans, our dreams. My father was right. William got what he wanted and then enlisted to escape me. He never loved me at all—!"

I smashed my fist down onto William's wrinkled face. The book flew onto the ground with such force that pages broke from the spine.

I sprang up and stalked away, my palms pressed to my eyes, hot tears scalding between my fingers. Here was actual proof William had lived his life without me, most likely forgotten me and married someone else. Oh, the shame of it. Father had been right all along. If only I could disappear forever, dissolve like mist in the sun—

"Rose, wait."

I looked back. Cleary held the remnants of the book—some pages and the water-stained cover. But something else, too. A thin sheet of paper that he was peeling from between two buckled pages and unfolding in the light.

"It's a letter."

"From William?" I hurried back.

Clary scanned it and shook his head.

"Seems to be from the pastor's wife. She's written to her sister." He lowered his head to read it, the crease between his brows deepening. He flipped it over and continued reading, his jaw clenched. When he came to the end, he sat back abruptly, crumpling the paper savagely in his hand, squeezing until his knuckles turned white.

"Cleary?"

He ignored me, glaring at the ground.

I inched closer, trailing my fingers near his fist. "What does it say?"

He shivered and looked up, his face rigid. Slowly, he smoothed the letter on his knee and held it out for me to read. There was no date and no address. Just some ink splats, as if someone had penned it in haste.

"Dearest sister, I write with sad news. Do you remember the poor young wretch who gave us such a fright that day at Loch Ard? The one with the dreadful mark on her face?"

I stopped reading, willing my eyes to close, not see anymore. But they betrayed me, and as my gaze crawled over the faded, looping handwriting, my blood slowly froze inside my veins.

"A while ago, she found herself expecting a child. Poor Jedrick was beside himself with shame. But the story gets worse, I'm afraid. The girl went mad with grief when her soldier was killed overseas. She drowned her wee child in the loch and then filled her own pockets with stones."

53
CLEARY

"It's a lie!" Rose jumped away from me, her features twisted in shock. "A wicked lie!"

My heart thumped erratically, and I couldn't bring myself to meet her gaze. Not just because of the shock of her striking the book from my hands, but because the words from the letter were pounding so loudly in my mind.

She drowned her wee child in the loch.

Could it really be true? As I gazed down the hill towards the house, everything clicked into place. The reason William never married her. The reason she was tethered here, trapped by a painful secret. And the reason she had buried her memories so deeply within her, they were nearly impossible to uncover—

Rose stamped her foot. "I can see your cogs turning. You believe what's in the letter!"

I folded the page in half. "It's gossip, that's all."

"But you're wondering if it's true. I can see it in your eyes, Cleary. You're worried about what I'm capable of." She clutched the front of her dress, her face grey, her features stark with shock. "You're joining the dots, aren't you? Racing ahead. Wondering if I'm a threat to you ... to your daughter!"

My throat tightened, but I shook my head. "No, I—"

"I'd never have hurt her, Cleary."

"I know, Rose. But why—" I flapped the letter lamely. "Why would the pastor's wife write such a thing? Did you ever meet her, offend her in some way? She said you gave them a fright."

"I forgot to wear my veil." Rose crumpled as the breath left her. "I was just a child, but some ladies saw me and screamed. It was our only encounter. I gave her no reason to make up such lies."

"Rose, I'm sorry." I sprang up from the log and approached her. "They were cruel to react that way. Writing those things in her letter was cruel, too."

She flinched away, her eyes blazing briefly in warning. Then she turned and fled into the trees, leaves swirling in a violent flurry behind her.

I should follow, make sure she was okay.

She was right, though. My cogs were turning.

What if the pastor's wife was telling the truth? Every entity had a tragic or violent history that kept them tethered to our world instead of moving on. And I couldn't ignore the way Rose had forcefully knocked that book out of my hands. I'd seen her manipulate the elements, creating mist and a windstorm—but this was next-level. What else was she capable of?

I rubbed my eyes, trying to keep the images at bay, but they rushed at me relentlessly. Rose holding her baby under the dark loch water, then jumping right in after. Her wild hair covering her face as she sank to the muddy bottom, weighed down by the rocks in her pockets. Her life gushing out of her in a surge of bubbles—

It's a wicked lie, Cleary.

Jamming the letter in my pocket, I collected the notebook from the ground and followed the trail into the trees where Rose had disappeared. I called to her for a while, but then gave up and headed home.

That night I stood at the window gazing into the darkness. I couldn't see her, but I could feel her presence nearby, like a bruise on my soul. Strong and palpable. As if she wasn't just tethered to the garden, but also bound to me.

The next day before school, Elsie walked up to the loch, but Rose wasn't there either. I dropping Elsie off and then returned home, searching all of Rose's favourite spots—the wild thorny arch looking over the valley, and the big weeping cedar behind her cottage. The orchard, with its snowfall of late season blossoms, and the knotted shadows beneath the lightning tree.

The week crawled by. Sometimes I sensed Rose watching us. I caught glimmers of her slipping among the tree shadows, or scooting along the pathways at dusk.

One night, a soft whimpering drew me along a winding trail. I followed a while, glimpsing her pale outline in the moonlight, but each time I drew close, she vanished once more into the darkness.

By Thursday, I feared the worst had happened. That she had somehow broken her tether and crossed over.

I dropped Elsie to school and then spent the rest of the morning brooding. Sitting under the lightning tree, its vast trunk solid against my back as I stared down across the valley.

The night we saw the fireflies, Rose had seemed happy, dipping her head to peek at me through her lashes, her eyes glittering in the firelight. Lord, my heart had nearly stopped. And then later at the cottage. How vulnerable she'd been, how uncertain. My hunter instinct had flared to life—not to banish her, but to protect her. Which went against everything I believed.

Rose had endured so much pain in her life. Her trust shattered by those who should have loved and protected her. Her grief over William. Over not knowing what became of her child. Yet despite her own sorrows, she was sensitive to other people's pain.

I admired her resilience and willingness to love again. She had taken my daughter under her wing and showed her affection, filling a role Elsie's own mother had refused. And she'd shared her memories with me, including private moments with William and the abuse from her father. It took courage, but she had trusted me to listen and understand.

And now, when she needed me most, it was time for me to trust her, too.

54
CLEARY

The sun warmed my back as I stood in an open patch of grass among the flowerbeds, breathing the sweet summer air and letting my senses unravel around me.

It was Friday afternoon, the November sun casting a golden haze over the hills in the distance. I had left Elsie in her room, her head bent over her desk, painting bright flowers and swirls on some clay hearts she'd made at school. *I'm going to hang them all over the garden, Dad. So Rose knows we love her.*

I inhaled deeply, letting my lids grow heavy. I rarely resorted to using my hunter's sense to track an entity, saving the effort for riskier situations, but I was worried about Rose after our discovery of the letter. I needed her to know that I was on her side. That together we'd sort this mess and get through it somehow.

A breeze lifted my hair, tickling the back of my neck. I wanted to scratch there, but forced my arms to stay relaxed at my sides.

With my mind, I reached through the sunlight and then the

shadows, seeking the icy ache that signalled an otherworldly presence. When I finally felt the tiny pulse of cold touch my awareness, faint as a solitary snowflake, the jolt of relief was electric.

"Rose."

I cut through the trees, making my way into the wild, craggy part of the garden and then veering uphill to the loch.

My stomach clenched when I saw her.

She stood with her back to me, her slender silhouette framed by the mist rising from the water. Her head bowed, her hair falling forward over her face, her whole body shaking as she sobbed into her hands.

I hated seeing her alone with no one to turn to. No one to gather her up and comfort her. It was my fault she was upset, and I needed to put things right.

"Rose, it's me." My voice barely disturbed the stillness. "Are you okay?"

She whirled around. She didn't look okay. Tears were rolling down her face, gluing strands of hair to her cheeks. She swiped at them and moved further along the bank, putting distance between us.

"Go away."

"I know you'd never do those things, Rose."

"You do?" Her voice caught on a sob. "That makes one of us."

"Hey, it's painful, I get that. But you don't have to go through it alone."

"You're wrong. I'm alone in ways you could never understand." She hugged her ribs, staring down at the dark column of her body reflected in the water's rippling surface. "Odette meant everything to me. She was one of those special souls destined to do something wonderful with their life. Like

Elsie. But something happened to her, and I know it was my fault."

"How can you know anything for certain? Until you face the memory head on?"

Her eyes flashed defiantly, seeking me through the shadows.

"What if the pastor's wife was right about me drowning my child ... and then myself? How do I face that?"

"Do you remember what you said in the cottage after the fireflies?" When she said nothing, I inched closer. "That you didn't know which was worse. Not knowing Odette's fate, or discovering something terrible. Well, I think it's better to know. Because then you can deal with it and find a way to heal."

She walked back along the bank towards me, her green eyes luminous in the gloom.

"Facing the truth is beyond me. It's too painful."

"Nothing's beyond you. Do you have any idea how powerful you are?"

She rolled her gaze up to the treetops. "You sound like William."

"Will you at least try something for me?"

She shook her head hesitantly. "Another crystal? Sorry, Cleary. The last time—"

"It's not a crystal. It's something much bigger, Rose. It's already inside of you."

She scoffed, looking back at me and knuckling the dampness under her eyes.

"A broken heart, you mean?"

"The other day, you struck William's photo with your fist. The book fell on the ground and broke apart, right?"

She shrugged. "That's how we found the letter."

"You did that, Rose. You made the book fall."

She glanced away, distracted. Moving suddenly, she caught

something from the air, a large brown moth. She closed her fingers around it, and when she opened them again, the moth sat withered and dead on her palm.

"Things happen when my emotions get out of control."

"What things?"

"My touch can kill flowers. Or insects." She showed me the lifeless moth on her palm, then blew it into the water. "My anger can create strong winds."

"Like your wild gale on the hillside that morning?"

She nodded. "And the night of the fireflies, my sadness brought the rain."

"The fog in the garden after dinner ... that was you, too."

"Yes."

"How do you do it?"

"I'm elemental, remember? Like the wind and the water. Just as the moon's gravitational pull affects the ocean tides, my emotions ripple outwards and influence the surrounding elements. At least, they do when they're intense enough."

"Like your anger at William, when you hit the book."

Her shoulders twitched, and she nodded. "But what does that have to do with Odette?"

"It's a long shot, but what if you sent your elemental energy through me? Maybe it'll spark one of your memories as a vision. So I see into *your* past, instead of William's. That way, we can solve the mystery without you having to confront it. I'll confront it for you."

"You'd do that?"

"What are friends for?"

"But I thought receiving visions directly from an entity was impossible."

"Just because it's never happened before doesn't mean it's

impossible. Just unlikely. But isn't it worth a try, to be free of a heavy burden?"

She stood rigidly, her eyes large and dark as her gaze drifted to the loch. A shiver rippled through her, and finally she nodded.

"I'd like to be free of it."

"Then let's give it a go. Could you become angry again now? Summon enough energy to affect the elements?"

She slumped, but a glimmer of understanding shone in her eyes. "I could, but only briefly. Too long, and it burns through me."

"Burns through you?"

"Harnessing my elemental energy leaves me weak. It depletes my life-force. I can stay connected for a few minutes, but afterwards I'm frail. I need time to hide away and repair myself."

"Can you always repair?"

She nodded. "Always. But it can take days. Even a week."

"Then we'd better get it right the first time. Focus on something that sets your soul on fire, makes your blood boil."

"Like what?"

"I don't know ... what about me? I seem to have a knack for irritating you."

I expected a smile, but as she shifted to face me, a spark ignited in her pale green eyes. She inhaled, her nostrils flaring as she inched closer. Her gaze darkened, a faint predatory glint in its depths as she trailed it over my jaw and mouth, and finally up to meet my eyes.

The aura flaring around her was suddenly so fiery that it singed my skin, shimmering and shifting as her emotion grew more intense.

But it wasn't anger.

And she wasn't sad anymore. She was—

"Cleary," she murmured huskily. Her pupils expanded, engulfing the lush green of her eyes until they were deep pools of blackness. "Take my hand."

Every tiny hair on the back of my neck bristled in response to her voice as my blood ignited, thumping so violently through my veins I thought I was going to die.

I reached for her hand.

Her touch was soft as a whisper, but as her fingers closed around mine—no longer just a cold gust, but actual warm flesh and blood fingers—my breath caught. Was this happening? How was I feeling her velvety skin, the presence of muscles and bones beneath, and the rapid beating of her pulse?

Clutching her slender fingers, I pulled her against my body, feeling her delicious warmth and curves as they pressed along my length. I cradled the back of her head, my knuckles lost in the silk curtain of her hair as I crushed my lips to hers, tasting her sweetness.

She reached up, tangling her fingers through my hair and pulling herself even closer, clinging so tightly it seemed nothing could tear us apart. In a rush of wild hunger, I plunged deeper into our kiss and just about devoured her. Inhaling her at close range was like getting drunk on midnight air ... it was wild violets and summer rain mingling with the taste of ripe peaches, and I never wanted to let her go—

The sensation of ice was abrupt.

Shocking. Electric.

A rush of familiar cold enveloped me, and my arms were suddenly empty. Rose was gone. Literally vanished. But our brief contact had triggered a vision, hopefully one of Roses's memories, something she was unable to face herself, just as I'd promised.

Yet I fought the giddiness, battling to stay conscious, wanting only to go after Rose and hold her again, or at least see that she was okay.

But the vision won. I moaned, crashing to my knees in the mud as snowflakes began to swirl and dance around my head, and the ache in my arms where Rose had just been yawned open and swallowed me, dragging me back into the past.

.

55
WILLIAM

1918

WILLIAM HURRIED through the dark garden, uphill through the snow, towards the berry patch, his thoughts churning. Why had Rose brought a child along this desolate track—their child, their little daughter, the joy of which was breaking his heart right now—up into the darkening garden on a freezing night like this?

"Probably to escape the old goat."

His breath puffed in the cold and the frosty air bit his lips and cheeks, making his injured scalp throb. No matter, there'd be time to heal later. All he cared about was holding his Rosebud again, kissing her lips, seeing her smile. He had been dreaming about that smile for two long, bitter years. It had sustained him through some hellish times and given him hope when the world around him seemed devoid of it.

Her skin would be just as soft as he remembered. The smell of her hair, the same sweet scent that had followed him during his years away, would mend his war-ravaged heart. When their lips met, he would be renewed. Become the man she needed.

"Rose—?" His voice echoed across the garden. He pictured her running down the slope towards him, clutching their child as she threw herself into his arms, the three of them laughing and crying all at once, finally together after all those hard and lonely times apart. "Rosalba, it's me!"

He quickened his step, smiling to himself.

He had a daughter. Lord, it was everything he'd wished for. Sweet Rose by his side. A little girl to rock in his arms, to smother in kisses. He'd teach her to ride a horse and catch rabbits. Grow things in the soil, as his own father had taught him. What a family they'd be! He made it his mission right then to give both his beautiful girls the happiest life possible.

Ahh, my Rosie girl, how I've missed you. But we'll make up the lost years, I promise.

He picked up pace. The ground became steeper, knotty with tree roots and stones. Dusk was deepening into night and a breeze rattled the leaves. Some dropped onto the track, only to swirl up again as he passed.

"Rose, are you here?"

Not much further to the berry patch. His hands began to shake. He'd seen unholy action on the battlefield, death and destruction all around him. And through all of it, he had somehow kept calm. But on the brink of seeing her, he felt like a nervous schoolboy ...

Lord, man. Don't fall apart now.

All those things her father said. About her being an unfit mother.

Well, the wicked old goat could go to hell. William would take Rose away with him tonight. He wouldn't even let her return to the house, just bundle her into his car and whisk her away down to his farmhouse in the valley. Buy her everything she and their little one needed. Start fresh, just the three of them, far from the shadows of Loch Ard. The farmhouse was modest, unlike Jedrick's grand house with its servants and crystal chandeliers, but it was warm and comfortable. And safe. Rose never had to see her poisonous father again.

His heart beat faster.

It was growing dark. As he approached the wall of brambles, a shiver ran up his spine. It was so cold in this part of the garden, so dank and uninviting. What had she been thinking, bringing her little daughter up here?

"Rose—?"

His poor Rosebud, how she must've worried over him. Bringing her child into the world, not knowing if he was dead or alive.

Before returning to Australia, he had lain immobile in a British hospital bed for months, unable to stave off the shakes long enough to write. Unable to see anything beyond a blur. A kindly nurse had written for him, and even posted the letters with her own stamps. He had waited for a reply, but none came. Perhaps the old man had waylaid the letters, stopped Rose from getting them. Or stopped her from replying. Well, William was here now. He would put things right—

He entered the weeping birch grove that surrounded the berry patch. He had planted the berry canes himself and later chosen the plumpest, sweetest berries to bring Rose on those nights they met at the piper's cottage. No berries clung to the vines now, and the leaves were gone.

"Rosie girl?" The shadows stirred in the clearing. "Where are you, love?"

He stopped in his tracks. Over there. On the ground. A clump of shadow huddled motionless as stone. Was someone here?

He stumbled closer. As his eyes adjusted, his heart shrivelled, blood roaring in his veins. His throat was dry as he crumpled to his knees.

"God, please ... no. Oh Rose, no ..."

56
CLEARY

NOW

"Rose!"

Clammy sweat coated my skin as the nausea rolled through me like an angry sea, making my stomach churn. My plan had backfired. Rose's elemental energy hadn't triggered a memory from her past, but simply another one of William's.

"Rose, are you here?"

Silence. Just the afternoon breeze whispering through dry leaves and the thumping pulse in my ears. Had I really held her? Flesh and blood, warm in my arms? It seemed like a dream, only the empty ache in my chest assuring me it had been real.

Wiping my mouth, I straightened and looked around.

I was no longer at the loch.

I had never been up here before. A small clearing walled in by blackberry vines and rampaging brambles. Neglected. Forgotten. Invaded by weeds.

As I walked further into the clearing, a clammy dampness settled over my skin and hair. The air felt dead, devoid of light and sustenance. Despite the blue sky, dank shadows swarmed under the tree canopies as though sunlight was not welcome to enter.

Then I recognised it. "The berry patch."

William had hurried up here that night, expecting to reunite with Rose and their little daughter.

"But you found something else, didn't you? What was it?"

Rose cradling her drowned child? Huddled and shivering on the ground, squeezing Odette's body tightly against her, mad with grief over what she'd done. Soaked and shivering among the blackberries, where nobody would think to look for her?

Maybe her father had already found her here, been unable to coax her back to the house. Had he spitefully sent William after her, knowing it would destroy him?

"You bloody old mongrel! How could you be so heartless?"

In the middle of the overgrown patch sat a mound of thick blackberry vines growing in an impenetrable clump. Thorns jutted from the canes like barbed wire, their tips gleaming poisonous red. What was underneath them—a birdbath or a crumbling old statue? I should leave it, get back to the house ... but something drew me over.

I tugged at one of the thicker canes, and a razor-sharp thorn sliced my palm. Blood welled, and I wiped it on my jeans.

"What are you hiding under your damn thorns?"

I gripped a length of vine between its barbs and wrestled it free. Thorns snagged my clothes, raking the length of my arm. The next vine whipped and clawed like a wild animal as I dragged it from the clump. It crossed my mind to return to the house for secateurs, but I was in a nervous rage after my vision, too impatient. In minutes, my hands and arms were slick with blood, but at last the tangled clump of vines yielded with a snap. I dragged it aside, revealing the block of shadow it had concealed.

A gravestone.

I crouched in front of it, rubbing away the lichen to reveal a weathered inscription.

> Rosalba Beatrice McGregor
> Odette Lilliam McGregor
> DIED 28 JULY 1917

I sank to my knees. Someone, probably Rose's father, had buried them together. William must have returned here in the winter of 1918, a year after Rose was already gone. This was what he had found that night—not Rose cradling her drowned child, after all, but the pair of them long dead and buried.

"Oh, Rose ... you and Odette died on the same day."

My nausea returned, but this time it wasn't a byproduct of my vision. I clenched my fists, fighting the torrent of panic constricting my chest. The words from the letter crashed through my brain.

She drowned her wee child in the loch and then filled her own pockets with stones.

"Rose wouldn't do that."

Would she? Crimes of passion were a common pattern among entities. The trauma and emotion would tether them here until they faced up to the consequences of their actions. Or until someone like me untethered them.

But Rose?

"She couldn't—"

The other night, as we sat together under the stars, watching the fireflies dance around us, I'd felt a deep sense of trust in Rose's company. And Elsie felt it, too—she always lit up and came out of her shell whenever Rose was near. We were starting to feel like a family.

But deep down, I knew it could never last. I was a hunter, so was Elsie. Rose was one of the others.

We were natural born enemies.

You think you know me, but you don't. I'm like the loch. Sunny on the surface but deadly beneath.

Leaning on the headstone, I traced my fingers over the names carved into the cold stone. Was the letter right? Did Rose drown her baby and then herself? Were my feelings for her blinding me to the truth?

As I crouched in the dying, shifting light, Rose's warning tolled in my brain. *Someone like me can cause a lot of damage.* Was I making the same mistake as my father? Had I let my guard down and already become too involved?

I got to my feet, lingering by the grave, unable to tear my gaze away from the two names. I had sworn to trust Rose, to have faith in her, and give her the benefit of any doubt. Yet I couldn't shake the feeling that something dark and unavoidable was waiting ahead of us, just beyond the shadows.

57
CLEARY

"She's amazing," Elsie gushed, pausing to gulp some lemonade from her glass as she beamed at her gran. "She took us to see the fireflies, and we slept under the stars. She also helped me figure out that I want to be a frog scientist when I grow up!"

We were lounging on Mum's back patio in her rambling East Melbourne home, streamers of light fanning through the dense forest of ferns and orchids, the air damp and green.

My mother turned to me with a knowing look. "That sounds wonderful. What does your dad think about her?"

Elsie didn't miss a beat. "He thinks she's super pretty. And smart. He renovated her cottage, and he saved her from drowning in the loch. And get this, Gran. When he talks to her, he actually *smiles*."

Mum's eyes widened. "Gosh!"

I got to my feet and stalked over to the rail, gripping it tightly as I gazed down at the lush pond below. I hated to break up their banter, but all this talk of Rose was like a thorn under my skin. My mother had already noticed the radiant glow on

Elsie's face, because she kept sending me appraising looks. The last thing I needed was another lecture about settling down, meeting someone nice, giving my daughter the things she needed most. Especially when the most obvious someone was out of bounds.

I nodded at Elsie to get her attention.

"Hey, kiddo. Give me a minute with your gran, okay?"

Elsie's glow vanished, quickly replaced by a scowl. She jutted her chin, ready to argue. "But we just—"

I threw my hands up in surrender and turned to my mother. "Okay, Mum. I've got this rash on my bum. Will you take a look?"

"Argh!" Elsie sprang up and stomped down the steps into the garden, heading for the turtle enclosure.

Mum was biting her lips. "There's no rash, is there?"

"Of course not."

"Ah, good. You had me worried."

"Ha ha."

"So what's up, boyo?" Her smile took me off guard, warm as the patchouli oil drifting from inside her house that wrapped around me like an old friend. Her hair was strawberry blonde today, flaming like pale copper in the afternoon light. The silver bracelets on her wrists jingled as she reached out and patted my shoulder. "Why so glum?"

"I found Rose's grave, Mum."

"Good," she said, though her brow creased ever so slightly. "Does Elsie know?"

"Not yet."

"She seems taken with Rose, more than the others. I know she formed a strong bond with the little Chinese girl some years ago, and she still talks about Lewis. But I've never seen her so happy. If I didn't know better, I'd say Rose is good for her."

"That's the problem. Rose is exactly what she needs."

Mum's eyebrows furrowed. "And you're worried she's becoming too attached?"

"If only it was that simple."

Mum reached for the mermaid teapot on the table and poured steaming tea into our mugs. She took a sip, cradling the mug in her hands, a frown tugging between her brows.

"Elsie's not the only one who's formed an attachment to Rose, is she?"

I blew out a breath and shook my head. "I've never met anyone like her, Mum. She's shy and sassy all at once, and she's been through hell, yet somehow she's still compassionate and sweet ... and—" I stopped and looked at the sky, suddenly lost for words.

"Lord," Mum whispered. "You've got it bad, Cleary."

"I've been having visions of the man who loved Rose. I feel everything he felt for her, but it doesn't stop with the visions. It pounds through me all the time until I can't tell where he ends and I begin. It's messing with my head."

"Ahh. We have a problem."

"Have you ever heard of a ghost becoming physical?"

"You mean like a poltergeist interacting with their surroundings?"

"I mean, so you can touch them."

Mum frowned. "Your father used to talk about an entity who bit him on the back as a child. It was part of what drove him to the hunt."

"Rose can summon rain or a storm with her emotions. But she can also manifest herself as flesh and blood."

Mum stared at me, her lips parting. "You've seen her do it?"

"I've touched her. Held her against me."

"Then you're already in too deep."

"It gets worse. I found an old letter that claims Rose killed her baby. I didn't want to believe it, but her headstone records that she and her child died on the same day."

Mum inhaled, all softness leaving her face. "Does she remember what happened?"

I shook my head. "She says she loved little Odette and would never have harmed her. And Mum, I want to believe her. I want to trust her so badly it hurts. But—"

"You're concerned about Elsie."

I gulped my tea, silence stretching between us. Hearing my fears spoken aloud made them seem terrifying, as if Rose was a threat, but I bristled up, wanting to defend her.

"She'd never intentionally hurt Elsie. I'd bet my life on it. But Mum, Rose is not like any of the others we've dealt with." My fingers tightened around the mug, heat seeping into my palms—in stark contrast to the icy dread trickling down my spine. "She's powerful. Unpredictable. It's like she's holding back a storm, and I can't help wondering what might happen if she lost control."

Mum was silent for a long time. Finally she put down her cup, silver bangles clinking.

"Unpredictable can be dangerous, love. More so when you're emotionally involved. Your father learned that the hard way."

"What do you mean?"

Slumping back in her chair, she let out a long sigh. "Years before you or your sisters were born, we lost a child. A little girl."

The words hit me with the force of a punch. "Mum, I'm sorry. I never knew."

"It's not something we spoke of. It was a horrible time. I guess we wanted to put it behind us." She tucked a strand of strawberry blonde hair behind her ear, her nose ring catching the light. "Many years later, your father became obsessed with a ghost. A delicate wraith who reminded him of our daughter. He wanted so much to believe it was her—"

"But you didn't?"

She shook her head. "No, this little one was nothing like our child. She was powerful and vengeful. One day she lost her temper over something trivial and ... well, you know how it ended, Cleary. You were there."

"Jeez, Mum."

"Love, you've got to understand." Her voice was softer than the silvery clink of her bracelets as she leaned forward. "Ghosts are not like us. They're stuck in limbo, caught between what was and what can never be. Can you imagine their frustration?"

"Rose is different. She has this ... presence. She's more alive than any ghost I've ever met."

"Presence or not, Cleary. A troubled soul is like a thorn bush. It may flower, but the thorns are always there, waiting."

I massaged the tension in my knuckles. "Ma, you know I'd be the first to step in and banish an entity. I've never shied from it before. But if I had to expel her forcefully, I don't think I'd be able to do it."

Mum looked across the garden, adjusting herself on the seat. "Do you remember what your father used to say? How true love is putting someone else's happiness before your own needs?"

"Yeah, I remember."

"When the time comes—and it will—you'll do whatever it takes to protect Elsie. Even if it means having to let go of someone you've come to care for."

I flexed my hands. I had come seeking answers, maybe even reassurance that I could make things work with Rose—despite the gravestone, and the letter, and all my private doubts—but this wasn't what I wanted to hear.

I turned my attention to the garden, where Elsie played beside the pond. Like Rose, my daughter also gravitated to water. Collecting tadpoles, skimming stones. Splashing around in the shallows. A shiver prickled over me. I imagined sweet little Odette, and Rose's small, powerful hands holding her under the water—

My mother sighed. "Oh, Cleary. Your father let his guard down. He got too close to an entity he had come to trust, one he wanted desperately to save. But the others are usually beyond saving. Eventually, Rose will have to leave."

"Mum, I'm not him. I'm not Dad."

"Of course, you're not." She reached out, her touch grounding. "But you're a father, and Elsie's your world. Remember that."

I scratched my stubble, hating the eventuality that was emerging. Mum was right. Our world and the spirit world could not co-exist safely or happily together for long. If something happened to Elsie, I'd never be able to live with myself.

Mum unwound a narrow leather bracelet from her wrist. Silver charms glinted as she passed it to me.

"This will block your visions," she said softly. "It's helped me in the past. Maybe it will bring you some clarity, too."

With a nod of thanks, I took the bracelet and wrapped it around my wrist.

"So what should I do, Ma?"

"Give Rose another chance to remember and confront what really happened to her child. If she faces her tethering event, it will make crossing over so much less painful for her. But if she refuses, there's only one thing you can do, Cleary. Light a fire on her grave and set her free."

58
CLEARY

As we returned to Loch Ard, the sun was beginning its descent behind the trees, casting long shadows over the house.

We unpacked the car and carried Mum's basket of goodies inside—a large container of raspberry cupcakes for Elsie, and a small box of taper candles for me. *Light them when you get home, Cleary. Let them burn until the moon rises, they'll strengthen your intuition.*

I lit the candles and stood at the bay window in the lounge room, gazing out across the garden as I breathed the scent of sandalwood and clary sage.

My mother was right. I had to make a decision soon. Today. If Rose refused to face her past and discover what really happened to her baby, then I needed time to prepare for the inevitable.

Each night, the moon was growing fuller, its lunar energies increasing. It would help Rose regenerate herself more quickly, restoring the life-force she'd lost by becoming physical the other day at the loch.

But she would still be weak.

All I had to do was wait till dark and salt her gravesite, then cast my intentions and set the soil alight. Within minutes, she'd be gone.

It's so real, this ache in my chest. What if the pain stays with me after she crosses over? What if I'm stuck with this feeling forever, longing for her, the way I'm longing for her right now?

"Man, you're such an overemotional coward. Stop moping, and do what needs to be done."

Elsie was seated at the kitchen table, engrossed in finishing some of her clay hearts, so I quietly slipped outside to look for Rose.

I checked all the places she loved to hide—the shadows under the cedar tree, the fern house, even the grassy slopes of the orchard. As I headed towards her cottage, squinting in the bright sun, a water dragon dived off the path in front of me, disappearing into the bushes.

I rapped loudly on Rose's door, and when she didn't answer, I went inside.

"Hey, we need to talk. Are you here?"

Everything was neat, just as I'd left it after the renovation. Only now a light layer of dust lay over the surfaces. The flowers Elsie had picked for Rose and placed in an old Vegemite jar were wilting. I wandered over to the window and noticed one of Elsie's clay hearts hanging by a dark blue string from the latch. It was deep pink with purple swirls, and delicate flowers carved across its face. Elsie must have snuck in and left it there as a surprise.

I'm going to hang them all over the garden, Dad. So Rose knows we love her.

My chest tightened. It was already too late.

In just a few short months, Rose had become a part of us,

just as we'd become part of her. I couldn't imagine our family without her, which somehow made her secrets all the more concerning. I wanted to trust that Elsie would always be safe around her—but could someone capable of drowning an innocent baby ever truly be trusted?

As I headed back down to the house, my mother's warning rang in my ears. *A troubled soul is like a thorn bush, Cleary. It may flower, but the thorns are always there, waiting.*

59
CLEARY

"Elsie—?" As I stepped inside the house and shut the door behind me, the silence met me like an avalanche. Instinctively, my neck tensed, but I forced a steadying breath. "Hey kid, you around?"

The dining table was empty, her clay and paints packed away. Whatever she was up to, she was awfully quiet. Hadn't she heard me come back? Usually, she'd spring out and start firing off questions about Rose. But the only sound was my boots on the polished floorboards as I thumped around in search of her. She wasn't in the lounge room or kitchen. I bounded upstairs, but her bedroom was empty, too.

"Possum, it's Dad. Where are you?"

I searched all of her typical hiding spots—the fairy tent in her room, and the book nook she'd made inside an old wardrobe where she sheltered when she was lonely or overwhelmed. Uneasiness gnawed at my bones as Jolene's accusing voice drifted back. *Being a single parent is no picnic, Cleary. You can barely commit to shaving every day, let alone raising a child—*

"Shit!"

A slideshow of worst-case scenarios started flashing through my mind. Elsie might have fallen and hit her head, be lying somewhere unconscious ... hit by a car on the road I kept telling her to stay away from ... gotten abducted by child predators. *If something happened to her, I won't survive it. I left her alone too long, didn't I? Dear God, she's just a kid. I forget that sometimes. My baby bird, so innocent and trusting, what if—*

"Jeez, man. Get a grip."

I ran outside and headed along the driveway to the front gates, jogged uphill a little way along the verge, my breathing heavy. The road looked tranquil. No plumes of dust or recent disturbance.

"Elsie!"

She'd been going to the loch a lot lately. Catching tadpoles, she said. More likely hoping to glimpse Rose. I cut up the rocky slope and ran along the ridge through the late afternoon shadows, stumbling in my haste. I was gasping for air by the time I reached the rise overlooking the loch. When I heard Elsie's soft voice in the stillness, my pulse began to jackhammer.

Stones skated under my boots as I loped down the ridge, and when I pushed through the thicket of trees and caught sight of her, I slumped in relief. She was crouched on the loch's muddy bank, singing quietly to herself and trailing her fingers in the water. Her dark hair had sprung out of its pigtail and tangled around her head like a dusky halo.

She seemed so small. Crouching by the dark water, all alone. So vulnerable.

I couldn't even be angry with her for going off without telling me. I was just so glad to see her unharmed. I slowed my pace as I approached her, not wanting to startle her or make her think I was cranky with her. As I got closer, I saw she had hung a few of her clay hearts along a nearby branch, several of them clinking together in the breeze.

"Hey, kiddo."

She sprang to her feet and whipped around, wide-eyed. Then she sagged.

"Oh. It's you."

"Expecting someone else?"

"Rose always finds me here."

I glanced over her shoulders to the shadows. "She does?"

"Yep. It's our special spot." Elsie fished in her pocket and took out another painted heart, holding it up for me to see. "I thought these would cheer her up, but I've been here a while and she hasn't showed—" She huffed out a sigh. "You look cross, Dad. Am I in trouble?"

My gaze went to the loch. A large tree trunk had fallen across it, forming a natural bridge, its surface furry with bright green moss. Despite it being summer, the blackish water looked freezing. And deep. Really deep.

I looked back at Elsie, wanting to lecture her for wandering off, for giving me one hell of a heart attack—but I was just so dang relieved to see her that the warning died on my lips.

"Nah, we're good. Come on, let's go home."

Elsie swung the heart by its string. "Can we go past the lightning tree so I can hang this up for her?"

I nodded, and we set off down the hill, walking in silence. I kept looking over my shoulder, half expecting Rose to emerge from the shadows, her life-force fully repaired.

I inhaled deeply, trying to release my panic from before. As the crisp, earthy garden scent filled my lungs, that afternoon by the loch came flooding back. Rose had been real and tangible in my arms, our kiss full of fire and tenderness, igniting a deep longing within me. It wasn't just physical desire, but the undeniable chemistry between us, as though fate had brought us together.

If only I knew why.

You think you know me, Cleary. But you don't. Someone like me can cause a lot of damage. Getting too close is a mistake.

The last half hour was a reality check. Mum was right. No matter my feelings for Rose, my first commitment was as a father. I'd let my guard slip. Let myself get too close to an entity I desperately wanted to save. But maybe Rose wasn't so different from other entities, after all. Maybe she was beyond saving, too.

60

ROSALBA

As I crouched in my bower under the atlas cedar, life coursed back through my veins. Despite the massive energy I had burned through at the loch the other day to become physical, I was healing fast. Almost back to normal.

Which shocked me ... yet also filled me with a lightness I hadn't known before now.

Being with Cleary in that way—being crushed in his arms, his lips on my mouth, the fiery intensity of his body against mine—drained me completely. It had taken all my strength to stay present and extend our kiss for as long as I could handle.

And yet now, somehow, it had also revived me.

My heart swelled. William said love had the power to heal. Finally, I understood. Love would heal me, too.

I drew my knees to my chest and hugged them against me, snuggling deeper into my bed of leaves. Cleary was right. With the right focus, I could overcome anything. Even the loss of my beautiful baby. With him by my side, I could manifest myself into flesh and blood. Become real, even briefly. If I practiced, maybe I could stretch it for longer? Minutes. An hour.

An entire day.

My heart soared. Becoming real for a day meant I could be with them. Not just as a shadow person on the edge of their lives, fluttering around the garden and seeing them when we chanced to cross paths—but a real, living part of their lives. Eating pizza at the table. Brushing Elsie's hair. Holding her hand. Being able to touch Cleary, hug him close, the way I had done a few days ago. Kiss him, and feel the warm, bare press of his skin against mine, our limbs twining together as we lay in front of a crackling fire in the cottage.

Once I could maintain a whole day of being physical, I could extend it to a week.

"Two weeks. A month."

Time was a funny thing. The way it swirled around you like autumn leaves or moonlight. Or fireflies. A cunning trickster, making you believe no escape from the past existed, when in fact it did.

What if you could become real ... permanently?

I bit my lip. A tear escaped, streaking like a raindrop down my flushed face. If my body hadn't been so frail, I'd have leapt to my feet and bounded around like a possum with its tail on fire. Was this joy?

I smiled, pressing my damp eyes against my knees.

"Come on, body. Hurry up and restore!"

I couldn't wait to see them. Tell them my plan.

So many secrets had already spilled out. What were a few more? Cleary believed in me. He trusted me. He'd said so. Even after reading what the pastor's wife had written, he had come after me, seeking me out to reassure me. *It's painful, Rose. I get that. But you don't have to go through it alone.* I now had the courage to confront it. Better yet, I had my family around me. We would face it together, just as Cleary had promised. With his support, I would heal from the past and move forward—

Voices erupted in the garden, drifting up from near the lightning tree. The soft piping of a baby bird and the gruff reply of her father. My heart squeezed and pumped like a tiny piston, firing lifeblood through me in a steady stream. I sat up, brushing leaves off my dress, picking them out of my hair. Still amazed by the speed of my recovery.

Do you have any idea how powerful you are?

I crawled out from under the atlas cedar and walked on shaky legs towards the sound of their quiet chatter. Hurrying along the track that led downhill, my energy growing stronger with each step. Soon, I could see them standing side by side beneath my old friend the tree.

Elsie was tying something onto a branch. When Cleary's big hand settled protectively on her shoulder, my heart melted.

They were the family I'd always yearned for, the people able to love me as I loved them. They knew who I truly was, and yet still accepted me.

I bit my lip, smiling. Picturing the three of us together, happy and laughing, or even sad sometimes, it didn't matter, because we'd always be there for one another. Through good times and the bad. It filled me with unbearable longing. Soon—very soon—my wish would come true.

My skin tingled as I stepped out of the lonely shadows of my old life and strode towards my new one. Finally, after a century, I was ready to take a chance on love.

61

CLEARY

"Where do you think she is, Dad?" Elsie finished attaching her clay heart to the branch, its red and green roses gleaming in the fading light. "I called out to her before, but she didn't answer."

"She's around somewhere."

"She'll find the hearts, won't she? She'll know they mean we love her, right?"

The sun hung low, casting golden light through the twisted limbs of the old gum tree we stood under. I forced a tight-lipped smile, watching the little ornament swing gently on its branch in the afternoon air.

"Come on. Let's go."

As we walked back along the trail towards home, I stole a glance at Elsie. She was swinging her arms happily as she marched along beside me. Her cheeks glowed pink from the sun, and a constellation of tiny freckles danced across her nose and cheeks. She kept darting her gaze hopefully uphill into the tree shadows, searching for Rose.

"Dad?"

"Hmm?"

"What's up? You look sad."

I took a deep breath. "Possum, have you ever felt scared around Rose?"

She looked incredulous. "What do you mean?"

"I dunno ... like she might hurt you?"

"Of course not, Dad! Why would you even say that?"

"She's one of the others, we can't—"

"Trust them, I know. But you're wrong this time."

"You know she can't stay here forever, Else."

"Why not?"

"Eventually, she'll have to cross over."

Elsie stopped walking. "What, no! We love her, Dad. You can't send her away."

"It's the only way she'll find peace."

She shaded her eyes against the late afternoon glare, searching my face. Her lip quivered, but her gaze was steady.

"You found her grave, didn't you?"

I nodded.

She glanced back up the hill to where we'd come from, and when she returned her attention to me, tears gleamed in her eyes.

"You're going to make her leave?"

My throat was suddenly tight. "I may not have to, kiddo. If Rose can confront the event that trapped her here, her tether will break without my help. She'll be free to cross over. You know that, right?"

"But we're a family."

"No, Else. You and I are a family. Rose is one of the others. She'll never be part of what we have."

"You're wrong, Daddy." She bit her trembling lip, dashing

away the tears. "We love her and she loves us. That's what a family is!"

"She can't stay, Elsie."

"Did something happen?"

I grimaced, remembering how I found Rose at the loch on Friday, and her deep unhappiness over her child. The need to protect her flooding through me. The kiss we shared, and the shock of her warm body as I drew her against me. And then finding her gravestone—

"She might have done something bad, Elsie. Really bad. In the time before."

Elsie tightened her lips. "Like what?"

"You remember how Lewis pushed his mum down the stairs, and how his mum died because of it?"

Elsie pondered this, then searched my face, frowning. "You think Rose killed someone?"

"Maybe."

"It was her dad, wasn't it? Because I kind of want to kill him, too. Did you know he whipped her?"

"It wasn't her dad. And I don't know what really happened. But it's not looking good, possum."

"Did you ask her?"

"She can't remember."

"Then ask her again."

"She doesn't want to, Elsie. It's too painful for her."

My daughter hugged her arms around herself the way Rose did when she was upset, and it ignited a fierce protectiveness inside me. I took a step closer, wanting to wrap her up and reassure her, but she backed away.

"Please, Dad. Just try to talk to her, okay?"

The pleading in her voice undid me. *Christ, man. You better be sure you know what you're doing.* With a sigh, I crouched at her level to look in her eyes.

"I know you think Rose is different from the others we've met. And I know you care about her, Elsie. I care for her, too. But she's very troubled. It's cruel to keep her here. We need to set her free."

"But Rose is happy. She loves being with us."

"She's also incredibly powerful. More than any entity I've seen. What if she got angry and accidentally hurt you—?"

Elsie gazed around the garden, battling her tears. "She never would, Dad. Not in a million years."

"You don't know that, kiddo. And to be honest, I'm not convinced we can completely trust her. We have to let her go. It's for the best."

Elsie drew her lips into a line, and ran at me suddenly, shoving me with all her strength.

"Leave Rose alone. She's my friend!"

I tried to grab her wrists, hoping to calm her. "Wait, Else. Listen—"

She ducked out of reach.

"No, you listen. If you do anything to her, I'll … I'll run away! I'll find my mum and tell her you're a hopeless dad. That you're mean and belt me. You'll never see me again." Turning and sprinting downhill, she veered off the path and vanished into the shadows behind the house.

When a door slammed inside, the silence that followed was brutal.

62

ROSALBA

STARING at the pretty painted heart swinging from its branch, its painted face winking red and green in the dying light, I gripped my throat. Fighting the slipstream of fire and ice pouring through my veins, as leaves swirled around my feet. I was like the heart, dangling by a slender thread, at the mercy of this fickle, confusing world.

She'll find the hearts, won't she, Dad? She'll know they mean we love her, right?

No one had ever made me anything before. This should have been one of those moments William used to talk about, those fleeting moments that were special enough to last a lifetime.

Instead, it burned like poison.

When dusk came down, I went along the trail to the house. As its windows sank into darkness, the lights blinked on. The moon climbed higher, and a hush fell over the garden. Only the raspy song of crickets filled the air, their wings fluttering frantically as they searched for mates. After a while, even they stopped. The silence grew eerie as night settled in.

Still, I stood watching, my arms locked around me, my fingers digging into my ribs. Cleary's words—the ones I'd overheard him telling his daughter—seeped through my system like acid. *Rose is powerful, Elsie. What if she got angry and hurt you?*

The hope building inside me earlier withered away, leaving only a bleak, crushing emptiness. What a fool I was to trust him. To believe all those things he said. I thought he cared about me. That we stood a chance. William used to say that true love had the power to transcend death and live forever. *It just keeps cycling back, life after life, always searching for its other half, never giving up until it finds its happy ever after.* I had pinned all my hopes on his theory being true.

Stupid. Stupid. I should have listened to my father. *You're a monster, Rosalba. No monster gets a happy ending.*

The lights in the house blinked off one by one.

Once again, I was on the outside looking in, as if Cleary and Elsie had closed their doors against me. Closed their hearts. I could not lie, it hurt. I felt hollowed out, as the new me withered and died, and the old me—the monstrous me—resurfaced.

My fingers clenched into fists. Blood roared through my veins. The air surrounding me seethed like volcanic steam. An eddy of dry leaves lifted and danced around me, swirling in spirals, creating miniature whirlwinds. Sighing and whispering, as if they too knew the sting of betrayal. *She might have done something bad, Elsie. In the time before—*

A door whispered open and shut, and Cleary emerged from the house shadows. He trudged uphill, his footsteps crunching on the gravel track that led around the cypress hedge towards the loch.

Was he searching for me? Planning to break my tether before I could hurt anyone else?

We need to set her free.

I followed him silently, staying hidden in the shadows as he made his way uphill. He walked fast, with a grim sense of purpose I'd never noticed in him before. Before he reached the loch, he veered off course and pushed between a thicket of overgrown trees, disappearing into the darkness.

I chased after him, my breath ragged as low-hanging tree branches whipped my face and arms. His strides were long and determined. Whatever he had in store for me wouldn't be good. My chest constricted. I wanted to lash out at him, to hurt him the way he'd hurt me. As if hearing my thoughts, the sky grew dark and foreboding. The wind picked up and sent leaves and debris swirling around my ankles.

Breathing hard, I entered an expanse that was wild and neglected, overrun with snarled and twisted bramble vines, the ground littered with fallen berries.

My feet dragged suddenly, fear creeping up my spine.

What could Cleary possibly want in this forsaken place? There was nothing here, just bushland and escaped blackberries. I had never ventured this way before. Never bothered. This part of the garden held no interest for me.

I usually avoided it.

Creeping through the darkness Cleary had disappeared into, I held my breath. As I approached a wall of brambles, the sour reek of rotting fruit overwhelmed me. I couldn't breathe. My steps slowed. Every instinct was shouting at me to turn and run. I knew this place, and just being near it filled my body with ice cold dread.

"The berry patch."

63

CLEARY

The sky darkened as storm clouds rolled in, casting a deep indigo hue over the garden. Shadows crept along the ground, slithering through the blackberry bushes towards Rose's grave.

As I paced in front of the headstone, I glanced down the hill to the house. All I could see was the peaked roof, its tiles gleaming like dragon scales in the moonlight. Elsie was asleep in her room, and I wanted her to stay that way. At least until this was over. She'd be heartbroken, of course. But I'd handle her later. Right now, I needed to deal with Rose.

I had sensed her in the garden tonight, observing the house from the cover of trees. If Elsie woke, she would have noticed her too. So I retreated up here, hoping Rose would follow.

Maybe seeing the grave would be enough to spark her memory, help her cross over without my intervention? That was what I wanted, right? For Rose to leave. For Elsie to be safe, and for life to return to normal.

The swollen moon broke through the clouds, casting a bright glow over the treetops, illuminating the twisted branches and tangled blackberry vines. I walked over to the gravestone and crouched in front of it, tracing my fingers over the names written there. Trying to get my head around letting her go.

Nothing I felt for Rose was real.

The need to touch her again, be near her. To protect her. The jolt each time I saw her, the rush of pleasure when she laughed, the ache that gripped me whenever she was sad—that all belonged to William. My feelings for her were nothing more than fallout from my visions, and Mum's charm had put an end to those. Once Rose was gone, her hold on me would vanish, too. Then I could move on. Pretend none of this ever happened...

Thunder boomed overhead, and the air was suddenly icy, sending my hunter radar into overdrive. I shot to my feet and whirled around.

Rose stood at the edge of the clearing, her midnight hair swirling around her in the cool night breeze. She was no longer the soft, vulnerable girl I had held and kissed by the loch. Something had changed. She was now a fierce goddess, shadows carving between her brows as she glared at me.

"What are you doing here, Cleary?"

A shiver ran across my shoulders. "There's something you need to see."

She made a scoffing noise. "Another of your lies?"

Ah, so she'd overheard. I stepped aside, gesturing at the grave.

"It's no lie, Rose."

Her gaze fell on it, and she frowned, a stillness settling over her. Her lips parted, and she seemed about to turn and run, but instead took one faltering step closer, and then another. As she approached the gravestone, her whole body started trembling.

She reached out, trailing her fingers over the names carved on its pitted face.

"Odette ... and me. We died on the same day?" She sank to her knees in front of the stone, looking around at me with huge, glassy eyes. "The pastor's wife was right. The letter, the rumours. It's all true. This is proof, isn't it?"

My voice came out sterner than I'd meant. "Only you can know that for sure, Rose."

She shook her head, as though in a daze. "It was me ... it's true, I did this. I drowned my poor little baby in the loch, just as they said. I really am a monster."

Even though I had hardened my heart towards her, seeing her buckle over in pain stirred my protector. All I wanted right then was to stride over and drag her against me, wrap my arms tightly around her and somehow hold her together.

Instead, I clenched my fists and stood my ground. Hating myself in that moment almost as much as I feared her.

64
ROSALBA

Silence roared around me, ringing in my ears. The clouds had rolled away with the storm, and the wind died down. The crescent moon hung low, casting a bright glow over the gravestone and the man who stood beside it.

He was speaking to me, but his words made no sense. He kept urging me to remember, to relive the day of my death. But it was too much to ask. I was already drowning in a sea of anguish, and couldn't bear to dredge up anything more.

I closed my eyes, wishing he'd shut up.

Wishing the grave would yawn open and swallow me.

All I could see was my baby, cradled in my arms, her round eyes peering up at me. *I lean in to kiss her soft cheek, the one with the mark, inhaling the scent of milk and baby powder. She grins toothlessly, her chubby little face framed by the soft white bunny rug I made for her. "You're perfect in every way," I whisper. "Oh, my darling, I'll never let you go—"*

Slowly I got to my feet, my joints aching, my blood sluggish and cold as it pounded through me. I looked at Cleary.

"How did you find the grave?"

His eyes were a little crazed, his hair raked about and his lips bitten.

"When we touched at the loch, I had another vision," he said hoarsely. "Only not one of your memories. It was William again, and he came up here, expecting to find you and Odette. But instead..."

"He found this." A hot, wet tear streaked down my cheek. "That's why we never married. By the time he returned, I was already dead."

"Yes."

I tried to tear my gaze away from Cleary, break the tension between us, but the sight of him trapped me.

The moon illuminated his face in shades of silver, making him seem even less a part of this physical realm than I was. Shadows bruised his eyes, while his mouth—grim and unsmiling, framed by his unshaven whiskers—looked as lush and inviting as it had the other day at the loch. He still reminded me of William. Yet in the past months, he had become his own person while William faded. Right now, though, with the proof of my crime casting a shadow across my feet, I longed for William's simple acceptance. For his unwavering belief in my goodness.

I swayed towards Cleary, wishing I had taken a different path in life—one where I had accepted William's proposal instead of letting fear keep me trapped here. Where I had escaped this cursed garden and gone to live in William's stone farmhouse by the river.

I sob caught in my throat.

Cleary was glowering at me. I remembered the brief, hot touch of his lips on mine at the loch, and my yearning for William disappeared. Heat rushed through my limbs, climbing through me till my skin burned. Even in the midst of my devastation, I still longed for this man who was going to be the end of me.

"Rose," he whispered, coming closer. "I know you're hurting right now. Seeing the grave was a shock. For me, too."

"Huh. I doubt that."

"You'll never find peace until you face the memory of how Odette died. Until you know for sure. Otherwise, it'll haunt you forever. Let me help you."

"I don't need your help." I backed away from him. "You tricked me. You're going to force me over against my will. I heard what you said to Elsie! You want me gone because you think I'm a danger to her."

His gaze flickered to the grave behind me, and when he looked back, his eyes were hard.

"*Are* you a danger?"

"Of course not!"

His face softened, and he sighed. "I know you care about her. I can't imagine how difficult it must be for you to be around her sometimes, after losing your own child. But, Rose—" He shifted closer, shadows deepening the lines in his face, his eyes glinting. "We're so close to the truth. If you keep resisting, keep turning away from your memories of Odette, what choice do I have? We can't spend our lives with the shadow of the past hanging over us."

"*My* past, you mean?"

His grim silence was answer enough.

I clasped my middle, digging my fingers into my ribcage.

"You never cared, Cleary. You only listened to my stories to use them against me. And now you want to break my tether and be rid of me."

"Maybe at the start, I wanted you to leave. Not anymore."

I curled my lips. "So many lies. And I gobbled them up, desperate that someone might love me. What a fool I must seem to you."

"There's nothing foolish about wanting love. But can you blame me for being cautious? After what you told me about Odette, and how scared you were that you'd hurt her? My gut is saying you'd never hurt anyone, least of all a child you dearly loved. And that includes Elsie. But how can I be sure?"

"You can't."

"I want to be. And I can be, if only you'll try harder to remember the day you and Odette died. Confront what happened, Rose. Make peace with it. If you don't, you'll live in a limbo land of grief and pain for the rest of eternity."

My legs sank against the gravestone, my fingers knotting in the fabric of my dress, as if every part of me was searching for something to grasp onto. Something to anchor me. To stop me from trembling. To stop the truth from spilling out.

"I don't need to confront it."

"Yeah, Rose. You do."

"I said no!"

"You're scared. I get that. But we need to know for sure."

I clawed my fingers, digging them into my thighs.

"I'm warning you, Cleary. Stop pushing me, before I do something we'll both regret."

He gestured at the ground around my feet.

"You don't seem to understand how vulnerable you are right now, ghost girl. Now that I've found your grave, I can break your tether in a flash. Sprinkle some black salt on the dirt, whisper an incantation. Set it alight. You'd be gone in seconds. Poof. Just like that. Whether you face anything or not."

"That's another lie!"

He rattled the matches in his pocket. "Will we try it and see?"

I gasped, feeling something small and scared wriggle to life inside me. He was bluffing, wasn't he? After everything we'd been through together, he wouldn't really force me to cross … would he?

"You can't hurt me, Cleary." My toes and fingers began to tingle. My blood raced hot and fast, my aura prickling and growing, like it did the other day at the loch when I ignited my elemental energy. When I became real. When Cleary kissed me. I clenched my fists, sidestepping him and heading out of the patch. "But I can hurt you. If you know what's good for you, leave me alone."

"Rose, wait."

He sprang at me and caught my wrist, swinging me around. Before I registered what was happening, he dragged me against his chest and trapped me in his arms.

I gasped as the raw heat of his body pulsed through me, shocking and electric. *Calm down, your rage is doing this, congealing in your cells, anchoring you to reality.* With a surge of energy, I managed to wriggle out of his hold for a moment, only for him to grab me back even tighter.

His grip dug into my waist as he crushed me against him. I thrashed and kicked, trying to break free, but he only tightened his hold, trapping me against his chest until I felt every ripple and clench of muscle beneath his shirt.

"Let me go!"

His breath warmed my face. "What happened to Odette at the loch? Think back … remember."

"No, I won't!"

"It's the only way you'll ever be free of the guilt. The fear."

He held me tighter, his eyes fixed on mine, his voice low and hypnotic. "Go back, Rose. Go back and see for yourself."

I struggled, but the sensation of being held was simply too strange. His heat, his scent, the strength of his energy wrapping me up, containing me. Trapping me. In the turmoil, I became aware that a small patch of skin on my breastbone was tingling.

"I'm sorry," Cleary whispered against my hair. "It's the only way."

"What's happ—?"

My blood turned to a rich, dark liquid inside my veins, fizzing and flooding through me like treacle. The taste of bread-and-butter pudding assaulted me, then cinnamon sticks and robust red wine. I saw myself wading into deep water, moss oozing between my toes, the snowflakes melting on my face, even though the sun was still shining down from a long-ago sky—

I gasped. There was something in Cleary's pocket.

The rosy quartz from the night we watched the fireflies. The one that transported me to the past. What had Cleary said? *Rose quartz ... it'll help you face buried memories.*

"Oh no, please."

I tried to escape, but then ... then...

The garden vanished, taking Cleary with it into a twilight haze. I sank into the shimmering blackness, clutching for Cleary, but when I cried out, it was not his name on my lips, but my daughter's.

"Odette—!"

65
ROSALBA

1917

"Odette?" My bare feet slipped on the icy ground, my breathing jagged as I strained up the incline. Clumps of snow still lay on the ground, quickly numbing my toes. Birthing a child had taken its toll on my body, and despite the passage of six months, I was not as nimble as before.

A thin wail carried on the early morning air. I ran harder, stumbling up the rocky slope.

"Odette!"

How long had she been up here? An hour ... more?

The cold was already throbbing in my own fingers and face, numbing my feet. How much worse for a wee baby? I dodged around boulders and fallen branches, racing up along the frozen track. Clouds stained the dawn sky a deep, menacing purple in. In the distance, something howled, an owl, but it made my blood churn and I stumbled in panic. Cold wasn't the only danger here. Hattie had seen dingoes lurking a few weeks ago as she walked home down the mountainside.

There were no more cries from Odette. Had I imagined that first one? It had been so frail and heart-wrenching, turning my blood colder than the snow I ran through. Was I already too late? How long could a baby survive out here? The sky was rolling with purplish clouds, getting ready to drop another snowfall.

When I reached the loch, I saw a small bundle at the water's edge. It wasn't a baby, surely? It looked so tiny, like a doll abandoned in the shallows. But then a wail drifted up and sent me racing to her side. Her rug had floated into the loch, and her little arm thrashed the water. I crashed to my knees and gathered her against me. She was alive. Breathing. But her eyes were glassy with fear and cold, her cries thin and tremulous. I pressed her tightly against me, murmuring reassurance as I tried to warm her with my body heat.

Me ... it was me who did this, wasn't it? The mud in my room and on my feet ... it was me, I know it. I brought her here, as Father had said I should. I abandoned her to the cold, just as he instructed. Why had I listened to him? Why would I do that? Did I still crave his approval and acceptance so desperately—?

Clutching my child in my arms, praying I'd found her in time to save her, I staggered back down the hill to the house. Up the front steps I ran, through the door and along the hall to the sitting room.

My father stood by the fireplace. Cooking smells drifted from the kitchen, onions and tomatoes and fried herb bread, but they only made my stomach churn all the harder. I joined him by the fire. Hunching my shoulders and dropping my gaze to the floor like a chastened dog, unable to meet his eyes. He knew what I had done, yet still he said nothing. Would he condemn me for my actions, call me a monster, and beat me in the stables like when I was small? Or was he secretly glad?

I rubbed my daughter's frozen little limbs.

It didn't matter what he thought. All I cared about now was getting Odette warm. But as I cuddled her and massaged the circulation back into her cold body, I noticed the mud. It was everywhere. Sliding off my legs onto the hearth, drying to scabby clumps in the fire's heat. Crusting on the hem of my nightgown, hardening on my skin. It had even found its way onto my father's shoes and the cuffs of his trousers, too.

Father shifted his weight. "You were restless last night, Rosalba."

That was all he said, and the cold flatness in his voice wrapped around me, condemning me. Locking me in a tiny, airless cell of guilt with no escape.

66

ROSALBA

NOW

I STUMBLED BACKWARDS, away from Cleary, already fading.

He came after me, but we could no longer touch. I couldn't catch my breath. Couldn't move. I wanted to flee, but something rooted me to the spot. The burden of my crime was consuming me, just as Cleary said it would.

You'll never find peace until you face it. It'll haunt you forever.

"What happened, Rose?" Cleary inched closer, his voice reassuring. "What did you see?"

The weight of what I had remembered was crushing me. I

couldn't keep this secret any longer. I crept my damp fingers around my waist, my heart breaking.

"My baby ... she—" I gulped, swiping at my tears. "It was so cold. Barely dawn and clumps of snow still lay on the ground. I found Odette in the mud by the loch. I gathered her up, crushing her against what little warmth remained in me—"

"She was all right, though?"

I nodded. "She seemed to be. Her screams got stronger, even as I held her and tried to soothe her. But Cleary, I did this to her. Brought her to the loch, crazed and half-asleep. My need to please my father stronger than the instinct to protect my child."

"Why would you say that, Rose?"

"He told me to abandon her in the snow. Because of her mark. He said it was kinder than letting her live a life of shame."

Cleary shifted. "Maybe he took her to the loch?"

"Oh no, no. It was me."

"Do you remember doing it?"

"No ... only kissing her goodnight and tucking her in."

"You said your father used to lock you in your bedroom. Why not that night?"

I frowned. "Perhaps he forgot."

"Did he often forget?"

"No, I don't think so. But he must have that night."

"Did he leave it unlocked on purpose?"

My shoulders sagged, and I nodded. "Maybe hoping I would take the opportunity."

"What did he say when you got back to the house?"

"He said ..." My hands trembled so hard I had to tuck them against me. "He said I'd been restless in the night. I'm certain he knew what I'd done, but that was all he said. That I'd been restless."

Shadows crept across Cleary's face, deepening his frown. "Tell me Odette survived."

A tear splashed down my cheek. I searched inside myself, but I already knew what I'd find. I had no recollections of her beyond that night. No more glimpses. No more memories. As though a veil of deep desolation was obscuring what had happened next.

I shook my head.

Cleary's eyes darkened with understanding, turning wildly black, as if the night had spilled into them like ink. Darker than loch water. Dark as mirrors. I saw myself reflected in them, and did not like what I saw.

My body tingled. The blood in my veins slowed.

Oblivion was calling to me, the need to hide away and restore myself after becoming physical before, after remembering. But I would not give myself that luxury. Whatever it cost, I would gladly pay any price. Cleary was right. I knew that now. I would find no rest until I confronted the memory of holding my baby under the water and watching the light fade from her beautiful, glass-blue eyes.

"You see, Cleary?" My words were a whisper, catching in my throat. "I really am a monster."

He did not answer, and I was glad. Shadows covered his face, the moonlight barely touching him now. He had seen beneath my surface to what I truly was, and now he was withdrawing from me.

Whatever love had spun its web around us was gone.

The garden grew quiet, as if all life had ceased. No possums scurrying up the trees, no worms burrowing in the dirt. No small creatures flitting about in search of food. There was just the eerie silence hanging over us, and the grave's shadow falling at our feet.

I stepped up to Cleary. My pulse thundered, and my gaze locked on his. Carefully, so as not to shock him with my icy touch, I flattened my hand against his shirt pocket.

The warm hardness of the quartz stone fizzed under my palm, stirring up a kaleidoscope of my childhood. The distant clang of cowbells, and the tangy sweetness of wild berries dancing on my tongue. Long afternoons spent lost in the pages of a book, the scent of old paper and ink folding around me like a friendly cocoon—

I was drifting, falling. Such a long way back.

Events spun around me, a blur of light and darkness. I didn't resist as they pulled me under, thrusting me back into a moment in time I had spent a century trying to forget. With a jolt that shook me to my core, I crash-landed back into the past.

67
ROSALBA

1917

"You were restless last night, Rosalba." My father rubbed his hands by the fire, his voice flat and trancelike. "Coming and going at all hours. What were you up to?"

I glared at him from the corner of my eye, hugging my baby against me. *As if you don't know.*

My muddy nightgown dripped onto the floor. Odette was sopping wet too, her small body possessed by shivers, her cries echoing off the walls. Though I rocked her and squeezed her tight, she would not settle.

My father did not notice her at all. He didn't notice the

wind howling through the front door I left open in my rush to reach the fire, nor the pools of water and mud on the floor. Oblivious to it all, he flared his nostrils as though relishing the aromas of herb bread and stewed vegetables that drifted from the kitchen like on any ordinary day.

Odette was heavy, so I knelt by the grate, rubbing her frozen little limbs. She cried as I showered her face with kisses, but soon the fire warmed her and she calmed. Pressing our faces together, I inhaled her sweet scent, my stomach churning over what had almost happened. My father was right. I wasn't fit to be a mother. Today, I would bring her to the church ladies and beg them to find her parents who could give her a better life.

How those ladies would scream if they saw me now.

Mud all over me. Saturating my torn nightgown, smearing my face and chest. Flaking off my bare feet. Drying in clumps on the floor.

It was even on my fathers' shoes. Not just smears, but wedges of it, thick crusts clinging to the edges of his soles and splattering his trouser cuffs. Almost as if—

A chill sank into my bones.

Why were my father's shoes muddy?

My gaze travelled slowly up to his face.

He was studying the pale rectangle of the window. There was nothing outside, just the grey morning haze, yet his jaw clenched, as if displeased by what he saw. Or maybe it was my sudden interest that bothered him. He glanced down, and for a split second, our eyes met.

His mouth fell open, and his cheeks caved inwards as he struggled to speak. Only a faint, airless whimper escaped his lips.

I went very still, until the ice in my bloodstream reached my heart and numbed it.

Without a word, I got to my feet. Cradling my child protectively, I crossed the room and slipped into the hallway, hurrying upstairs. In my room, I removed Odette's wet clothes and dressed her in warm dry ones, then wrapped her in a clean blanket. I stripped out of my ruined nightdress and left it on the floor, shivering in the cold as I dragged on a warm dress and coat, stuffing some things into a small carpetbag.

Back downstairs, I crept towards the front door.

I was halfway there when Father called to me. He emerged into the hallway, holding a wide-necked metal flask, his face as grey as the winter sky.

"It's bitter outside, Rosalba. Will you at least take some soup?"

Needles pricked the backs of my eyes.

Throughout my life, I was a burden, a weight on him. Yet even now, I longed to please him. Longed for his acceptance, for a last shred of kindness. His soup offering was too little too late, and I wanted to refuse it. But that neglected little girl inside me quickened, needing a final breadcrumb of his elusive esteem to take with me into the terrifying world that awaited us beyond the safety of our home.

I retraced my steps and took the flask he offered. As I did, I saw a fleck of mud on his sleeve. He caught me looking and absently brushed at the spot.

"Your mother was a great beauty, Rosalba. She was famed for it, even back in Scotland. People would visit us just to admire her. Did you know that?"

I clutched my baby tightly.

"Beauty isn't everything, Father." I hadn't meant to respond, but the words came out on their own, with a fierceness I hadn't known I possessed. "It's what's inside a person's heart that matters most."

Before he could reply, I turned away and hastened into the hall. Bypassing the puddles of mud and melted snow I'd let in before, I walked outside into the frosty morning, clasping my precious bundle in my arms as I closed the door of my father's house behind me forever.

68

CLEARY

NOW

Shadows swarmed out of nowhere, gathering around Rose as if to shield her from the light. She was clutching the sides of her dress, her body rigid, and then she seemed to collapse into herself, absorbing all light and energy and gravity, reflecting only darkness, as clouds blocked the moon.

"My father," she whispered. "His shoes..."

I froze in place, unable to breathe. Was this how it ended? She was coming untethered, wasn't she? Any moment now, she would wink out of existence in front of me and be lost—

"Rose?"

I stepped as close as I dared, wanting to touch her, to bring her back to me. To hold her close again, but of course that was impossible now. I could only stare at her in the pitch blackness, my heart pounding as the shadows constricted around her fragile form.

Every muscle in my body was wound like a bowstring. I wasn't ready for her to go. Could I stop this from happening, turn back the clock somehow and buy us more time? An hour, a few minutes? Long enough to tell her...

You love her, you idiot. Not because of William, or the visions. You love her for who she is now, and for who she's making you become. You want her to stay around so you can see where it leads, only now it's too late...

I reached out to grab her hand, but my fingers passed through her. She recoiled, and the darkness retreated from around her, the bright moon emerging from behind the clouds, turning everything gold.

"Cleary?" She inhaled suddenly, as if returning from some distant place, her eyes locking on mine, the words leaving her in a rush. "I didn't hurt my baby. I never took her to the loch that night. It was him."

"Your father?"

She nodded. "His shoes were crusted in mud. Hard, flaky mud. Like it was drying there for hours." A tear streaked down her cheek, and she swiped it away. "He must have come into my room and taken Odette from the crib while I slept, and then returned later to splash the mud around."

"He knew you'd blame yourself."

"Yes. He knew I'd be so full of horror and self-loathing that nothing else would make sense—" Her lips trembled, tears pooling in her eyes. She turned her gaze upwards, blinking rapidly to hold back the flood. Slowly, her features softened and she let out a deep, shaking sigh. "I knew something was wrong when I woke up. I felt groggy. Confused. My tongue was furry and my head throbbed."

"He drugged you?"

Her eyes widened, and she laced her fingers in front of her, squeezing until the knuckles blanched.

"The piper grew medicinal herbs in his garden behind the cottage. Valerian among them. Old Malcolm liked to sip it before bed for his insomnia. After he died, it grew wild at the back of the cottage. Father could have easily added some to my bedtime tea."

The big ripe moon glowed brighter as the last clouds scattered, leaving a trail of stars in their wake.

"Rose, you know what this means …. don't you?"

She looked uncertain. "Please don't make me remember anymore. At least, not tonight. My poor heart can't take it."

"I'm not asking you to remember. I'm asking you to forget."

She frowned. "Forget?"

"If facing this last memory was your tethering event, you'd be gone by now."

"Oh."

Digging my fists into my pockets, I eased out a breath. "I think your own death was the trauma that trapped you here. You've buried it deep for a reason. It's the source of your anger, and possibly the source of your power, too. But once you face it and remember, then your tether will break."

"I thought that's what you wanted?"

I shook my head slowly, studying her face. The alluring contrast of the dark side with her mark, and the radiant glow of the other, her eyes sparkling. She appeared ethereal in the moon's golden light, with her delicate features and shimmering dress, her dark locks falling over her shoulders.

I swayed closer, the power of our bond consuming me like a tidal wave. "Everything's changed," I whispered. "I want you to forget the past. I should have listened to my instincts and trusted you, but I was scared. I let you down and I'm sorry."

She gazed back at me for the longest time, her eyes wide and luminous, then a tiny smiled tugged her lips.

"You were right to be wary. I'm not the most reliable person on the planet. Running off all the time. Attacking you with a gale of leaves. Screaming in your ear."

"Hey, no one's perfect, right?" I laughed softly, wanting so badly to kiss her, to hold her close, the way I'd done at the loch. "Besides, there's nothing to prove by remembering how you died. Not anymore. Whatever happened at the end, I know your intentions were good."

She looked up at me. "Is that enough, though? Maybe—" She swallowed, and her eyes darkened. "Maybe good intentions aren't enough."

"They are for me."

"My father said I was a monster. I always thought—"

"That he was right?" I clawed my fingers through my hair. If only I could comfort her without touch, but my repertoire was limited. I'd never wanted to comfort an entity before meeting Rose. Never needed to. All I had were words, and I feared they wouldn't be enough. "Your father forced you to wear a veil, Rose. He imprisoned you in your bedroom. He beat you and called you terrible names, insisting the outside world would hunt and kill you. Then he tried to murder your child. If anyone's the bloody monster, it's him."

She nodded, but her eyes stayed wary. "I still don't know what happened to Odette. Or to me. Or why we died on the same day."

"Could you live with not knowing?"

She stepped back, searching the shadows, as if her father was waiting there to pass judgement.

"I don't know."

"As long as you don't remember how you died, then your tether will remain intact." I inched closer until the chill of her skin touched the heat in mine. "Will you stay, Rose?"

The light returned to her eyes. "In the garden?"

"I mean stay with us. With me and Elsie." My heart thumped so hard it hurt my chest, but I knew this was right. Not just for me, but for my daughter as well. Rose was a perfect fit for us. We needed her. And she needed us. "We won't be a conventional family, but we can figure it out as we go along. What do you say?"

She searched my face with wide-eyed curiosity, her lips curling up in a shy smile. As her smile grew, tiny crescent moons reflected in her eyes, and she inhaled deeply.

"I've never felt part of a family before, Cleary. I wouldn't know how."

"It's easy." I laughed huskily. "We just hang out together and drive each other completely crazy for the rest of eternity."

She nodded, rolling her eyes a little. "You and I could manage that. Easily. Not so sure about Elsie. She doesn't drive me crazy at all."

"Oh, she will. She can be an incorrigible pest when she wants to be. But that's part of being a family, too. Accepting each other, flaws and all. Knowing the worst about them and loving them anyway."

"Was it like that with your family?" she asked softly.

I leaned in to see her face in the dark, inhaling the intoxicating scent of violets and crushed eucalyptus leaves.

"Yeah, we're a pretty accepting bunch. We still drive each

other nuts, though. But I'd do anything for my sisters and mum. Anything."

"Do you think they'd accept me?"

I hesitated. "Once my sisters get over the shock, then yes, I believe they would. With open arms."

"Your mum?"

"She might take a bit of convincing. But once she gets to know you, she'll come around."

"Even if I'm ..." She flicked her gaze down at herself and shrugged. "You know."

"An entity? I promise after five minutes they won't even notice."

"But they're hunters."

"My dad had this saying. 'True love means putting someone else's happiness before your own needs.' He lived by those words until the day he died. My sisters and mum and I live by them too. It's our family motto."

"Like how you put Elsie's happiness first?"

"Ahh." I shook my head. "Honestly, I haven't been the best dad. You opened my eyes to that. I've been carrying guilt since my own father died, and it's kept me constantly moving. But that's all changed. Did you know Elsie's dream is to find her forever home?"

Rose's eyes shone as she nodded. "She told me."

"Well, I think we've found our forever, Rose." I leaned in until our bodies were almost touching. Until I could feel the cold blaze of her skin against mine, and the icy puff of her breath on my lips. "It's here at Loch Ard ... with you. If you'll have us?"

"Cleary, I—"

A sound cut her off, a distant rumble, out of place in the quiet night. Like the revving of a car motor.

Rose stiffened. The dreamy look in her eyes vanished, replaced by a frown. As she glanced downhill towards the front gate, her hand came up and she clawed her hair forward over her mark.

"Rose, what's wrong?"

Then I heard it. Drunken yelling. Shouts and the screech of tyres as a vehicle roared up the mountain road towards us.

69
ROSALBA

Cleary changed before my eyes. No longer the big soft bear who had just revealed his inner self to me—but suddenly the hunter, his shoulders tightening and a glint in his eyes that sent shivers over my skin. He followed my gaze down the hill to where a dark mass of trees concealed the front gate.

"We've got visitors." He drew himself tall, his face creasing. "At this hour?"

"It's just kids. They've been here before."

"What do they want?"

"To ... blow off steam, I guess. They hear stories about me in town and come here to see firsthand."

"I'll fix it, Rose. Go back to the house and keep Elsie company. If she wakes up while they're making that racket, she'll be terrified."

"Be careful, Cleary. They might be armed."

He nodded, searching my face, then strode down the dirt track toward the gate. I ducked through the hedge and took a shortcut back towards the house.

Barely an hour ago, my heart was breaking, but now a glow spread through me, warming every inch of my soul. It was happening at last. One day soon, I would feel Cleary's arms wrapped around me again. I would melt under the intoxicating thrill of his lips crushing mine. We would picnic under the stars with Elsie, watching the fireflies. And yes, we'd probably drive each other crazy for the rest of eternity...

"Because that's what families do," I said softly, hurrying through the warm night. *True love means putting someone else's happiness before your own needs.* "I've never had a family motto before, but now—"

"Rose?" A small voice piped through the darkness. "Where are you?"

I whirled around. Torch light rippled across the trees surrounding the loch, and something, maybe a pebble, plopped loudly into the water.

"Elsie?"

When she didn't reply, I changed direction and hurried uphill again. She was supposed to be asleep in the house. Why was she at the loch? *Looking for you, of course.*

I started running up the slope towards the loch, leaping over the pathways to cut under low-hanging branches and weave between tree trunks and boulders. The scent of damp earth and pine needles assaulted me as I approached the water, my mind reeling back to that terrible moment long ago when I'd found another child in the shallows—

When I saw her, a cold sweat flushed over me. She was inching along the fallen trunk that spanned one side of the loch to the other, her arms outstretched as she navigated its mossy surface, agile as a monkey. Her flashlight jerked around in her hand, casting crazy ripples over the water.

"Elsie—"

She stopped, shadows carving her pixie face. Her cheeks shone with tears and her eyes were puffy, as if she'd been crying.

"Rose! I thought you left us."

"Please come back to shore."

Her arms swung out for balance as she peered back at me. Below her, the murky water resembled black glass, its bright wavelets catching the torch beam.

Elsie hiccupped a sob. "I woke up and Dad was gone. I got scared and came up here. Then I heard you arguing, but I couldn't find you. I thought he was going to send you away."

"Oh, sweetheart. I'm not going anywhere."

"You sounded really upset, Rose. So I came to the loch because it's where you always find me."

"Your dad and I needed to sort a few things out. I'm sorry we scared you."

"Dad said you were miserable. That we were cruel to keep you here, and he had to set you free."

"That's all changed, my love. I promise. Now hop off that log and I'll tell you some exciting news."

"Oh ... what? Tell me now!"

"I'm staying, Elsie. We're going to be a family. The three of us together, always."

Her eyes widened, and she let out a squeal. She quickly turned back, her torchlight making crazy patterns through the leaves as she nimbly scampered along the dead tree, her arms outstretched for balance. I breathed a sigh, my muscles unlocking—

The crack of rifle fire split the night like a thunderclap. Elsie cried out, and her foot shot out from under her. She slithered off the log, hitting the water with a splash, her scream cut short as the loch swallowed her.

I scrambled into the muddy shallows, my heart punching

my throat. The flashlight's beam flickered from beneath the rippling water, but there was no sign of Elsie.

When she didn't surface, I plunged into the black water after her. Flailing my limbs to propel myself under the log bridge, cursing my younger self for never learning to swim. I pushed past water weeds, deeper down into the murk, following the hazy light until I saw her. Bubbles erupted around her as she kicked and writhed, frantically kicking her legs as she tried to break free from the gnarled roots twined around her ankle.

There wasn't time to resurface and call for Cleary. If he'd reached the gate, he was at least ten minutes away. Elsie only had a minute or so before she'd start to drown.

She looked up and saw me, her eyes wide and frightened in the rippling torchlight. Her hair floated around her face, and tiny bubbles escaped from her mouth. I dived down and reached for her ankle, grasping at the fibrous roots to wrench them loose, but my fingers passed through them like mist.

I lunged towards her with outstretched arms, instinctively wanting to gather her against me so I could drag her free. She put her arms out to me, too, but my hands passed through her, as they had with the roots. *I can't touch her, can't help her. She's going to drown right in front of me. A real mother, a mother of flesh and blood, could save her. It's killing me that I can't—*

Unless ...

Unless I could harness enough of my elemental power to become physical. Not just for a heartbeat, or a few seconds. Long enough to drag Elsie free and get her to the surface. But that would burn through more energy than I knew how to muster.

A chill trickled into my bones. Maybe there was a way to harness that much energy. A way to become flesh and blood for long enough to save her. It would cost me everything I had, but without Elsie I'd have nothing, anyway. No family. No three of us together. No always.

Reaching out, I gently brushed my fingertips against Elsie's cheek, trying to convey all the love and comfort I could through a simple touch. Our eyes met, and I poured every ounce of reassurance into my gaze.

"I love you," I mouthed, and she gave a brief nod, her own lips trembling as tiny bubbles escaped.

With a deep breath, I closed my eyes and concentrated with all my might, conjuring the most painful memory of all.

70
ROSALBA

1917

Snow lay thick in the garden, glowing in the dawn light like a soft grey blanket. I had always loved it. Running through it, rolling snowballs. Eating it—the tang of ice on my tongue as a child, plucking frosty clumps straight from the branches and slurping them down as I grinned up at the winter-blue sky.

Now I feared it.

Go back to the house, it said. *Foolish girl, you are making a terrible mistake.*

Why did the snow sound like my father?

Ignoring it, I hurried towards the western trail. Loch Ard's vast garden had always been my playground, my sanctuary. The place I could escape into unseen. Now the tall trees and deep shadows sheltered me as I fled along the track, perhaps for the last time. My baby in one arm, wrapped in her lacy blanket, my bag in the other as I forced my feet to take one step, then another through the snow.

Already my shoes were sodden. My dress clung wetly to my legs. My feet were numb, the icy chill creeping into my bones. The gravel path soon ended and the way between the trees got steeper, harder to navigate as the shadows grew denser. A loose stone wobbled under my foot, and I tumbled sideways, hitting the ground on my knees.

A wail lifted from the bundle of blankets. It rose into the morning, gaining strength and climbing higher until it shattered the pearly sky.

I rocked Odette against me. "Quiet, love. Mama's here. Please, shush."

I held her tightly, quietly trembling, as I looked up and saw we were almost at the lightning tree. The sight of its powerful arms holding up the sky gave me strength. Getting to my feet, I grabbed my bag and stumbled on.

By the time we reached the tree, my arms ached from Odette's weight, and my legs shook so violently they seemed about to give way.

I sat on the big stump near the tree. Odette was still grizzling, so I unbuttoned my blouse and nursed her, keeping her face sheltered from the drifting snow with a corner of my shawl.

Soon she snuggled against me, fast asleep.

I should get to my feet and walk down to the gate. But the shock of finding her at the loch, and then comprehending what my father had done, had drained my spirit. Shivers rolled through me. My limbs trembled, and the gate seemed too far.

Some soup would warm me.

I took out the flask and poured the steaming liquid into the lid cup. It was warm and delicious, if slightly bitter from the greens floating in it. Perhaps a little too salty, which was strange because Father was never generous with the salt. I drank half the soup, keeping the rest for when I reached the town. I had saved a little money, stolen from my father's desk drawer, but it wouldn't go far.

I wiped out the lid and screwed it back onto the flask. The soup had warmed me, so why did I feel so strange? I got to my feet, but then sat quickly again, my head spinning. My limbs were rubbery, my stomach cramping. My tongue tingled. What was happening to me? I blinked, trying to clear the sudden haze from my eyes.

The soup ... was there something in the soup?

Had my father mistakenly used the wrong herbs...

Or perhaps intentionally?

The truth struck like a lightning bolt. My father had betrayed me. He had tried to kill my child, and now ... now...

I dropped the metal flask into the snow, kicking it away.

My father had poisoned me. He wanted me to die, knowing my child would die with me. He had stolen our future, everything we had hoped for. But really, why was I surprised? Hadn't he always stripped away my dignity and confidence with his beatings and mind games? Hadn't he called me a monster while inflicting his own monstrous punishments on me?

The veil lifted from my eyes, and my life's path unwound before me. The love denied. The guilt of surviving my birth while my mother died. The burden of polluting the world with my ugliness. Losing William to war and being forced to question his loyalty.

And now, the cruellest twist of all. My baby, the one precious person who loved me unconditionally and who I loved beyond reason, was slipping from my arms. She would die here in the snow beside me ... and after we were gone, my father would continue spreading lies about us, to make himself seem all the more pious and put-upon.

A dark energy knotted in my chest, shattering my faith in him and in all of humankind. My heart splintered like glass, leaving behind sharp fragments that pierced every inch of my being. From the wreckage sprang the monster my fourteen-year-old self had brought to life while kneeling on thorns in the stables. *You're a monster, Rosalba ... and no monster gets a happy ending.*

"You made sure of that, Father."

The air grew damper, a chill settling in. My teeth began to chatter uncontrollably, and each shiver sent a jolt of cold through my body. I couldn't seem to stop the violent tremors that spread from head to toe.

Dragging off my shawl, I wrapped it tightly around Odette and held her close. She was sleeping soundly. Her little face turned towards me, her lashes making dark half-moons on her cheeks.

If only William was here.

When I shut my eyes, he seemed nearby. His smile warming us, his love glowing like a beacon, calling us to him. When I opened them again, the snowy garden blurred around me and we were alone.

I tore the emerald ring off the chain around my neck.

Probing with my fingers, I pressed it into the folds of Odette's blanket, working it gently, tucking it against her warm little side. Praying for a miracle. For William to return in time to save her. He would understand the ring's significance and know that I had been here. Waiting for him. Thinking of him at the end. Remembering our promise to meet again on the other side of death.

My head nodded forward.

Odette began to slip from my arms. Rather than drop her, I slithered off the log and sat on the ground in the snow. Somehow, I was lying down, and the snow gathered me into its icy embrace. My eyes became heavy, and I gave up the struggle of keeping them open. Sleep was claiming me, and I couldn't fight it. Soon I would slide under its spell and everything I loved would be lost to me. If only I could stay here, under the protective arms of my tree. Stay until William found us. At least until I knew my baby was safe.

I drew my shawl up over our faces. *My body heat, my breath. Please, let them be enough to keep her alive for as long as possible. Perhaps someone will find us here, take pity on my baby and give her the life I cannot.* With the last of my strength, I tilted my head and pressed my frozen lips against her brow.

"Whatever happens, I'll watch over you, sweet girl. Always, I promise. And one day, we'll meet again in a far happier place than this."

71
CLEARY

NOW

As I jogged down the driveway towards the front gates, another shot rang across the night. I saw a white ute parked on the other side of the gates, and three teen boys laughing and bantering.

The kid who had fired the rifle stood like a gangly sentinel, puffed up and proud. The others stalked up to the gates, kicking the posts and jeering as if they were trying to attract someone's attention.

Well, they'd succeeded.

The one cradling the rifle wandered inside the gates and took aim at a tree, firing off two quick rounds.

"Hey!" I bellowed, charging towards them, my fists clenched, ready to do battle. "What the hell are you doing? This is private property!"

All three faces snapped around. The kid with the rifle recoiled, his face going slack. As he lowered the weapon, a shot rang out, shattering the silence and making all three of them jump.

I staggered sideways.

Taking another step, I sank onto one knee, feeling like I'd been punched the entire length of my body. A spot over my hip burned, as if a hot poker was drilling into me. I tried to stand, but my leg refused to do anything but tremble. A river of sticky blood gushed down my side, hot against my skin.

The boy who fired the shot lurched backwards. His face hollowed out and he started towards the ute, the others scrambling to follow him.

I got to my feet and loped towards them. My legs wobbled unsteadily, but a roar bellowed out of me. The biggest of the three boys flinched, and I locked my eyes on him.

"This ends now."

As I approached, they jostled into the car and started the motor. I wrenched open the driver's side door and dragged the kid from the seat. He wasn't the shooter, but he'd do. I gripped my fingers around his throat and shoved him hard against the car.

He let out a yelp. "Shit, man! What the—?"

"Shut up." I glared into the car, making eye contact with the other two. "Take a hard look at my face. I'm the crazy bastard who lives here now. If any of you idiots turn up here again, I'll skin you alive and hang you up to dry on those trees you were firing at. You get me?"

The boy I'd pinned against the car twitched, his eyes

bugging. I tightened my stranglehold on him to drive home my point. His face jerked up and down as he tried to nod. His fingers came up, and he started clawing at my hand.

Let go, you'll kill him.

Blood poured out of the wound in my side. I could feel it coursing down my hip in a hot stream, soaking into my jeans. My leg buckled, and I gave the guy a final, threatening shove.

"Bugger off home and warn your parents there's a lawsuit on the way. And stay the hell off my—"

A scream from somewhere behind me in the garden cut off my words. I unclamped my hand from the boy's throat and staggered backwards. The kid dived back into the vehicle and it roared to life, screeching away down the mountain road, its tyres skidding and churning up gravel.

"Rose—?"

The shout hadn't come from the house, but from somewhere deep in the garden. I turned around and hobbled up the steep driveway, my palm clamped against my side.

The house lay in darkness. Not even the glow of Elsie's night light shone from her window. Good. Elsie must have slept through it. As I turned to survey the vast, shadowy garden, a wave of lightheadedness washed over me. My mouth filled with saliva and my vision blurred. My leg went dead again, and I stumbled on the gravel. When had the night gotten so dark? I stopped to get my bearings, swaying unsteadily—

"Cleary!"

My body jolted to attention. Rose's cry echoed around me, rebounding from all sides. Adrenaline pumped through me, burning my veins like petrol.

"Rose! Where are you?"

My words echoed across the garden, but there was no response. I staggered uphill towards where the cry had come from, casting out my feelers, registering how weak they suddenly were. If only I could locate the small, cold pulse of her presence, I could find her, even in the pitch dark. But why couldn't I sense her?

Had she remembered something more, despite my warning? Had her tether broken? Was she already lost to me?

"Rose, hang on. I'll find you."

I ripped off my T-shirt and pressed it against the bleeding wound on my hip, limping up the track. Shadows flickered and retreated as I stumbled over rocks and tree roots, loose stones crunching under my boots.

The only thing guiding me now was the moon's golden light, urging me deeper into the silent darkness of the garden—and the hope that I would find her in time.

72
ROSALBA

Darkness splashed around me on all sides as moonlight speared through the tangled branches above. The icy loch water glistened like ink, tiny wavelets lapping my face, stinging my eyes as I paddled with one arm, fighting to keep Elsie's face above the water.

"Cleary!" I screamed again.

My voice tore into the night as I clutched Elsie against me. Praying her father would reach us before I returned to non-physical form and Elsie slithered back into the water.

Elsie's violent coughing only seemed to bring more water into her lungs. I could hear the gurgling sound as she gasped for breath, her body rigid with effort. She was trying to cry, but the air kept catching in her throat, her little lungs rattling as they struggled to breathe.

Kicking hard with my legs to keep our heads above water, I thumped my fist between her shoulder blades, trying to dislodge the water she was choking on. When she didn't respond, I thumped again. And again. At last, she started retching up big gulps of water. Even when she could breathe freely again, she seemed disoriented, thrashing against me.

"Elsie, it's okay." The calm in my voice hid the panicked racing of my heart, but she quickly responded to it. "Hold on to me, love. Can you do that?"

She lifted her thin arms and wound them around my neck, sobbing against me. But at least now I could focus on getting us to the bank. It seemed miles away. If I lost my grip on my physical form, and Elsie slipped out of my arms into the water, she might not have the strength to swim up again.

I had never stayed physical for this long, and I was holding it with surprising ease. But how long would it last?

"Hang on, Elsie." I pressed my lips to her cold forehead. "You'll be alright. He'll find us soon."

I held her tightly with one arm and thrashed the water with the other, kicking my legs as I aimed for the shallows. My progress was minimal. My legs were struggling now, twitching and cramping as my body grew more exhausted. The shore seemed impossibly far away. My fingertips tingled as the feeling drained out of my legs. I was growing weaker, my elemental energy ebbing away.

Elsie started sliding from my arms and back into the water. I gritted my teeth, and once again forced myself to remember my last moments under the lightning tree with Odette in my arms, picturing every heartbreaking detail.

Snow is falling harder, banking up against my body as I lie on the ground with Odette cradled against me. Her thin cries drift in the icy air, but I'm helpless to do anything. Whatever poison flows in my veins has numbed my limbs, slowed my lungs, turned my blood thinner than water. It's so cold, and I'm trying to pass all my remaining body warmth to her, to keep her alive as long as possible. The same words replay in my mind. Please, someone. Pass by this way and find her. But no one comes. My baby's going to die. And I'll die with her, praying to the emptiness and breathing her milky scent for the last time—

I moaned softly, my blood swelling in my veins, the energy rising through me like a dark tide. This was the last of my reserves, but it flowed through my limbs, a powerful surge that fed my waning elemental powers. My grip on Elsie tightened. I had lost one child, but so help me, I would not lose this one, too.

I strained every muscle in my body, flailing through the water until my foot finally hit something solid—thick, squishy mud. I planted my other foot and slowly gripped with my toes, inching my way forward until I could stand upright. The murky water swirled around me as I gained enough footing to progress more quickly.

Soon I was wading through the waist-deep water, gripping the shivering girl in my arms, almost at the shore.

"Cleary!"

My voice rasped through the dark, my pulse thumping in my ears like the echo of gunfire. Where was he? Lying hurt somewhere, unable to hear me? How much longer could I hold my physical body? My blood thundered in my ears, my cells vibrating unsteadily, the telltale prickling and numbness slowly returning to my fingers and toes.

Picking up pace, I pushed my legs harder through the sludgy water. Finally, the thick mud released my ankles, and I staggered across the shallows, collapsing onto the bank with Elsie in my arms.

Elsie's sobs shook her slight frame as I held her tightly, gasping for air and trying to calm my rapid breathing.

I stroked her wet face. "Are you all right?"

She nodded, tears mingling with the water dripping down her face. "I'm sorry, Rose. I didn't mean to fall in."

"Hush, love." I took her hand and pulled her close again. "As long as you're okay, that's all that matters."

She pulled back suddenly, her eyes wide. "I can feel you, Rose! How am I touching you right now?"

"I can harness my emotions like a power source. If they're strong enough, they can influence things around me. I can make it rain or bring on a fog. This time, I used it to manifest physically in your world."

Elsie coughed, wiping her mouth delicately on her wrist, her eyes huge and dark as they searched my face.

"How long will it last?"

"Not much longer."

I held up my trembling hand in the moonlight, already feeling the tingle of retreating energy. The airy ropes that bound me to this realm were starting to fray and unravel. Fine filaments, once strong as steel, were slowly eroding as all my old anger and fear drained away, and a feeling of calm flooded my being. *Soon*, my spirit whispered to me. Say your goodbyes, because ... *soon*.

Cleary burst through the trees, staggering towards us, his chest and belly gleaming slick and wet, his eyes glassy and crazed. His boots splashed through the shallows as he rushed over and gently took Elsie from my arms, crouching in front of her and examining her face.

"Are you hurt?"

"I'm okay, Dad. Rose saved me."

Cleary frowned over at me, hugging Elsie against him as she clung to him. The smell of blood radiated off his skin, so hot and metallic I could taste it on my lips. Moonlight caught a deep red stain on his side.

"You're bleeding," I whispered.

I inched closer, wanting to offer help, then withdrew my hand when he shook his head. His eyes shone in the dark and something passed between us, a silent understanding. He didn't want to frighten Elsie any more than she already was.

He pulled back and looked back at her, his face softening. "You were supposed to be asleep, kiddo."

"I heard you arguing with Rose, and I wanted to stop her from leaving."

Cleary rocked back on his heels. "And this is where she always finds you?"

Elsie nodded. "She dived under and pulled me out of the tree roots. I thought I was going to drown, but then—" She glanced down and gasped, staring at Cleary's waist. "Dad, you're hurt!"

"I'm okay. It looks worse than it is."

I leaned closer, my hair brushing against his arm, as I examined the wound in his side. "It looks deep."

"A stray bullet nicked me. Nothing a few stitches won't fix."

"Oh dear. And the boys?"

He dragged in a breath, his face pale in the darkness. "They won't be back anytime soon."

"You've lost a lot of blood," I said, resting my fingertips on his chest, feeling the crash of his pulse. "You need a doctor. And so does Elsie. She's taken in some water, she should be examined."

Cleary gathered Elsie against him again and pressed a kiss to her wet hair, looking over at me.

"I'll get us to the hospital ... but first I need to know you're okay, Rose. You would've burned through a lot of energy to do this. I don't understand, though. You're still here. Shouldn't you be restoring yourself right now?"

The tingling in my fingers grew more intense. I wriggled them absently as I studied the two people before me, committing every detail of their faces to memory. The life-force coursing through me was fading. Time was running out.

"I tapped into some potent emotions, Cleary. My energy's ebbing. We don't have long."

"What are you saying?"

"Elsie was drowning. Becoming physical was the only way I could save her. So I drew on my last hours with Odette. The day we both died."

Cleary shook his head. "Please tell me you didn't."

I nodded, tears streaming down my cheeks.

"I remembered everything, Cleary. Right up to my final breath."

His face twisted, his features tightening. "Your tether?"

"It's broken. My crossing has started."

"No ... no, Rose. This isn't happening."

I reached for his hand and squeezed it gently. "I had to confront that memory in order to save Elsie. I needed to tap into its power. And I'd do it again in a heartbeat."

He gazed around wildly, as if seeking a way out. Across the loch to the fallen tree. Up at the black sky where stars twinkled through the twisted branches over us. Finally, he looked at me, his warm fingers tightening around mine.

"What did you remember?"

I inhaled shakily and told him everything in a breathless rush. My father's odd behaviour, and me packing my bags, fleeing the house with Odette in my arms.

"It was the soup," I explained, my voice trembling. "My father poisoned it, and I stopped to rest under the lightning tree, where we used to wait for William. When I understood what was happening, I covered us with my shawl and held Odette tightly ... as she—" Tears streamed down my face, hot and salty, as I choked on a sob.

"Hey, come here."

Cleary gently grasped my hand and drew me over beside him, wrapping his arm around me. Elsie shuffled closer and rested her head against my shoulder. I shut my eyes, savouring their warmth, their solidness. I had a family, and it was everything I hoped it would be. Everything I'd dreamed. *Say your goodbyes, because soon...*

"Rose?" Cleary cupped my face in his palm, searching my eyes. "Can you fight it?"

I shook my head. "If only I could. I'd give anything to stay. I love you both so much, it kills me to leave."

"Leave?" Elsie's eyes widened. "You said you were staying. That we're going to be a family."

"I want to stay," I told her gently. "With all my heart. But it's just not possible now."

"You were real." Her little face twisted, tears welling. "You pulled me from the tree roots and held on to me so I wouldn't sink into the water again. Why do you have to go?"

"It's my time," I told her as tenderly as I could. "But don't be sad, my beautiful girl. I'll watch over you always, I promise. I'll watch over you both."

Cleary reached for me suddenly, drawing me closer and pressing his forehead to mine. The shock of contact was electric. I trembled against him, feeling the heat radiating from his bare skin as I tasted the sweetness of his lips and breathed in his familiar scent. My fingers dug into his shoulders as I clung to him, desperately trying to hold on to this moment that would have to last me forever. But then the lines between us began to blur. The warmth in my body retreated, making way for the cold. When a shiver rippled across Cleary's chest, I knew it had started.

My crossing.

If there was a way to re-tether myself, to be trapped here with the people I loved, even though it meant a lonely forever, I would cling to it with all my might.

But there wasn't.

It was time to say goodbye.

I pulled back with a sob. Elsie flung herself into my arms, and we held tight for a few precious moments. When she sank to her knees with a disappointed cry and began to weep inconsolably, I braced myself for what would come next.

73
CLEARY

MOONLIGHT PENETRATED THE THICK CANOPY, casting distorted shadows on us. The dense aroma of blood mingled with damp earth and pine filled my nostrils as I grappled for breath.

"Rose, don't leave."

Her eyes reflected the icy lunar glow, strands of hair falling over her face as she shook her head.

"It's time, Cleary. I'm ready."

Panic welled up as warm blood oozed out from my side, trickling through my fingers. This couldn't be goodbye. Not like this. Not yet. She might be ready, but how could I let her just slip away without trying?

"Pull yourself together, Rose. You've done it before." My words rasped in the night air. "Stay with us. Elsie needs you … I need you too. It took me a lifetime to find you. Now that I have, I can't bear to let you go."

Her lips trembled as she smiled.

"You'll be all right, Cleary. You'll find your happy ever after.

It just won't be with me."

A fist-sized knot tightened in my throat as I searched her face, hating that I was trying so hard to commit it to memory. I wanted to keep denying the truth, because I just couldn't face losing her. But as the moon rose higher, and shadows stretched and darkened around us, I knew she was right. *Once her tether is broken and she leaves, she can never come back.*

Elsie cuddled closer to me, her quiet sobs shaking her small frame. I held her protectively, gently stroking her hair, trying to comfort her, as my gaze fixed on Rose.

"I need to know you'll be all right, Rose. That wherever you are, you'll think of us from time to time. And know that we'll never stop thinking of you."

Rose looked up at the stars, shadows flitting over her face.

"William used to say that our souls live on after we die. That they keep cycling back, life after life, seeking the other half of themselves."

"You think William's soul is inside of me?"

When she looked back at me, her smile was full of longing. "I thought so at first. But you're not him, Cleary. You are your own person. I thought fate had finally brought us back together, but I was wrong."

"Instead, it's about to tear us apart."

"Yes."

Elsie let go of me and stared at Rose with wide eyes, a solitary tear clinging to her lashes. "Maybe you can find a way to come back to us?"

Rose sighed softly. "If only I could. I'd be back with you both in a flash."

Elsie blinked, and the tear splashed onto her cheek. "Promise you'll try?"

"I promise." Rose's face crumpled, tears falling even as she smiled. "Oh Elsie, I love you so very much. Remember that, sweet girl."

"I love you too, Rose."

Elsie started sobbing again and buried her face in her hands. I drew her against my good side and held her tightly. As the heavy crescent moon shifted between the branches, its glow became blinding. The trees cast long, ominous shadows that stretched towards Rose, as though trying to regain their hold on her. Her delicate features flickered, and I reached out to her.

"Rose?" A surge of grief gripped me—raw and unfamiliar, clawing its way up from a place that had lain dormant in me till now. She was fading like a valley mist dispersing in the sun. I knew what came next. I had seen it countless times, only now it was breaking me in two.

"Wherever you go next, remember you're part of a family now. A real family."

"I'll remember." Her words came faintly, as if already drifting from another world, but her eyes remained fiercely locked to mine. As she leaned in closer, the chill from her breath brushed my lips. "I promise."

"Hey, ghost girl," I whispered, swallowing hard as I drowned in her eyes for the last time. "I love you."

Her face crumpled into a luminous smile. She nodded, her lips quivering as tears spilled down her cheeks. They glistened like rain in the moonlight, but her smile only grew wider. And then, right before my eyes, she fluttered out of existence like a candle flame.

74
ROSALBA

A MOMENT ago it was night. Now the air shimmered with flakes of gold and silver. The sun was setting, casting a soft pink hue that sparkled above me like a veil of diamonds.

Cleary's words lingered in the twilight, already fading from my mind like a softly whispered promise from a long-ago dream.

Hey, ghost girl.

I braced myself for the wrenching pain of loss ... but instead I felt a sense of weightlessness. As my ties to the living world weakened, I grew lighter, and a new connection beckoned me from beyond. Perhaps the answers I had been searching for were not in this life, but waiting for me on the other side of death.

As I gazed around, my lips parted. "What is this place?"

It was Loch Ard, yet not as I'd ever seen it before.

I had wandered away from the loch and reached a gap in the fence, the grassy paddock on the other side teeming with butterflies. The surrounding garden seemed washed clean, its shadows clear and pure, its dark memories banished.

A breeze whispered through the treetops, lifting the syrupy perfume of the flowers, and fluttering the lacy ferns. Even the loch no longer scared me—it was just a body of water, giving life to the dragonflies and the frogs who inhabited its muddy hollows. A part of my past that was neither good nor bad, but simply a thread woven through time.

Rosebud...

I should go. The sun was calling to me. Not the sun, the light. The bright buttery-white light. It felt warm on my skin, and so very welcoming. I walked into the paddock, the tall grass tickling my legs as I approached the glowing sunbeams. But then I paused again. With only one stride to cross over, why was I hesitating?

"It's only a step, my Rosebud."

I gasped. Fresh tears stung my eyes. I knew that voice.

"William?"

He emerged from the brightness and stood before me, exactly as I remembered him. Young and broad as an oak, his blue eyes glowing in the sun, his smile as wide as the sky.

"I'm right here, Rose. I've always been here."

Dressed in a green shirt flecked with grass, his trousers rolled up to reveal tanned bare feet, exactly as I first saw him that day by the willow. I flew into his arms, yelping with joy. He crushed me against him, his strong embrace enfolding me. It felt so good to be held. Really held. Not just fleetingly, for a few precious, stolen moments, but truly held. For too long I'd been a creature of shadows, of mist. But now ... now I was—

I pulled back. "How is this possible? Am I alive again?"

"In a way, yes. A different kind of alive."

A laugh bubbled out of me. "I've no idea what that means, but as long as we're together again, I don't care. Just please tell me you're real?"

William's arms wrapped tightly around me. "I'm a hundred percent real, my love."

And so he was. Real and solid, a grounding force amid the chaos of my emotions. As I buried my face in his shoulder, the weight of my past life slowly slipped away, leaving behind only the warmth and brightness of my present.

Elsie and Cleary were unreachable, but they would always be a part of me, like branches on a tree that led back to a shared root. Our paths would cross again, just as streams eventually merge back into a mighty river. We were family now, and family endured.

William gently squeezed my fingers. "It's time, Rosebud. Are you ready?"

I smiled. Time was a curious thing, wasn't it? The way it slipped through your fingers like water droplets or falling leaves. Or quickening heartbeats. The way it made you believe there were no other moments than this one, but all the while twisting and turning, looping back and forth without end.

"I'm ready. But William?"

"Yes, love?"

"Now that I'm here, where shall we go?"

He linked his arm in mine and his eyes crinkled as he patted my hand. "Why Rose, we can go wherever your heart desires. We can do whatever will make you happiest."

I looked back over my shoulder towards the loch. The garden beyond our shimmering patch of sunlight was now shadowy, the sounds muted. I heard the faint sound of a young girl crying and a deep, soothing voice trying to comfort her. An overwhelming sense of longing swept over me. I searched William's eyes.

"I waited so long to find you again ... yet I feel our journey's not quite over."

His eyes locked onto mine, and his brow creased with what might have been regret.

"We can't go back to our old lives, if that's what you're thinking."

"Ah ... no, I suppose not."

"But we can go forward."

"Forward?" I shook my head, fearing I had misunderstood. "Oh, if only that was true! I know we can't change the past, but I want to make it right. I want to experience the love that we missed out on before. I want to hold our little girl in my arms and watch her grow up. I want us to be a family, William. Not just in this dreamlike place. But for real. My father used to say there'd be no happy ending for me. I want to prove him wrong."

William's dark pupils seemed to soften. "Anything's possible, Rosie girl. If you put your mind to it." He leaned in close, his muscular arm wrapping protectively around my waist as he pulled me against him again, his breath tickling my forehead as his lips brushed my skin. "We can start over. From the beginning. Create a new life for ourselves and fulfil the destiny we missed out on last time. What do you say, Rose. Will we take a chance on love?"

I pulled back, nodding, my pulse flying, my heart brimming over.

"Only this time, we'll take control of our story. We won't let anyone convince us otherwise. We'll claim our happy ever after, William. We'll spend the next lifetime together, just as we always planned. And this time around, we'll get it right."

75
ROWAN

NOW

Wake up, Rowan. My lashes fluttered and I blinked, breathing the cool air as my eyes adjusted to the faint rectangle of my bedroom window. My dream faded, leaving the impression of wide skirts swishing around my ankles and a heaviness leaving my body, as though I'd grown wings.

"Crazy woman." I rubbed my eyes, looking around. "Wings indeed."

The first thing to greet me was always my plants—potted ferns and fiddle leaf figs, a hundred varieties of peperomia—their pots arranged in neat rows along the groaning shelves. Usually my plants grounded me, but today everything felt …

extra. As though the light was clearer, and the air surrounding me faintly electrified. As if I'd woken up—not just from a good night's rest—but from thirty-plus years of sleepwalking through my life.

Weird.

Swinging out of bed, I shrugged into my dressing gown. My dream had been as vivid as always. The towering gum trees, the golden rays of sunlight filtering through the canopy. The giddy sense of homesickness creeping over me, like I needed to return there ... if only I knew where 'there' was. The dream always came to me on nights when I was most tired or feeling fragile. Ever since my gran died, really.

The voice from inside my dream lingered.

Wake up, Rowan ... it's time to start living.

Strange. Maybe I shouldn't have eaten all that curry last night. As I crossed my room and drew aside the curtains, a feeling of disorientation washed over me. My apartment was small and cramped, with limited natural light, but it all looked in order. *So why does it suddenly feel like I've emerged into a life I no longer recognise? Like something really important is missing?*

I pressed my forehead against the cold windowpane. Below me the city was coming to life, cars and vans whizzing by on Balaclava Road, their headlights cutting through the dawn as they dodged trams rushing towards their morning stops. It all felt familiar, yet strange. As if my dream was real and the city was an illusion.

My gran always said there was more to life than what we could see. Other layers of existence we could sense but not always interact with. Spirits and such, moving behind the veil that separated our world from theirs, and sometimes slipping through it to trespass amongst us. I never held much store for all that ... until right now. The dream I could barely remember seemed somehow more real and vital to me than the life I'd just woken into.

"Definitely something in that curry."

I showered and dressed, then stood in front of the mirror applying my usual layers. Sunscreen, concealer, setting powder, just like my actress mother had shown me all those years ago. Then I brewed coffee and drank it on the way to the tram stop.

Wake up ... it's time.

I sighed. Maybe this was the start of a mid-life crisis. In a few months, I'd be thirty-five. Most of my friends were married with kids and mortgages, well into living their best lives. My grandmother had taught me long ago not to bother comparing myself to others. After all, I was the one with the career everyone envied—production assistant with one of Australian television's hottest gardening shows. So why did I feel something was misplaced? As if I was a ghost, drifting through life, unable to find my anchor?

I felt for the slender gold chain around my neck, touching the smooth surface of my grandmother's emerald ring. It had been her prized possession, a family heirloom, all she had left of her own mother. As I closed my eyes and took a deep breath, I felt her calming presence wash over me. The ring was too small to wear on my finger, so I always kept it close to my heart. She had given it to me during her last days, and now it was my most cherished possession, too.

But as I climbed onto the tram and tapped my card, clinging to the handrail as we rattled off along the busy road, that feeling of disorientation washed over me again. Something had definitely shifted. The noisy traffic outside blurred past, while the flashes of sunlit trees from my dream called out to me.

Go and claim your happy ever after.

Crazy. It sounded like something Gran would say. But for

me, love and fairytale endings were just a fantasy. After countless rejections and disappointments, I had learned that love never came easily. Guys seemed keen enough at the start, acting offhand like nothing bothered them. After my makeup came off, they disappeared without a second glance.

I took out the book I'd been reading, hoping to get lost in it, but the tram abruptly stopped and my gum leaf bookmark fluttered to the gritty floor. A stream of people got off, trampling the poor leaf under their feet. As I stared down at it, Gran's words echoed in my mind. *True love is worth fighting for, Rowan. We all need to kiss a few frogs before finding our prince.* I shut my book with a bang. That was easy for Gran to say. She had married a wonderful man who adored her till the day he died. She found her prince, while most men I dated were cane toads.

"I'm done with kissing frogs, Gran," I muttered under my breath. "It's just not going to happen for me, okay?"

The tram jolted to a stop, and I stepped off onto the bustling street. My heels clacked against the footpath as I made my way down Swanston Street towards the towering network building, trying to clear my head for the upcoming production meeting. On the last day of filming our latest garden makeover, I couldn't afford distractions.

But as I pushed through the glass and steel doors into the foyer, the giddy feeling from my dream lingered, shooting goosebumps over my skin. *It's time to take control of your story, Rowan. You need to wake up...*

76
ROWAN

After the meeting, I hopped in a taxi and made my way to Lygon Street. The bustling streets faded away as I stepped through an iron gate and entered a small inner-city garden. In just a few days, the Digger's Delight team had transformed the neglected backyard into a private oasis. The once barren space was now filled with life—a paved area for entertaining, native trees in pots, and raised beds overflowing with vibrant succulents. Under the clear autumn sky, brightly hued lorikeets were squabbling over the sparse blooms of a newly planted bottlebrush tree.

I inhaled the cool air, filling my lungs. Morning was the highlight of my day, filled with potential. Like life was resetting itself, and all I needed to do was exhale the old to make space for the new—

"Rowan?" A man's voice cut through the babble of other voices behind me. "I need you over here, now."

Markus sounded irate, and I wasn't quite ready to take on that energy ... at least not yet. Shading my eyes from the bright

April sun, I watched the lorikeets lift into the sky and flap away. *How would it feel to have that kind of freedom, with no one dictating your actions or judging you, with no limitations holding you back?*

I tucked a strand of hair behind my ear. "Bloody wonderful, I expect."

Not that I could complain. I loved being a production assistant. Or at least I had—until recently. Working on Digger's used to bring me joy, but that had changed twelve months ago.

Across the garden, a blond man was barking instructions to the camera operator. Marcus Dolby had charmed us when he arrived from another network, and our ratings soared. But behind the scenes was a different story.

I walked over to a garden bed and collected the rake abandoned on the ground. My nostrils flared at the scent of newly laid earth, and it brought back the yearning I'd felt earlier. I tightened my grip on the rake handle, relishing its roughness on my palm. My grandmother's hands had been calloused from years of tending to her garden. She could grow anything, even in unlikely places. Her stories about a magical garden of snowflakes and ice had enchanted me as a child, and I still obsessed over it sometimes. Gran had been my best friend and mentor, gone for fifteen years, and I still missed her deeply.

On a whim, I began to rake the soil, breaking up clumps and smoothing it out. The crew was busy setting up the barbecue area, their voices a dull hum in the background. A drop of sweat trailed down my cheek. I resisted the urge to wipe it away, not wanting to ruin the layers of makeup I painstakingly applied only a few hours ago for work.

Gripping the rake, I moved it back and forth, the tines scooping up debris as I walked along, pebbles crunching beneath my heels. The warm autumn air filled my lungs, and I fell into a familiar rhythm, rekindling a connection with the earth that I'd lost in my busy years of city life. Ironically, my rented apartment had no garden, only a concrete courtyard with zero greenery.

As I lost myself in the tempo of my task, last night's dream drifted back, and another wave of longing washed over me. In my dream, I'd been racing barefoot through a vast, misty garden—

My feet pound the trail as I pass lush flowerbeds, fruit trees, and a shady lake. Through the gap in a bramble hedge, I glimpse a small gravestone, but keep going, trailing my fingers over the soft flower petals, over the rough bark and the prickly blackberry canes, moving silently between each shrub and daisy bed and tree, my bare feet barely touching the ground. "Wake up, Rowan," a man's voice whispers nearby. "It's time to claim our—"

"Dammit, Rowan. Didn't you hear me calling?"

I lurched to attention, dropping the rake like a hot potato and cursing softly under my breath.

Marcus stalked towards me, dodging wheelbarrows and bags of potting soil. His spiky fair hair caught the morning sun, his pale brows knotted. With his sharp jawline and piercing eyes, he'd once caught my attention. But learning who he was beneath that charming smile quickly deterred me. How could I have dated someone so shallow and mean-spirited?

He stopped in front of me, spreading his palms. "What's wrong with you?"

I dusted my hands on my trousers. "Just doing my job."

"You're not getting paid to flick dirt around. What part of production assistant don't you understand?"

I narrowed my eyes, standing tall, glaring down my nose at him. "I get all of it, Marcus. Especially workplace health and safety. Rakes shouldn't be left lying around, remember? You should mention that to the new presenter before someone gets hurt." My jaw clenched as I stared him down, hands on my hips and sunglasses perched on top of my head.

Marcus crawled his gaze over my cheek, and when I refused to back down, he glanced away.

"Today's the big reveal," he said slowly through his teeth, as if addressing a disobedient child. "The owners are arriving at eleven. I've just found out that the caterer bailed on us at the last minute. I need you to fix it."

I picked up the rake, meeting his glare with one of my own, and stalked off, muttering under my breath.

"So much for the promising new day. Thanks, idiot."

Was this my future? Every day walking on eggshells around my toxic boss's volcanic temper and enduring his demeaning treatment? He was punishing me for his bruised ego. I got that. But did I really want to spend my professional life with a boss who diminished and showed no respect towards me? *Think of the job, Rowan. How hard you worked to get it. What you've sacrificed along the way.* It was true. This job meant everything to me. It was the hub my life revolved around. I had no family, not even a cat. Or goldfish. This was it for me. I was one of those women who'd chosen a career over everything else, and I would not let that annoying sleazebag derail me.

"Maybe that's what my dream was trying to tell me. I need to wake up and take control of my story."

I hooked my finger under the delicate chain around my neck, calming myself with the comforting weight of Gran's emerald. *Think how proud Gran would have been seeing you on national television. What if she's watching from the afterlife, cheering you on?* A soft blanket of calm settled over me as her voice echoed in my mind. *This is your dream job, Rowan. Don't let anyone ruin it for you.*

The rest of the day flew by in a blur of phone calls, set preparation, ferrying the owners from the airport, a last-minute trip to Bunnings to replace a malfunctioning water feature, and finally the grand reveal that went predictably well.

After the film crew finished packing their equipment into the vans, I took a breather to look around. Once again, the Digger's Delight team had outdone themselves. A new barbecue stood proudly on the paved space, with large lounge chairs surrounding it. Potted grevilleas framed the area, their yellow flower spikes drooping earthwards. Mounds of freshly dug earth sat on the sidelines like small forgotten graves.

I shivered as a gust of something cold prickled over me. Weird. Why was I thinking about graves? Memories of my dream resurfaced, bringing back the homesick feeling. I had dreamed of a gravestone in the shadows, and pathways winding past a small shady lake, and blackberry vines growing rampant through the flowerbeds—

"Rowan?"

I whipped around. Marcus was on the warpath again, judging by his frown. He jogged over and cornered me. His dark grey pants and T-shirt contrasted starkly with the bright bed of mixed perennials we had spent the week planting—and his scowl made my mood sink lower.

I sighed. "What's up, Marcus?"

He shook his head. "You were a million miles away. Again. Didn't you see me gesturing? That new presenter rambled on forever. It was embarrassing. Not to mention getting all his facts wrong. What a nightmare."

"Then give *me* a chance. I'm a certified landscaper with an outstanding track record. I could design the garden, as well as present the segment—"

He pulled back, aghast. "What, you in front of the camera?"

I held his gaze. "That's what a presenter does."

"Jeez, Rowan." He sighed through his teeth, checking his clipboard. "Still harping on this, are we? You'll get a segment when I think you're ready for one."

"And when will that be, Marcus?"

"When you pay attention to what I say, instead of doing your own thing."

"But—"

His phone rang. He showed me his palm and walked off.

I glared after him. Our friction wasn't just about work. I should never have agreed to date him. I'd known after the first boring dinner that he was all wrong for me. Just totally ... wrong. Definitely a cane toad. Besides, he had joked about doing me a favour by inviting me out. When he pressed for a second date, I blankly refused. The shock on his face had given him away. *How can someone like you refuse a babe magnet like me? Most women would kill for the chance—*

Well, I wasn't most women. Lifting my hand, I patted the backs of my fingers over my cheek. My skin felt hot, vaguely sticky from the layers of sunscreen and thick makeup.

"Go to hell, Marcus. I don't need your approval. Or your pity."

Although I did need the job, and the promised promotion he'd been dangling over me for the past year. But my doubts lingered. *Am I truly satisfied working for Digger's Delight? Shouldn't I use my inheritance from Gran to pursue my childhood dream of owning a landscaping business?* As the smell of crushed gum leaves enveloped me, I hugged myself tightly, longing to get back to my roots and nurture a garden with my own hands.

I'd spent my happiest moments in Gran's wonderful rose garden in Prahran, learning from her and sharing a sense of purpose with her. Gardening wasn't just a hobby for us, it was a way to make the world better. After she passed away, I found myself gravitating to television, probably to impress my mother. Mum had starred in a TV soap since she was sixteen and was hugely successful. Yet underneath my drive to impress her was a yearning to find my way back to Gran and her strong values through gardening. I wanted to feel connected again—not just to the earth, but to Gran as well. And to myself.

I looked across the newly created terrace and sighed. I'd been so swept up in working for Digger's that I'd lost sight of my old plans. Maybe it was time to revive them? All I needed was one happy customer to get started. What was holding me back?

Marcus's voice drifted from the new pergola. He was still on his phone, barking orders. His words were unclear, but his irritable tone was familiar. He had used it on me a few months back—right after I refused to sleep with him. *You owe me, Rowan. Remember who helped you climb the ladder, you ungrateful bitch. I'll ruin you. Whatever you try to do, I'll be right there behind you, making sure you fail.*

It wasn't only Marcus, though. He was just the current voice of my lifelong insecurity, reminding me how far I had to fall if my dreams crashed and burned. If only I could break the pattern somehow. At the ripe old age of thirty-five, it felt well and truly ingrained.

I tipped back my head and gazed up at the sky, picturing my grandmother's face—a perfect mirror image of my own—smiling down at me.

"Hey, Gran? I need a sign. A really obvious one I can't miss, preferably with glitter. Help me out, would you?"

77
CLEARY

In the months following Rose's untethering, the garden returned to the wilderness it had been before we arrived.

As the winter chill descended, a thick blanket of mist clung to the mountain like a ghostly veil. The flowerbeds were overrun with tangled blackberry bushes, their bare prickly canes dominating the landscape like gnarled bones.

I had been inactive while the bullet wound in my side knitted back together. But even after it healed, I continued avoiding the garden. It felt empty to me now. Empty and dejected.

Some days I stood at the window, searching the tree shadows for a flicker of movement, hoping to glimpse a willowy figure with wild dark hair. Other days—the bleakest ones—I convinced myself Rose had never existed beyond my warped imagination.

A light snow fell in mid-July, and in August a gale wind sent leaves flying in wild gusts that drew me back again to the window.

Still I couldn't venture out. The lavender had wilted, and the once lush flowerbeds were dry and thirsty for water. Even the tallest trees seemed ragged and unloved. As if the garden's spark had gone out.

I pulled the curtains shut and sat in front of the television, although I had no intention of turning it on. Beer cans littered the coffee table, and as I stared at the blank screen, the familiar ache descended on me. *I hope you found peace, Rose. You, of all people, deserve it. But God help me, this place is desolate without you.*

My renovation work around the house had stalled, and even simple tasks like ironing Elsie's school uniform or keeping up with the washing felt like climbing a mountain. I mowed the lawn sometimes to keep the snakes away, but that was all. I needed to snap out of it, but no matter how I berated myself, the weight of my grief held me down.

When Elsie arrived home from the school bus, she found me still in the same spot. She said nothing, but joined me on the couch. We ate takeaway while watching her favourite garden makeover show, Digger's Delight. In the past it had always cheered her up, but lately, neither of us smiled much. We simply ate silently, watching the transformation unfold as if gardening was the furthermost thing from our minds.

One afternoon, I paused in the doorway.

The late sunlight cast a golden glow over the dining table with its colourful mismatched chairs. Elsie sat bowed forward, her hair falling over her face. Since Rose left us all those months ago, Elsie had grown her hair past her shoulders and seemed to take solace in hiding behind the messy strands.

"Want me to brush it for you, kiddo?"

"Nah, I'm good." Her fingers were deftly scrawling her gel pen over a sheet of fancy pink writing paper, a birthday present from her gran. She paused as I stepped into the room, lowering her head so her hair obscured her work.

I wandered over. "Watcha doin'?"

She bent closer over her page, shielding it from view with her arm.

"Writing a letter."

My lips twitched into a smile. "Since when do you write letters?"

"Since now." She sat up straighter and adjusted her glasses—another development in the last few months.

"You're writing to your gran?"

"Nope."

"Who, then?"

She shook her head. "It's a secret."

I raised an eyebrow and tried to peek over her shoulder, but she tipped her head forward and let her hair fall over her face again. I hated seeing her mimic Rose's habit of hiding behind her hair, but if it helped to heal the ache in her heart, then who was I to stop her?

I leaned against the kitchen counter, watching her.

"Alright, kiddo," I murmured. "Keep your secret, then. Remember, I'm here for you if you ever need to talk."

"I'm okay, Dad."

The sadness in her voice broke my heart. I could see it in her eyes, too, mirroring the desolation that had lingered with me since Rose vanished from our lives. I wanted to protect Elsie from the darkness that was consuming us, but I couldn't shield her forever.

Despite Rose's promise, I knew she could never find her way back to us.

At the kitchen bench, I began preparing dinner, pulling out salad and ham from the fridge and assembling sandwiches. In all the years I'd been a hunter, I had never seen anyone return from the afterlife. Or ever wanted them to … until now. But once a being's connection to our world was severed, they couldn't come back. And no amount of wishing or hoping was going to change that.

Later, as I tucked Elsie into bed, she looked up at me with teary eyes.

"Dad?"

"Hey, kiddo … what's up?"

Her lip trembled as she tugged her pyjamas sleeves down over her hands. "Remember when we talked about being rolling stones and always moving on?"

"Hmm."

"I guess it's time, isn't it? Now that we've done our job here."

My throat tightened. We were going to break ties. With the garden. And with our memories of Rose. I wasn't entirely sure I was ready. I may have come to terms with the finality of losing Rose, but that didn't mean I was finished wallowing. If Elsie had moved on, though, it was a good thing … wasn't it? I sat back, stretching my legs so I could stare at my boots.

"You want to leave Loch Ard?"

She sighed dejectedly. "A rolling stone gathers no moss."

"Right."

"Trouble is … I still really like moss."

"Yeah." I sent her a sly glance and winked. "It's kinda growing on me, too."

She rolled her eyes, sitting up to punch the lumps out of her pillow. "Moss bogs you down, Dad. You end up stalagnating, remember?"

"Stagnating? Yeah …" I did remember. My fear of getting stuck, having to face the things I hated about myself. The things

I regretted. But Rose had taught me the importance of a family motto. I'd given ours enough lip service over the years, but it wasn't until I met Rose that I properly understood it. *True love means putting someone else's happiness before your own needs.*

I picked up my daughter's teddy bear, her best-loved one with the missing eye and torn ear. Tucking it gently into the bed next to her, I smiled.

"Maybe it's time we stopped chasing after something that was never meant to be caught. How about we settle down and gather some moss instead?"

Elsie looked up into my face, surprised. "Really, Dad?"

I shrugged, gazing around at the room with its fairy lights and high white ceiling. Elsie's book piles and her reading tent, and the cheery curtains my mum had sewed for her.

Elsie had made this room into her own quirky sanctuary, with feathers and pinecones and leaves she collected in the garden. A garland of clay hearts like the ones she'd made for Rose hung across one wall. It made me remember what Rose had said the afternoon we picnicked above the cottage. *Deep down, you believe you don't deserve a stable, settled life. And maybe you don't need one. But Cleary, your daughter does.*

The heavy weight I'd barely registered I'd been carrying lifted off my shoulders and fell away. I looked back at Elsie.

"This place seems as good as any."

"We can stay?" Her voice quivered. "At Loch Ard?"

"Forever, if you want."

"Oh Daddy, I'd love that!" Scrambling up, she threw herself into my arms and clung tightly.

As I pressed a kiss to her warm hair, relief washed over me. We would stay and create new memories in this place we both loved. And if Rose continued to haunt me, then so be it. Elsie and I had each other, and that was all that mattered.

78
ROWAN

The icy Melbourne winter had finally loosened its grip on the city. It was now September, and the first signs of spring had arrived. Despite the lingering chill in the air, the blooming flowers and chirping birds brought a sense of renewal.

As I entered the network meeting room, the pungent mix of lemon furniture polish and sticky pastries wafted around me. Team members sat around a long table, chatting as they shuffled papers and stirred cream into their coffee. I took my place at the table, sipping my hot chocolate, waiting for Marcus to finish his call. We were meeting to discuss projects for the following season, and a pile of printouts sat in the middle of the table. Mostly emails from people requesting garden makeovers. A few letters. One caught my eye instantly. The envelope was hot pink ... and was that *glitter*?

I plucked it off the pile and tore it open, wondering if this could be the sign I'd asked Gran for all those months ago. Large, neat handwriting scrawled across the letter, and the border of vibrant, sparkly flowers made me smile.

Marcus pocketed his phone and looked over. "What've you got there, Rowan?"

"Hmm. Could be good. It's a huge historical garden up in the mountains, an hour north of here. Grieving single dad. Cute kid. What do you think?"

His jaw worked. "How do you know the kid's cute?"

I raised the letter, unable to contain my grin. "Glittery flowers?"

Marcus suppressed an eye-roll. "Not likely."

"Let me read it out. I think our viewers will like it." I smoothed the paper on the table. "Dear Digger's, I'm not allowed to watch much telly. Dad says it'll turn me into a zombie. He only lets me have an hour, and I use it to watch your show. I like how everyone gets so happy when they see what you've done to their yard. Ours is probably too big for your team. It's really old with tall trees. A god awful mess, Dad calls it. There are fireflies and a loch. Even an orchard! It's super cool. I reckon if you came here and saw it for yourself, you'd really like it. You might want to put it on your show. I hope so. Dad's sad all the time lately. We lost someone we loved, and a new garden would cheer him up. Love from your biggest fan, Elsie."

Marcus snorted. "What else have we got?"

I waved the letter. "What's wrong with this one? It's adorable."

"Kids surprising their parents—it's old news. We've already done two this season. To be honest, I've had a gut-full of heart-broken single parents."

Was it my imagination, or did the glare he gave me hold some sort of subtext?

"Besides," he went on, "we don't do extensive gardens. Quarter-acre lots are the max for us. Compact backyards we can knock over in a couple of days." Reaching across the table, he plucked the letter from my grasp and crumpled it into a ball, hurling it at the bin. It bounced off the rim and landed under a nearby chair. Gripping the table's edge, he looked around at us expectantly.

"What's next?"

Later, after they'd all gone, I lingered at the table, making a production of sorting my briefcase. My gaze kept darting towards the girl's crumpled up letter on the floor.

The garden she described—fireflies and an orchard—sounded like a slice of paradise I needed to know more about. Marcus was right, though. A brooding single dad wasn't anything special—at least not for us. Every week, we chose an ordinary family down on their luck. We sent them away for the weekend and made over their garden. It was good solid TV, but we needed more big-impact stories with lots of drama that attracted high ratings. We all knew Marcus was the high priest of ratings, worshipped in the industry. His word was gospel because he knew his stuff.

As I walked across the sleek, glass-walled meeting room, I glimpsed my reflection in one of the floor-to-ceiling mirrors. Makeup caked my face, the layers of concealer and powder making it look shiny and mask-like. I hated having to wear so much make-up. In the cutthroat world of television, even behind-the-scenes appearances mattered. It was all about projecting an image. If you didn't conform, you were out.

How had Marcus phrased it on my first day? *We have certain standards to uphold, Rowan. I'm sure you won't mind doing whatever you can to blend in.*

Standards, huh. Where were his standards? Six months ago he'd promised me a hands-on role in the show, even offering tips for presenting myself on camera. It was only later, after my refusal to jump into bed with him, that he'd changed his tune.

I walked over and stared down at the crumpled letter.

Just seeing the pink paper made me smile, remembering my own childhood love for all things pink. But it wasn't just the paper that drew me in. The way Elsie described her garden, with its rambling mysteries and tall trees, transported me back to the magical, ice-spangled landscape from my grandmother's stories.

Elsie's garden seemed magical, too.

I picked up the crumpled letter and smoothed the creases, then tucked it into my bag. It didn't deserve to be swept up with the rubbish. The least I could do was write Elsie back a reply. Was it the sign I'd been hoping for? The really obvious sign I couldn't miss? It was glittery, after all. And pink.

My smile widened. "Thanks, Gran."

As I approached the door to the meeting room, indistinct words floated towards me from the hallway. Marcus's low voice blended with a high-pitched whisper I assumed belonged to the new presenter. I hesitated, unsure if I should interrupt their conversation. Before I could decide, Marcus continued speaking in his hushed tone.

"Don't worry, Rick. I've got your back, mate. There's no way I'm putting her in front of the camera." He let out a smug chuckle, clearly pleased with himself. "We can't have a face like that scaring off viewers, now can we?"

I froze as his words sank in. Tears sprang into my eyes, but I dashed them away and stood tall, shoving through the door so hard that it struck the wall with a clatter. Both men turned, and Marcus's smile fell away. His eyes widened. For the first time since I'd known him, he seemed at a loss for words.

I didn't have the same problem.

"Beauty isn't everything, Marcus," I said calmly. "It's what's inside a person that really matters. I know this job inside out, and would have made a great presenter. If you'd bothered to give me a chance."

"For goodness sake, Rowan. Why are you still lurking around, eavesdropping? I thought you'd gone home to your sad little life an hour ago."

"Actually, I'm handing in my notice."

My jaw clenched. I hadn't meant to say that. The words tumbled out before I could stop them, and instantly I wanted to suck them back in. But I squared my shoulders, keeping my gaze firmly fixed on Marcus, suddenly not caring what he thought. "As of now. I can't work in a place where I'm constantly belittled and judged based on my appearance. I'll be lodging a complaint about you to the network. Then I'm branching out on my own."

"You won't make it."

"Just watch me."

He seemed taken aback by my sudden boldness, but then his face hardened. "Fine," he said coldly. "But you'll regret this. Don't come crawling back when your little side project fails."

"Oh, I won't be back. My only regret is not escaping your toxic presence sooner."

Leaving them both gaping after me, I stalked along the hallway and out into the fresh air, feeling lighter—and far more terrified—than I ever had before.

79
ROWAN

Two hours north of Melbourne, I drove into the leafy main street of Woodhill, a tiny boutique village nestled beside a river at the foot of a small mountain range.

Wide streets took me past a clock tower and quaint shops that whispered of bygone times. As I turned off the main street and drove beyond the town, the landscape transformed into lush green farmland.

The air was crisp with the scent of eucalyptus as I continued up into the hills, along a rugged dirt road that led up through thick bushland. Winding down my windows, I breathed in the eucalyptus-scented air.

The closer I got to the mountain, the faster my heart raced and the sweatier my palms became around the steering wheel. Quitting a stable job to pursue my passions—what was I thinking? As someone who had always valued stability and shrank from unnecessary risks, I should have been shaking in my boots. Instead, a whirlwind of excitement and freedom was sweeping through me. If only Gran could see me now. What would she say?

It's time to take control and claim your happy ever after.

Maybe there would be happiness in my future. Digging in the soil, planting things and watching them grow. Hauling around patio chairs and constructing worm farms and raised veggie beds. Best of all, being my own boss and finally doing what I most loved.

The road narrowed, meandering higher into the hills. When a white gate appeared up ahead, I pulled over. As I cut the motor, a blanket of tranquility settled over me, broken only by the call of a kookaburra, and somewhere in the distance, a droning lawn mower.

Pulling over, I checked the address on Elsie's letter.

It was early on Saturday, the morning sunlight peeking through the trees. I had worn my lucky green dress and black Funkis clogs—not the most garden-friendly attire, but it was a winning combo that always gave me a confidence boost. Fake it till you make it, right? That was what I told myself as I stepped out onto the gravel verge and locked my car.

Meeting new people always made me nervous, but after getting past the initial awkwardness, it usually went smoothly. There was a lot riding on today—an alternative career path, my reputation—but I had a good feeling about it.

Taking a deep breath, I smoothed my hands over the soft denim of my jacket.

"Okay, let's do this."

My clogs crunched on the gravel as I walked through the open gates. Passing under a peeling, hand painted property sign —LOCH ARD—I strode up the driveway towards a beautiful old sandstone house. Sunlight poked through the leaves of a stunning paperbark cherry tree, and the scent of cypress pine mingled with the tang of newly mown grass. As I approached the house, weedy beds of pink and white native daisies greeted me. Further up the hill, tangled blackberry vines and gorse ran rampant.

I smiled. It was like stepping into a fairytale, or back in time to my grandmother's garden, with her stories of delicate snowflakes and glittering icicles. And then there was the house itself, standing tall and elegant amidst the chaos of nature. It reminded me of Sleeping Beauty, hidden away from the world by layers of vines and thorns. Only I was the one waking up, rubbing my eyes. Coming to terms with my new reality. The scent of blooming flowers, freshly cut grass, and chirping birds engulfed me as I hurried along the path. The crisp spring breeze danced around my skin, sending goosebumps skating over my arms. The thought of transforming this untamed garden into a stunning oasis filled my spirit so fully I could barely hold back a little squeal.

Bypassing the house, I followed the sound of voices, making my way through more weed-choked flowerbeds. Withered dahlias nodded from their dry stalks, crying out to be pruned, while native sarsaparilla escaped into the trees. The garden was calling to me, and I couldn't wait to get started.

"I'll get to you soon," I whispered. "I just need to convince the owner to give me the job."

The scent of fresh cut grass swam around me, and I spotted a large barn behind the house. A man stood in front of it, his back to me as he raked grass clippings into a pile. Intricate tattoos peeked out from under the sleeves of his T-shirt, accentuating his muscular arms.

As the sun beat down, my skin prickled in protest and a thin layer of sweat formed on my forehead. With a deep breath, I approached him.

"Hello there."

He turned towards me, his intense blue eyes meeting mine.

I gave a little wave. "I'm Rowan Kowalski ... from Digger's Delight? I've been trying to call, but your phone was out of range. I hope it's okay, just showing up like this?"

He dropped the rake and stepped towards me, frowning. "Rose?"

"Um no, it's Rowan." I ventured closer, my heart sinking. "Elsie wrote and said you might be up for a garden overhaul. I'm not with Digger's anymore. I've branched out alone. But I'd like to offer you a free consultation, in exchange for before and after photos I can post on my new website ..."

He kept staring, completely immobile.

I lifted my chin. So much for my first successful solo venture. It was cursed before it began. Doomed by a clueless man staring at my face like a fool in headlights. My jaw clenched as I fought the urge to march up and slap that dumbstruck look off his handsome face.

"Never mind." I turned to go.

"Hey, wait. Rowan—?"

When I glanced back, he gave an awkward little wave of his own. His eyes were wide and somehow haunted as they searched my face, roaming every inch as if unable to believe what he was seeing.

I pressed my knuckles gently against my cheek. The skin was warm and sticky from my sunscreen and thick concealer. Not that it hid much in the bright sunlight. My cheek must be glowing like a beacon. My heart shrivelled smaller than the dahlias as Marcus's words echoed back to me. *We can't have a face like that scaring off viewers, can we?* But rather than my usual defeat, a stab of anger made me straighten my shoulders and glare back at this rude man.

"I've got another birthmark on my arse if you'd like to gawk at that one, too?"

His lips parted, and a hungry look flitted into his eyes. Then he seemed to catch himself, raking shaky fingers through his hair.

"Ah God, no. I'm sorry. It's just that you're so—"

So *what*, familiar? Because seeing him now at close range made me wonder the same thing.

I glared at him. "Have we met before?"

His jaw dropped open, but before he could reply, a bicycle bell rang shrilly and a girl of about nine rode out from behind the barn. She wore denim shorts with embroidered flowers, and her dark hair had escaped its ponytail and hung over her face.

When she saw me, she skidded to a stop. Frowning, she tucked her hair behind her ear, and then her jaw just about hit her chest. Scrambling off the bike, she let it crash into the dirt and raced towards us. With a yell, she flung herself into my arms.

"Rose!" she cried. "You came back, like you promised! How did you ... what—?"

"Whoa, there." I caught her in a hug and then untangled myself. "I'm Rowan Kowalski, from Digger's Delight ... you must be Elsie? You wrote me a letter, right?" I pulled the pink sheet of paper from my jacket pocket and flapped it like a peace offering.

"Rowan?" Elsie slumped. "But you look like Rose. And sound like her, too."

The devastation on her face took me off guard. "Ah, sweetie. Was Rose your mum?"

She went still, her cheeks flushing. "I wanted her to be."

"I'm sorry. You must miss her."

The girl nodded, her eyes like saucers. "But you're exactly like her."

"Your Rose sounds like an amazing person," I said, trying to lighten the mood.

They both stared. Neither of them so much as cracking a smile.

I sighed inwardly. Hiding behind the scenes, like I'd done at Digger's for the past fifteen years, kept me safe from confrontations like this one. It wasn't the first time my face had stopped someone in their tracks. Sadly, it wouldn't be the last.

"I can see it's not a good time." Adjusting my bag over my shoulder, I rumpled the letter back into my pocket and walked away.

"Wait." The man caught up with me. "I'm sorry. We didn't mean to be rude. We're just in shock. My daughter's right. You look exactly like someone we lost recently. She was special to us both. We didn't intend to make you feel unwelcome. You said Elsie wrote to you?"

"It was a surprise," Elsie chimed in.

Judging by her wide eyes, she was the surprised one.

The man offered his hand, and I shook it, registering his warm skin and rough callouses. He was trying to smile, but the gleam in his eyes made it seem like he was coming undone.

"Why don't you stay a minute, Rowan? We can show you around. You've come a long way. At least let me get you a lemonade."

Up close, his eyes were a stormy winter-sky blue. There was grass in his hair and sweat marks on his shirt. A glittery pink hair band circled his wrist.

"I don't know." I sighed. "To be honest, I'm not even sure why I came here. A hunch, I suppose. I was looking for a sign and after reading Elsie's letter, I thought I'd found it. Now I think coming here was a bad idea."

Small fingers closed around my hand.

Elsie was gazing into my face with such yearning that it stole my breath. Her pixie face was rosy pink, and huge tears welled in her eyes, splashing down her freckled cheeks.

"Rowan?"

My heart went out to her, and I slumped. She had one blue eye identical to her father's, while the other iris was pale grey-green … the same hue as mine.

I swallowed the sudden lump in my throat. "Yeah?"

"Rose really was the coolest. Would you like to see her cottage?"

I hesitated. Probably I should walk away now, strike the whole encounter down to experience. The last thing I needed was a weird entanglement with a sweet young girl and her grieving dad. I gazed up the hill to where Elsie had pointed. A steep terracotta tiled roof peeped between the trees, looking like something from a fairytale. I pictured Sleeping Beauty curled in a tiny comfy bed, surrounded by dust and dried flowers … and a little wooden cot with peeling paint and cobwebs between the rungs—

I frowned, shaking off the random image.

"It does look intriguing. Maybe just a quick peek." Then I could escape back to the city and forget Loch Ard had ever existed.

80

ROWAN

I FOLLOWED Cleary and Elsie up a wide gravel path to a charming cottage.

Ivy climbed its stone walls, and butter-yellow curtains adorned the windows, the rustic front door begging me to open it and peek inside. A few minutes ago, I'd been planning to leave as quickly as possible, escaping back to the predictability of city life, where everything was familiar and within my control. But as Cleary ushered me up the steps, my pulse quickened. It was all so familiar. Had I been here before?

"Oh, my ... how divine."

Cleary gestured at the door. "In you go, it's not locked." Then he stood aside with his arms crossed tightly over his chest, his gaze turned away as though distracted by the deep shadows congregating under the cypress hedge.

I pushed open the weathered door and stepped inside. Antique furniture filled the living room, and a beautiful old stone fireplace featured on the back wall. The rear of the cottage held a restored kitchenette, opposite a newly renovated bathroom with clawfoot bath and pedestal vanity, a large vintage mirror taking up most of the wall.

At the end of a narrow hallway, I stumbled upon a small bedroom. A single bed stood in front of a window, where a little ceramic heart dangled from the latch. Sunlight streamed through the panes, falling on an antique wooden cot pushed into the corner.

Frowning, I went over, goosebumps racing over my skin.

Had Gran brought me here as a little kid? No, I'd have remembered Loch Ard and the garden. I inhaled deeply, taking in the musty scent of violets. It reminded me of Gran's house when I was a child, and a comforting sense of nostalgia washed over me.

I ran my fingertips over the cot's dusty safety rail, collecting cobwebs. Why did this room feel so familiar?

"Something's going on here, Gran. I have no idea what—"

"Rowan?" Cleary's voice cut through the serene silence of the cottage. "Are you alright in there?"

I hurried back outside, rubbing the chill off my arms.

"The cottage is lovely, Cleary. So peaceful. Like coming home." I looked away quickly. Why had I said that? Totally sappy, and now a flush was creeping up into my cheeks. I needed to create a distraction.

I pointed up the hill. "What's up there?"

Cleary tore his gaze off the hedge and glanced at me.

"Come on, I'll show you." He hurried ahead of us, leaving Elsie and me to trail behind.

As we walked uphill, the path became even more overgrown with tall grass and wildflowers. We trudged through the tangled landscape, ignoring the thorns and prickly vines, until we reached an antique shade house, home to a colony of leggy tree ferns.

"Watch your step here," Cleary warned, gesturing at a fallen branch that lay across the track and disappeared into a riot of blackberries. "It needs a good clearing out. The garden has lovely old bones, though."

My plan to make a fast getaway was quickly fading. Elsie's bright smile and Cleary's solid presence captivated me. Their passion for this place was contagious, and the garden itself was weaving its magic around me. Here was a project that called to something within me, a yearning I couldn't explain.

"Over there could be a kitchen garden," I found myself saying, pointing to a sunny patch. "And a pergola here, draped in native sarsaparilla." The words tumbled out before I could stop them, my professional eye assessing the layout, imagining the garden waking from its long slumber.

Cleary's lips curved upwards, revealing the slightest hint of dimples behind his gingery scruff, the warmth of his smile reaching his eyes. When his gaze lingered a touch too long on my face, I found myself not minding. For a man who seemed perpetually braced for disappointment, that glimpse made me wonder if there was another side to him. A side I might enjoy getting to know.

Leaves crunched underfoot as we took a downhill track through the tangled growth. Cleary led the way along a narrow track, his movements deliberate and sure. Elsie trailed beside me, her hand occasionally brushing against mine, her gaze gravitating to my face. Suddenly, she swooped ahead and collected something from the ground. It was a fallen gum leaf, its yellowing surface flecked with green and purple lichen.

"Will we be on telly?" she asked, twirling the leaf.

"I'm not with Digger's any more, Elsie. Are you disappointed?"

She shook her head. "Why'd you leave?"

"My gran had a wonderful garden. I'd like to get my hands in the soil, like she used to. I've spent too long behind a desk. It's time to have some fun."

"I know what!" Her face lit up. "You could live in Rose's cottage. It'd save you driving back to Melbourne every day. And Dad wouldn't mind."

"Ah, well. I'd have to think about that."

"It's really quiet up here. No one to bother you. Just the birds and insects, and sometimes the owls hooting at night."

"I'm okay with owls."

"Sometimes it's super windy, and all the leaves fly about the place. Do you like leaves, Rowan?"

"Oh, I love them." I crouched lower so our faces were level. "Just between you and me, sometimes I use them as little bookmarks."

"Me too!" She beamed, taking my hand and placing her gum leaf gently on my palm. "Here you go, something to remember us by."

I tucked it carefully into my pocket and glanced through my lashes at her father. He was frowning up the hill, but I could tell he was listening intently. Still purposefully ignoring me, though.

After the awkwardness of our initial meeting, he was keeping a low profile, which was probably for the best. As much as his quiet intensity intrigued me, the last thing I needed right now was another messy workplace involvement gone wrong.

Elsie pointed up the hill. "The fireflies come out in summer. We can show you sometime, if you'd like?"

Hmm. Fireflies would make a perfect photo for my website, swarming and glowing against the night sky with the floodlit shade house in the background. Everywhere I looked was inspiration, and I was starting to view my future with new enthusiasm.

"That'd be wonderful."

We arrived at a large open clearing, dominated by a tall, ancient tree, its limbs twisted and blackened by a long-ago lightning strike. The bark was gnarled, the limbs stooped, like an old sentinel weary from battles past.

From one of the lower branches dangled a clay heart, like the one I'd seen in the back room of the cottage, only cracked and weathered. It swung gently, the sunlight picking out a delicate pattern of etched roses.

Cleary folded his arms across his chest, the muscles in his jaw working as his gaze roamed up the tree. "Quite the eyesore, isn't it? I've been meaning to cut it down and open up the view, but ..." He trailed off, sighing. "I can't seem to bring myself to do it."

Elsie went over and sat on a fallen log, squinting at me through the dappled light.

"Rose called it the lightning tree. It was special to her."

I remained silent, studying the tree. Its raw, sculptural form spoke of resilience, a testament to time passing and the scars that came with it. This marred old tree had watched over the garden, maybe for centuries. It belonged here as much as the soil beneath our feet. To remove it would erase a chapter of the garden's history.

"Cleary, don't cut it down."

His eyebrows shot up, but then his expression softened. "You don't think it ruins the view?"

I went closer, gazing up at the gnarled branches. "That large central branch, do you see it? The way it curves upwards ... like it's defying the storm that tried to take it down. It's beautiful."

Elsie sprang up, her gaze following mine.

"I can see it, Rowan! Look, Dad."

Cleary had frozen in place. I ventured closer to the tree, still gazing up. The gnarled branches stretched toward the sky, each twist telling a story.

"It's a survivor ... Why not celebrate that? Build a seat around it, maybe? You could sit here and admire the view."

"I love it!" Elsie gave Cleary a meaningful look. "Please, Dad. Build us a bench."

Cleary's eyes remained on the tree. "Hmm. It could be a pleasant spot to watch the sunset."

I pressed my palm against the weathered bark, tracing the rugged patterns carved by nature's fury. Like the tree, I had weathered storms. The teasing at school, people's shocked looks, enduring my mother's makeup lessons. Being left on Gran's doorstep. Then losing Gran and struggling to navigate a life where I never fit in ...

At least, until now.

Tears pricked my eyes. Lord, where did that come from? I must be getting soft. I'd never been a crybaby. I turned my head, meaning to pretend absorption in the view. But as I shifted away, my collar caught on a twig and the chain around my neck snapped.

Gran's ring slithered off and bounced against the trunk, flying off into a blackberry bush.

"What's that?" Elsie sprang up and came over. "It looks valuable."

"It is to me." I ran over to the tangled bush and crouched down. Frantically patting my hand under the prickly vines as irrational fear seized me. What if had slipped down a crack in the earth? What if I never found it, my last link to Gran gone forever? "It belonged to my gran," I told Elsie, unable to stop the catch in my voice. "It's all I have left of her."

"Dad, do something!"

Cleary crouched down in front of the bush, reaching his hand under the prickly tangle. As he felt around, the sharp thorns tore across his forearm, leaving a trail of tiny red beads along his skin, mixing in with the intricate designs of his tattoos.

He withdrew his hand, frowning down at the small, shiny object on his palm.

My grandmother's emerald ring glinted like a chip of green ice in the sun. As I breathed a sigh of thanks and reached for it, Cleary flinched, closing his fist around the ring. His face hollowing as he stumbled over to the tree and braced his other hand against its trunk.

"Oh no," Elsie said softly and came over beside me, taking my hand. "It's happening again."

"What's happening ... Cleary, are you okay?"

He was staring at his fist, as though in a trance. As he stood there, his chest expanded and contracted with each heavy breath, his taut muscles rippling beneath his skin. His jaw clenched so tightly that a vein in his temple bulged. He looked like a fierce god caught in battle against an unseen enemy.

"Is he having a seizure?" Or, God help me, a heart attack? I let go of Elsie's hand and started patting my pockets for my phone. "Don't worry, sweetie. Try to stay calm. I'm calling an ambulance."

"Rowan, there's no reception here. And even if there was, they wouldn't be able to help him."

I looked down at her small face, upturned like a serious sunflower. She seemed strangely resigned for someone whose dad was on the brink of collapse.

"Why not?"

"This always happens when he touches something belonging to an entity."

I stared at her, blinking. "An entity?"

"You know. Ghosts. Things that go bump in the night. Ghouls. Glimmers. Spirits. Glimpses from the corner of your eye, you name it. They don't bother me, but if Dad so much as looks sideways at one ..." She frowned over at her father and sighed. "He falls to pieces."

81

WILLIAM

1978

William plodded through the white gates, gazing around as his old heart raced. The place had changed since he'd chugged up this driveway in 1918 behind the wheel of his father's Model T Ford. It was wild and overgrown, neglected. Yet the meandering pathways he'd built and the tall elms he had planted made it seem like only yesterday.

As he crunched up the gravel, gripping the slender stems of three white rosebuds, he whistled softly.

It was no surprise they called her Briar Rose. The once beautiful garden at Loch Ard was now a tangled web of thorns and briars, vines choking out all other growth. The atmosphere was eerie, as if the grounds were under a spell that kept the outside world at bay. Insects buzzed and fluttered, providing the only signs of life in the otherwise still environment. Butterflies, beetles, and dragonflies worked tirelessly, bringing life to the deathly stillness.

A lifetime had passed since he last came here, but that icy winter's day after his return from the war remained vivid in his mind. His encounter with Jedrick McGregor, Rose's father. His trek uphill through the snow to the berry patch, the cold gnawing at his heart, dread growing inside him the closer he got. Then seeing the grave. Slowly understanding that everything he had survived the war for was gone.

So long ago.

And now, the rumours.

Someone had seen her. Heard her crying at night.

William strolled up the winding path, gazing around at the vibrant flowers and lush greenery. Each step held a memory —Rose peeking at him from behind the willow tree, and then later, seeing her face for the first time, his heart skipping a beat at the raw challenge in her eyes.

Will you reject me too, William? Will you run screaming?

He wiped a hand over his face. The sun blazed overhead, but he felt no warmth. His gaze kept drifting, searching the shadows. Was she here? Aware of him, spying from the dark places between the trees? God, how he longed to see her one last time before he died.

"Rosalba?"

He laughed softly. Old fool. Here he was in his twilight time, chasing ghosts. All his life he'd felt lost without her, lacking direction and purpose. Was that why he was here?

Hoping that one more glimpse of her would give his life meaning again, even as he approached the end?

He'd be eighty-seven on Sunday. Over six decades ago, he had made her a promise. *Nothing will keep us apart, Rosie girl. Not even death.*

"It still stands, Rose. I'll wait for you. Forever if I have to."

He followed a trail uphill to the shade house. Its wrought iron roof glinted in the sun, and blackberry vines pushed through the bars, choking the leggy tree ferns reaching up towards the light. If only someone loved this place like he did, and could restore its glory. Rose deserved to be remembered, and this garden was the perfect memorial.

William ...

He whirled around, but it was only the wind in the trees. Trudging on, he climbed the overgrown track, avoiding tree roots emerging through the soil. His legs weren't what they used to be, and uneven ground was a minefield for an old bloke like him. When he pushed through the hedgerow of bramble berries and saw the gravestone, he caught his breath.

There was his Rosebud, the love of his life. And their little one, Odette. The daughter he'd never met, but who haunted him to this day.

"Bloody Jedrick and his poisonous lies."

When Rose's father lay dying in the hospital, William had gone to see him. Jedrick wanted to talk. To offload a secret he had buried inside himself long ago and kept from the world.

It was me who found Rosalba's body, he told William, clutching the younger man's forearm as the light slowly faded from of his eyes. *She lay frozen in the snow, under the old tree. Her hands curled protectively around nothing. Maybe dingoes carried the baby off. Or someone discovered her and took pity. But*

William, I carved the child's name on the headstone alongside Rose's for one reason only ...

"To break my heart," William said aloud, surprised by the strength of his bitterness. And Jedrick had succeeded, too. William's heart never recovered. He avoided getting close to anyone after he lost Rose. Lingering on the fringe of society, keeping to himself. Gardening had saved him. Getting his hands in the soil, making things grow. Though none of his gardens compared to Loch Ard ... or the joy he had briefly found here.

Did he believe Jedrick's confession about the child?

Maybe. Maybe not. But deep down, he hoped it was true. Somewhere in the world, the daughter he'd made with Rose still lived and thrived, content and loved within her own family.

He swiped the back of his hand across his damp face.

"I'll be with you soon, Rosie girl. Our waiting will be over—"

He bent and carefully placed the white rosebuds on the grave. As he turned to go, spears of sunlight flickered between the trees further up the slope.

A figure emerged from the shadows.

Dappled light played over her delicate features, the wind teasing her hair. William's breath caught. Was it really her?

She was exactly as he remembered. Young and willowy, beautiful in her favourite green dress. Her glossy dark locks falling forward, covering her mark, her gaze wary. He wanted to rush up the slope and gather her against him, beg her forgiveness. Shower her in all the love he'd pent up over a lifetime. But he was suddenly breathless with fear of scaring her away.

Instead, he lifted his hand in a wave.

She froze in place. Her fingers fluttered by her side, and she raised her hand in a furtive gesture. Did she not recognise him? Of course not. He'd been young and strong in his soldier's uniform when she saw him last. Now he was an old man with white hair.

The wind picked up suddenly, blowing leaves around his ankles in a whirlwind of dust and grit. He looked down, startled, and something lodged in his eye. The gust subsided, and when he cleared his eyes, the woman had vanished.

82
CLEARY

NOW

As I stumbled, grasping onto the lightning tree's thick trunk to stay upright, my gaze locked onto Rowan's face.

Despite layers of makeup, the distinctive mark on her cheek stood out against her pale, shocked expression.

A single thought hammered through my brain. *It's her, Rose ... she's the one you wished into being all those years ago in the past. What you most wanted for Odette ... it's her.* I had no proof, of course. Only her astonishing resemblance to Rose, and the inkling that I knew her. Not to mention my racing pulse whenever I stole a glance at her, which was often—

"Cleary, are you okay?"

"Yeah," I rasped. "Give me a minute."

Elsie darted forward, peering into my face. "Who did you see?"

I looked over her shoulder at Rowan, but Elsie bobbed back into my line of sight. "It's okay, Dad. She knows about the visions. I told her."

"Jeez, kid—"

"Who was it this time, Daddy ... was it Rose?"

I shook my head, standing upright. My joints creaked as I walked over to Rowan. Reaching for her hand, I pressed the emerald ring into her palm, closing her fingers over it.

"I believe this is yours."

She nodded, sliding the ring into her pocket, distracted. "Elsie said you see ... things."

"Yeah." I dragged my hands over my face, swallowing the last of the nausea. "Visions. Weird, right?"

She shrugged. "Not really. But I am curious about the ring. What did you see?"

"You said it belonged to your grandmother?"

"That's right. Why?"

My body trembled, but not from the vision. I had seen that ring before. The exact one with the fleck of darker green at its core, like a tiny heart.

William had given it to Rose on the hillside before he left for war. The man in my vision was no young soldier, but a bitter old man at the end of his life. Yet his heartache gave me hope. Perhaps Rose had returned to us, after all.

She lay frozen in the snow, Jedrick had said. *Her hands curled protectively around nothing. Maybe dingoes carried the baby off. Or someone discovered her and took pity.*

My legs quaked as I trudged across the clearing, crushing brittle leaves and twigs under my boots. I motioned for Rowan to follow me.

"You said before that you weren't sure why you came here. I think I know."

83
CLEARY

Rowan stared at the grave, her brows creasing as she walked over, her feet crunching on dry blackberry leaves. She crouched in front of the weathered stone, trailing her fingers over the names engraved there.

"Rosalba ... Odette." Standing slowly, she turned back to look at me. "Who were they, mother and daughter?"

"Yes."

"I'm sure this is just a bizarre coincidence, but my grandmother's name was Odette. She was born in January, 1917." She glanced at Elsie, then wandered back over to the grave. "Gran was Odette Lilliam Makepeace. Neither are common names, are they?"

I shook my head. "Definitely not."

Rowan tugged her long hair out of its ponytail and let it fall around her flushed face. When she wrapped her arms tightly around her midsection, buckling slightly into herself, she resembled Rose so much it was eerie.

"This isn't just a coincidence, is it?" she whispered.

I hesitated, then shook my head, remembering my vision of William. "Odette isn't buried here, Rowan. She didn't die in 1917. There was a mistake. Her mother was poisoned, and died under that old tree we saw. But when her father discovered her body, Odette wasn't with her. I'm guessing someone found the child alive."

"What are you saying?"

I gestured at the headstone. "Rosalba's little girl Odette—"

"Was my gran."

Elsie gasped, then slapped her hands over her mouth, staring at Rowan wide-eyed. Rowan's lips quivered and her eyes filled. She placed a hand over her heart and looked at me.

"I want to say you're wrong, Cleary. But I can't." She blinked around, the dappled tree shadows moving over her face. "Gran used to talk about a garden just like this one. Her mum was a wonderful storyteller, and Gran told those same stories to me. Fairytales about snow queens and magic icicles, and a garden so vast you could lose yourself in there and never be found. Gran also told her own story. How she was adopted and raised by my great-grandmother. And how this—" She lifted the emerald ring from her pocket and tilted it in the sunlight, making it glint like a chip of green ice. "How they found this ring tucked into the crocheted rug she was wrapped in."

Elsie lowered her hands, her eyes round and wet as she looked across at me.

"It's our Odette, isn't it, Dad?"

I nodded. "What was she like?"

"My gran?" Rowan pulled out a clean hanky and gently wiped Elsie's damp cheeks, then tucked it into her pocket. "She was everything to me," she said quietly. She rolled her shoulders and eased out a breath, glancing back at the gravestone. "I remember being dropped off at Granny Odette's house when I was seven years old. My mum had already explained that her jet-setting lifestyle wasn't suitable for a child. She was an actress, the star of a successful TV series. There were always parties back then. Lots of people around. I used to wonder if she was ashamed of my birthmark. Years later, she admitted she was trying to protect me." Rowan ran her fingers lightly over her cheek. "Thankfully, Granny Odette also had a mark and never made me feel like an outcast. She became my rock, my confidant, and my champion. It's funny, but not having her around left me diminished somehow. As though I misplaced an enormous chunk of myself that I've never been able to recover. I felt lost, like a ghost haunting my own life."

"A ghost?"

"I know! Weird, right?"

I swayed closer, captivated by her words. Her skin was fine and smooth, her mark paler through the heavy makeup than Rose's had been. She held herself differently too, tall and poised, exuding confidence.

"I'm sorry," I murmured. "You must really miss your gran."

"Every moment of every day." Rowan's eyes glowed warmly, and she smiled. "I was twenty when she passed away in 2008. She was ninety-one. An age gap of seventy years, but she was my bestie. I'll never forget the love and support she gave me, especially since my own parents weren't around. I had a wonderful life with Gran. Gardens were more my thing than television, anyway. I only regret that it's taken me so long to understand that."

"What else do you know about her background?"

Rowan shrugged. "Sadly, not much. Her mother was Hattie Makepeace—her adoptive mother, that is. Hattie was a lady's maid in Melbourne who never married, scandalous back in the 1920s. Raising a child alone in those days would have been hard. But she was devoted to Gran, utterly adored her."

"And your gran's father?"

"All she knew about him was that he died in the war."

I scratched at my stubble, frowning. "I've heard that name before. Hattie Makepeace. Rose mentioned her a few times."

"Oh?"

"Hattie worked here as a housekeeper during the first war. She and Rose became friends."

"Wait, I'm confused." Rowan gestured towards the grave. "You mean Rosalba? I thought …" Her words drifted off, and she frowned from me to Elsie and back again.

I hesitated. To the wider world, I was just a guy who flipped houses. The number one unspoken rule for ghost hunters was secrecy, but lying to Rowan was not on the cards. I only hoped she wouldn't bolt when she learned the truth.

Elsie caught my eye. "Go on, Dad. Tell her."

Rowan frowned at Elsie, then at me. "Tell me what?"

"Rosalba Beatrice McGregor, your great-grandmother … was also *our* Rose," I said as gently as I could. "She lived in the garden when we bought the place. We got to know her really well."

"*Really* well," Elsie echoed, her voice trailing sadly. "We were going to be a family."

Rowan wound her arms around her middle, her gaze growing wary. "Sorry, I'm not following. Rosalba died in…" She gestured towards the gravestone. "She died over a hundred years ago, Cleary. What are you talking about?"

Elsie's lip trembled as she went over and slid her arms around Rowan's waist and hugged her.

"Dad doesn't just see visions, Rowan. He sees other things, too."

Rowan tenderly ran her fingers through Elsie's dark locks, absently tucking away the stray strands. Her gaze lingered on my face, searching for something, yet her green eyes gave nothing away. After a long pause, she let out a deep exhale.

"You're talking about ghosts?"

I nodded. "Yeah."

"As in paranormal investigations?"

"Ah ... something like that."

Elsie tipped back her head and gazed up into Rowan's face. "I see them too, Rowan. It runs in the family. We're hunters. It's like a job for us. We make friends with them and help them cross over to the other side."

Rowan's eyebrows arched, and the hand caressing Elsie's hair stilled.

"You make friends with them?"

Elsie nodded. "Sometimes they get a bit tetchy and zip off, but mostly they're a lot of fun to hang out with."

Rowan's brow furrowed as she stared at my daughter.

"Gran could see them, as well."

Elsie took a step back. "Really?"

Rowan nodded, then blew out a long breath. "Just shimmers or shadows, and never for very long. She saw an old man, once. Another time she said a big white cat was hanging around her garden shed, but I just thought it was another of her stories." She looked pointedly at me, then shook her head. "As far as I know, she never befriended them. But she would probably think what you do is pretty cool."

"You're not turned off us?" Elsie wiped her eyes on the back of her hand, gazing raptly at her new best friend. "You don't think we're weird?"

Rowan's lips curved upwards, and a deep, warm laugh escaped from her throat.

"Well, let's not get too carried away," she said with a playful glint in her eye. "But I must admit, I am intrigued. Will you tell me more about this Rose of yours?"

Elsie's shoulders straightened, her hand darting up as if she was in class.

"Rose was awesome. She knew all the plant names, and she told me I could be a scientist one day and study frog hollows. She loved William, but he went to war and never came home. She was a good mum, but her little baby died. At least, that's what we thought. Only now ..." Her words cut off, and when she looked at me, bless her, those big adorable eyes were full of tears. "Dad?"

A shiver went through me. I stepped up to my daughter and smoothed my fingers gently over her head, the way Rowan had done before.

"Come on, it's nearly lunchtime. What do you say we invite Rowan to stay for pizza, and we can catch her up on the rest of the story while we eat?" Flutters rippled through me as I met Rowan's green gaze. "Hungry?"

She tipped her head to one side, regarding me. The green dress hugged her curves, bringing out the depth of her dark hair and brightening her pale eyes, making them hypnotic. My gaze drifted downward to her legs. Did she really have a birthmark on her bottom? I caught myself staring and glanced back up.

Her eyes crinkled at the corners, and a smile lit her beautiful face. "I thought you'd never ask."

84
ROWAN

THREE MONTHS LATER

On a warm December afternoon, as the sun sank behind the mountain, Cleary and Elsie strolled up to the cottage with a picnic basket full of goodies and a plaid blanket. I greeted them on the verandah, peeling off my gardening gloves and brushing grass from my jeans.

"Hey, you two. What's up?"

Elsie raced ahead of her father, pulling a small parcel out of her pocket and thrusting it into my hands.

"I made it for you, Rowan."

"Aww, Elsie. No one's ever made me anything before."

As I loosened the ribbon and peeled back the wrapping

paper, I froze, my lips dropping open. It was a small clay heart with delicate flowers etched on its surface. *Like the one in my bedroom out the back ... and all the weathered ones hanging through the garden.* Elsie had hung them there so Rose would know they loved her, and now, cradling the fragile creation in my palms, I could sense their love surrounding me as well.

I gave her a hug, kissing the top of her silky head.

"I adore it, thank you."

"Where will you hang it?"

I dashed back inside the cottage and looped the string over the window latch, facing the heart outwards. Then I went back outside and the three of us stood in the warm air, watching sway gently against the glass.

Cleary shuffled beside me on the gravel, scraping his nails through his whiskers and grinning.

"We have another surprise for you, Rowan."

Elsie grabbed my hand. "Have you ever danced in the moonlight with fireflies?"

I couldn't help laughing. "Um, no."

"Eaten cake under the stars?"

"Never."

"Ran through the misty garden at midnight?"

"Only in my dreams."

She released my hand and skipped a little way uphill along the gravel trail, calling back.

"Well, your dreams are about to come true!"

Mystified, I glanced over at Cleary, but he only shrugged and picked up the picnic basket. His gaze lingered on mine though, and his slow smile was full of warmth.

"Elsie planned the whole thing. She wanted you to know how happy we are that you stayed."

A flush burned up my neck and pooled in my cheeks.

Sometimes, like now, I felt naked and exposed without the heavy makeup I'd given up wearing since moving to Loch Ard. I lowered my face behind my hair, peering at Cleary from behind the thick strands.

"Okay," I murmured. "I'm officially intrigued."

Cleary's smile faltered. He reached over and tucked my hair back behind my ear, then—so softly I might have imagined it—gently touched my cheek.

"You don't have to hide from us, Rowan. We love you just as you are."

I opened my mouth to reply, but nothing came out. Not even a squeak. So I bit my lips together and smiled, hoping that was enough. I had always held back from people a little, wary of being judged and rejected, defensiveness bristling up around me like a shield. But being here at Loch Ard had somehow dislodged all my old fears. There was nothing holding me back now.

Side by side, we headed up the hill after Elsie. The track led around a stand of giant cypresses, then the landscape opened up to a glorious view of the valley below. We sat on the rug under a gum tree, taking in the scenery and talking. At dusk, the fireflies came out. Elsie took my hand, and we cavorted among them, giggling and making up silly songs. It was the most fun I'd had in … ever. When I finally flopped onto the rug with Cleary, he patted the spot beside him and I shuffled closer.

"I've got something for you, too." He reached into his pocket, bringing out a small heart-shaped stone and placing it on the rug between us.

I looked at it. "Rose quartz. It opens the heart and inspires love and compassion."

"It's also for clarity." His voice was suddenly husky. "It'll help you find your way back to that misplaced part of yourself

... that you lost after your gran died. Here—" He nudged it closer. "It's yours now."

I cradled the stone in my palm. He was right. Already I could feel its soft energy pulsing against my skin like butterfly wings. I curled my fingers around it and looked back at him.

My missing pieces were already falling into place, but not because of the quartz. I had found my way back to the garden in my dreams and made it my home. My landscaping business was thriving. And now, here I was, taking a chance on a man with walls around his heart and a young girl with stars in her eyes. Nothing had ever felt more right.

Cleary was smiling at me. "Hey, ghost girl," he said softly.

Impulsively, I leaned over and kissed him.

His lips were warm, and his whiskers tickled my skin. I should have pulled back then. My kiss was supposed to be fleeting, like a promise. But suddenly, it became so much more. Cleary's hand slid to the back of my head and he drew me closer, wrapping me in his arms as our kiss deepened. I melted into him, gliding my hands up over his shoulders, burying my fingers into the wild silk of his hair. He smelled of wood smoke and night air, and as his heat enveloped me, a sigh escaped. *How did I ever think I could survive without this? Without him? Was there room in my life for love, after all?*

When we pulled away from each other, our breaths ragged and quick, I snuggled into the warmth of him, nestling against his side on the worn rug, our fingers interlaced.

As the fireflies danced in the darkness and Elsie's lively chatter filled the glade as she played nearby, the night settled over us like a soft, familiar blanket.

Cleary pressed his lips against the side of my head in a gentle kiss, making me smile. Ghost girl, he'd called me. I liked it, but I didn't feel like a ghost anymore. And I wasn't lost. Instead, I felt alive and connected to this dark garden in ways I never thought possible. As if every moment in my life had led me here, to this night, with this man, and this one point in time.

I traced the rough geography of his knuckles with my fingers, feeling the ridges and scars.

"Time is a funny thing, isn't it?"

His lips curved into a smile, his eyes lighting up as he looked at me. "What makes you say that?"

"It always seems in a rush. Slipping away like smoke or a shooting star. Darting out of reach like fireflies. We say we're running out of time, that we only live once ... but what if it just keeps looping us back around? Taking us on different journeys, and then bringing us back to this one perfect moment?"

"That's quite an idea. I like it."

"Do you ever feel like you've been here before?"

The firelight flickered over our faces, warming our skin as it cast us into an intimate world of shadow and light. Cleary shifted against me, our bodies close, his lips making feather-light contact with my fingertips.

"More times than I can count. You?"

"Before I came to Loch Ard, not so much. But since being here with you and Elsie? It happens all the time." My fingers tangled in his hair, pulling him against me until our faces were so close I could feel his breath on my skin. "But none of it matters, does it? The past doesn't matter, time doesn't matter."

Cleary smiled, leaning in till his mouth was nearly touching mine.

"Why's that, love?"

"This moment, right now, is all that matters," I whispered against his lips. "Because it belongs to us. For all of time."

DEAR READER

Thank you so much for reading THE GHOST OF BRIAR ROSE—I hope you enjoyed it! If you did, please consider telling your friends and family, and leaving a quick review on the store where you bought it. I'd be very grateful, as reviews help get the attention of other readers.

If you'd like to learn more about me and my other books, check out my website at annaromer.com

Happy Reading!

ABOUT THE AUTHOR

Anna Romer is an internationally bestselling Australian author of mystery and romance, both historical and contemporary, with elements of paranormal woven in—ghosts, haunted houses, and fairytales. She's also working on a stockpile of dark romantic fantasy novels.

She lives on Australia's beautiful eastern coast, and when she's not writing she's a keen gardener, knitter, bushwalker and conservationist.

ALSO BY ANNA ROMER

Lyrebird Hill

Under the Midnight Sky

Thornwood House

Beyond the Orchard

Printed by Libri Plureos GmbH in Hamburg, Germany